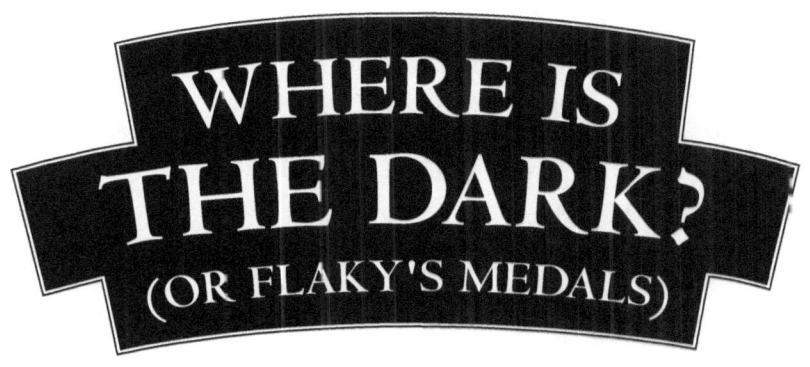

WHERE IS THE DARK?
(OR FLAKY'S MEDALS)

AN UNDERSIDE ADVENTURE

BY

RAY LEWIS HALLIDAY

U K Book Publishing.com

Editing, design, typesetting and publishing by UK Book Publishing

www.ukbookpublishing.com

ISBN: 978-1-917329-87-3

WHERE IS THE DARK?

(OR FLAKY'S MEDALS)

FOREWORD

Many of our traditional stories, fairy tales or legends are richly populated with wonderous creatures. Why is it that we no longer see them? The reason is simple. Most of them left.

Now, these non-humans, these "mythical" beings, occupy a subterranean realm, beneath our feet but away from our prying eyes. This place is home to dragons, witches, wizards, fairies, goblins, elves, and many others. This world has various names. Amongst those beings known as elves, it is called Underside.

In the part of this domain that is controlled by the elves, their largest city is called Hollow Earth. Primarily as a result of its size, Hollow Earth has become the elvish Capital of Underside. It also functions as the administrative, financial, and political centre for the elves.

CHAPTER ONE

Underside recovers

I n the last few months, Underside had faced major disruptions to its everyday life.

Underside had experienced its first terrorist, in countless decades. A character calling himself The Dark, whose sole aim was the sabotage of all the daily activities of the elves. His attempts at violent disruption had so far proved harmless or ineffective. Many elves felt that this was deliberate; that The Dark did not truly mean anyone any harm. Others believed that it was only a matter of time until someone was hurt.

Furthermore, the magic dust supply, which was held in Hollow Earth, had been corrupted, by fairy spies with assistance from The Dark. The dust was essential for the smooth running of Underside and allowed the elves to live far longer than their human counterparts.

Recreating the supply of magic dust had been a monumental challenge. Removing the residual corrupted dust or its effects was an even larger challenge. One still being met.

Additionally, the "current" Santa had decided to retire, with an intention of finding a replacement.

[Yes, there is a "real" Santa Claus but, of course, he is not immortal. I am sure that you never imagined he was. The

elves had taken on Santa's duties when Saint Nicholas died but even though elves are long-lived, each Santa has to relinquish the festive outfit at some point. Finding a good replacement is never an easy task.]

Any of these events were dramatic enough to disrupt the smooth running of Underside. However, if there is an opportunity for fate to complicate things further, fate always accepts that opportunity readily.

[As I am certain you must have observed yourself.]

If fate had a personality, it would be that of mischievous meddler. So it was, that this mischievous meddler added various skirmishes, minor conflicts and battles with the fairies and the goblins, the sworn enemies of the elves, into the already complicated mix.

These clashes culminated inevitably, in a climactic battle, which became known as The Battle of Southern Field. This was arguably the most confusing battle ever to have occurred or possibly not occurred, depending on your point of view. Thousands were injured, with hundreds seemingly mortally wounded, on both sides in The Battle of Southern Field. As a result of intervention by Merlin, with the assistance of other witches and wizards, they disappeared from the battlefield, only to reappear, miraculously recovered shortly afterwards.

The last battle, if it could be called that, was an attempted charge by the enemy. For much of the fighting, the elves had been outnumbered. The arrival of the dworfs, long-time allies of the elves, changed the numerical balance.

[Dworfs are not to be confused with dwarfs or dwarves. In essence, dworfs are elves. Merely, elves who delayed their departure to Underside for as long as they could and have steadfastly refused to partake of the magic dust used by other elves. Due to their preferred locations, these elves habitually called themselves Deep Wood or Forest elves. The acronym D.W.Or.F. was developed from this. Eventually, the DWORF elves became known simply as dworfs.]

As they realised suddenly that they were now outnumbered, the fairies and goblins had retreated without a single moment of actual fighting.

History requires every battle to have a title. The elves, with some amusement, decided to call this battle The Big Non-Event.

Similarly, history requires every war to have a title. The elves decided to call the hostilities with the fairies and goblins, The Great Non-War.

✲✲✲

Underside was recuperating from all of the disruptions to its everyday life.

This recovery was painfully slow. Nonetheless, Underside *was* recovering.

The Great Non-War with the goblins and fairies had finished over three months ago. Or so it was believed by the majority of Underside's elvish population.

Most elves were not sure exactly what had happened, but they knew that their preparations for Christmas, the single most important date in the elvish calendar, were significantly behind schedule.

Most elves were not Potter Teasready. As newly appointed leader of the High Council of Elves and Commander of the elvish armed forces, Potter knew exactly what had occurred.

[Potter's name is not unusual for an elf. Traditionally, elves select names that we, as humans, might consider strange, amusing, or downright ridiculous. Of course, elves consider human names to be equally strange.]

Naturally, the "back of the bar experts" that could be found in any of Underside's many hostelries, also felt they knew exactly what had occurred.

In the village of Little Merritiddle, there were two such experts, Ewan Earth, and his cousin Helen Earth. They ran the local village shop "Down to Earth", which sold every conceivable essential household item that villagers might require *[with a few, in all probability, that no-one would ever require]*. These items were packed (reasonably safely) into an astonishingly small display space, together with a surprising array of local grocery produce.

When not in their shop or at one of their many suppliers, the Earths could usually be found seated at "their table" in The Flooded Meadow, or The Meadow, as most villagers knew it. They were not outstanding in appearance, being of average height for elves with sandy hair, light, brownish fawn eyes and faces in an unfortunate, dull, rusk-like hue. However, they were so practised in the art of the confident pronouncement and always agreeing with each other, that their disadvantageous similarity to a biscuit was easily ignored.

As was often the case, they had been joined by Onion Gravy, the village handyperson, and his supposed assistant, Flaky Pastry.

A less likely working relationship was difficult to imagine. Flaky was a kind, helpful natured but undeniably foolish elf, who tackled everything with unlimited enthusiasm. Regrettably, this enthusiasm was usually accompanied by stupendous, ludicrous inanity or clumsiness. Of the two, Onion was the "brains" of the outfit. Although not particularly intelligent, his years of working provided him with considerable, practical "common sense". He had a pleasant, placid, patient nature, which was often required when working with Flaky.

In addition to their personality differences, Onion and Flaky did not resemble each other in their outward appearance. Flaky looked exactly as you would imagine any unintelligent, incapable, accident prone idiot would look. A look that was not improved by his pale skin, which was similar to the colour of a mushroom stalk, or his equally pale, blue eyes. He perpetually looked like someone who had been "dragged through a hedge backwards", without knowing how or by whom. His yellow, straw-like hair was constantly sticking up on end, in keeping with his usual untidy clothing and dishevelled appearance. He was six feet four inches tall, but his habit of adopting an embarrassed stoop made him look shorter. Despite his extremely healthy appetite, he always remained exceptionally thin and gangly.

Elves who knew Flaky were convinced that he "burnt off" excess calories by his natural, nervous energy or in redoing tasks he had failed to complete successfully on his first attempt. Alternatively, they were aware that his clumsiness meant he regularly wasted time and effort struggling to pick up or relocate items he had knocked over.

With eyes and hair, the colour of gravy and fresh onion-coloured skin, Onion lived up to his name. He was shorter than

Flaky at six feet two, but he appeared larger due to his sturdy build and his tendency to "stand tall". When working he wore a battered, old, stained cap shoved down over his hair. With his muscular arms, and clothes which were invariably spattered with paint, he looked like every elf's idea of a stereotypical handyperson.

Onion promised Flaky's mum that he would look after Flaky, once she had gone. She was not dead, merely departed to Hollow Earth, but Onion had heard nothing from her in the three years since she left. Onion kept his word to her so Flaky became his responsibility as well as his "charity case". Flaky now fulfilled the role of local "fetcher and carrier" and helper (or occasional hindrance) to Onion.

Today, the topic of choice at The Meadow was the recent war, with The Battle of Southern Field as the featured specialist subject.

'Must have used magic,' stated Helen. 'We know that Merlin was around during the battle. We also know he had other wizards with him and even some witches.'

'Yes, stands to reason they used magic,' agreed Ewan. 'It's the only way to take injured fighters, cure them and return them fighting fit a few seconds later. They must have used that large Hospital room at Hollow Earth, as we discussed before.'

'That's what *I* said,' added Flaky. 'Magic whizzy pop-pops. Disappearing with whizzy pop-pops, then coming back with more whizzy pop-pops.' He sat back in his chair beaming with satisfaction.

Unfortunately, Flaky had forgotten that he was sitting on a stool. As Onion helped Flaky back to his feet, Ewan and Helen stared at Flaky with a mixture of amusement and disbelief. They had heard him propound his "whizzy pop-pops" theory previously.

'I suppose that schoolteacher must have known what he was doing. Old Teapot?' said Onion.

'Teasready,' corrected Helen and Ewan simultaneously.

'Not yours, Flaky,' said Helen, Ewan, and Onion, in unison. Flaky sat back down on his stool.

'You need to learn his name, Onion,' stated Helen. 'After all, he's allocating war repair work to every available handyman, including you.'

'And he is the leader of just about everything nowadays' said Ewan. 'The council, the elvish armed forces and no doubt that new police force.'

'Not sure about the police force, Ewan. I hear that other ex-teacher, Kuppa Broth, is in charge of that.'

'Yes. I believe you're right, Helen. Looks like we missed our vocation running the shop. Should have been teachers. Might have ended up running the whole place instead.'

'I didn't know you missed your holiday,' said Flaky. 'Were you going anywhere nice?'

The other three looked at him in amazement.

Onion sighed. 'Vocation, Flaky. Not vacation!'

✿✿✿

Underside was buzzing, as the elves were working to catch up with lost time.

As Potter signed yet another bundle of overtime forms, he sighed, quietly yearning for the "good old days" when marking pupil's homework, as a history schoolteacher, was the most challenging task he undertook. As council leader, the problems facing him nowadays were on a far larger scale.

Potter wandered outside to stand in the in the doorway of the Council Hall, looking out over Underside, as he had just over three months earlier. He had been accompanied on that occasion by Wendy Panboil, his long-time friend.

[His potential life partner if he would just "wake up and smell the roses".]

As Potter's closest, most supportive friend, Wendy often provided him with much needed reassurance. Despite being the leader of the council and a highly regarded elf, Potter often lacked Wendy's quiet, self-confidence. He loved having her as a friend but baulked at the idea of romantic entanglement. Not only was Wendy highly intelligent but also, she was generally thought of as eye-catching. She was six feet one in height with a maple syrup toned face and bright blue eyes, beneath long, straight jet-black hair.

In comparison, Potter considered himself to be unremarkable in both intelligence and looks. In truth, Potter's lack of self-confidence meant his personal assessment was overly critical. It could be said that his appearance was unremarkable for an elf. He was six feet three with short, neatly cut dark-brown hair and skin resembling a freshly made cup of coffee, with just a "dash" of milk. All of these features were typical for many elves, but Potter's lively, hazel-coloured eyes displayed his innate intelligence. An intelligence that had successfully carried the elves through the recent war. Despite this, Potter was convinced Wendy could never be interested in him romantically. In Potter's mind, she was simply "too special".

Potter was so deep in reverie that he passed Wendy a barley twist sweet, without really noticing her presence. As he went to help himself to a sweet, he stopped, turning abruptly.

'Wendy, where did you spring from? Have you been here long?'

'Just a couple of minutes,' said Wendy putting her arm around him, fondly. 'I could see you were deep in thought so I decided I would wait until you were ready. I've finished for the day, at the school, so I've come to drag you to The Bell.'

Ye Olde Sleigh Bell or The Bell as it was usually called was the local pub for many of Hollow Earth's school teachers, council members, elite guards, and members of the recently formed police force. Unsurprisingly, there was rarely any "trouble" at The Bell!

'I'd love to, Wendy, but with all this work...' said Potter.

'No buts, Potter! You need a break. Coming?' asked Wendy.

Potter gave a small, resigned smile and shrugged. He knew when he was beaten. Wendy took a barley twist from Potter's bag and popped it in his mouth.

'Ok, let's go,' mumbled Potter. 'Maybe I'll try this new pint I've heard they've got on tap.'

'What Dark 'n' Dangerous? Brave lad!'

As they strolled to the pub, hand-in-hand, Potter could not help continuing to ruminate on recent episodes.

Turning to his companion, he wondered, 'Did I do the right thing, Wendy?'

'You know you did, Pottsie,' said Wendy, putting her arm around him. 'You did what was needed to save countless lives.'

'That's what I keep telling myself, but I can't help feeling guilty about the chaos I've caused.'

Potter's feelings of guilt were understandable. Knowing the potential for massive bloodshed, Potter had employed magic. He had asked Merlin to create a Field Hospital with a self-contained time bubble. With the help of some other wizards and witches, Merlin had treated injured, severely wounded, or mortally wounded soldiers within this bubble, using a combination of magic and medicine. Although in reality, such treatments took a period of weeks or months, the soldiers thought no time had passed. Fighters were returned almost instantaneously to the battlefield apparently unharmed.

Potter knew that his actions had saved the lives of thousands of combatants but at what cost to their sanity?

Conflict on the scale of the recent war had not been experienced by Underside's elves in an exceptionally lengthy period of time. Most of the elves involved in previous wars had forgotten (or chosen to forget) what it had felt like to undergo serious 'life or death' warfare. They had forgotten the nightmares or the occasional bouts of panic and depression that followed. The elves of Underside had no concept of the condition known by humans as Post-Traumatic Stress Disorder or PTSD.

In addition, no elf had ever experienced what many had in The Great Non-War's Battle of Southern Field. To be wounded but not wounded, killed but not killed were unique experiences for all of the elves involved.

Potter hoped that the consequences of the war would be short-lived and temporary, but he had no answer for the thousands of individuals who were convinced that they still existed but were also, somehow, actually dead or "meant to be dead". He had no choice but to refer them to those experts more used to dealing with problems of the mind – Underside's ever-growing population of psychologists, psychiatrists, mediums, faith healers and spiritualists.

In order to create the illusion that wounded combatants had magically reappeared on the battlefield moments after departing, Merlin and his companions had used a great deal of immensely powerful magic or devices to distort time.

Such actions have inevitable after-effects. Time itself had been "bent". Even with Merlin's advice, Potter did not know how to manage the "time leaks" being experienced everywhere, throughout Underside. How do you explain to an elf that the figure he has just seen entering his house, which looks remarkably like him, is him, in fact, but just five minutes into his own future? It was impossible. Fortunately, Merlin was convinced the "time leaks" were dissipating and time would soon stabilise.

CHAPTER TWO
Potter prepares for a meeting

P otter could not begin to imagine how the elves would ever remove fully the residual corrupted dust that still remained. He knew it might take years. It might be something they could never resolve. Effects had been felt throughout Underside.

Bizarrely, in Little Merritiddle, Flaky Pastry had benefited positively from the corrupted dust still blowing around the village. Flaky remained as dense as he always had been, but he had acquired one or two new skills.

Strangely, he was now a faster cyclist than previously; able to travel at extraordinary, but nonetheless uncontrolled, dangerous speeds.

Although Flaky could travel faster, courtesy of the corrupted dust, his road-sense had not improved. In his attempts to dodge potholes, Flaky had always been inclined to zigzag wildly across cycle paths or roads and veer suddenly, without signalling, when he realised that he needed to turn. Now, his increased velocity meant that every zig, every zag, every last-minute swerve created increasingly huge risks for all other cycle path or road users. It was not unusual for Flaky to leave a trail of chaos behind him, while he cycled on entirely oblivious.

However, foremost of his new skills was dog walking. In the past, most dogs ignored Flaky or simply avoided him, presumably confused as to what he was. Now, Flaky was like a magnet to every canine. Every dog "loved" him and wanted to be with him.

Onion quickly spotted an opportunity. There were ten dog owners in the village with limited time to walk their dogs. Onion swiftly drafted an advert for the Merritiddle Mercury. "Local dog walker available. Excellent rates. Your dog has never lived until he has been taken out by Pastry. Contact the following number and ask for Gravy."

The villagers received Onion and Flaky's new business enterprise with enthusiasm. They all agreed that Flaky was the best dog walker they had ever seen.

Helen and Ewan held a marginally different view.

'Thank goodness, he's finally found something he can actually do!' said Helen.

'Yes, without breaking anything!' agreed Ewan.

✿✿✿

At his desk in the council chambers, Potter absent-mindedly placed a barley twist sweet in his mouth. He allowed himself a small, resigned shrug accompanied by an even smaller smile. Both might be considered Potter Teasready trademark gestures. Potter had begun to realise that being a leader in peacetime was notably different from the wartime role he had recently fulfilled. This experience had provided him with an insight into the practicalities of leadership during warfare, but he remained unsure regarding his leadership duties when there were no battles to be fought. Those duties clearly involved him attending far more meetings than he had experienced previously and required him to process substantially more paperwork.

Potter became aware of a figure standing in front of his desk.

'The minutes of the last council meeting, Potter,' said Ena Minnit, as she passed across a thick wad of papers, a quirky smile playing across her lips, 'with the agenda for the meeting next month.'

Ena was recognised as the most natural and gifted administrator in Underside. Her knowledge and experience had earned her a place on the High Council of Elves five years earlier. After these five years, she was seen as the ultimate council administrator. Any council member, with a query, automatically sought Ena's help.

Recently, she became one of Santa's official helpers, as a member of the Honorary Order of the Helpers of Santa (or H.O.H.O.S.) – a singular honour afforded to only a select few elves. Naturally, Ena soon took administrative control for the H.O.H.O.S. as one of her new duties.

Ena's deep brown skin, dark almost black hair, brown eyes, and general, serious nature deceived many elves into assuming she was a "typical" humourless administrator. In reality, although a quiet individual, Ena had a good sense of humour.

Potter hated the mountains of paperwork that his new role embraced but, he reassured himself, at least with Ena in charge of council administration, the punctuation and spelling of the meeting minutes were bound to be correct. Correct grammar or spelling had been beyond most of Potter's young history students. He almost laughed aloud as he recalled the fact that some could not even spell the word history correctly.

Potter ran his finger down the agenda items for the next meeting. It was to be a special meeting, covering three principal areas. The first item was to be a summary of the events of The

Great Non-War. Related to this, there were to be reports on the war's after-effects, both physical and mental.

The second item consisted of a series of reports from their field agents (spies) on the current status of the goblin and fairy armies, including any unusual activities.

The third item on the agenda was locating and appointing a new Santa Claus. The most important agenda item, in the minds of all the elves, that would be attending the meeting. Mark Tyme's "retirement" had left a worrying gap. Not only had Mark been Potter's predecessor, as council leader, but previously he had also been the nominated Santa. For all elves, there could be no "real" Christmas, without a "proper" Santa.

[Decades earlier, the elves agreed with the humans that they would continue the work of Saint Nicholas. Eventually, this has resulted in them "providing" a Santa, who is a "proper" Santa (i.e. not somebody hired to play the role, at a Christmas party, in a shopping mall grotto, in a department store, or, most importantly, not your dad wearing a Santa hat and a red dressing gown, with cotton wool stuck to the lapels). Any elf is honoured if nominated to fulfil the role of the "real, proper" Santa. Periodically, when this Santa dies or retires, a new one has to be appointed.]

Due to the sensitivity of the items being discussed, Potter had decided that this meeting needed to be held in a "safe" location.

It was agreed that a secure briefing room at the Southern border outpost met all requirements.

In addition to preparing for the upcoming meeting, Potter had busied himself on one task upon which he had placed the highest priority. Certain individuals had demonstrated bravery or ingenuity during the recent conflict that required recognition.

In a quiet ceremony, it had been Potter's honour to present the appropriate awards to the individuals concerned. He had presented both Frank Leigh and Derrie Farmer with the Elite Cross for bravery, for their refusal to leave each other's side despite severe injuries. Baton Burg and Redd Shoos had both been injured when they had charged into approximately fifty enemy soldiers, to seal a gap in the ranks of the elvish forces. Both were awarded the Underside Medal of Honour. The most prestigious award was the Elite Star of Honour, which Potter presented to Cotten Shirt, for conspicuous bravery and sacrifice.

Knowing Potter's emotional nature, Wendy was impressed and surprised that he completed these presentations without needing to wipe away any tears. Unbeknown to her, so was Potter.

CHAPTER THREE
Appearances can be deceptive

At the Southern border of Underside, two members of the Elvish Elite could be seen, standing on guard.

This was not unusual. Guarding the borders of elvish Underside was one of the most important roles undertaken by the Elvish Elite, the prime military arm of the elvish world. What was unusual was the appearance of the two guards. They did not possess that indefinable military bearing or the typical large muscular build of an Elite guard. Their uniforms looked as though they were intended for other individuals. All in all, these guards seemed ill at ease and uncomfortable.

In reality, these were not two highly trained members of the Elite. More exactly, they were two volunteers, dressed in Elvish Elite guard uniforms.

Following the Great Non-War, there was a shortage of Elite Guards, who were physically and psychologically fit for duty. Potter had put out a request for volunteers. He knew, that with the possibility of fairy or goblin spies in the area, it was important to retain the appearance of a fully staffed Elite force.

No individuals appreciated this more than two Victorian soldiers, who after the Crimean war, approximately one hundred and fifty years before, had joined an expedition exploring the Amazon. Following a climbing mishap, they had stumbled into a cave system, which led into Underside and specifically to a small, remote village near the southern border, called Little Merritiddle. Now, approximately one hundred and fifty years later, Sir Roger Derringer Carruthers and Lord Claude Remington Ponsonby-Smyth were accepted not only as residents of the village but also as honorary elves. When the Great Non-War commenced, Carruthers and "Ponsers" volunteered for service, offering their extensive previous warfare experience. Both now served as Captains in the Elvish Elite.

On hearing Potter's request, Carruthers had "volunteered" Onion Gravy and Flaky Pastry. As a Little Merritiddle resident, he felt that the village should be represented.

'If you gentlemen could drag yourselves away from your commitments for a few weeks in order to help the Elite, it would be extremely helpful and gratefully accepted, I am sure. I imagine dog walking and repair works could be delayed for a short while.'

Private Flaky Pastry of the Auxiliary Special Reserves Volunteer Unit stamped his feet, in an attempt to get some feeling back into his toes.

[As any guard will tell you, it is not the cold alone that gets to you but the standing around for hours in that cold.]

'Guard Duty again, Onion. Why do we always get guard duty? When the captain volunteered us, I thought we'd be doing exciting stuff like shooting guns, sticking things with those rifle knives, driving big trucks or marching up and down to show off our smart uniforms. But it's always guard duty, Onion!'

'Maybe it's coz they trust us, Flaky,' replied Private Onion Gravy of the same Auxiliary Special Reserves Volunteer Unit, 'or maybe they think it's what we're good at.'

'Everyone always tells me that I'm not good at anything. Doing this guarding thing, all I do is get cold. I'm freezing again, Onion!'

'Never mind, Flaky. We're due to be relieved soon.'

'Oh good, I really need to go to the toilet.'

'No, not that kind of relief, Flaky! We'll be relieved by the new guards coming on duty. Then we can go inside and get warm.'

'Yes, and I can go to the toilet.'

'Yes, yes, if you must. So anyway, not much more guard duty today.'

'Good, then we can get our reward, can't we?'

'Reward? What reward?'

'You know! The reward! They said we'd get a free bed and a board and a roof over our heads if we did guard duty. I've got none of them, yet.'

'What are you on about?' asked Onion Gravy. 'You've got all of that, Flaky.'

'All I got is an uncomfortable bunk in the barracks. I've got no bed and where's my board?' asked the rather literally minded Private Pastry.

'Oh, good grief, Flaky! It's not an actual board, is it? What would you do with an actual board, anyway?'

'Don't know, Onion. If I had one, I could find out. What about this roof I'm supposed to have over my head?'

Both volunteer guards were standing in wooden guard huts. Onion Gravy looked up meaningfully at the pointed roof above his head.

'What do you call that then...?'

Private Gravy then looked up at the cavern roof, which could just be made out in the gloom, many yards above.

'...and what do you think that is up there?'

This intellectually stimulating conversation was interrupted abruptly by a commanding voice. Both guards stood immediately to attention.

'Good afternoon, gentlemen. Please, stand easy. Can you direct me to the room where the briefing meeting is taking place?'

'Of course, Captain Ponsonby-Smyth. Across the square, first door on the right, sir,' indicated Private Gravy, with unexpected efficiency. 'May I ask, will Captain Carruthers be attending, sir?'

'Yes, he will. I should imagine he will be along shortly. Thank you...Private Gravy, isn't it? One of our volunteers?'

'Yes, sir!'

'Oh, and with regard to your complaints which I could not help but overhear...Private Pastry, is it?'

'Sir?'

'You make some valid points. I will raise them on your behalf. Don't look so worried, Private. I will not mention you by name. The phrase "some of the men have said" will be sufficient.

'Right Ho, men! Stand up as straight as you can, shoulders back and puff those chests out. You need to make it appear to any enemy scouts that they are looking at regular Elite guards. They will be looking at you from a distance, and from a distance, appearances can be deceptive.'

Captain Ponsonby-Smyth smiled, signalling back to the guards with a reassuring "thumbs up" as he wandered across the square.

Very shortly after this exchange, Privates Tommie Gunne and Lodge Quarters arrived to relieve Onion and Flaky. As they trundled off to the barracks, Flaky could still be heard bemoaning his lack of bed, board, and roof.

Having been informed by Onion that Captain Carruthers was due to arrive shortly, the new guards were determined not to get caught out when he arrived. They stood at what could only be described as semi-attention. Alert and watchful. The complete picture of guarding perfection.

In general, the Elite's "regular", experienced guards did not approve of the use of volunteers.

'I don't think it's right, Tommie,' commented Lodge Quarters, 'using volunteers for guard duty. Did you see the state of those two?'

'Yes, embarrassing. Still, at least now we're here, we can ensure the border will be guarded correctly,' replied Tommie.

Ten minutes after Ponsonby-Smyth had departed, Private Gunne spotted Captain Carruthers approaching.

Private Quarters snapped to attention, with an inch-perfect salute.

'Across the square and turn right for the briefing meeting, Sah!' he barked out.

'Thank you, Private…' said Carruthers.

'Private Quarters, Sah!'

'Indeed. Well done. You may relax.'

'Yes, Sah!'

Once Carruthers had departed, Private Gunne turned to his fellow guard and chuckled.

'Blimey, Lodge! And you say I crawl to the officers!'

✳✳✳

These exchanges were observed with keen interest by four figures concealed in rocks a short distance from the border post.

Cranberry Relish broke the silence that the four fairies had been keeping.

'Did the two guards standing on duty seem odd to you, Trixie?'

'Yes,' replied Trixie Bell. 'From my experience, members of the Elite are usually fully focused on the job. They don't waste time chatting to each other.'

'I don't think they normally feel the cold, do they?' asked Garlic Pie.

The others turned to look at the only female in the party.

'You're quite right, Garlic,' agreed Trixie. 'I have never before seen one stamping his feet to keep warm. Very strange.'

'I can understand it, though,' said Petunia Twinkle. 'I'm quite cold as well. Wish I'd worn another layer.'

'Weren't you the one who said you were fed up with being a messenger and wanted a change? So, you thought you'd try a spot of spying instead?' said Trixie.

'I didn't realise it would be so cold,' replied Petunia.

'Yes, well, that's field work for you. Sitting around for hours on end, cold and miserable with nothing much to show for it apart from stiff, aching bones and a dusty rear end. It's not as glamorous as many fairies think but it is essential,' observed Trixie.

'I noticed that their uniforms seemed a bit large as well. They didn't quite have the build to fill them,' noted Garlic.

[Yes, fairies do have unusual names. Males tend to have the names given mostly to small, sparkly female fairies in films, while females are universally named after food

stuffs – in particular, vegetable dishes. I am not sure about Cranberry's name. He is most definitely a male fairy but with a name perhaps more suited to a female. I expect the parents are to blame!]

'I'm not too worried. The soldiers that came on duty to relieve them looked far more like the Elite guards I would expect to see,' said Trixie.

'Perhaps the other two are trainees,' mused Garlic. 'Not fully fighting fit or fully trained yet.'

'That would make sense,' noted Petunia.

'Probably nothing of note to report back, really,' summarised Trixie. 'I think we'll keep an eye on things for the next few days but if nothing much changes, we'll report back to the prince. Tell him that the Elvish Elite have recovered from the battle and seem to be back to normal. I don't expect he'll be incredibly pleased.'

'Do you mind if I pop back and get a blanket, Trixie?' asked Petunia.

'A blanket? Really?'

CHAPTER FOUR

A briefing. Part One, the fairies

The briefing room was already packed when Carruthers arrived. Representing the military were General Karel Zingor, Captain Sandy Aird, Captain Ponsonby-Smyth and now Captain Carruthers. Covering the update reports on the fairies and goblins were Merlin and Arthur Moe. Mark Tyme, Mary Tyme, Bingo Houzey Houzey, Lottie Houzey Houzey and Ena Minnit would report on the search for a new Santa. Hazel Nutt and Wendy Panboil were reporting on the aftermath of the Great Non-War.

In his past career as a history teacher, Potter had been present at remarkably few meetings. He had never chaired any which he had attended. He was used to addressing young elves. He found the idea of chairing a meeting with so many adult elves extremely daunting. He realised that he was not entirely sure how he was supposed to proceed, but he knew everyone was waiting for him to speak. Potter called the meeting to order.

'Good afternoon, everyone, and thank you all for coming. I've arranged for this meeting so that we can review the effects of The Great Non-War, look at what we know of the enemy's current activities, and lest we forget, report progress on the search for a new Santa now that Mark has decided to stand down after so many years of wonderful, admirable service.

'So firstly, perhaps I can ask you to start us off, Hazel?'

As well as being a senior member of the Council, as head teacher of "Hollow Earth College for Elves", the largest and most prestigious school in Underside, Hazel Nutt commanded enormous respect in the community. At the school, younger pupils were wary of this five feet eleven, serious, stern teacher who customarily wore her red hair tied back from her unsmiling, pale, pink face. To council members, she was seen as level-headed, intelligent, and fair-minded. The perfect person to consult with the various experts providing physical health care or mental health care to the recovering troops. Wendy Panboil was assisting her.

Like Hazel, Wendy was intelligent and level-headed. Likewise, her seniority on the council and at the school granted her the same kind of respect as Hazel.

'The physical recovery of the Elite has been very quick, as you might expect,' stated Hazel. 'They have a fine selection of "aches and pains", but they are trained soldiers, so this does not bother them. Their mental health is another matter altogether. From what I have been told some troops appear to be almost unaffected by events. I consider these soldiers ready for service whenever required. However, I recommend that their health checks are maintained as problems may arise in the future.'

Hazel paused before continuing.

'Of the other troops, most function quite well during the day but have a variety of problems at night. Some have enormous difficulty sleeping. Some suffer from dreadful nightmares, often shouting out or screaming in their sleep, or just wake during the night in a panic without knowing why. Many are puzzled by events during the battle, being convinced that they were gravely injured or killed. They cannot understand how they experienced that whilst apparently remaining on the battlefield unharmed. Those who attribute it to a waking dream or hallucinations manage to continue with their lives with limited disruption. I also consider that these soldiers are ready for action, but again, regular checks on their health should be made. Lastly, there are those who were most seriously wounded. For the most part, they are ready for service now. It seems that if you know you were badly hurt but were fully aware of the recovery process, your desire to "get back to action" overrides any difficulties you might have.'

'Thank you, Hazel. Very succinct, as usual,' said Potter.

'May I ask, Mistress Nutt? Have you been able to compile a list of those guards who are now available to re-join their units for action?' asked General Zingor. The general was the overall Elite commander and the chief military advisor to Potter Teasready.

Similar to Hazel and Wendy, General Zingor was afforded tremendous respect. This respect was well earned. It reflected her sixty years' experience as well as her unquestioned intelligence. An intelligence that shone from her eyes, which were often described as flinty blue by her troops. The general was never seen in public in anything other than her full uniform, which accentuated the authority that her six feet two inches height commanded. Her hair, which mimicked the tone of a dark conker, was habitually tied neatly in a ponytail with her sandstone-coloured face set in a stern "no nonsense" expression.

Hazel leant over in brief, whispered conversation with Wendy.

'Yes, Wendy has compiled a list.'

'Excellent,' replied the general. 'Can you pass copies to Captain Aird, Captain Carruthers, and Captain Ponsonby-

Smyth? I understand that it has been necessary for the captains to use volunteers so that any enemy spies would not notice our depleted ranks. The sooner we can dispense with volunteers the better. Captain Aird, I will leave you to consult with Captain Carruthers and Captain Ponsonby-Smyth on that subject and report back to me once we are back to, say, ninety percent strength.'

'Yes, General,' said Captain Aird, with his customary dark-eyed frown accompanied by a less familiar slight blush appearing on his tan-coloured face. He brushed his hand awkwardly through his short chestnut-toned hair. The captain did not suffer fools gladly but tended to act foolishly himself when spoken to by the general. His uneasy embarrassment resulted from an emotional conflict. He was attracted to the general whilst, at the same time, completely intimidated by her.

Ponsers gave Carruthers a knowing grin, while absentmindedly stroking his bushy, fair-haired moustache and sideburns, a habit shared in part with Carruthers who regularly brushed his hand over his short black moustache. Carruthers returned his friend's smile. They were both aware of the reason behind Captain Aird's discomfiture.

If the general noticed the captain's embarrassment, she did not show it. Not only was the captain a long-serving officer but he was also the commander at the South Border. As such, the general trusted Captain Aird implicitly. In the general's mind this granted him seniority over the other two captains.

[I am sure the fact that Captain Aird is an elf while Carruthers and Ponsers are humans has no bearing whatsoever. Every elf I have spoken to assures me that they are not prejudiced against humans. Some even berated

me with comments such as "Of course not. The very idea!"
or "Elves are not like that! How dare you suggest such
a thing?".]

Once Wendy had passed copies of her "fit for duty" list,
Potter continued.

'Wendy, I believe you can update us on the state of those
volunteer elves, who unexpectantly found themselves involved
in the battle?' asked Potter.

'Indeed, Potter. I am afraid their situation is similar to that
of the regular troops only much worse. It may take some of
them months or possibly years to recover properly. However,
strange as it might seem, since our Christmas preparations have
been so hugely disrupted, some may recover more quickly with
something important like Christmas to focus on. As every elf
in Underside knows that we "own" Christmas and it cannot
happen correctly without us, catching up on the Christmas
backlog will take their mind off their own worries.'

'We can only hope,' agreed Potter.

[You might have noted that on the subject of Christmas,
modesty is a rarity amongst the elves.]

In much the same way that the fairies had spied on the elves,
the elves had spied on both the fairies and the goblins. Potter
asked Merlin and Arthur Moe to update the meeting.

Like Ena Minnit, Arthur Moe was a senior council member.
Being a quiet elf, his contribution to the council or elvish society
in general, was regularly undervalued. In reality, Arthur was
sharply intelligent with deductive abilities that, were he
interested, would have ensured him an outstanding career as a

detective. Arthur and Ena were close friends. Arthur desired to be more in Ena's life than just her friend but was unsure of Ena's feelings. Ena had been married previously but was widowed when her husband, Henny, was killed in an unfortunate accident in The Teddy Bear Stuffing Factory. Now, she had realised that she was more than "just fond" of Arthur and was wondering if he might become her future husband.

Arthur's looks were so similar to Ena's that elves, who were unacquainted with the couple, had thought they must be siblings. Arthur had a marginally lighter skin tone with the same shade of brown eyes, but whereas Ena's hair was "almost black", Arthur's hair was undoubtedly as black as the beard, which he was in the habit of rubbing whenever he was thinking hard about something.

As newly appointed Head of Classified Intelligence and Secret Services [C.I.S.S. *for short]*, (a role for which Arthur was perfectly suited), Arthur was first to speak.

'Following the war, the fairies are in disarray.

'We know that, just before The Great Non-War, Queen Parsnip Mash plotted to overthrow her husband, King Elderberry Flower. She was imprisoned but escaped with the help of her sister Lady Butternut Risotto and a small contingent of soldiers.'

The head of the fairy royal family was King Elderberry, a tall, calm individual with bluish-green skin and notably pointed ears. Appropriately, his hair was royal blue in colour. His eyes were a striking purple tone in keeping with his name. Unfortunately, as a result of his slow, dull manner of speaking or writing, he was often deemed boring.

Elderberry's son, Prince Dandelion Trinket, was remarkably similar in appearance to the king, but while he had inherited his father's pointed ears, his skin had a lighter bluish-green tone, his hair was lighter with a greenish tinge, and he had yellowish-green eyes. Fortunately, he had a speedier speaking and writing style than his father.

The king's traitorous wife Parsnip and her sister Butternut had been blessed with neither Elderberry's good looks nor his placid temperament. In every respect, they were not the embodiment of royalty. They were best described as the absolute opposite of regal splendour.

Parsnip's appearance suited her name. She had pallid, creamy-brown skin, with dull, khaki toned eyes, and peculiar stubbily pointed ears. Her long, straggly hair was an unattractive muddy-green colour. She was reasonably tall but her odd habit of crouching like a boxer while clenching her fingers into a fist, made her seem shorter.

Butternut was a similar height to her sister with not dissimilar looks. She had the same unusually stubbily pointed ears, which are undoubtedly a family genetic trait. Her skin was an excessively pale pink, not improved by her lifeless, pale beige eyes. Her only redeeming quality was her neat, tidy blue-green hair.

The sisters shared the same bad-tempered, fiery, astonishingly unpleasant temperament. Both of them appeared to believe that when communicating, with another person, that individual would only hear what they said, if they were bawled at. It is almost as though they were told in the past, "never whisper, always shout".

[Which they now do – very loudly!]

After a small cough to clear his throat, Arthur continued his summary.

'The Queen has returned with a larger force of troops, loyal to her. I say loyal but I should explain that loyal may not be the best word to use here. Both Parsnip and Butternut are fearsome, angry, noisy individuals who *demand* loyalty from their followers. Their idea of command is bellowing deafeningly. Their commands were so thunderous, we could hear them, even though we were watching at a distance. Their followers do as they are told as they are too scared to disobey their orders.'

'The Queen's forces are currently besieging the King's castle,' added Merlin.

'Although the King's army vastly outnumbers the Queen's, his troops are still recovering from battle, whereas the Queen's troops are fresher as they were not involved in any of the fighting. Ultimately, we think that the King will be victorious through sheer weight of numbers, but at the moment there is a stalemate.'

[It is important to understand the fairies featured in this adventure. They are not those miniature individuals with shiny, sparkly names or lovable, bubbly natures depicted in so many television programmes, films or greeting cards. They are not those, at times, unbearably cute little bundles of fluttery, winged happiness, always involved in harmless, mischievous fun. More accurately, such creatures are more likely to be representations of imps, pixies, or sprites.

Although, there are respectable fairies such as Elderberry, they are not the norm. Typically, the fairies in this story have no true decency. They are sharply intelligent but theirs is a cunning, devious, self-serving intelligence. At their worst, they can be downright nasty. Historically, these are the beings that ruined your crops, soured your milk, set fire to your outhouses, or stole your children. The latter being a feat requiring unusual daring or bravery, both of which are not typical for the average, small and "wiry" fairy.

Fairies do have the expected pointy ears, often accompanied by slim, lengthy, hooked noses. A male will reach five feet to five feet nine inches in height. Females are shorter, typically only reaching between four feet nine and five feet six. Fairy hair and skin tones are as varied as a paint chart.

Flitting about on gossamer wings is also not normal for fairies. Remarkably few fairies grow wings. Those that do, find them an embarrassing association with their "jolly" little cousins. They tend to keep this fact to themselves, hiding the unwanted, appendages beneath their clothing.]

※※※

The Queen was "encouraging" her soldiers.

'CALL THAT FIGHTING?' she yelled over the sound of the conflict. 'YOU ATTACK LIKE A BUNCH OF SISSY TWO YEAR OLDS! YOU, MAN, GIVE ME THAT PIKE. I'LL SHOW YOU HOW TO FIGHT LIKE A REAL FAIRY!'

"Call me a sissy?" thought the fairy trooper. "Give her my pike? I'd like to stab her with it!" However, despite what he was thinking, the fairy passed his pike to the Queen, saying meekly, 'Yes, your Majesty.'

In an aside to her sister, Parsnip said, 'It is the only way to make these idiots fight. Yell at them until the message gets through their thick skulls.'

The sissy, pike-less, idiotic, thick-skulled fairy, who was still within earshot, was wondering where he might find a replacement pike. He was also wondering which part of the Queen's anatomy might most benefit from a sharp pike applied to it when he did obtain one.

Lady Butternut had seen some of the Queen's troops being beaten back by a group of the King's castle guards (the toughest of the King's men). Considering this to be merely slacking by the Queen's troops, she added her own words of "encouragement" to those of Queen Parsnip.

'YOU LOT!' she cried, waving her arms around dramatically. 'WHAT ARE YOU DOING? I WANT TO SEE YOU FIGHTING LIKE PROPER FAIRIES!'

With that, Butternut grabbed a sword from one of the fighters. Finding it too heavy to hold in one hand, she took it in both hands. With an extreme effort she raised it above her head and ran forward, flailing the sword about madly. She was joined almost immediately by the Queen who rushed in, laying about her with the pike. Butternut and Parsnip were soon overcome by the King's soldiers.

Seeing their leaders being beaten to the floor, the Queen's other fairy soldiers found themselves in two minds. Should they allow these obnoxious harridans to be captured or should they wade in to rescue them? Eventually, and it must be said, with quite considerable reluctance, they leapt into the fray. After several minutes of fierce fighting, Queen Parsnip and Lady Butternut were dragged to safety. As the "ladies" were not suitably attired for combat, they were now somewhat dishevelled with a multitude of cuts or tears in their clothing.

In an attempt to regain some degree of composure and dignity, the Queen took a deep breath before muttering quietly. 'I suppose a thank you is in order.' Then regaining her more usual demeanour, she bawled, 'AND WILL SOMEONE FIND US SOME ARMOUR AND WEAPONS?'

Inside the castle walls, away from the battle, everything was peaceful. Almost tranquil.

King Elderberry Flower relaxed on his throne. He glanced down at Tulip Garland, the fairy standing in front of him.

Tulip was one of the king's messengers. But Tulip was convinced he was more than just one of the messengers. He had nominated himself as the king's "favourite messenger". He had short, slicked-back black hair with matching black eyes set in a dreary grey face. Eyes that were often thought of, by other fairies, as "beady". An arrogant, self-important, extremely "affected" fairy. Although, he was five feet ten inches tall, he was so obsequiously, subservient to his monarch that he rarely stood to his full height.

'How goes the battle, Tulip?' the king asked languidly. 'Are we close to defeating my traitorous wife and her treacherous sister?'

'They continue to barricade the castle walls, Sire, but the Queen's soldiers seem rather dispirited. I feel that without the Queen's shouts of encouragement, many would be willing to give up and go home.'

'Hmm, shouts of encouragement? Do you mean, in fact, screaming insults at them, berating them for their perceived fighting inabilities? Advising them that a four-year-old could do better? That kind of encouragement? I have seen those techniques employed by Her Majesty previously. We would have to say that they did not impress us. The Queen is a strong believer in the arts of aggression and bullying, as indeed is her horrendous sister. Fortunately, we feel that this gives our troops an advantage. Unlike my wife, I hope that I am judged to be a good ruler, who cares for his subjects. Someone to whom his subjects feel loyalty and respect, resulting from fair and decent treatment not obedience through fear.'

'Yes indeed, your Majesty. Exactly that,' replied Tulip, bowing so far forward that he was almost crouching.

'Good, good. Now, our supply lines. Do they remain open?'

'The enemy temporarily breached one tunnel, Sire, but we blocked it before they were able to gain access to the castle. All of the other tunnels are clear, and we have ample food and drink for six months.'

'Excellent, Tulip. As you know, my son Prince Dandelion is coordinating our intelligence gathering, just outside the elvish southern border. I wish to send him a short message of support. Perhaps you would like to take a short break while I compose it.'

King Elderberry Flower was a popular ruler but known for his rather dull and tedious manner of speaking, which was reflected in his missives. Tulip knew that a "short message" from the King might take three to four hours for him to compose and would, most probably, run to eight to ten pages. He withdrew, deciding he had time for a large, four-course meal.

CHAPTER FIVE

A briefing. Part Two, the goblins

Potter gave a small smile and an equally small shrug. He raised an eyebrow, while placing a bag of barley twist sweets in the centre of the table.

'Help yourself, everyone. So, no immediate threat from the fairies then, Arthur? Merlin? What about the goblins?'

As a species, goblins had startingly limited intelligence. It could be argued that they compensated for this with their overly aggressive natures and massive physical build. A typical goblin was approximately six feet in height with an astonishingly huge, muscular body.

It was a challenge to distinguish individual goblins. All goblins had dark grey, incredibly leathery skin, dark grey eyes, moderately pointed ears and large noses. Their hair was usually grey, black, or deep reddish-brown. All of them were amazingly dense.

[Some goblins are so lacking in logical thought or commonsense that, although intelligent, in comparison with a house brick or plank, the difference could be described as marginal.]

Both males and females wore shapeless, animal-skin, knee-length garments hung from one shoulder. The only other attire they would wear is armour when going into battle. All goblins tended towards violently aggressive, brutish behaviour with females generally being more aggressive than males.

With their large stature combined with their indisputable idiocy, it would be reasonable to imagine that goblins were courageous fighters. This was simply not the case. In large groups they often "thundered about", yelling and shouting. Whilst this might have seemed exceedingly menacing to others, in truth, it is primarily just a show of force. All bluster and no substance. They hoped that their opponents would run away in fear. However, goblins enjoyed "a good fight". They would happily wade into each other with no provocation, if they knew they were stronger than their opponents, had caught them off-guard or outnumbered them, but most were notoriously lacking in true bravery.

'As Arthur and I were keeping a close check on the activities of the fairies, we dispatched a small team of elves to observe the goblins,' said Merlin, with the small smile of someone who knows what they are about to say next.

'Their reports were extremely peculiar. Initially, they informed us that the goblins had held a huge feast, as though they had just won the war. Then, as seems customary for goblins, most fell asleep, undoubtedly recovering from the vast volumes of food that they had consumed. The following day, our agents thought that a disagreement had arisen, but they later decided that they were actually watching the goblins training for battle.'

At this point, Arthur interjected.

'I have seen this myself in the past. Their training is exceptionally violent. Almost impossible to distinguish this from genuine fighting. I am not surprised that our operatives did not realise what they were seeing, at first. I was surprised, as was everyone else, by what happened next, according to our observers. The goblins being monitored were attacked suddenly by other goblins, with a different appearance.'

'Different? In what way?' asked Potter.

'I was told that, mainly, it was a difference in their colouring and their clothing,' Arthur explained. 'There was no discernible difference in height or build. All of these "new" goblins, if I can call them that, were around six foot tall with the typical goblin strong muscular build. All were, just like their counterparts, excessively aggressive and equally stupid. I was informed that several of the newcomers even accidentally attacked their own comrades.

The skin and hair colour of the attacking goblins is markedly different. As you know, we are used to seeing the grey-skinned, grey-eyed goblins with their drab grey or brown hair, with just one or two standing out from the rest with black hair. Apparently, these strangers have brown or reddish leathery skin with blond, light brown, or auburn hair. The new arrivals also favour a long piece of fur-covered animal hide suspended from one shoulder, but most additionally sport brightly coloured cloths around their necks, held in place with large brass buckles.'

Arthur paused for breath.

'Merlin and I have decided to split up. I will join with our scouts currently watching the goblins. I will see for myself whether these new goblins are likely to pose a future threat to Underside and report back at the proper time.'

'I will continue to monitor the ongoing battle between the two fairy contingents,' added Merlin. 'I will report back to you, Potter, when the fighting ceases. I suspect this will be very shortly, with victory to the King's forces.'

Merlin was an elf with mixed parenthood. His father was an elf but also the prominent wizard of his time. His mother was part-elf, part-fairy and additionally a powerful practising, witch. With such a background and lineage, it was inevitable that Merlin would become the most powerful wizard in Underside. Despite his mixed genetic background, he considered himself, primarily, to be an elf. His appearance supported his position in Underside society. He was six feet four with an authoritative bearing and commanding voice.

[In case it had crossed your mind, this Merlin is the same character that is featured in the tales of King Arthur, but, at the same time, he is markedly different from the way he is portrayed in those stories. Notably, he does not have the countenance of an old man. Neither his hair nor his beard is unkempt or white. He does not wear a white flowing robe or carry a hefty, ancient, gnarled wooden staff.

Merlin is the individual with the most time travel experience in Underside, using a time travel device. Please do not ask me how this works. I have no idea!

Suffice it to say that it allowed Merlin to travel to the point where King Arthur and his round table existed. Satisfying himself that Arthur was indeed the one "true" King of England, subsequently Merlin travelled back to the time of Arthur's childhood. There, he contrived to embed a sword in a stone, held in place by a magic spell. He further established the myth that only the true king of England could remove the sword from the stone. During the multiple attempts to remove the sword from the stone, the cunning wizard ensured the spell was always active, but whenever Arthur attempted to lift the sword, he deactivated the spell temporarily. In this way, Arthur's right to rule was verified. Although, in reality, these activities took several weeks, by returning to Underside shortly after he left, the Underside elves barely noticed his absence. Merlin continued to check on King Arthur's progress periodically, but, his visits were only ever occasional and fleeting.]

Merlin had a neatly trimmed beard with lengthy, neatly cut hair, both of which were earthy brown in colour. However, his most striking feature was his twinkling dark chocolate eyes that gave the impression that his mid-brown face was perpetually preparing to break into a smile. A well-informed smile but a smile, nonetheless.

✷✷✷

Hammer Legbreaker, the goblin King whispered to his wife, Queen Avalanche Jawcrusher, using his "indoor voice".

'WHO DESE GOBLINS DAT ATTACKING US, DEN?' he asked.

[It is a strange, self-evident truth that goblin Kings are unable to talk quietly. Their quietest whispers are deafeningly loud. You do not want to be in the vicinity if a goblin king decides to shout. I can only assume that their loud vocalisations result from a need to command their troops in battle. Alternatively, it might be that having taken part in so many noisy wars, they can no longer hear

properly and do not realise they are shouting. Who knows?
I certainly will not be asking one of them!]

King Hammer was a typical goblin. Huge, muscular, terrifying but not very bright. However, he was also brave and very loyal to his people, which made him a much-respected leader. Hammer never wore a crown to mark him out as the king, although, at six feet six inches in height, he was easily identifiable. As an alternative to a crown, when he was not fighting, he sported a leather helmet, of inconsequential size. Around this was a metallic headband. From that two further metallic bands were attached to the headband. One passed over the top of the helmet from side to side, the other from front to back.

Naturally, Hammer was also fierce, merciless, and unforgiving to his enemies. As a result, Hammer was unable to imagine who might be attacking them.

[Of course, in truth, Hammer was unable to imagine much at all. If asked what he thought about imagination (assuming that he could understand the question or formulate a meaningful answer), Hammer might suggest that imagination was "dat fing for der weedies" or "der clever fing wot der Queen do".]

Queen Avalanche smiled at her husband, patting him affectionately on the arm.

'I believe these are our cousins from the North,' stated Avalanche. Noting her husband's bewildered look, she provided him with a simplified explanation. 'The North goblins, my love.'

'NORTH GOBLINS?' the King murmured. 'DEM ALL DEAD. ME SITTING ON DERE BONES.'

This statement was true. In part.

In a past battle, Hammer's goblins had slaughtered an extremely substantial number of North Goblins in a devastating, deadly family feud. Hammer had ordered his throne to be constructed from their bones. So he was, indeed, sitting on their bones as he had stated.

'I believe these are the remaining family members of the North Goblins you slew, my dear,' explained Avalanche. 'I expect that they wish to remove the bones, in order to give their relatives a proper burial.'

Avalanche was a hobgoblin rather than a goblin. Hobgoblins were not those terrifyingly gargantuan monsters often depicted in films. They were largely indistinguishable from other goblins in appearance with, if anything, a modest stature in comparison. Queen Avalanche was five feet ten inches tall with a slight build. The most significant difference was their intellectual capacity. If compared with an average human, a hobgoblin was reasonably intelligent with an acceptable reasoning ability. Hobgoblins were a rarity, caused by a minor genetic deviation. Their numbers remained low as they would pair with a goblin, whenever a suitable hobgoblin partner was unavailable. Resulting offspring were inevitably regular goblins. On the other hand, a match between two hobgoblins, although exceptionally rare, resulted in a hobgoblin such as Avalanche. An exceptionally intelligent hobgoblin. This meant that whenever any thinking or explaining was required from goblin royalty, the Queen always provided this.

'Perhaps we might talk with them rather than fighting them, Hammer?' Avalanche wondered.

'NO, BASH FIRST! TALK LATER! NOT GETTING DERE BONES BACK!'

With that King Hammer leapt off his throne to join the fray, stopping only to pick up a massive club and his equally massive, serrated sword, the blade of which was approximately four feet in length.

CHAPTER SIX

A briefing. Part Three,
search for a new Santa

'Therefore, as things stand,' summarised Potter, 'our enemies are too busy fighting each other to worry about us. That situation may be only short-term, but it is good news, nonetheless. That leaves one final but particularly important item on our agenda. The search for a new Santa.

'Mark, how are you progressing with that tricky subject?'

Mark Tyme was the most recent occupant of the role of Santa, as well as the previous leader of the Council, although this was not obvious from his appearance. Mark was similar to many "average" elves. He had mid-brown skin, dark, almost black eyes, deep brown hair and a "just beginning to grey" deep brown beard. None of these were unusual. His height, at six feet two inches, was also average for a male elf. Mark's wife Mary, a senior council member, was similarly average. She also had deep brown hair with mid-brown skin, but light brown eyes. Like her husband, her height, at five feet eleven, was not unusual for a female elf.

'It is proving very tricky, as you suspect, Potter,' stated Mark. 'We have been inundated with volunteers. Thousands, in fact, but these are all enthusiastic elves wishing to uphold the elvish traditions of Christmas.'

'I'm not sure if I fully understand the problem, Mark,' stated Potter.

'Maybe I can help to explain,' offered Mary. 'The problem is that we need a candidate who will be a Santa for the humans. Not a Santa for the elves.'

'Our search needs to be refocused. Mary and I have identified a possible individual Topside, who might suit our needs if he can be convinced to take on the job,' added Mark.

[Topside is the elvish name for planet Earth's surface. In other words, where we humans reside.]

'This individual is half-human, half-elf although he is not aware of his elvish ancestry,' Mark explained. 'Some of you may recall his father, Ty Upbowes, a fine upstanding elf. On a visit to Topside, Ty met and fell in love with a human called Teidi Mason. You may recall the council's feeling on that subject, Potter. While we did not agree with Ty's decision to marry Teidi and live Topside, we could understand the choice he made.'

'Yes, indeed,' said Mary. 'At the time, such inter-racial marriages were unheard of. This relationship set a precedent. We did not even know if any offspring would be possible or whether they would be healthy. Since then, there have been two other such marriages and thankfully, all of the resulting children have been fit and well.

'When Ty was killed most unfortunately, in a traffic accident, Teidi decided to bring their son up on her own, as a human. She shortened her surname to Bowes and took a revised first name of Violet. Her son, originally named Archer, has grown up believing himself to be a normal human with the name Benjamin Leonard Dennis Bowes.'

46

[Yes, Benny, Lenny, Denny Bowes. Although Teidi now resides Topside as Violet, she still remembers Ty's elvish heritage. Out of respect, she has endeavoured to follow the bizarre naming conventions, peculiar to all elves, when renaming her son.]

'Over the years I have kept a close eye on the boy,' said Mark. 'His growth pattern was strange for ten or eleven years resulting in overly large hands and feet. Eventually his body caught up with his appendages so that he now looks remarkably normal. At six foot five, he is tall for a human and well-built, but otherwise he does not stand out as unusual.

'On the other hand, his childhood was not ideal, and he was subject to verbal bullying. He has struggled to find his way as an adult, tending to drift aimlessly from job to job. Despite that he seems quite happy and stable with an excellent sense of humour. I feel that with the right encouragement and support, he might just be the Santa we are looking for.'

'That sounds like a challenge, Mark,' said Potter, 'but, with your and Mary's experience, I am sure you will succeed.' He looked around the table. 'Any other business?'

'Have we seen or heard anything from The Dark recently?' asked Ena Minnit. 'He seems worryingly quiet.'

'No, we haven't. His silence worries me as well. It has been three, nearly four months since we heard from him. I would prefer to hear one of his intrusive, taunting broadcasts. Annoying as they were, he could never resist providing clues to his next terrorism attempt. The current silence is disturbing.'

'So, we have no idea what he might be up to, Potter?' said Ena.

47

'Exactly,' responded Potter. 'Kuppa wonders if he might be just keeping out of sight while he plans his next move, but she has told her people to report anything unusual.'

Potter slipped a barley twist sweet into his mouth. He sucked on it pensively.

'Does anyone have a further question?' he said. 'No? Excellent, I think this meeting is concluded. Shall we make our way to The Bell?'

CHAPTER SEVEN
Kuppa's police spring into action

Hollow Earth's brand-new Chief of Police, Kuppa Broth sat in her brand-new chair at her brand-new desk in her brand-new office in the brand-new Police Headquarters. There was an incredibly good reason everything was brand-new. Until very recently, Hollow Earth had not possessed a Police force.

Kuppa understood the importance of appearance. With her grey/green skin, green eyes and long, naturally silver coloured hair, she was aware that, even amongst her fellow elves, her appearance was unusual. She needed to ensure elves were not distracted by this and would take her seriously as Chief of Police. By tying back her hair into a tight bun and wearing the formal, purple, and dark blue police uniform with matching cap, she presented a formidable, serious demeanour.

It had taken Kuppa the best part of three months to create the new police force, from scratch. During that time, her largest headache was recruitment. More accurately, the recruitment of suitable officers.

The Hollow Earth Police Force consisted of two branches, each with their own specific and important duties. The Hollow Earth Detective Division (H.E.D.D.) had quickly earned the nickname The Heads (or as they were called sneeringly by their uniformed colleagues, The Big Heads). They were, as you would expect, the investigative branch. The Detectives. The Hollow Earth Police Patrol (H.E.P.P.) or HO.P.P. as it was generally referred to, consisted of the uniformed patrol police. The HOPP officers were usually called Hoppers.

Potter had called for volunteers to swell the ranks of the Elite during The Great Non-War. On the conclusion of the war, many of these untrained elves were keen to continue "in uniform" and happily volunteered to join the new police force. Amongst these volunteers, there were those who merely wanted the new police uniform (the same much-admired purple and dark blue uniform with bright, shiny buttons which Kuppa was wearing), but they quickly discovered that a vigorous two-month training course lay ahead of them. This was designed and run by Sergeant March Doubletime.

Sergeant Doubletime, since promoted to Chief Inspector Doubletime, was an "old school" elite guard sergeant. At approximately six feet eight in height with the military bearing and musculature of a long-serving soldier, recruits were disinclined to argue with him. His deep brown hair and neat moustache ensured that his light acorn coloured skin did not detract from his overall presentation as a sergeant to be respected.

The description of what was required from any participant on the Sergeant's course together with the equally exacting entry form was enough to slim the number of eager applicants down by half. Anyone graduating from his course (approximately 90% – Doubletime hated failure) was guaranteed to be a first-rate police constable. A Hopper on whom the force could rely.

Recruiting and training the Heads had proved more challenging, but gradually, Kuppa had managed to find elves with the necessary mix of intelligence, curiosity, puzzle-solving, and determination required to become a detective. Although members of The Heads possessed uniforms, these were considered to be "dress uniforms" only to be worn on special occasions. The detectives' usual attire was "plain clothes".

Kuppa had not anticipated the vast mountains of paperwork involved in her role as Chief of Police but as she gradually learnt the art of delegation, the burden was diminishing. All the same, she was delighted at the interruption her ringing phone provided.

'Hello.'

'Ah, Sir, er Ma'am, er Chief, sorry for disturbing you it seems that something important has come up.'

Kuppa smiled. Appropriate forms of address were still being established across the force. 'Please just call me Chief. Now, to whom am I talking?' she asked.

'Sorry, Chief. It's Constable Hill Walker. We had an urgent call from a member of the public. They say that someone has found a body in the river!'

'OK, Constable Walker. What's the location?'

'Not far, Chief. About five miles upstream. Just before you arrive at Babbsley Reach.'

'Right, Constable, get there as quick as you can and secure the scene. Take a couple of colleagues with you. No-one is to touch anything until I get there. Cordon the area off with that bright orange tape we have.'

'You mean the tape with "Police Investigation" printed on it, Chief?'

'Yes, that's the one. Now get going, Constable. No time to lose.'

When Kuppa arrived at the site approximately fifteen minutes later, she was met by an awkward, embarrassed-looking police officer with "worried" light brown eyes, standing just ahead of a taped-off area. Two other constables stood to one side attempting, quite unsuccessfully, to look as though they were not really there. Both looked ill at ease and self-conscious. They were holding onto a young slightly built elf of average height, with a light blue complexion and deep green hair, who also looked as though he did not want to be there.

'Constable Walker, Chief,' declared the foremost officer, doffing his cap to reveal coffee-toned hair, covering his orange-coloured face. 'To my shame, I'm the one who rang you.'

'Shame?' queried Kuppa.

'Yes, I think your time has been wasted. If you care to have a look for yourself, Chief, you will see what I mean.'

Walker lifted the tape so that Kuppa could pass through. They walked to the bank of the river. Sure enough, there was a body floating in the river, but it was not the body of an elf. Kuppa looked closely.

'What exactly is that, Constable?'

'It appears to be the body of a crocodile, Chief.'

Walker was correct. The body was that of a small to medium-size crocodile. The body was extremely battered, bruised, and ripped.

There was a large waterfall to the north end of Hollow Earth. The water fell in torrents from Topside. The waterfall dropped down from approximately two miles above the river, having thundered through a labyrinth of crevices and perilous rocky openings. It was likely that the animal had slipped through one such opening and been smashed and killed as it fell through.

Stifling the loud laugh that she could feel rising in the back of her throat, Kuppa turned to Walker.

'So, we do have a body but thankfully not that of an elf. Do we know who reported this?'

'Oh yes, Chief. It was a student at the University. The young elf over there. The one being restrained by Barry and Cole. You saw him as you walked in.'

'Barry and Cole?'

'Sorry, Chief. Constables Barry Tone and Cole Slorre. That's Barry with the green face and black hair. He had his cap knocked off while arresting this young elf. Cole is the other officer, Chief.'

Kuppa smiled reassuringly at Constable Walker. He was an inexperienced PC, who would, in time, learn that stating the obvious to senior officers was unnecessary. She decided to ignore it, at this time. 'Please continue, Constable.'

With a look of relief, PC Walker returned to his summary. 'I have already warned the young fellow that wasting Police time is an offence and that he may be arrested.'

'Arrested? Oh, I don't think that will be necessary. If this were a prank, there would be other students looking on, enjoying events as they unfold and waiting to see the outcome. Since I cannot see a large number of onlookers, we should proceed on the assumption that this was an honest mistake by a civic-minded citizen. Tell him he is free to go, with our apologies, and to please carry on reporting anything unusual he sees in the future. I would far rather risk that we look foolish occasionally than miss something profoundly important because people are too nervous to come forward and tell us.'

'Yes, Chief.'

'Now, let us see if we can retrieve that body. We need to decide what we do next.'

Constable Slorre stepped forward, removing his cap. Like PC Tone he had black hair but his was contrasted with a light face, closely resembling the colour of an unripe banana.

'I saw two other Hoppers on patrol earlier in this area, Chief,' he reported. 'Constables Rockearth and Boncebasher. With their muscle power they will have the body ashore in no time.'

(Towards the end of The Great Non-War, three goblins had been captured. They had decided to join forces with the elves. Granite Rockearth, Mountain Boncebasher and Cliff Wallbreaker had since been drafted into the new police force. This decision was a calculated risk by Potter. Arguing that the elvish community now incorporated dworfs, he felt that they should also embrace the goblins, for reasons of racial diversity. He admitted that there were likely to be issues with the astonishing lack of intelligence displayed by the goblins. Despite this, he was optimistically confident that they would improve by serving with other officers. He reasoned that surely something would "rub off" and they would gradually learn by carrying out the role of police officers. Other elves were not so sure!)

'Sounds like an excellent suggestion,' agreed Kuppa. 'Then what?' she wondered aloud. 'The Hollow Earth Zoo will not want it. Our scientists might wish to study it but…I think not. Our main job now is storage and disposal. Actually, no. Alternatively, we need the services of my good friend, Dusty Baker.'

Dusty Baker was recognised as the best butcher in Hollow Earth. Despite his family's long tradition of bread and cake baking, as a youngster Dusty found himself drawn to meat. Now, no-one could prepare meat like Dusty. From tender steaks, succulent sausages, meaty chops to juicy burgers, Dusty was unsurpassed.

Kuppa continued thinking aloud. 'I know just who to contact to move this carcass.'

She picked up her phone. 'Hello, Onion? Are you anywhere near Babbsley Reach at the moment? You are? Excellent, I have a little job for you, if you're interested. Our vehicles? No, not yet. They are almost ready, but they are just finishing the police livery. Should take delivery of the first patrol cars next week. Anyway, meet you shortly on Babbsley Reach village green. Bye for now.'

✳✳✳

Kuppa and Dusty had known each other since childhood. Dusty was delighted to help out his friend. Placing a white cap over his light brown hair, he soon set to work preparing the crocodile meat, with a wide smile on his beige-toned face.

It was not long before crocodile steaks, croc burgers and "crocsages" (crocodile sausages) were firm favourites with the elves. When an alligator from Hollow Earth passed away, from old age, the obvious supply and demand issue, that was about to arise, was temporarily averted.

At The Bell, the demand for crocodile-based food was high. Unfortunately, every elf felt it obligatory to tell the same one or two croc jokes when ordering. Doris Aupen (Hollow Earth's favourite bartender) was wearying of hearing the same, obvious crocodile jokes. She wanted to hear new croc gags, so she placed a large sign by the hatch where the food was served.

WARNING

IF YOU SAY, "Croc Burger, Doris, and make it snappy" YOU MAY BE BANNED

BUT HALF-PRICE SANDWICH FOR ANY
ORIGINAL CROC JOKE

This had the desired effect. Customers would order their meal before considering their croc joke offerings. There were those who were quick to think of an appropriate witticism, but most sat wracking their brains in an attempt to think of something different.

That evening, Potter wandered in with Wendy.

'What can I get you both?' Doris asked.

'Definitely not that Dark 'n' Dangerous I tried the other night, Doris,' said Potter. 'Marvellous pint but after just two I woke with a thunderous headache the next morning.'

Wendy laughed. 'Two? You had three and helped me with the last of my Tree-light as well! But you were extremely distracted. That is why we insisted you came to the pub in the first place.'

'Oh, that's right. I did have three, didn't I? Cannot imagine why in Underside I had any of your Tree-light though. I don't even like lager!'

'After three pints of Dark 'n' Dangerous, you did not care,' said Doris.

'Well tonight, I shall play safe. A pint of Sleigh Bell Best please, Doris. What will you have, Wendy?'

'I think I will stick to my regular favourite, Pottsie. A pint of good old Hollow Earth IPA please, Doris.'

[Wendy and her sister Candy were the only elves that used the name Pottsie as their affectionate nickname for Potter.]

'Certainly, my lovelies,' replied Doris. 'Any food orders?'

'Well, I think I must try one of these croc burger baguettes,' said Wendy. 'How about you, Pottsie?'

'Yes, good idea. I've heard that crocodile tastes like mild chicken with a slight fishy edge. I'm keen to try it. Can you make it two croc burger baguettes, Doris? Thanks.'

'Actually, Doris, did you hear the quiet crocodile?' asked Potter.

'Quiet crocodile? No, I didn't.'

'Nor did its victims!'

Doris sniggered. 'Oh, that is good. I like that!'

'How would you rate it on a *scale* of one to ten?' asked Wendy.

'Scale? Oh, very clever. Well, two crocodile jokes I haven't heard before. Well done! Deserves two half-price meals,' said Doris.

Doris Aupen is the epitome of a female bartender. Cheerful and friendly with a welcoming smile, she is the first face that new guests or regulars see when they visit "The Bell". This is hardly surprising as Doris's cottage backs onto the pub, with a top floor sitting over the bar. Getting to work on time is not a problem for Doris. She is always the first to arrive and the last to leave.

Only a select few elves know that Doris is a co-owner of the pub with her business partner, Bob Downe, who resides in the cottage adjacent to the pub. Bob has a variety of roles which he undertakes for The Bell. In addition to helping Doris with the pub's accounts, Bob orders in all the food and drinks, as well as ensuring the drink barrels are replenished regularly. At six feet five with his short, brown hair (hair clipper setting number two), slate grey face, dark, bushy eyebrows bridging his piercing purple eyes, together with his barrel-lifting physique, Bob can appear menacing. In reality, he is a happy, friendly elf with an excellent sense of humour.

Both Doris and Bob like the pub to be meticulously clean, so they pitch in together on cleaning duties. Bob is at his happiest when he is cooking. He relishes not only the act of cooking but also discovering and trying new recipes. Bob is rarely seen "front of house", apart from those occasions when there is trouble in the bar. With a clientele consisting primarily of teachers, elite guards and police officers, such occasions are incredibly rare.

By appearance, Doris is a buxom elf with unnaturally white-blonde hair. However, Doris's look is manufactured. In the case of her hair colour, this is manufactured by Lottie and Bingo's company and purchased by Doris in a bottle labelled "House of Houzey Hair Colourant, Sun-Kissed, Shade 9". Doris is not overweight or particularly buxom but has manufactured that look by always wearing clothes that are slightly too tight for her. As with all elves, she retains a youthful appearance but for reasons known only to herself she always feels the need to layer on an unnecessary amount of make-up.

There is no doubt in the minds of the regulars at The Bell that Doris is "made" for the role of bartender. Undoubtedly, Doris would agree. She is never happier than when she is working in the pub.

The Bell does not employ any other elves but on occasion Doris has help from friends or relatives. Doris has a cousin Wade Aupen who runs a hairdressing salon with his long-time partner, Maurice Dance – or Monsieur Maurice as he likes to be called. At times, Wade finds Maurice irritating. He has been heard to comment that "he never had all of these airs and graces until he visited those Topside salons in London". As their salon specialises in unusual styles and haircuts, it glories in the name "Mystery Cuts". Naturally, this is a title conjured up by Maurice.

Wade and Maurice have an adopted daughter, Gates Aupen, who works in the salon but, on occasion, helps her "Auntie Doris" in the bar.

CHAPTER EIGHT
Kuppa's new police facilities

It had been a busy day for Onion Gravy and Flaky Pastry. Having returned from their short, unimpressive stint as stand-in Elite guards, they had returned to their more usual activities.

Recently, Onion had expanded his village handyperson business to encompass all of the villages in the area – Great and Little Merritiddle, Upper and Lower Tinkerton, Great Riverstop, Lower Riverstop, Dingleberry, Greater Dingleberry and Babbsley Reach. His van had new red paintwork decorated with the logo "Gravy and Pastry Limited".

[The words "Pastry Limited" seemed appropriate to many villagers.]

Onion was busy attempting to renovate three properties in different villages at the same time while Flaky collected and delivered wood and spare parts for him.

With the money he was now earning for dog walking on top of his regular pay as Onion's assistant, Flaky had saved enough to replace his battered old tricycle. With Onion's help, he had purchased a new tricycle with a "power assist" feature. Again, with Onion's guidance, he had arranged to have extra large tyres fitted. Flaky had a bad, past history with potholes. Onion assured him that with these new features, pothole problems were "a thing of the past". Flaky was unsure, so he continued swerving to avoid as many potholes as he could.

Onion fitted a towbar with a flatbed cart to the trike so that Flaky could ferry around Onion's supplies. Although still astonishingly stupid, Flaky was in danger of becoming quite useful in practical ways. When Kuppa's call came through, Onion was working in Lower Tinkerton, so he dispatched Flaky to meet Kuppa in Babbsley Reach with his tricycle and cart. He told Flaky that the extra exercise would do him good, but secretly he did not want a smelly, crocodile carcass in his newly decorated van.

Flaky cycled away happily. His new tricycle made cycling amazingly easy. He bounced over the occasional pothole that he failed to avoid. Climbing hills was no problem with "power assist". He was enjoying himself immensely. At first, he did not see the figure cycling towards him.

'Hello, Flaky,' he called out as another Flaky cycled past with a large, dead crocodile in his cart.

'Oh, hello Flaky,' replied the other Flaky.

Flaky stopped pedalling to look over his shoulder at his doppelganger. As he watched, the other Flaky gradually faded until he had disappeared completely. Flaky rubbed his eyes. He was often confused but, even Flaky knew what had just happened was extremely unusual.

'I'll tell Onion what happened when I get back. He'll know what to do.'

Flaky continued his journey to Babbsley Reach to collect the dead crocodile from Kuppa.

By the time he was returning, Flaky had recovered his composure and was appreciating his ride again.

'Hello, Flaky,' called out another Flaky who was heading towards Babbsley Reach.

'Oh, hello Flaky,' replied Flaky.

Flaky did not look back. He was too scared. "I'm being ghosted by me!" he thought.

[The word haunted was not in his vocabulary!]

'Onion will not believe me, but I know that happened just now. I'll have to tell him about this as well. I expect he will get cross and tell me not to be so silly.'

Flaky could not know that he had just stumbled upon one of the time leaks that Potter was so worried about.

✿✿✿

The incident with the crocodile body made Kuppa realise that her new police force was not just lacking in vehicles but also in scientific equipment and experts. After work that evening, she went to The Bell for a quick drink and something to eat. Her boyfriend Redd Shooz, a private in the Elite, was on duty that night so she hoped she might see someone she knew. Kuppa hated drinking and eating alone. She was delighted when she spotted Potter and Wendy.

'Hello Potter, Wendy, may I join you? I am all alone tonight as Redd is on the night guard watch.'

'Of course, Kuppa. It's not nice being on your own,' said Wendy. 'Hazel is joining us later, as she is also at a loose end. Cotten's back in Hospital overnight for a routine check. Hazel thinks he is fine but his injuries in the War were extensive, so the doctors want to keep an eye on him.'

(During a temporary cessation of fighting during The Great Non-War, Sergeant Cotten Shirt and Hazel had become extremely close and were now "walking out together".)

'Good to see you, Kuppa,' added Potter. 'It's been a while You have been busy with your new police duties, I imagine?'

'Yes, although our only real excitement turned out to be the body of a crocodile. Still, rather that than an elf. Is that croc meat that you are eating?'

'Oh, yes,' said Wendy. 'Crocsage baguette. Surprisingly good.'

'Mm looks lovely. I'll just pop to the bar and place my orders.'

Kuppa returned shortly with a pint of "Armpit".

(Bell Ringer's Armpit had been introduced originally as a Christmas special but due to its popularity, Doris had kept it on offer.)

'I know you are on your own time, Potter, but can I just mention something for you to consider tomorrow?' asked Kuppa. 'I have been watching a few Topside police television programmes recently. Two or three are quite entertaining but my main reason for watching was research. I needed to understand more about the modern, scientific policing methods we should introduce. Relying on Merlin and our other wizard and witch allies was fine as a short-term solution, but we cannot continue to expect them to drop whatever they are doing whenever we need assistance.'

'I see. You make a good point,' conceded Potter. 'I assume you will need to employ specialists in addition to purchasing a significant quantity of equipment?'

'Naturally. Will that be a problem, Potter?'

Potter popped a barley twist in his mouth, gave a small smile and a shrug.

'I hope not but, as we are talking about a prodigious investment by the council, anything I agree in principle now will be subject to ratification at the next Council meeting. Is that acceptable to you, Kuppa?'

It was Kuppa's turn to smile. Potter's solutions to the challenges thrown up by The Great Non-War had been extreme, but nonetheless, they had proved popular with the whole Council. She knew that if Potter proposed something, the other Council members would follow his lead.

'Thank you, Potter, that will be fine. I think we will be talking about considerable expense but most of it will be "one-off". My first concern is forensics. I need a forensics unit set up, staffed with forensics scientists. We may not have people who can carry out forensics so training may be necessary. Next will be a police mortuary to store the bodies. I am sure "The Hollow Earth Crematorium" will be able to help with this and provide morticians. Finally, we will need a DNA analyst. This is a very new science for elves so it may be difficult to find the right candidate.'

There was a terrible cacophony of noise from behind the bar. It sounded like a carillon of discordant bells, punctuated with muffled screams and small cries for help. It was as though heavy items were falling on someone's head.

[Which they were!]

The "someone" was Flaky Pastry. While retrieving a bag of tools from a shelf, he had knocked into the shelf, dislodging everything. Flaky appeared from underneath a small pile of tools. As he stood, two glasses toppled down. Amazingly, Flaky caught them both. Holding them up, he smiled triumphantly.

Just then a bottle dropped onto his head. Flaky fell over once more but swiftly reappeared.

'I'm OK,' he said before passing out. Luckily, Flaky was not hurt and was soon explaining himself.

'Sorry, Mistress Kuppa. I was just collecting these tools for Onion. He forgot them.'

Looking embarrassed and awkward, Flaky muttered, 'I'm just leaving now.' Flaky departed as only Flaky can, dropping tools out every few feet until he realised he was holding the tool bag upside down.

Potter laughed. 'Good old Flaky! You can always rely on him to create an interesting or amusing diversion! Right, Kuppa, I will come over to your office in the morning and you can give me the full details. Now, more importantly, who's for another drink? And don't let that baguette go cold, Kuppa.'

CHAPTER NINE
Flaky's news

Flaky shot back to Little Merritiddle as fast as his tricycle would carry him, making full use of his power assist feature. After dropping off Onion's tools, Flaky walked round to The Meadow. As expected, Onion had joined Helen and Ewan Earth at "their table" in The Meadow. Currently, the Earths were offering their expertise on the subject of crocodile-based sandwiches, as a small supply had been obtained on a trial basis.

'Apparently, these croc burgers, croc steaks, and other crocodile products are very popular in Hollow Earth,' mused Helen Earth. 'Seems unnatural to me. Crocodiles are predators. They usually eat other creatures. They are not normally the ones being eaten.'

'No, it stands to reason,' agreed Ewan. 'It cannot be right for crocodiles to be eaten. I am happy to eat beef burgers and fish fingers but not croc burgers. I will not be buying any.'

'So, you think it's all a bit fishy, then,' said Onion, attempting a joke.

Onion's attempt at humour was ignored by Ewan and Helen, who merely looked at him strangely. At this point, Flaky joined the conversation.

'You should hear what I heard in that Sleigh Bell pub in Hollow Earth,' he said.

Onion, Helen, and Ewan stared at Flaky, expectantly, waiting for him to say something further. Flaky sat there with the wide grin of secret knowledge adorning his face. He seemed to have forgotten completely that he had been talking.

'What did you hear, Flaky?' asked Onion finally.

'Oh yes. It was Mistress Broth talking about these hens.'

'Mistress Broth?' queried Helen. 'That schoolteacher that's setting up some police force in Hollow Earth?'

'Yes, Mistress Kuppa Broth. She's very nice and really clever but she seemed worried about these hens.'

'Hens?' asked Onion. 'What hens?'

'Well, she was with that Potter man, you know the one, Mr Teapot, and that other nice schoolteacher. I think she's called Wendy Panhandle.'

'Right' said Ewan. 'Kuppa Broth was talking with Potter Teasready and Wendy Panboil?'

'Yes, that's who I meant,' said Flaky.

'Talking to them about hens?' Ewan continued.

'Yes, she has four hens sick, and she was quite rude to Mr Teasready.'

'Rude to him?' said Helen.

'Yes, she called him a nit. Four hens sick, you nit. That's what she said to him. And the hens must be really sick as she was looking for people to carry out the hens.'

'This is all very strange, Flaky,' said Helen. 'Are you sure you heard this correctly?'

'Yes, and there was more,' said Flaky, who was beginning to enjoy his new role of informant.

[Although he would not know what the word informant means.]

'Kuppa was also talking about someone called Terry.'

'Terry?' asked Onion.

'Yes, I think the hens must have died, as she said she needed More Terry to keep the dead bodies.'

'More Terry? I have not come across a butcher with that name,' Ewan observed.

'Yes, and Kuppa must have been upset by the dead hens as she said she needed more tissues. I think being upset made her hungry as well as she also talked about dinner and … a list, for some reason.'

'Dinner and a list? You've excelled yourself this time, Flaky. The most confusing you have ever been,' stated Ewan.

'Thank you,' replied Flaky, cheerfully ignoring the sarcasm.

'This is going to take time to sort out,' said Ewan. 'Who's for another drink?'

✿✿✿

In fact, Helen and Ewan puzzled over Flaky's incomprehensible ramblings for a full two weeks before they could work out the meanings. Finally, they concluded that "four hens sick, you nit" was "forensic unit", "More Terry" was "mortuary", "more tissues" was "morticians" and "dinner and a list" was really "DNA analyst".

At times, understanding Flaky's pronouncements was akin to attempting to translate an ancient forgotten script, belonging to a lost civilisation, without an artefact equivalent to the Rosetta Stone. Whenever "big" words were involved that Flaky had never heard previously, interpretation was particularly difficult.

CHAPTER TEN
Onion delivers

After a few days, Potter contacted Kuppa with good news. He had managed to find two elves who had studied forensic science.

Dawn Lite had attended a college course whilst on an extended visit Topside. She had "topped up" the information she had gained from the course with hours of further online investigation. Dawn told Potter that she considered her forensic knowledge extensive but untested. She was eager to put her knowledge to use. At the same time gaining valuable, practical skills.

Blue Berrie was a self-taught enthusiast, having taken an interest in the subject and then researched it online. Potter felt that Blue would need support from Dawn, as the more formally trained colleague.

Kuppa had yet to locate a DNA specialist. Potter had sent through details of other elves who were interested in joining the police force. It was clear to Kuppa that her best chance was Diamond Werk. Potter knew Diamond as a former pupil. On her details, he had added a notation to the effect that although Diamond's parents, Brick and Crystal Werk, were "tried and trusted" building contractors, Diamond's interests lay elsewhere. Diamond's passion was mathematics. Additionally, she had a keen interest in all branches of science and computing with excellent skills in all areas. Kuppa realised that with such obvious intelligence, knowledge and flexibility, Diamond might be just the person she needed.

The next morning, Potter rang with further news.

'Hi Kuppa. You will be pleased to hear that your scientific equipment has arrived. I arranged for it to be delivered to Gravy and Pastry Limited, in Little Merritiddle. They will bring it down to you.'

'Gravy and Pastry? What, Onion and Flaky? Are you trying to give me heart failure, Potter? Most of that equipment is fragile. I cannot imagine what state it will be in if Flaky gets his hands on it!'

'It is OK, Kuppa, really. Onion has promised me that everything will be packed protectively, and he is sending Flaky off on one or two other jobs to keep him out of the way.'

'He had better, Potter! If anything gets damaged it could put my operation back by weeks, possibly months. Why are we using Onion, anyway?'

'Necessity, Kuppa. If I could have used one of the bigger, more established companies I would have. The freight haulage company, which is based near our western border, were worried about their safety around our border. They were concerned about the recent fighting and the continued unrest amongst the fairies and goblins. In truth, they did not want to deliver anywhere near the border. I persuaded them to deliver just inside our borders. Naturally, I suggested Little Merritiddle as it is near to the border and has a delivery company.'

'Hmm, how much was the bribe, Potter?' asked Kuppa.

'Sizeable, but worth it to ensure you receive everything.'

***

Onion had been true to his word. As soon as Flaky arrived back from his dog walking, Onion sent him off to deliver wood to four of the local villages. The wood was needed to allow Onion to complete the various renovation and rejuvenation tasks he was undertaking. Having the wood ready and waiting for him would save time.

Onion was very carefully loading his new van with boxes, ensuring each box was the correct way up and surrounded by protective packing material. Unexpectedly, he was interrupted by a familiar voice behind him.

'What's ELIGARE?' asked Flaky holding a box.

Onion quickly but cautiously retrieved the box from Flaky. He placed it (right side up) in his van with the other boxes. He listened carefully as he loaded it. He was relieved when he heard no tell-tale sounds of breakage from within the box.

'You had the box upside down. It says "FRAGILE" and you shouldn't be touching any of those boxes at all. What are you doing here? You've only been gone five minutes!'

'Sorry, Onion. I picked up the wood from the store but, I couldn't remember where I had to deliver it.'

'Where's the list I gave you?' said Onion.

'In my pocket,' answered Flaky. He had a silly grin on his face that suggested he was quite pleased with himself. 'I've kept it safe.'

Onion sighed. 'Well, try reading it. It tells you what to deliver to each village.'

'Oh right.'

'Now get moving, Flaky. People are waiting on you. When you are finished get over to The Meadow and get your lunch. I'll try to join you there when I'm done.'

Onion sighed again, as Flaky left. 'What on earth did I do to deserve Flaky?' he muttered to himself. 'Sometimes, it's like looking after a small child!'

***

When Kuppa spotted the arrival of Onion's van sporting its new, bright, shiny red paint she was surprised. With its new logo of Gravy and Pastry Limited, it appeared quite professional. She was quite delighted when Onion opened the rear doors, revealing a substantial collection of boxes, each wrapped in protective packaging and securely tied into the van. Onion loaded the first few boxes onto a shiny, new hand barrow. He gently manoeuvred the barrow onto the van's tail-lift. He lowered the tail-lift, which Kuppa noticed descended smoothly and quietly.

Kuppa greeted Onion with a smile.

'Good morning, Onion. Is this a new van? It looks very smart.'

'Not new, Kuppa, but as good as new. It's been completely overhauled and reconditioned,' said Onion, beaming with pride.

Onion was very comfortable with his old van. He would never dream of replacing it, unless absolutely necessary. Nonetheless, with the profits from his recent unexpected, additional work, Onion had purchased a new motor for it, a new battery, a new tail-lift, the new barrow, and the straps to hold cargo securely in place. Not forgetting, of course, the new paintwork he had commissioned. Further to that, Onion had also had the seats re-upholstered and reconditioned, new suspension fitted and four new tyres. Onion had also spent out on a new heater and a new air conditioning system. His van truly was "as good as new".

'So where do you want the boxes put, Kuppa?' Onion asked.

Kuppa was temporarily taken aback at this unusually efficient version of Onion. Then again, Kuppa had failed to realise that practical work was where Onion excelled. Intellectually, Onion was not the brightest elf around, but he could tackle any task involving the use of his hands. It was the skill that made him such a useful handyperson.

Kuppa soon found her voice.

'We have put a room aside for all of the boxes. Follow me and I will introduce you to Dawn and Blue, our new scientific specialists, who will be using all of this wonderful apparatus. They will help you unload and position the boxes.'

CHAPTER ELEVEN
An incident at The Meadow

F rank and Pearly Wisdom were the owners of The Meadow in Little Merritiddle. It would be challenging to find a more disparate couple.

Pearly was approximately five feet ten inches in height with a slim build, but it was her colouring that most people noticed. Her face was a gentle, welcoming, sandy brown tone, which was not particularly unusual. It was the colour of her hair that stood out. It was deep brown, verging on black, with a natural blueish-green highlight. An exceptional shade even for an elf. Pearly's bright, blue eyes seemed to sparkle, reflecting her relaxed, "easy going", pleasant personality. She loved running the pub. Pearly could not imagine that there was any better employment in Underside.

Frank was a fraction over six feet two in height, with pale, almost white hair, which he kept cropped in what he considered a military style. Regrettably, as Frank's complexion was pallid, virtually ashen, this meant that in some light he appeared to have no hair whatsoever, just a white head. Frank had extremely dark brown eyes, which many of the pub's customers found menacing. These together with his semi-permanent dour expression, revealed Frank's true personality to be anything other than welcoming. In reality, he did not share Pearly's enthusiasm for the work. He would rather have been the owner of a restaurant. He considered the pub customers (or punters as he liked to call them), to be an intrusive nuisance. A necessary nuisance, but a nuisance, nonetheless. For their part, the regulars of the pub, tolerated Frank's gloomy, often angry, behaviour with amusement. As Onion once commented, 'He's a dreadful misery but he's a fantastic cook.'

Frank and Pearly had just completed setting everything out for the evening trade.

Frank was hoping to shoot a couple of rabbits so that they could prepare rabbit casserole as a special for the next day. By preference, Frank preferred to use a crossbow rather than a shotgun as it caused less damage to the rabbits. He had just loaded his crossbow, prior to leaving, when Flaky walked in.

Flaky's sudden appearance together with his greeting call of 'Hello, Frank!' caught Frank by surprise. Frank jumped, shooting himself in the foot with the crossbow bolt.

[I expect very few of us have experience of this kind of pain, but I imagine it must really, really hurt.]

'Oh, *@#, *@#!' screamed Frank.

[Or something else that I would prefer not to include, in case a small child sees this.]

'Pearly! Pearly!' yelled Frank. 'Quickly, get me to the Hospital! I've hurt myself badly! I'm bleeding all over the floor! Call Helen and Ewan. See if they can cover the pub for us!'

Flaky stood there in confusion, wondering if it was something he had said or done.

Onion arrived in time to see Pearly driving off down the road at breakneck speed. He could see Frank sitting next to her, in the passenger seat, with a pained expression on his face.

As he walked into the bar, he spotted Flaky standing looking rather uncomfortable. Helen and Ewan Earth were waiting behind the bar.

Hoping for a sensible reply, which he knew was unlikely if he asked Flaky, Onion said to Helen and Ewan, 'What's going on? Where are Pearly and Frank dashing off to?'

'The Hospital. It's Frank's own fault. He shot himself in the foot,' Ewan replied.

'Why, what did he say?' asked Onion.

Ewan looked puzzled at first. 'No, it is not what he *said*. Apparently, Flaky arrived and said Hello. Frank jumped and shot a crossbow bolt through his foot.'

It was not a shock to Onion that Flaky was involved with the incident. Somehow, where Flaky was concerned, it was inevitable.

'A crossbow bolt! In the pub?' asked Onion. 'Are you sure you had nothing to do with this, Flaky?'

'I only said Hello,' said Flaky. 'Honest, Onion! I'm sorry, I didn't mean to make Frank hurt himself. I always get it wrong, don't I?'

Onion could see that Flaky was upset, close to tears.

'Don't be hard on Flaky, Onion,' said Helen. 'As Ewan said, this was Frank's own fault. Fancy holding a loaded crossbow inside the bar! Asking for an accident if you ask me.'

'Yes, couldn't agree more,' added Ewan, 'as they were leaving, I heard Pearly telling Frank off. Told him what a silly fool he was, for loading the crossbow in the pub. When she asked him what he was thinking, he mumbled something about trying to save time. I don't think Pearly was impressed!'

'No, I should think not! Extremely dangerous. Stands to reason that someone was bound to get hurt,' said Helen.

Onion walked across to Flaky. 'Have you had anything to eat yet, Flaky?'

When Flaky said, 'No, I didn't feel hungry,' Onion knew that Flaky was genuinely shaken up.

Onion put his arm around Flaky's shoulders.

'It's alright. I know you did nothing wrong. Come on, let's look at the menu.'

Secretly, Onion was incredibly pleased. It made a pleasant change to hear that an accident was not Flaky's fault. Usually, he could be confident that something like this *was* Flaky's fault, especially given Flaky's track record with Frank.

Years back, before Frank and Pearly were married, Frank was sole owner of the pub. Pearly White, as she was then, was Frank's bartender. One evening, Pearly called to say she was not well. As Flaky was the only person sitting in the pub at that time, Frank asked him if he could help.

[With the benefit of hindsight, Frank realised that this was not one of his better ideas.]

As usual, Flaky's enthusiasm vastly outweighed his abilities. He happily agreed to collect used glasses for Frank. Unfortunately, as Flaky walked behind the bar, carrying a full tray, he tripped. As he fell forward, smashing all of the glasses, the tray slid out of his hands and under Frank's feet. In trying to keep his balance, Frank knocked three drinks off the bar and accidentally tipped a pint over Ewan Earth who had just arrived and was waiting at the bar, to be served.

Helen Earth was just behind Ewan and luckily avoided the beer deluge. She immediately took charge.

'Flaky, best if you take a seat, dear.'

She chuckled as she looked at her cousin, who was soaked and dripping beer slowly onto the floor.

'Ewan, looking at the state you are in, you should pop home and change. Frank, I can help you clean up that mess in a minute. Anything needing to be delivered to a table?'

'Oh thanks, Helen. These two meals are for table four.'

When Pearly proposed to Frank, they decided that the obvious venue, for their wedding, was The Meadow. Pearly, who often felt sorry for Flaky, wanted him to be part of the proceedings. She was not put off by past problems when she was organising the event. Pearly decided that Flaky might be useful in marshalling vehicles into the car park. The resulting mess of carts, bikes, cars, and taxis was amazing. No-one could imagine how Flaky had caused so much chaos in a mere fifteen minutes. Frank bravely attempted to stay calm, as he extricated everyone from their various means of transport.

Frank sent Flaky to act as usher to the guests as they arrived. His attempt was remembered for many years after. He stood at the entrance to the room, where the ceremony was being held, solemnly asking each guest in turn, "Guide or Broom?"!

Afterwards, Pearly tried to improve Frank's decidedly sour mood.

'Flaky can't help it, Frank. He means well. He's just not too bright.'

'Means well? Not too bright?' snarled Frank. 'Wherever he goes, whatever he does, it is disastrous. He nearly ruined the wedding.'

'Oh, I wouldn't go that far, Frank.'

'Really! No-one knew where to sit because of his ridiculous attempt at ushering so I had to sort that out. Then I spent over an hour getting the car park clear, after the ceremony. Not how I wanted to spend my wedding day!'

'I think it's just that Flaky doesn't always grasp things first time and he is a bit unlucky. Let's enjoy the rest of the day, shall we?' said Pearly.

'Unlucky? No, I think it's more than that. I know you feel sorry for him, but I just think that Flaky is the stupidest elf I have ever met!'

[With this history behind them, perhaps it was no wonder that Frank jumped when Flaky appeared suddenly.]

CHAPTER TWELVE

The Tymes arrive in London

M ark and Mary Tyme had travelled to London, using one of Santa's secret entrances to Topside. Their mission was to find the son of Ty and Teidi Upbowes or Violet Bowes as she was now known. Their intention was to talk with him; hopefully to persuade him to become the new Santa Claus. They decided that their best course of action was to visit their friend Bingo Houzey Houzey.

[Bingo Houzey Houzey, a senior member of the Council, is unique in elvish society. To begin with, his surname is unusual. Few elves have a double-barrelled surname. Even fewer elves have a double-barrelled surname, where both names are the same. In this respect, Bingo's surname is a rarity indeed.

Bingo has a brother and two sisters, as his mother gave birth to quadruplets. This is also quite unexpected, even extraordinary amongst elves. Bingo was originally named Spick but has changed his first name several times before settling on Bingo. Once again, few elves do this.

In Underside, Bingo is the storekeeper for the elves. The elf who can supply the elves with virtually anything they require. If it is not in his store, he can get it for you. This means, however, that Bingo spends almost as much time Topside as in Underside. Which brings its own complications.

Lottie Houzey Houzey, a senior member of the Council and Bingo's wife, also splits her time between Underside and Topside, which brings her the same type of complication as Bingo.

Bingo has two stores (amongst several) that he sees as the gems in the Houzey & Houzey business. One of these is the store in Hollow Earth, the other the store in central London.]

At the time of Mark and Mary's visit, Lottie was managing the store in Hollow Earth with Bingo managing the London store, under the guise of his own great-grandson, Franklin Houzey.

[For those of you interested further, there is a (very) detailed section on Bingo and Lottie at the end of this chapter... I can only apologise!]

As soon as Mark and Mary entered Bingo's store, he greeted them warmly.

'Mark, Mary, what a pleasant surprise. I didn't expect to see you here in London. There must be a special reason for your visit. What can I help you with?'

'We're looking for someone, Bingo, and hoping you can help us find him.'

'Sorry, my name's Franklin, not Bingo' said Franklin (Bingo) with a wink and a slightly apologetic grin. 'So, who is it you're looking for?'

'Ty and Teidi's son, Archer,' replied Mary. 'We think he might be called Benjamin now.'

'Oh yes, I know Benny. Before Ty died in that accident, he asked me to keep an eye on Teidi and Benny, should anything ever happen to him. I told him not to be foolish, but Ty had a feeling of foreboding, some kind of premonition. It was as if he knew that something would happen to him. So, reluctantly, I agreed. Since Ty's death I have kept in close contact with Teidi and Benny. To Teidi, who now calls herself Violet, I am a good friend; to Benny, a surrogate uncle.'

'That's incredible, Bi…Franklin!' Mark exclaimed. 'We did not imagine finding Benny would be so straightforward. Where would he be, at the moment?'

'I've no idea where he is right now,' said Franklin, 'but I know exactly where Benny will be this evening. I am going to watch him try his hand at stand-up comedy tonight.'

'Stand-up comedy?' asked Mark. 'We heard he was struggling to find something he liked, having tried various jobs but we thought he had settled on teaching.'

'That's true, in part,' admitted Franklin. 'He was teaching for three months but before that he tried any job he could get. For a while he was a janitor, then a bouncer at a nightclub, then a painter and decorator. He followed that with attempts to become an artist and an author, before moving on to become a children's entertainer, which he still does as that pays the rent on his flat. You say you heard he was trying to find something he likes?' Franklin asked.

'Yes, that's what we were told,' said Mary.

'Well, let me give you a more accurate picture. An honest one from someone who cares for the boy but is aware of both his abilities and his shortcomings. At best, he was only an average janitor, an average bouncer and a poor painter and decorator. He had major difficulties as a teacher. He was too nice. He could not control the children.'

'What about those other jobs he tried?' said Mark.

'Mixed results,' said Franklin. 'I read some of his writings. They weren't bad but they lacked that something, that vital spark you need to be successful. His artwork, on the other hand, is excellent. His drawings and paintings are marvellous. Of course, the problem with art is getting your work recognised. He has sold two or three pieces but that is all. Aside from the art, he is an excellent children's entertainer so that's why I want to see his stand-up routine tonight. I think it is something he might be good at, as long as he remembers it is an adult audience he is playing to. Where his long-term future lies, I cannot be sure.'

'I see,' said Mark. 'Where is he booked for this comedy performance? We would really like to speak with him.'

'I have the address, but it isn't really a booking, as such,' explained Franklin. 'The performers pay a small fee to get a five-minute slot in the hope of a future, real booking.'

'Ah, that gives me an idea for how I might approach him to see if he might be open to a proposition,' said Mark.

***

Currently, Benny Bowes was visiting his mother. This did not occur often. Benny did not share a strong, loving bond with his mother. His occasional visits did not occur because he loved to see her. He just felt an obligation to stay in touch with his only living relative. Something his mother did not reciprocate. On no occasion had she instigated contact with her son. Despite countless invites, Benny's mother had never visited him at any of his many flats or "house shares". As a result, he saw no need to visit her for any length of time. However, Benny's mother inadvertently extended all of his visits with her "tea ritual". Something that always tried his patience.

As soon as Benny turned up at his mother's house, she insisted on making him a cup of tea, but waiting for his mother to make a cup of tea was just like watching paint dry. More accurately, it was like watching paint dry, that had been applied poorly and hastily by a DIY painter with more enthusiasm than skill.

[You might have experienced this yourself. The DIY "expert" insists on tackling the task, without any assistance. "I know what I'm doing. I've done this before." You sit waiting for ages, fighting off the boredom, only for the end result to be a complete let-down.]

Typically, Benny's mother would turn up about thirty minutes after he arrived, presenting him with a mug of grey liquid with unidentified "bits" floating in it. Benny would, out of respect to his mother, dutifully sip the stone-cold "tea" for a while, carefully sieving the bits (usually tea leaves) through his teeth.

If Benny was lucky, the phone rang while he was there. "Saved by the bell!" That gave him an opportunity to empty his cup into a pot plant, as well as a reason to excuse himself and leave. He never understood what his mother did during her tea preparation, since he had never been allowed to enter the kitchen while his mother was making the tea. For reasons unknown to him, his mother hated anyone entering the "domain" of her kitchen.

As a result, Benny had never found out why his mother took so long preparing one cup of tea, but he had his suspicions. He knew she was easily distracted. The "Ooh" and "Aah" sounds that he heard periodically suggested his mother was looking at online pictures of animals or babies. Occasionally, she punctuated this with "Oh, I've won something!", indicating she had now moved to a gambling website. It was little wonder that making a drink took her so long.

Benny considered himself lucky that his mother remembered he was there at all. Benny did not mind. He had not been "close" to her for years. They were always polite to each other when they met. On the surface, his mother always seemed pleased to see him, but Benny suspected that his mother would not notice if his visits ceased completely.

Benny had tried untold times to mend their broken relationship without ever knowing why or how it had become broken. He had suggested visiting somewhere like a museum or going out one evening for a meal or to the cinema. His mother turned down all of his offers. In particular, she would not contemplate venturing out after dark. "Not with that Jim the Slasher about" she would say. Benny had never had the heart to tell her the real name of the Victorian killer she was referring to or that he would have died decades ago. Therefore, he knew for certain that there was no point mentioning that night's performance to his mother.

ADDENDUM TO
CHAPTER TWELVE
Bingo's family history

[Unfortunately (or fortunately depending on your viewpoint), this Addendum is that detailed section on Bingo and Lottie, that I mentioned earlier. Naturally, you may not wish to expend any time reading this. That is up to you entirely, but if you do read it, you may find that it provides you with a few diverting minutes. Should you feel afterwards that your time has not been well spent (or even wasted), as I said before, I can only apologise!]

As has been noted previously, an elf with a double-barrelled surname was unusual in elvish society. An elf sporting a double-barrelled surname where both names were the same was downright peculiar. As might be expected, the reason for this was equally peculiar.

Bingo's mother, Pristine Houzey had fallen for one of her very distant cousins, Perfect Houzey. When it came to the wedding, their families did not expect any disputes in choosing their married name. It was straightforward. Surely, they would simply become Mr and Mrs Houzey.

Unfortunately, both elves tended to believe stubbornly that they were always correct. Both were also exceptionally proud of their family histories as well as their family name. Pity the elf that spelt Houzey incorrectly.

As with all elves, the members of both Houzey families loved nothing better than a good squabble. They could bicker for hours on any subject.

In reality it was no surprise, that the moment Perfect suggested they become Mr and Mrs Houzey, Pristine objected. Pristine pointed out that no-one would know whose Houzey this was. Was it Houzey from her family's side or Houzey from Perfect's side? After three weeks of pointless, circular bickering, Pristine's mother Flawless, stepped in with a compromise solution to the stalemate.

Finally, Flawless's suggestion of Houzey Houzey was agreed upon although neither elf ever accepted that their Houzey was the second in the surname.

When the Houzey Houzeys decided to have a child, another peculiarity occurred. Amongst elves, multiple births were infrequent. It was a rare couple indeed that had twins so for the Houzey Houzeys to have quadruplets was an unheard-of event.

For a short while, the Houzey Houzeys were "celebrities", with all of their family, friends and neighbours clamouring to see Spick, Fresh, Neat and Tidy. Presumably, to avoid either Pristine or Perfect claiming favouritism, nature provided them with two boys, Spick and Neat, and with two girls, Fresh and Tidy.

In time, although Fresh, Neat, and Tidy kept their given names, Spick grew to dislike his, so he considered alternatives. Initially, he tried Immaculate, Spotless, then Clean before settling on Smart. For five or six years, he continued to be known as Smart until a visit to Topside introduced him to the word Bingo. As Bingo Houzey Houzey, he felt he finally had a name of which he could be proud.

As you might imagine, whilst Bingo Houzey Houzey's name was popular with other elves in Underside, the nature of Bingo's business meant he spent a substantial amount of time Topside. Topside his name was problematic. As a first name Bingo became too readily confused with the game of the same name, while the unusual double-barrelled Houzey Houzey caused too many questions, with far too much time spent by Bingo in answering them.

Reluctantly, as a result, when Bingo set up his Topside business, he replaced the name Bingo with Tobias. Additionally, to the disdain and consternation of his parents (who threatened to disown him at one stage), he dropped one Houzey from his name. He placated them to an extent by calling his business Houzey & Houzey.

Bingo was a typical long-lived elf. *[500 to 900 years of age is common.]*

Such longevity brought logistical difficulties. As Bingo resided in Topside as often as he resided in Underside, he knew that he could not live indefinitely Topside, in the guise of Tobias Houzey.

By the astute use of ever-changing facial hair, hair dye, or even shaving his head bald, Bingo had been able to let Tobias "die" to be succeeded by Bingo taking on the role of Tobias Houzey's "son" Jeremiah. Following that Bingo became Tobias's "grandson" Arnold.

As mentioned already, Bingo was currently running Houzey & Houzey as his own "great-grandson" Franklin Houzey, a well-respected elderly businessperson. Bingo expected to need Franklin to "pass over" within the next few years. In preparation, Franklin's "son" Norman had "covered" the running of the business on those occasions when Franklin was "away". As you might expect he was already named in Franklin's will as sole beneficiary.

Luckily for Bingo, the employees of Houzey & Houzey saw no problem with the regular absence of Mrs Houzey over the years. It was always accepted that she was busy elsewhere, running other parts of the business.

However, Bingo's wife Lottie "popped up" periodically, at noteworthy events, in a variety of disguises as each version of Mrs Houzey. By the clever use of wigs, make up, facial or body padding, wearing high heels or just standing "tall" in one or two cases or "slumping" down in others, Lottie contrived to look suitably different for every wife she played.

Bingo arranged for each Houzey to be painted for posterity, insisting that Lottie was always included on each portrait with them. Visitors to Bingo's office would regularly remark on the family likeness of each Mr Houzey, through the generations, but strangely none noted any similarities in any of the various females.

CHAPTER THIRTEEN
Mark meets Benny

I n the centre of London's "theatre land" there are numerous theatres. Some are large, some are small, some are new and smart or old but well preserved. Some are not. One old, less well-preserved theatre could be found (with difficulty) in a quiet alley behind an old cinema which had been repurposed as a gym and bingo hall. The only indication of the theatre's presence was a flickering neon sign stating "T E A T R". The missing H and second E had ceased working a few years earlier.

Inside the theatre was a small crowd that had turned up for an advertised "comedy night". It was clear to any neutral observer that the crowd was enjoying the theatre's cheap alcohol more than the acts they had seen so far. The previous act, Nikky Jackson, had been greeted with total silence throughout his performance and had left to the sounds of a slow handclap and jeering.

The theatre's manager stepped up to the microphone.

'Right, you lucky people. Our next act is new to the circuit. Let's hear it for Sosso!'

After a short pause, a tall figure wearing a green wig, red shirt, blue spotted bowtie, a huge ill-fitting yellow suit with massive black and yellow shoes, plodded slowly onto the stage. His feet slapped as he walked. This sound was the only sound that could be heard as the audience sat waiting impassively. The new arrival's face was white, with a green nose and a question mark across each eye. His lips were painted green to match his nose. He leant across into the mike, pausing for a moment before speaking.

'I bet I know what you're thinking. Who's this clown?'

This was greeted with an almost polite, light chuckle of laughter from a few members of the audience. It wasn't much but it was a start.

'My name is not Sosso it is actually SoSo. Yes, I know but, my parents did not have high expectations!' There were a few smiles at this comment.

'Well, good evening, everyone. It's good to see you all here. Did anyone have trouble getting here? The roads are so congested nowadays, aren't they? But I like driving despite all the traffic. I have such a terrific car! I expect some of you saw it parked outside. It's the pink one with two green doors, two blue doors, a yellow boot, and a red roof. It cost a fortune since I bought all of the extras I could afford. But it draws too much attention to me.

'I was driving along the other day minding my own business and trying out the comedy distress feature. ...Sorry, you don't have that one? It's where the wheels all wobble as if they are barely attached and black smoke bellows out of the back.

'So anyway, I was driving along, and a police car pulled in front of me. So, of course, I stopped immediately, using the clown brake feature. All four doors flew open, the bonnet popped up, the boot door fell off and a rubber chicken shot out of the sunroof. I was delighted. Money well spent I thought!' SoSo was pleased to see a few more smiles following this remark.

'Well, the officer came up to me and asked me to get out. Then he said, "Excuse me, sir, do you think this vehicle is safe to take out on the road?"

'So, I laughed. He laughed. I laughed some more...

'... Police cells really are quite small, aren't they?

'That was not my first run in with the boys or girls in blue. You may find it hard to believe, people, but I was stopped twice last week for speeding. I was *so* pleased! The police officer who stopped me on the second occasion wasn't pleased at all. He walked up to the front of my car, took a long look, no doubt admiring its distinctive features, and said "Sir, you were speeding, *again*." I said "Again?" "Yes, sir, I stopped you this morning for speeding," he replied. So naturally I laughed and said, "How do you know it was me?"

'As I said before, police cells are quite small, aren't they?'

SoSo turned to his audience.

'We haven't got any police in tonight, have we?

'We have? Aah, you're doing an outstanding job, officer. What day is it we're due in court?' This finally achieved a handful of laughs from the audience.

As this died down, SoSo stood looking at his watch and saying periodically, 'Seven out of ten. Eight out of ten. Six out of ten.' He looked up. 'Sorry everyone, just marking time!' There were some smiles with quite a few groans. Music to SoSo's ears.

SoSo glanced at his watch again. 'Well, as you all know, every act only gets five minutes, and my time is up. Thank you for putting up with me. Hope to see you again soon.'

At this point, a stagehand walked on with a bucket and a mop handle, which he dropped at SoSo's feet. SoSo removed his green wig to reveal a mass of short, spiky green hair beneath. He attached the wig, which could now clearly be seen to be a green mop head, to the mop handle and started to mop the floor. SoSo glanced up from his mopping, commenting, 'My parents always said that if I worked hard, some day I would clean up.'

Smiling, the clown looked down into the audience.

'There is a woman in the front row who has just turned to her partner and said, "I told you he was wearing a mop head as a wig." There is no fooling some people, is there?'

With that SoSo foot-slapped his way off the stage, mopping as he went. He departed to a ripple of genuine laughter and applause.

As he sat removing his SoSo clown make up, in the small dressing room shared by all of the performers, Benny was quietly pleased with how his act had been received. "That went well," he thought. "I think they liked it. Who knows, maybe I could make a go of it as a stand-up comedian. I hope this green hair dye isn't permanent," Benny mused, as he continued wiping his face clean.

After a few minutes, Benny took himself off to the toilet to wash the dye out of his hair over one of the sinks. He was pleased to see the green colour washing out quite easily. The door opened and another man came in to use the facilities. After he had finished, the man came to the adjacent sink to wash his hands. He glanced across to Benny.

'I caught your act earlier. I thought you were very good, very funny. Far better than mine. I was the act before you. The crowd hated me. Deathly silence throughout, then slow handclap as I left the stage!'

'Oh, that was you, was it? Sorry they treated you that way. I am sure you did your best.'

'I expect most of it was alcohol-fuelled but if I am honest my act wasn't that good. I am Mark Tyme by the way, although I used the name Nikky Jackson tonight.'

Benny dried his hair on a handful of paper towels. There was barely any sign of the green dye. He stared at his reflection in the mirror, which showed his natural mahogany brown hair, and deep brown eyes. Benny's face had that scrubbed pink look only achieved by fervent cleaning, but it was gradually regaining its natural "lightly tanned" hue.

'Not bad. It will do,' he declared.

He turned to speak with this new, unexpected companion.

'Pleased to meet you, Mark. My name is Benjamin Bowes, although you can call me Benny. Most people do.'

'Well, I am pleased to meet you as well, Benny. Benny Bowes? Is your mother called Violet Bowes by any chance?'

'Yes!' exclaimed Benny. Then, as he considered the oddness of this situation, he became concerned. He looked at Mark suspiciously.

'Sorry, you know my mother? How is that, then? She isn't very sociable.'

Seeing the expression on Benny's face, Mark guessed that Benny did not trust him. He was not surprised. His revelation must have come as a shock to Benny. In fact, Benny wondered if he was being set up for a scam. Who was this perfect stranger, who just happened to know his mother? Who just happened to be the act on before him? What were the chances of that?

'I don't know your mother as she is now,' confessed Mark. 'I knew her and her husband Ty, many years ago,' he added.

'You say you knew my father? That's a bit difficult for me to believe. Actually, this all seems very strange to me.' Benny turned to leave.

'Look, I can see that you are wary of talking with someone you have only just met, in the toilets,' said Mark.

'Here,' he said, passing Benny a card. 'I am staying at this hotel with my wife for the rest of the week. We are just sightseeing, but we will be in the hotel bar tomorrow lunchtime from about half past twelve. If you decide to join us, perhaps we can buy you lunch and tell you a bit more about your parents? If you want to check on us beforehand, you can always speak with Reception. We are in room 25.'

Benny took the card, albeit hesitantly.

'I'll think about it,' he said, walking out of the door. As he collected his things from the dressing room, Benny knew that he *would* go the following day. He had nothing to lose. He might find out something about his father but, more importantly, he might enjoy a good lunch. It was a long time since he had enjoyed the pleasure of a decent meal.

Mark departed shortly after Benny, making sure to walk in a different direction. He was disappointed in himself. He had hoped for a more positive outcome, but he knew that he had only succeeded in creating mistrust in Benny's mind.

As Santa, Mark was practised at speaking with children. He was less successful with adults. Admittedly he could talk, with authority and confidence, in formal circumstances such as council meetings. Mark could chat happily at length, with his friends and acquaintances (for too long, Mary often commented).

When Mark spoke with someone that he did not know, the consequences of the conversation were never certain. He knew that his attempts to make a friendly or sociable introduction often resulted in an effect that was the exact opposite of his intention. Unfortunately, recipients of his attempts usually became guarded, questioning his motives.

Mark needed to talk with Mary. Mary was far better than he was at gaining people's trust.

CHAPTER FOURTEEN

A return

A mysterious, shady figure strode along an unused, winding passageway, lighting his way with a wooden torch. The top half of the torch had been dipped into an unknown, tar-like substance. As the torch burnt, it produced a thick, dark smoke which partially obscured the figure from sight as he proceeded on his way, turning into one side passage after another.

In addition to the dense, smoky fog, the torch discharged a bitter, eye-wateringly powerful stench. This did not bother the figure. In fact, he counted on the smoke and smell not only to disguise his whereabouts, but also to deter any other elf from venturing along the path.

Finally, the figure arrived at his destination. Before him was a large rock, with an apparent, recent landslide of marginally smaller rocks. The figure reached around the large rock until his fingers located the small crevice, for which they were searching. There was a click. As he withdrew his hand, a slow, scraping noise commenced. The large rock, together with the smaller rocks, slid open. The figure stepped through the entrance into the dusty, murky cave beyond. He pressed a button on the wall, causing the rock-door to close behind him.

Brushing aside a collection of unwanted cobwebs, which had accumulated in his absence, the figure lit two other foul-smelling torches, which were mounted on the wall, from the torch he was holding. Once he had installed that torch on the wall, he surveyed his surroundings, with his hands on his hips.

'Ah, Home Sweet Home,' he announced.

The Dark had returned.

There was no natural light or warmth in The Dark's chosen abode. The murky, pungent smoke clouds from the freshly lit torches merely added to the cavern's depressing gloom. Water trickled slowly down the walls, puddling on the floor below. The Dark had chosen not to install modern heating or bright lighting. He preferred the cave as it was – dark, cold, and damp.

'Perfect!' whispered The Dark.

Giggling to himself insanely, the terrorist briefly imitated the galloping motion of a horse, as he circled the cave's interior before half-skipping, half-jumping over to a far wall. Stopping, the hooded figure raised both hands in the air. Slowly, dramatically, he lowered his hands until they reached two panels. Both contained a single button. With a theatrical gesture worthy of any great actor, he struck the buttons simultaneously.

'Let the fun begin!' The Dark announced to the empty room. As he said this, the whirring noise, of distant generators, commenced. In the ceiling above, small, weak lights shone down. The Dark danced across to the bank of twenty to thirty TV monitor screens now faintly lit by the ceiling lights. One by one, four screens leapt into life, showing images of the rocky corridor he had used in gaining access to his "lair".

'So far, so good, my beauties,' he cackled.

For reasons that only The Dark might understand, he dropped forward into a perfect handstand. He hand-walked to a large, soot-blackened stone fireplace. Stacked beside this were enough logs to last the resident at least three years. Righting himself, he piled four logs into the fireplace. Collecting an unlit wooden torch from the wall, he strolled over to the lit torches on the entrance wall, which were now burning fiercely, bellowing acrid blue smoke across the cave. Lighting his torch from one on the wall, he strolled back to the fireplace, whistling tunelessly. He placed the torch under the log-pile until the logs were alight.

The Dark had set a timer on his screens, so they would turn on and off automatically, over a period of twenty-four hours. He had ensured that they would not, under any circumstances, be turned on all at once.

Periodically, two or three TV monitors would turn off, adding to the illusion of usage by multiple individuals. It was The Dark's aim, with this seemingly random sequence, to avoid any possibility of creating an electrical "spike" that might draw attention to his whereabouts. Only an unbalanced character would consider learning the sequence, in which the screens turned on or off.

The Dark had.

He sat down and scooted himself across the floor, until he was positioned in front of one of the blank screens. He snapped his fingers, hooting with hysterical pleasure as the screen lit up.

'Time to put a fire under these elves,' he said, laughing coldly.

CHAPTER FIFTEEN
Kuppa has order
established for her

At Police Headquarters, Kuppa Broth puffed out her cheeks before exhaling loudly. Sitting back in her chair with measurable satisfaction, she surveyed her desk. Immediately in front of her, the desk was bare.

At the edge of Kuppa's desk sat four trays. On the left of these four, there was a tray marked with "For action". She was pleased to see that it continued to remain empty. Just to the right of this was a tray marked "Review/Follow-up" containing two files. Kuppa knew what was in each of these files. Further, she knew that both were cases she could not progress currently. There were two further trays, "No action needed" and "Completed cases". Both trays were stacked high, but Kuppa was unconcerned, knowing that the contents would disappear before long.

Kuppa considered herself extremely lucky. Two of her uniformed constables had volunteered to "sort out" her paperwork backlog and introduce a paperwork filing system for her. They had certainly delivered on their promise.

When Kuppa first took on her new role as chief of the brand-new police force, she had found herself drowning in a veritable mountain of paperwork. It was a mountain that she had found both daunting and exhausting. She had no idea how to tackle it.

PC Jersey Pullover liked creating order out of disorder. To Jersey, Kuppa's paperwork mound was an exciting challenge. It was a mountain he dearly wanted to scale. In his mind, he envisaged himself as an intrepid mountaineer climbing from the foothills of the stack to the very summit of the mountain.

Before midday, of his second day working on the task, Jersey had worked through the backlog and identified the categories, that now made up the titles on Kuppa's desk trays.

In addition to his joy in creating order from chaos, Jersey also loved to create computer systems. By the end of the third day, he had set up a basic computer system. He knew his system would need "fine tuning", but Jersey looked forward to changing and developing it, as required. In particular, he could not wait to hear the computing requirements of the chief's new specialists. He knew nothing of forensic science but, to Jersey, information was information and systems were systems.

[Elvish society is an odd mix of the old and the new. Computers are used but while they are embraced by those up-to-date elves, who are more attuned to the modern world, they remain worryingly strange, "new-fangled machines" for many elves. Therefore, a computer specialist is a rarity. Someone with Jersey's enthusiasm for computers is even rarer. I imagine that Jersey might be considered the elves' first "computer nerd".]

Jersey's appearance was not unusual. He was average height with a light blue complexion with dark green eyes. This was nicely balanced by his short, navy hair, which blended in well with his uniform. Despite his acceptable looks, most of the other Hoppers felt that PC Pullover's love of paperwork or his excited attachment to computer "mysticism" marked him as eccentric and peculiar. Further to this, they thought he was too quiet, too bookish for police work. Jersey did not share their doubts. He knew his worth. He was determined to prove that any doubts his colleagues had, were misplaced.

PC Avva Biscuit was one of Jersey's few real friends in the police force. Like Jersey she was of average height with a pleasant, light orange face, and chestnut toned eyes. Avva wore her ochre-coloured hair in a style that other female elves described as "a bob". She was not sure why it was known as that, but she was unconcerned. She liked the style, which she was certain looked suitably neat for a police officer.

Avva Biscuit knew that, to her friend Jersey, nothing was more enjoyable than establishing order from disorder or creating a new computer system. Avva's interest lay in retaining order once it had been established. She loved nothing more than filing. On her first day, she purchased two hundred files, twenty desk trays and a large, varied supply of stationery. As Jersey worked through the paperwork, defining categories, Avva created the files for each. One was labelled The Dark. It was easily the largest file.

Avva decided to place the remaining empty files on four shelves, waiting to be filled. Finally, she created the trays which now resided on Kuppa's desk.

Avva also established the simple procedures by which information arrived at or left Kuppa's desk. Anything requiring Kuppa's attention was placed in her "For action" tray. Anything "urgent" was either passed to Kuppa directly or placed in the centre of her desk if she was unavailable. Avva kept a regular check on Kuppa's "No action needed" and "Completed cases" trays. Whenever these trays were becoming full, she took the contents for filing.

Most of the other Hoppers had no concept of filing. Had they known, it is likely that they would have avoided it like the worst type of virulent disease. They had no idea of what Avva did, but they were convinced that it was not "proper police work". Nonetheless, over time, they developed a grudging admiration for the officer who could find any information that the police held on file.

[Avva is not the elves' first filing clerk. That "honour" should go to Ena Minnit, the elf who keeps control and order for both the High Council of Elves and the Honorary Order of the Helpers of Santa (or H.O.H.O.S.) but Avva is, most probably, the first elf to turn filing into an art form.]

Avva had no idea what the filing requirements of the new forensic detectives would be. Additionally, she was not aware that the forensic scientists had already begun to start collecting data for the computer systems, which they wanted Jersey to create.

Kuppa had agreed to three teams being set up to collect information from known criminals. Each team would have Diamond, Dawn or Blue accompanying them to collect fingerprints and DNA samples.

Each team also included one of the goblins to "persuade" any uncooperative felons that it was in their interests to comply with the requests. The goblins developed "encouraging phrases" such as "Do der fingerprint fing, not get der fingers broke" or "Give der sample, not get der jaw broke". These phrases were very convincing for most. As a precaution, each team contained a young, fit Hopper to catch any villain that tried to elude this "voluntary" process, by running away.

Before long, Avva had created an enormous collection of files with a description of each individual, with any identifying characteristics, their fingerprints, and the DNA sample. Each file also listed all of their known crimes. She also created files for unidentified fingerprints and DNA, found at crime scenes.

Jersey updated his computer system to allow for the added information, while Avva designed the procedures that would be required to provide and maintain this information on Jersey's system. All three of the specialists worked tirelessly to enter the current data onto the systems.

The scientists, the detective Heads and the uniformed Hoppers of Kuppa's new police force were ready now to tackle anything. Or so they thought.

CHAPTER SIXTEEN
The Dark creates disorder

The Dark sat back in a chair surveying the everyday life of the elves, as it unfolded on the screens in front of him. He was dressed from head to toe in black. His favoured colour scheme. Although partially lit by the glow from his screens and the muted overhead bulbs, his face remained obscured, thrown into shadow by the dim light from the fire behind him and the wavering flickers from the lit torches on the wall.

The torches sputtered as water dripped down from the cavern wall, hissing as each drop hit them. The colony of bats, which shared The Dark's cave with him, crowded together. They gave off a continuous gentle rustle as they moved around, each attempting to obtain the best position for themselves. The Dark loved all of the sounds of the cave. He was quite relaxed. There was nowhere he would rather be. This was his real home.

'Time for some music,' The Dark stated, to the empty space around him.

From his private collection of dark, scary, dramatic music, he selected 'Night on Bald Mountain' by Mussorgsky.

[If you want to listen along with "Uncle Dark", you can find this piece on a host of classical music collections. The

title might not be familiar, but I'm sure you will know the
music straightaway as soon as you hear it.]

Immediately the orchestra started playing, The Dark leapt to his feet, prancing around the room as though possessed by a demon. As the music concluded, he slumped back into his chair. Rolling over to a particular screen, he watched, with barely concealed delight, as it showed two thieves expertly stealing a wallet from an unsuspecting elf, before disappearing into a side alley.

'Oh well done, gentlemen!' The Dark proclaimed to his non-existent audience.

'Smoothly executed indeed, wasn't it?' he asked. Spinning about in his chair, he looked around, smiling expectantly. Abruptly, as though he had just remembered his solitude, the smile fell from his face to be replaced by a scowl.

'Suit yourselves,' he muttered. 'Some people have no appreciation for true art!'

With most of his face continuing to remain hidden from view, only the scowl was visible. Had anyone been present to witness his grim visage, they might have assumed they were seeing someone wearing a mask.

[This is a reasonable assumption, as The Dark often wears
a black mask to conceal his identity.]

In reality, the scowl disguised The Dark's true feelings. In the minds of most elves, he was seen as a terrifying legend. An almost mythical, master criminal. The first name on Kuppa's "most wanted" list. The most frightening terrorist since Sedge (Mad Jack) Warbler, a notorious villain from fifty years previously. Mad Jack was accused of completing an array of nefarious deeds, culminating in blowing up a train, killing himself and ten passengers, as well as injuring sixty-three others, of which fifteen suffered serious injuries.

In comparison with Mad Jack, The Dark considered himself a failure. To date, he had failed in his attempt, with three fairy allies, to corrupt Hollow Earth's magic dust supply. Similarly, he had failed to disrupt the firework display at Lake Cavern, the cavern which contained the largest lake in Hollow Earth. Finally, he had failed to disrupt the Christmas Plus Party at the Council buildings.

[Christmas Plus is the name the elves give to the day after Christmas Day.]

The Dark felt it was essential for him to make a "statement" terrorist act but, he knew that he needed time to prepare, without any interference. Kuppa's new police force worried him. He knew he was the top priority for Kuppa and, therefore her police force. The Dark realised that keeping Kuppa's police busy with a wealth of crimes would distract them from him and his true purpose.

In the last four months, he had set up a network, consisting of as many criminals as he could locate, in Hollow Earth. He had gathered together every thief, burglar, trickster, fraudster, and con artist that were available "for hire". In fact, every type of miscreant currently plying their criminal "trade" that he could persuade to work for him.

The list was extensive but not excessively long, as most elves are hardworking, law-abiding citizens.

The Dark sat at the centre of this network, using his CCTV cameras to watch the comings or goings of the elvish community. He began to target unsuspecting elves when they left their properties empty. He passed the information to his associates to advise them when a cottage, house or business was unoccupied, making theft both easy and safe. He also started to encourage his pickpocket confederates. For them, he highlighted any individual, currently carrying a hefty sum of money.

The Dark further directed his thieves to those members of the criminal fraternity who could "fence" their stolen goods. In this scenario, everyone was a winner, apart from the unfortunate victims. It was "easy pickings" for the thieves and a regular supply of stolen goods that the fences could sell on. They all profited, and The Dark took a percentage as the information provider.

The Dark remained a hidden presence. He used "runners" to pass on his messages. He was never seen, even by the runners. It was important that no-one could identify him, should the police become involved.

The sudden crimewave that resulted from The Dark's unlawful network of villains starting their nefarious activities, caught the police unawares. Kuppa's new police officers were still familiarising themselves with their duties. They were not prepared for a massive increase in criminal activity and struggled to cope. It was a steep learning curve for them. In future years, looking back, all but a handful of Kuppa's detective Heads and uniformed Hoppers would comment on how much they had learnt "on the job" during this period.

The Dark was overjoyed. He had wanted to create disorder. Disturbance in elvish society. Something to interfere with their daily routine. He could barely believe the chaos that his followers created in a few days. As The Dark had hoped, the chaos deflected Kuppa from her search for him. With so many offences to solve, Kuppa had no time to worry about The Dark's apparent absence or what he might be doing.

However, regardless of the recent crimewave, Kuppa was not deflected entirely from her purpose. She was determined to locate The Dark. As soon as the situation allowed, she intended to discover his plans, ensuring he was unable to complete whatever felony he was aiming to commit. As Chief of Police, Kuppa considered the safety of Underside's citizens to be paramount. She would not allow The Dark to threaten that safety. Kuppa's pursuit of The Dark remained her top priority, but as she sat at her desk, she was vexed by several questions, which she had written on a large board in the main office, with a space under each for possible answers.

The questions listed were:

Who is The Dark?

What is The Dark planning?

Why have we not heard from The Dark recently?

When will The Dark strike next?

Where will The Dark strike?

To one side of these, Kuppa had written one question in capitals and underlined it for emphasis. The question was:

Where is The Dark?

Watching the confusion of the police, on his screens, as they stumbled around from one crime scene to another, The Dark was unable to contain his joy. He bounced excitedly in his chair.

'Brilliant! Brilliant!' he yelled. 'Oh, well done, team! Oh, well done, me!'

***

Prior to the recent outburst of criminal activities, Kuppa had felt more organised with her new administrative procedures in place. Unaware of the bedlam that The Dark was about to unleash, she had decided she had time to visit the "laboratory", where her specialists had set up their equipment. As she started to walk down the corridor, a voice called out.

'Wait up, Kuppa. Can I join you?' said Potter. 'I want to see how you are getting on.'

This statement was true but, as council leader, Potter also needed to see where the council's money was being spent.

Amongst her numerous duties, Ena Minnit was the council's treasurer. She had pointed out to Potter the substantial amounts being spent by Kuppa to set up her police force.

'You need to pay her a visit, Potter. We all trust Kuppa, but the council is investing a tremendous amount. We need to see something for it.'

Kuppa was delighted to show Potter the new laboratory and introduce her new specialists to him. He was pleased to finally meet them and amazed at Kuppa's progress to date. Sucking on a barley twist sweet, he smiled, offering the bag to everyone. Kuppa helped herself but the three scientists declined, out of misplaced politeness. They were taken aback by the mild-mannered, very pleasant elf in front of them. Was this truly the semi-legendary Potter Teasready, who had successfully led the elves to victory over the combined might of the fairy and goblin armies?

Kuppa then proceeded to introduce Potter to her "administrators".

'I would be lost without these two invaluable officers, Potter. PC Jersey Pullover has created and maintains our computer systems. PC Avva Biscuit set up all of the procedures to provide the information for Jersey's systems and that allow me to manage my work.'

'Well done, all of you,' said Potter.

'So, Potter, what do you think of Hollow Earth's new police force? Will the council think it is money well spent?'

Potter gave Kuppa a small but encouraging smile. 'I think everyone on the council will be impressed.'

'I am sure that they would love to see this for themselves,' he added.

'Do you think you might arrange a date for a conducted tour or maybe an Open Day?'

'I would be delighted, Potter,' Kuppa replied.

Potter provided Kuppa with one of his customary, slightly awkward shrugs.

'All we need now is a few crimes for your officers to investigate,' he commented.

'Yes indeed,' said Kuppa.

At this stage, neither of them could be aware of the havoc that was about to be created by The Dark.

CHAPTER SEVENTEEN
Mark's revelation

Mary and Mark Tyme sat in the bar/restaurant area of the Goodfellows Hotel. It was 12:40. Both wondered if Benny would show up.

'I'm beginning to think I made him suspicious of my motives. I expect he's convinced himself by now that I'm a criminal or some kind of sexual predator. Probably spent this morning trying to find my name on a register,' said Mark.

'Oh, Mark, don't be so hard on yourself. We both knew there was a risk he might not turn up but it's still early. He's bound to be wary. I doubt that he has been looking for you on any register but he may be finding it difficult to decide whether to come or not,' said Mary.

'Yes, you're probably right, Mary. When it comes to judging people, you usually are.'

'Let's give him a bit more time. If he hasn't appeared by 1:30, it probably means he's not coming, but actually, I'm fairly sure he will meet us,' Mary stated confidently.

'What makes you so certain?' asked Mark.

'Well, two things. Firstly, you told me how thin he is. I expect he hasn't had a good meal in weeks, and you offered him a free lunch. Secondly, I think I've just spotted him through the window, crossing the road towards us.'

Mark laughed. As he did so, Benny entered the bar.

'Over here,' Mary called out. 'Pleased to see you. Glad you could join us. We didn't meet last night. I'm Mary, Mark's wife. Please pull up a chair and join us.'

'Pleased to meet you, Mary,' Benny said. 'Good to see you again, Mark and a nicer venue than the Theatre toilets last night,' he continued, smiling broadly.

'Yes, sorry about that. You must have found my approach rather strange,' Mark replied.

'Not at all. I was quite intrigued.'

'Well, I'm quite intrigued by "Venison in cherry sauce", if I'm honest,' Mary commented, looking at the menu. 'Are you hungry, Benny?'

'Oh yes, starving,' said Benny.

'Well, I suggest we order, and we can have a chat while we wait for the food to arrive,' said Mary.

With their orders placed, Benny raised the subject of his parents.

'Mark, Mary, you say you knew both my parents. How is it that my mother has never mentioned you to me?'

'We knew your father very well, before you were born. We met your mother shortly before they decided to move ... here. We knew your father as Ty Upbowes not Ty Bowes.'

'Ty Upbowes?'

'Yes,' confirmed Mary. 'When we met your mother, she was not called Violet. Ty introduced her to us as Teidi Mason. Later when your parents married, she became Teidi Upbowes.'

'Ty Upbowes and Teidi Upbowes? I didn't know any of this. It's a lot to take in, if it's true.'

'It's all true and I'm afraid there's a lot more you don't know, Benny. Did you mother explain how your father died?' asked Mark.

'Yes, she told me it was in a car accident, not here but where she was living at the time. I think it might be one of those typical, little English villages. A place called Hollow Earth.'

'That is mostly correct except the accident was with a horse and cart, not a car, and Hollow Earth is not, in any way, a typical English village,' said Mark. 'I think Ty's death affected your mother hugely and was probably why she decided to change her name to Violet Bowes and your name from Archer.'

'Sorry, did you say my name was originally Archer?'

'Yes,' said Mary. 'Archer Upbowes.'

'You mean to say I've been saddled with Benjamin Leonard Dennis Bowes all my life when I could have been Archer Upbowes or even just Archer Bowes?'

'Yes, your mother renamed you,' said Mary. 'We don't know much about her thinking, but we've been told that she wanted you to have a more 'traditional' name than Archer. From what we've been told, your mother could not decide which name she liked the most so, in the end, she gave you her three favourites.'

Benny chuckled. 'Yes, sounds like her. The least decisive person I've ever met but she did bring me up, all on her own. So, I'm thankful to her for that, but I wish she'd told me more about my father. I don't even know where he is buried.'

Mary and Mark exchanged a glance. After a few seconds, they nodded to each other, in silent agreement.

'If you are willing to trust us, we can take you to Hollow Earth and we can visit your father's memorial,' said Mary. 'I should warn you that it's a bit of a journey and you need to prepare yourself for some surprises.'

'That's fine. After the surprises I've already had, I think I can handle a few more. When could you take me?'

'If you're free, we could go tomorrow,' said Mark.

'I've nothing planned. What time will we leave?' asked Benny.

'Meet us here tomorrow morning at nine,' said Mark. 'We have a small walk from here back to where we are parked and then, as Mary put it, a bit of a journey.'

'Ah, I think I see our lunches being brought,' declared Mary.

CHAPTER EIGHTEEN
The Goblin fighting continues

The goblins were still fighting but the progress of the battle had slowed. Although both sides continued half-heartedly to fight, tiredness was creeping in. They had fought each other to a standstill, with bodies stacked in large numbers, around the combatants. There was no uniformity to the colour of the deceased goblins. The mound contained an equal number of dark grey skinned or reddish skinned bodies. Plainly, there had been no clear winner, to date, in this fight. It was that least satisfactory of battle outcomes – a draw.

Many of the goblins were confused, which was not unusual for goblins. None of them could remember why they were fighting.

'Wot fighting dese red goblins for?' asked Drumnail Rockfall, whose grey skin with his drab grey hair was typical colouration for one of Hammer's goblins.

'Coz King sez,' replied Gravel Blackhead, the nearest thing there was to King Hammer Legbreaker's right hand man (or goblin). Gravel was further differentiated from many goblins by his black hair.

'If King sez, den dat wot we do den. Who dese red goblins den, Gravel?'

'Dey Norf goblins. King not like dem. Dey want our bones.'

Drumnail had no idea what a North Goblin was or for that matter, what North was, but he did not say anything. Drumnail was marginally less lacking in intelligence than an average goblin. He was a proud goblin warrior. He knew that proud goblin warriors were never stupid and did not ask foolish questions, like "Wot Norf?", "Wot Norf goblin?" or "Why dey red?"

'Not get my bones,' declared Drumnail, settling on that part of Gravel's sentence that he grasped most clearly. 'Need der bones for der standing up and fings.'

'Not get my bones, neiver,' agreed Earthquake Mallethand, another grey skinned, grey-haired goblin. 'Need der bones for der running and uvver fings.'

'Yeah, need der bones for der standing, der running, der hitting and der stabbing,' added Drumnail.

'And der chopping and der bashing,' said Earthquake, who was beginning to enjoy himself.

Amongst this group of goblins, one stood out from the rest. As a general rule, goblins only have hair on their heads. They do not grow body hair. Axecutter Gravelface was the exception to that rule. His extensive deep brown hair covered all of his grey-skinned body.

'Fight dem if try get my bones,' said Axecutter, unintentionally changing the focus of this highly intellectual and engaging discussion.

'Already fighting dem,' said Gravel.

'Oh yeah, fight dem already,' said Axecutter.

'Wot do next den?' asked Drumnail.

'Dunno. See wot King sez,' said Gravel.

Even the two Kings were struggling to remember why they were battling each other. Goblin Kings always lead their goblin armies into battle. Inevitably, the two kings now faced each other across the battlefield. They were too weary to renew their fight.

'WOT DOING? WHY FIGHTING?' King Hammer asked in a quiet, respectful, non-provocative voice.

'WANT DER BONES BACK. BURY DER DEAD FAMILY AND FINGS. DER BRUVVERS, FARVERS, MUVVERS, UNCLES, BOYS, GIRLS, AND FINGS,' replied the North Goblin King, Mountain Stonewall, in an equally quiet, respectful voice.

Mountain was similar in appearance to his subjects, with a reddish, leathery-skinned muscular build, brown eyes, and auburn hair. At six feet two inches in height, he was not exceptionally tall for a North goblin. He was identifiable as the king by his disproportionately massive brass buckle, which held a vivid crimson scarf in place. In the centre of this buckle was a huge garnet gemstone. Mountain did not wear a crown, but when he was not in the midst of battle, he was known, instead, to wear a modest, fur covered cap, previously owned by his father.

[A first name of Mountain is common amongst goblins, in deference to the great goblin hero, King Mountain Longspear, who had once ruled over all goblins.]

An unexpected silence descended. Both Kings watched, in disbelief, as the remaining ranks of goblins parted, allowing a single figure to approach. A stately figure with dark grey skin, stern, grey eyes and long, black hair. On top of the figure's head was a gold crown embellished with jewels. The figure was wearing a full length, tailored dress, hung neatly from both shoulders, and held at the waist by a belt, with jewels matching those in the crown. The figure stopped immediately in front of the two monarchs.

117

'Right!' said Queen Avalanche. 'There will be no more fighting. We will settle this by talking. You have made enough dead goblins. You are getting nowhere. Besides, these bodies will soon start to smell. They need to be taken away to be buried.'

[I am no expert, but I understand that all dead bodies smell. Also, I've been told that as goblins smell even when they are alive, the bodies of dead goblins really, really stink.]

Hammer took one look at his wife's face. It had on it the expression he knew you did not argue with. Mountain had never met Avalanche, but he recognised that look. He had seen it many times on his own wife's face.

'YEAH, STOP DER FIGHT,' said Hammer. 'WE DO DER TALK, AVALANCHE.'

'YEAH, DO DAT FING DEN,' agreed Mountain, glancing around at his wife, Queen Snowstorm Headbreaker, who had just arrived.

Snowstorm's entrance created a similar impact to that of Avalanche. She had a similar regal bearing, with a silver, bejewelled crown, topping her long, wavy hair. Snowstorm's hair was extremely blonde. Virtually white in colour. Unlike her husband's reddish brown, leathery skin, her complexion was a noticeably softer, pale pink. Her usual, warm, light brown eyes were matching Avalanche's severity. Like all of her subjects, she wore a fur-covered animal hide, but similarly to her cousin, she had shaped this into a full-length dress. Although this hung only from her left shoulder, a wide, silver toned sash adorned her right shoulder. This attached to her dress with an insignificant clasp at the back, but with an ornate silver buckle at the front. Around her waist was a loosely strung belt, decorated with countless tiny jewels.

'Yes,' said Queen Snowstorm, who was an intelligent hobgoblin like her counterpart, Queen Avalanche. 'You will stop the fighting right now, Mountain. Queen Avalanche and I will sit down to discuss a solution that will suit both you and Hammer. In the meantime, Avalanche, do you think we should get the men to clear these bodies away?'

'Excellent idea, Snowstorm. Hammer, did I see Gravel and Earthquake just now? Oh, and Drumnail and Axecutter. All of you, remove the bodies of our warriors now.'

The Goblins all looked at King Hammer.

'DO WOT DER QUEEN SED,' said Hammer. 'NOW!'

(Hammer forgot to use his "indoor" voice when he emphasised the word "Now". As a result, the ground under him shook, starting a small landslide while a nearby boulder cracked down its length, falling into two halves.)

The four goblins rushed to carry out their King's orders.

'Who have we got nearby?' Snowstorm asked Mountain.

'HEADSPLITTER TREETRUNK, BOULDER DAGGERTHRUST JUST DERE. KNIFECUT CLUBFACE AND DER BRUVVER, STONEBASHER CLUBFACE OVER DERE,' whispered Mountain.

Headsplitter was typical of his kind with reddish, leathery skin. Boulder had a similar aspect. Both were large, muscular goblins with light brown hair. The Clubface brothers were a comparable size to their colleagues but exhibited a brown body with auburn hair. Knifecut was the senior of the pair, by two years, but the brothers were so similar in appearance that they were easily mistaken for identical twins.

[Naturally, as goblins all tend to look alike anyway, this is not surprising.]

'You four, remove the bodies of our dead warriors now,' commanded Snowstorm.

The goblins ignored her, which was a perilous choice to make.

'*YOU, RIGHT NOW!* DO WOT DER QUEEN SED,' ordered Mountain.

(Like Hammer, Mountain also forgot to use his "indoor voice" at the beginning of his sentence. A further boulder cracked in half, while the previously halved boulder disintegrated into a mass of pieces, so tiny that they were barely discernible from the dust raining down from a second landslide.)

The four goblins fell over each other as they hurried to comply with their King's orders.

It did not cross the minds of the two Queens to check where the goblins placed the bodies they had removed. Obviously, nothing of any significance crossed the minds of the two goblin Kings. As a result, when the goblins "removed" the bodies they merely placed them to one side in a large pile, out of immediate sight. This was guaranteed, in time, to set new records in odoriferous unpleasantness, additionally attracting record swarms of insects.

Queen Avalanche and Queen Snowstorm had decided that with "give and take" on both sides, a solution to the current conflict could be found.

'It does seem unfair that Hammer's throne is made from the bones of your family members. The trouble is that he really likes his throne. He does not want to give it up and he gets very stubborn about such things. It's all bash and stab until he gets his way,' Avalanche explained.

'I know just what you mean. Mountain is very similar. He decided that he had to have the bones back, but he did not even think about talking to Hammer first. Just attacked,' said Snowstorm.

'Any idea on how we can avoid more fighting?' asked Avalanche.

'We are hunters,' stated Snowstorm. 'We have a large store of animal furs and skins, which make good leather. Most of our goblins are fighters but some are good at making things. Do you think King Hammer would give up his throne, if we made him an even better one from leather and fur?'

'That's a good idea. I think he would if I explain it to him. He is not a young King anymore. Sitting on bones is not really comfortable at his age. Bone thrones are really for young Kings.'

Queen Avalanche was surprised how easily King Hammer accepted the idea.

'YEAH, WANT DER NEW FRONE WIV FUR AND LEVVER. BETTER DAN BONES. DEY HARD TO DO DER SITTING ON. WE MAKE DER SWAP.'

Now the fighting had stopped, the goblins stood around wondering what to do.

'Wot do now?' asked Cutslash Bladegrinder, a North goblin.

'Dunno. Eat der food, do der sleep, den fight someone else?' suggested Drumnail.

'Who fight den?' asked OneEye Hookhand, another reddish skinned North goblin, with light, fair hair.

[OneEye Hookhand was well named as he did actually only have one eye (an eye which was blue but red-rimmed and bleary through eyestrain) and a hook for one of his hands. I suspect OneEye Hookhand was a name he gave himself unless his parents were unusually talented seers of the future.]

'Fight der sneaky fairies,' called out a voice from the back of the goblin horde.

'Yeah, don't like der fairies. Got der stupid names,' agreed Axecutter.

'Yeah, hate der fairies. Fink more cleverer dan goblins. Fight der fairies,' said Cutslash.

Before long, most of the goblins had agreed that they must fight the fairies.

Silently, the figure owning the voice at the rear of the crowd, stole away. The Dark was elated. This was exactly the result for which he had hoped. Next stop, King Elderberry's castle.

CHAPTER NINETEEN
The Fairy fighting continues

At King Elderberry's castle, the fairies were still fighting but the defending fairies were gradually pushing back the attacking forces of Queen Parsnip Mash and Lady Butternut Risotto. Realistically, their forces were insufficient to storm the castle. Their initial successes were entirely due to the ferocity of Parsnip and Butternut.

The majority of fairy Lords felt no loyalty to the Queen or her sister, considering both of them to be rude, bad tempered and brutish. Certainly not deserving of their respect. As a result, the King's defending army had been markedly strengthened by reinforcements from all of those fairies who were loyal to their ruler. In particular, the King was indebted to the support from Lord Photinia Pink, Duke Azalea Blossom, Duchess Carrot Ragout and Count Ceanothus Lilac, all of whom had provided their best soldiers to assist His Majesty.

The King was safely ensconced inside the castle with his son, Prince Dandelion Trinket.

'It is of continuing concern to us that your traitorous mother and her equally treacherous sister persist with their efforts to storm our castle,' said King Elderberry. 'We find this unacceptable and tiresome. They have become a nuisance. A nuisance for which we must find a solution quickly. Do you not think so, Dandelion?'

Dandelion knew that whenever his father employed the royal "we", it meant that he was sorely vexed and really required nothing other than acceptance of whatever he was saying.

'A nuisance indeed, your Majesty,' agreed Dandelion, who wondered exactly where his father was going with this. Dandelion was aware that his grandfather, the old king, would have had Parsnip and Butternut beheaded and their heads displayed on spikes atop the castle walls. He hoped his father was not contemplating that particular form of punishment. Despite their terrible tempers or their bullying approach to ruling, he was fond of both his aunt and his mother. His aunt had always been kind to him and given great presents, and his mother was the woman who had raised him.

[Well, his mother and about fifty servants, anyway.]

Dandelion realised that his father had just spoken.

'Sorry, Father, you were saying?'

'We have made our mind up, Dandelion. We will have our most skilful fairies cast an expulsion spell on the Queen and her sister, to last fifty years. They will be expelled from the kingdom into the hinterlands. The spell will ensure that they are never again able to enter our realm.'

Dandelion was cautious in his reply. 'That seems very fair, Father.'

In truth, Dandelion was horrified. For any fairy, expulsion was worse than death. However, Dandelion knew when to keep his counsel. It was clear that his father was in no mood to discuss the matter.

A few hours later, on the battleground, Queen Parsnip and Lady Butternut had been pushed together with their warriors around them, holding off the King's soldiers.

'What now, Parsnip? I think we are defeated,' declared Butternut.

'I think you are right. We are surrounded. We must withdraw at once,' said Parsnip.

Even in defeat, Parsnip persisted in yelling at her troops. She was convinced that this was the only way to gain their respect and loyalty.

'RETREAT!' she commanded royally. 'RETREAT TO THE BORDERS!'

As her armies withdrew, the Queen issued a further order.

'CHARGE!' she bellowed.

All of her fighters stopped in their tracks. They were confused. What exactly did their Queen want them to do? They had never previously received the instruction to retreat followed seconds later by the instruction to charge.

This confusion resulted from Parsnip's inexperience in battle. Fortunately, she was able to clarify her meaning, quickly and of course, noisily.

'WHAT ARE YOU ALL WAITING FOR?' Parsnip roared. 'ARE YOU ALL DEAF? RETREAT TO THE BORDERS NOW, AT ONCE! COME ON! CHARGE TO THE BORDERS STRAIGHTAWAY! THAT'S AN ORDER!'

'YOU HEARD THE QUEEN!' bawled Butternut. 'GET MOVING!'

Parsnip and Butternut burst through the ranks of the King's army, racing for the borders.

As the defeated army sped towards the border, the respect and loyalty the soldiers had for Parsnip became fully apparent. Most quickly decided that staying with the Queen or her sister was unlikely to be rewarding or good for their health. They either "retreated" to their homes or turned back to the castle to throw themselves on the mercy of the King. By the time she reached the border, it was only necessary to use two hands to count the numbers of Queen Parsnip's remaining followers.

'Halt!' a voice commanded. Parsnip found herself surrounded by a vast number of the king's soldiers. 'Put them in chains!' their commander ordered.

'Your Majesty, at the king's command you and your sister are to be held here. Here you will await the arrival of The Seven. As I am sure you are aware, these are the seven most powerful fairy magicians in the realm and are led by Lavender Bushel. He has cast a spell on your chains himself. No degree of trickery or spell on your part will set you free, as I am sure Lavender will explain. When he and the others of The Seven arrive, they will cast an expulsion spell, expelling you from all fairy realms for fifty years.'

Butternut gasped. 'No, no, not that. Anything but that! Tell the king, I am sorry. I beg for mercy.'

Parsnip was incensed. She had no intention of meekly accepting the sentence passed by the king. She snarled, 'HE WOULD NOT DARE! HE COULD NOT. I DEMAND TO SPEAK WITH MY HUSBAND AT ONCE!'

'It is out of my control; my Ladies,' said the commander. 'The king considers this to be a commuted sentence for treason. The alternative is beheading. An alternative I have permission to offer to you, should you request it. The king has stated that he will not discuss the matter with either of you nor will he listen to any requests for mercy. Do either of you wish to request beheading?'

There was no reply. 'I will take your silence as an acceptance of the expulsion sentence to be passed on you. The Seven will be here shortly.'

Parsnip muttered to her sister, 'This is not the end of it. We will find a way to return. That idiot Elderberry will pay dearly for this insult.'

CHAPTER TWENTY

Tulip and Bluebell
with the King

L ater, shortly after the departure of the invading armies, Tulip Garland arrived at the castle with a message for the King. Tulip, an arrogant, self-opinionated fairy, considered himself to be the King's number one messenger. Both King Elderberry and Prince Dandelion were aware of Tulip's presumptive self-assessment, but it was something they tolerated. Good messengers were hard to find.

Elderberry and Dandelion were surprised to see that Tulip was accompanied by another fairy. An unusual development. It was not like Tulip to share his news with another.

'Ah, Tulip. I believe you have been to visit our agents. Those that we tasked with the surveillance of our goblin neighbours. You bring news for us, I assume. Good news I hope, but first, who is this fairy that you have brought with you?' asked King Elderberry.

'Greetings, your Majesty, your Highness. I had thought to bring you news of continued fighting amongst the goblins but then I chanced upon this fellow on the road. He had updated news. May I suggest he tells it to you, himself?'

On receiving a nod of approval from his father, Prince Dandelion spoke.

'What is your name, fairy?'

The fairy in question was tall and wiry but, he was stooped so low in his subservient stance that he appeared shorter and stockier.

'If it is permitted, Highness, my name is Bluebell Meadow.'

'Well, Bluebell, what is your news and how did you come by it?'

'I was lost, your Highness. I had taken Brownie, my chestnut mare, for a ride, when a bird spooked her. I was thrown off and she galloped away. I was quite shaken and dazed. I wandered around trying to find Brownie. I'm not sure how long I searched but eventually I heard goblin voices shouting things like "hate der fairies, fight der fairies". I was very scared, but I crept up behind some rocks to look. I saw hundreds of goblins. Some of them were strange looking. They had brown or red skin, not grey. I left quickly and ran into your noble messenger, Sire Garland.'

'Thank you, Bluebell. You have performed an excellent service to your King,' said Elderberry. 'Tulip would you be so kind as to escort Mister Meadow to the kitchen for light refreshments? After which find the poor fellow a horse, so that he might make his way home. Dandelion, we have much to discuss. War with the goblins is an unexpected development.'

Following an absolutely huge "light refreshment", Bluebell rode back towards elvish territory on a magnificent black stallion. En route, he threw away his bright yellow wig, his fake hooked nose and removed the false points attached to his ears.

As he neared the outskirts of Hollow Earth, Bluebell Meadow released his horse into a nearby field. He knew that a horse with saddle and bridle would draw attention, but he was not concerned. A lucky elf would benefit, and it was unlikely that any questions would be asked. Bluebell walked for approximately a mile before turning off into a narrow lane, which did not appear to lead anywhere. Shortly, he stopped at a tree. Hanging from an old branch stump was a small black rucksack. Stepping behind the tree, he changed swiftly out of the clothes he was wearing.

When Bluebell emerged, he was dressed completely in black, with a hooded top and black mask shielding his face. Collecting the rucksack from the tree branch, he filled it speedily with the discarded outfit he had been wearing. Shouldering the rucksack, he walked down the lane, for a further few minutes, before disappearing suddenly. He turned down an unknown, disused, winding pathway. As Bluebell proceeded on his way, he began to whistle tunelessly. He started to laugh quietly but, after only a brief time, this laughter turned into a recognisable, manic cackle. The cackle of The Dark, arriving home.

The Dark was delighted with his work. The goblins were poised to attack the fairies, and the fairies were now preparing to fight the goblins. This should keep them all occupied for an acceptably lengthy time, he thought. There was little chance that they would be joining forces, to attack the elves, in the near future. Additionally, there was little chance that they would be ruining The Dark's plans again.

The Dark enjoyed his many disguises, as they allowed him to pass unnoticed amongst the other residents of Underside. None were retained beyond a day or two at the most. The only exception was the one essential, elvish "alter ego" of Cornflower Blue, that he had no choice but to keep. The Dark would have no further use for his recently invented Bluebell Meadow persona. At the same time that he had disposed of Bluebell's fake nose, false ears, and wig, he had also discarded that specific identity from his mind.

CHAPTER TWENTY-ONE
Flaky sees a murder

The Dark's network consisted, for the most part, of "sensible" felons. They had no particular loyalty to The Dark, but they had little doubt that he had made their criminal lives considerably easier. They knew they were better off as part of his network than plying their illegal trade alone.

The Dark had let it be known that he did not want any aggressive acts committed. 'It's unnecessary, untidy, and foolish. More importantly, it will draw unwanted attention to our group. As members of my network, you have my protection. I will not accept any of you carrying out any violence. Be warned. You will not like the consequences of defiance.'

The majority of The Dark's band of crooks could see the sense in this warning. They were quite content to benefit from the general disruption being caused to elvish society, by their activities. As many were heard to say, "why rock the boat?".

[Yes, elves use that phrase as well.]

However, for some villains, they either lacked the intelligence to understand that it was possible to commit crime without using their fists, a cosh, a knuckleduster, an iron bar, a crossbow or an alternative weapon, or the violence was so ingrained in their being that they did not desire to perform "harmless" crime. They wished to execute their crimes with maximum force, irrespective of any consequences. In such circumstances, it was inevitable that someone would get hurt, eventually.

The Dark had offered a robber the "opportunity" to break into the house of Peter Howte, a jeweller with a large shop in the Galaxy Mall. "Howte's luxury jewellery and fashion accessories (Bespoke engagement and wedding rings our speciality)" was considered *the* place to visit for "Top of the Range" jewellery items.

The Dark had noted that Peter Howte, the founder, and proprietor of Howte's, restocked his shop on the first Tuesday of every other month. On the Monday preceding the restock, Peter brought home any items that he had been unable to sell. Items that did not appeal to customers of Howte's. These were kept in a safe overnight and delivered to Peter's sister shop, in one of the Mall's smaller, quieter arcades. This sister shop, "Petra's", offered "Quality new and second-hand jewellery, at reasonable prices".

The Dark had obtained the combination of Peter's safe and had noted that Peter, without fail, took a one-hour lunch between midday and one. One of The Dark's trusted runners had passed this information to Morty Vicker, one of the network's sensible crooks, in a quiet corner of the mall. Unfortunately, the instruction was overheard, by Isaac Lubbe, an ex-associate of Morty's, with whom Morty had hoped never to have any further dealings.

Isaac was a large elf, with an unusual appearance. When Isaac was not around, other elves had remarked on his incredible similarity to a coconut. His facial colouration mimicked the off-white tone of the inside of one, while his coarse hair bore an astonishing resemblance to the "hair" on a coconut husk. He was an exceptionally strong and thuggish elf with a ferocious temper. His approach in all matters, was to act first and ask questions after. He was known for "muscling in" wherever it suited him and never accepting "no" as an answer to any question when he finally decided to ask it.

Morty was despondent when he spotted Isaac approaching him. He had not seen Isaac for three months and they had not parted on the best of terms. In fact, Isaac had accused Morty of swindling him, after their last job together. He was surprised to see a small, crooked smile on Isaac's face. It did not bode well.

'Got yourself a nice little earner then, Mr Vicker?' said Isaac. 'You'll be needing someone to help out then, won't you, Mr Vicker?'

'No, I'm fine, thank you, Mr Lubbe,' Morty said, attempting to depart.

Isaac grabbed Morty's shoulder with his huge hand. A hand that would not have looked out of place on the end of a gorilla's arm. He pulled Morty back towards him.

'And I said, you'll be needing someone to help you then, won't you, Mr Vicker?' repeated Isaac, with barely concealed menace.

Morty was an intelligent, non-violent elf of "modest" build, who knew better than to argue with Isaac. Wiping a small bead of sweat from his pale green face, before pushing his hand through his short, navy coloured hair, Morty hesitatingly replied.

'Do you know what, Mr Lubbe? I think I need someone to help me with this job. Are you free at midday next Monday?'

'Oh yes, I'm free,' said Isaac with his friendliest grin, which was guaranteed to induce terror in the bravest of Hollow Earth's inhabitants.

'It's number 4, Galaxy Rise, Mr Lubbe,' said Morty. 'The owner leaves at midday prompt, so meet me there at five past.

There are cameras, so you need some kind of covering to hide your face. Have you still got that hood from our last job? The one that covers your whole head apart from your eyes. No real names while we are working. I will be Mr Day and you, Mr Night.'

'Yeah, got all that. Number 4 it is, at five past twelve on Monday, Mr Vicker. I will be there as Mr Night, face nicely hidden in the hood. I always said we were good partners. You with the brains and me with the brawn.'

'Well remember, Mr Lubbe, no violence. The Dark does not want any violence.'

'Of course. Of course, Mr Vicker. We would not want to upset Mr Dark now, would we?' said Isaac.

Morty was not convinced by Isaac's apparent sincerity. He recognised sarcasm when he heard it.

The Dark who was watching this interchange on one of his screens, with interest, found himself in agreement with Isaac Lubbe or, at least, his words.

'No, you are quite correct, Mr Lubbe. You would not want to upset me.'

✿✿✿

The following Monday, the two thieves entered Peter Howte's house. They accessed the back door of his property, via a small alley. With the casual ease of years of practice, Isaac prised the door open with a crowbar. Within a few minutes, they had made their way to a room, at the front of the house. They had been informed that the safe was hidden behind a portrait of Peter Howte, in that room. There were six paintings, one of which might be considered a portrait. This portrait was clearly the work of an amateur artist, with limited ability. It bore extraordinarily little resemblance to Mr Howte. This delayed the robbers for a couple of minutes while they checked the other paintings, before deciding that this had to be the portrait in question. Once they located the safe behind the painting, it was a matter of moments for them to open it and for Isaac to scoop up the valuables in one of his massive hands.

Isaac swiftly walked back through the house, then departed at a run down the alley. Morty, being smaller, lighter, and fitter, quickly caught up with him.

'Hey, half of that's mine!' yelled Morty.

'Yeah well, you stiffed me on our last job, so maybe I'll keep all of this. It will remind you not to cheat me next time, won't it? Eh...Mr Day?' growled Isaac.

'Not a chance, Mr Night. We share it out between us. Right now!'

Morty attempted to grab the jewellery. This was a mistake. Isaac shoved him away. 'No-one double crosses me,' he said, before stabbing Morty with a knife. Morty groaned, falling to the floor.

'You won't get away with this,' he said, gasping for breath. 'The Dark won't stand for it.'

'The Dark? I don't care what he thinks. We never see him, anyway. Who's gonna tell him? You? I don't leave any witnesses!' As Isaac said that he stabbed Morty a second time.

As Isaac made to leave, he ran straight into Peter Howte, who had returned home early. Peter had forgotten to take his keys with him, but he knew he could get in at the back of the house, as he always kept a back door key under a stone, in the flowerbed.

'What are you doing here?' Peter demanded. 'That's my jewellery. Give it here, at once!'

'I've had enough of this!' Isaac shouted, before stabbing Peter in the stomach and running off.

Neither Morty nor Isaac had noticed the figure in the alley across from theirs when they arrived. Flaky Pastry had just delivered a bookcase to one of Onion Gravy's customers.

Flaky watched the thieves break into the house. Flaky was foolish, quite possibly the most foolish elf in the realm, but even he knew when to keep quiet and hidden from view. He stared in amazement at the fights that followed, shortly after the thieves left the house. When the big thief stabbed the smaller thief, Flaky was so shocked that he almost cried out. He was used to Onion clamping a hand over his mouth, to keep him quiet, as it happened with such regularity. On this occasion, Flaky clamped his own hand over his mouth.

Flaky was paralysed with utter terror, when the big robber stabbed Peter Howte, as well. He stood for several minutes, trembling at the horrific scenes he had just witnessed. Without Onion to tell him, he did not know what to do next. He tried to think what Onion would say. He was sure that Onion would tell him to wait.

'Wait!' said Flaky's imaginary version of Onion. 'Check that the big, scary elf has gone. Let's call him Mr Stabby. Right, look *very* carefully. Has Mr Stabby gone?'

Flaky peeked out, nervously. 'Yes, Mr Stabby's gone,' he said to imaginary Onion.

'Good. What do you do next, Flaky?' asked imaginary Onion.

'Start crying?' asked Flaky.

'No, not that. It won't help,' said imaginary Onion. 'You can do that later.'

'Yes, Onion,' said Flaky.

'Come on, Flaky! Think!' demanded imaginary Onion, with irritation. 'Think, what do you do next?'

'Run away, Onion?' Flaky asked, uncertainly.

'No, that also won't help, will it?' queried imaginary Onion.

'No, Onion,' said Flaky.

'Come on, Flaky! You *can* do this!' said imaginary Onion. 'Just think. What would I do?'

'Get help?'

'Yes, Flaky! Get help. Find a police officer!' said imaginary Onion.

'Yes, yes! That's it, that's it!' muttered Flaky. 'Thank you, Onion.'

Looking up, Flaky realised that imaginary Onion had disappeared.

Flaky collected his tricycle. He dashed down the road, making full use of his power assist feature.

'Get help, Flaky! Tell Onion. Find a police officer,' he said repeatedly as he went.

CHAPTER TWENTY-TWO
Flaky reports a murder

The dramatic increase in minor crimes was straining Kuppa's resources.

'We're struggling to catch up with all of the crimes, March,' she commented to Chief Inspector March Doubletime, her second in command. 'Have we had any good news?'

'A little, Kuppa, but only a little,' the Inspector replied.

'At the moment, I will take a little. It is better than no good news, March. What have we got?'

'The forensic team are proving useful. We have recovered some stolen property with identifiable fingerprints, which the team have matched to known villains on our records. We have also found fingerprints at certain sites, which have had break-ins.'

'Well, that is good news. Right, bring in anyone whose fingerprints have been matched. We have grounds to arrest them and charge them. Draw up search warrants for their homes. We may be able to retrieve other stolen goods and link them to other offences or find fingerprints belonging to their associates. The more criminals we have in jail, the less of them out on the streets for us to deal with. Excellent work, March. I know you were worried about becoming a Chief Inspector, but this shows I was right to choose you.'

'Thank you, Kuppa. We do have another problem, unfortunately.'

'Another problem? Minor or serious?'

'A bit of both, really. Every crime scene has to be taped off and secured by one of our Hoppers, who then attends to assist the investigating Head and the forensic expert. As you know, we send out the Hoppers in teams of three. Every time one of them is left at a crime scene, we have to "juggle" the other officers to ensure we continue with teams of three. Regrettably, it means at least one reformed team is patrolling with inappropriate personnel.'

'Inappropriate, March?'

'Yes. You remember we agreed that the goblins should not work together?'

'Of course. A goblin should always have two Hoppers with him, as the goblins require a degree of supervision.'

'Yes, Kuppa. Well today because we were so short of available Hoppers, I was forced to create a team with two of the goblins and one of our less experienced officers. Totally inappropriate I know, but I was running out of options.'

'I see. Well, it cannot be helped in the current circumstances. We will just have to hope they do not have to deal with anything major.'

Flaky was becoming ever more confused, as he cycled along. Finally, he saw three police officers coming towards him. He skidded to a halt in front of them.

'Get Kuppa. Tell police! Find Flaky! Help officer Onion!' he blurted out.

'Who Flaky, den?' asked PC Cliff Wallbreaker.

'Dunno. Who dis Onion officer?' added PC Granite Rockearth.

PC Sally Forth was inexperienced but she knew from recollection of her basic training, that this was not the correct approach. Tucking a loose strand of her wavy, rich, earthy-toned hair under the peak of her cap, she revealed a light peach coloured face with pleasant mid-brown eyes.

'Hold on, officers,' she called out. 'We need to know this elf's name first. What is your name, Sir?' she said, addressing Flaky. Flaky looked behind him. He was never called Sir. He knew the police officer could not be talking to him.

PC Forth tried again, this time looking pointedly at Flaky.

'What is your name?'

Flaky stared at her for a moment before stammering out a reply.

'Onion Pastry. No, no, Flaky Gravy. No, that's wrong.'

PC Forth smiled reassuringly at him. 'Take a deep breath and try again.'

Flaky took a deep breath and muttered, 'Flaky Pastry. Yes, I'm Flaky Pastry.'

'Good,' said PC Forth. 'Now, what can we do for you, Sir?'

Slowly, Flaky's confused brain worked out that the nice, smiling police lady was still talking to him.

'Seen a big elf, Mr Stabby,' he declared.

PC Granite Rockearth remembered they had been told they should write everything down. He pulled out his notebook. 'Der big elf. Stabby,' he said to himself. Granite could not write, so he drew a picture of a big figure, looking vaguely like an elf. Next to this he drew a knife.

'So, this big elf, he upset you?' said PC Forth.

'He done a stabbing. Deaded another elf. I think they were both thieves,' said Flaky. 'Then the big thief stabbed Mr Howte from the Mall.'

'I see. Can you show us where this happened?'

'Yes, I'll take you,' said Flaky, leaping back onto his tricycle. He cycled off with the three officers running behind, endeavouring to keep up.

'So, dat der Flaky, den,' said Cliff, running as fast as his short goblin legs could carry him. 'But who der Onion officer, den?'

'Dunno,' said Granite, puffing and wheezing. 'Doan like all dis runnin. Make der talk hard!'

Flaky stopped at the entrance to the alley behind the Galaxy Rise houses.

Peter Howte was sitting propped up against a hedge, bleeding badly. Peter was a slight-built, black haired elf with pale, grey skin, which currently had paled into a paler grey than usual.

'Flaky, I'm hurt. Can you help me?'

'The police are coming, Mr Howte,' said Flaky.

At that moment, Sally Forth arrived.

'Mr Howte? I am PC Forth, but you can call me Sally. I will call for a ward van to get you to hospital urgently.'

She could see that he was holding his jacket to the wound in his midriff. Leaning over, she said, 'Press your jacket tight to your stomach, Mr Howte. It'll hurt but it will slow the bleeding until the van medics arrive. I will make sure they hurry and send a proper van and not a bike.'

[For reasons I cannot explain, some words filter down from the human world into the elvish world while others do not. Therefore, elves have the word hospital but not ambulance. They have wards in their hospitals, so ward van makes sense to them. However, what makes no sense is the fact that they use bicycles and motorbikes on hospital business, which they also call ward vans.]

As soon as she had finished her call, PC Forth turned back to Flaky.

'Mr Pastry, you say another elf was stabbed. Where was that?'

There was a pause as Flaky looked around. Finally, he realised that not only was he "Sir" but also, he was "Mr Pastry".

Flaky answered. 'It was just down here, Mistress…er, Police lady, …er, officer Sally,' said Flaky, leading her further down the alley.

Morty was lying on his back in a large pool of blood. Sally felt for a pulse. It was clear that a ward van would be too late for him. She drew a chalk line around his body and taped off the area, as she had been shown on her training course.

Sally had a problem. Technically, she was the junior officer of the three. Officers Wallbreaker and Rockearth had several weeks of police experience compared to her one week. On the other hand, she knew that when it came to the number of usable brain cells available to each, she outranked them dramatically. Sally decided to take charge.

'Officer Rockearth, can you guard that body I've taped off over there, until the forensic team arrives?'

'Yeah, me guard der dead body fing. Me good at der guarding.'

'Thank you, Officer Rockearth.'

Sally walked back up the alley to where she could see another puddle of blood, next to where Peter Howte was sitting.

'Is this where you were stabbed, Mr Howte?'

Peter Howte nodded. Sally taped around the puddle.

'Officer Wallbreaker, we need another good guard to look after this evidence, until forensics get here.'

'I do dat, Officer Forth. Make sure der blood doan go,' said Cliff. As usual, Cliff was keen and enthusiastic. Astonishingly inane, but keen and enthusiastic.

Sally contacted police headquarters to report the murder and attempted murder, explaining that officers Wallbreaker and Rockearth were waiting at the crime scene.

Sally smiled at Flaky. 'Mr Pastry, we need to go to the police station, so you can tell people what happened. Can you give me a lift there if I climb in your cart?'

'Y... yes, Police Officer Sally,' Flaky replied.

When Kuppa heard what had occurred, she was impressed with the actions taken by PC Sally Forth and overjoyed to hear that she had two witnesses. As one was about to go to hospital, she knew they would need to wait before interviewing him. When she heard that the other was called Mr Pastry, her heart sank, and she picked up her phone.

'Hi Onion, it's Kuppa. Flaky's seen a murder and is coming into the police station. Can you come and act as interpreter?'

CHAPTER TWENTY-THREE
Flaky is questioned

The next hour passed as everyone, who knew Flaky, had expected. For PC Sally Forth, Flaky's explanations were a bizarre insight into the strange, confused chaos of his mind.

'So, Mr Pastry…sorry, Flaky, can you describe this "big elf" to me again?' asked Sally. (She had learnt to address him as Flaky, on the advice of his employer, Mr Onion Gravy, who also seemed to act as Flaky's carer. "He'll get worried if you call him Mr Pastry. He won't be sure you're talking to him," Onion had explained.)

Flaky grinned widely. 'Yes, PC Officer Sally, I can.' Flaky continued to sit, smiling happily at everyone and offering no further information.

'Flaky? Do you think you could describe him to us, right now?' asked Kuppa.

'Yes, sorry, Officer Chief, Mist Kuppa. I got it wrong again, didn't I?'

'That's alright, Flaky,' said Kuppa reassuringly. 'Please describe the elf you saw.'

'That's easy, Mist Chief Kuppa. He was a big elf, with big muscles. Like this!' (Flaky held his arms out wide, indicating an elf approximately five feet wide.)

'A very big elf indeed,' said Kuppa. Beside her, PC Forth bit her lower lip, in order to avoid laughing.

'What was he wearing, Flaky?' Kuppa continued.

'I'm not sure,' muttered Flaky.

'Maybe I can help, Kuppa?' offered Onion.

Kuppa nodded.

Onion leant forward, patting the top of Flaky's hand, in a surprisingly comforting way. 'Now Flaky, what colour shoes was he wearing?' said Onion.

'Black shoes, Onion.'

'Good. What about his trousers, Flaky?'

'I'm not sure. That alley was very dark and scary, Onion.'

'Have a guess, Flaky. Same as the shoes?'

'No, no. Not black. I think dark blue, possibly or were they dark green?'

'Good, good, Flaky. You're doing very well,' said Onion. 'What about his top? Do you remember?'

'Oh yes, Onion. I saw his top. It was a dark brown jumper.'

'Excellent,' said Kuppa. 'Now, can you describe his face, Flaky?'

'His head was funny, Chief Mist Kuppa. All black and he had no ears, nose, or mouth. Just horrible staring eyes.'

Kuppa wrote "full head covering" in her notebook.

'Well, thank you, Flaky. You have been extremely helpful,' said Kuppa. 'You can go home now. Oh, and Flaky, Mr Teasready awards a "Citizen of the Month" medal each month. I will recommend you for this month's medal. Officer Forth, can you escort Mr Gravy and Mr Pastry to their vehicles? Please come back straightaway, as I would like a word, before I forget.'

'Yes, Chief,' said Sally, wondering what the Chief wanted.

Flaky almost floated out to his tricycle. "A medal", he thought. "For me?"

When PC Sally Forth returned, she was astonished to see that Kuppa was beaming at her.

'Don't look so worried, Sally. I just wanted to praise you for an absolutely perfect piece of police work, especially given the team with which you were working. I shall be putting a commendation in your file. If you continue with that standard of policing, I can see you progressing to Sergeant very quickly. Keep up the good work!'

'Thank you, Chief,' said Sally, with a stunned look on her face.

✿✿✿

Three days later, an elf rushed up to three Hoppers who were patrolling the streets near the Galaxy Mall.

'Officers, you need to come quickly! Some shoppers are holding on to an elf with stolen jewellery. This way,' she said.

For the briefest moment, none of them moved. Then the senior officer, Sergeant Brass Button took control.

'You two, follow me,' he ordered the two PCs, before running quickly after the elf who had reported the problem.

As he caught up with her, the Sergeant knew that he needed to find out the identity of this elf.

'Sorry, Mistress, could you just tell me your name?'

'It's Mist Ruby Sleeper, Sergeant, not Mistress,' Ruby stated slightly huffily, with an irritated expression, which surprised the Sergeant. His first impression of Ruby was of a young elf with a pleasing, light pink face. Those elves who knew Ruby Sleeper well, would have advised him that her peppery red hair was a better indication of her nature than her deceptively sweet-natured face.

'My apologies, Mist Sleeper,' said the Sergeant, 'please continue to lead the way.'

Sergeant Brass Button was well named. His oatmeal-coloured complexion was magnificently balanced by his brassy beard and hair. (All regulation cut, of course.) He was not an overly tall elf at five feet ten inches but compensated for his relative lack of stature with a well-toned, muscular physique. Due to his unusual shape, finding a suitable uniform for him had proved difficult. All of them, including the one he was wearing, made it seem that he was overweight rather than powerfully built.

Button liked to think that he kept himself fit and healthy. Nonetheless, he struggled to keep up with Ruby Sleeper, who was considerably younger than the sergeant.

The two PCs accompanying the sergeant were also much younger than he was but, they held themselves to a less intense fitness regime. It was a struggle for them to keep in touch with him.

'Brass can certainly get a shift on when he tries,' commented PC Brekkie Rawle, chuckling to her partner. Brekkie, an average height, pale blue elf with maroon hair, was an elf with "acceptable" fitness. (At least, that was March Doubletime's judgement on Brekkie's final police fitness assessment, following her training.)

'He's fitter than he looks,' agreed PC Willie Woantee, a lanky, scrawny elf with a mid-brown face and hair the colour of a muddy pool. Willie, like many elves, did not exercise if he could avoid it. He saw no need, as the magic dust pervading Underside removed all the fitness concerns the elves might have.

Most elves are proud of their names. This was not the case with Willie Woantee. "Might change my name," he confided to Brekkie Rawle. "My name makes me sound indecisive."

When PCs Rawle and Woantee caught up with Sergeant Button, he was in the midst of a large crowd. The crowd were sitting on a large, well-muscled elf, while the sergeant held him in a headlock. He had been punched once by the offender and was determined to avoid a repeat performance.

> ***[The Dark was, as usual, watching proceedings. He was pleased that some of his helpers had galvanised the shoppers into action. He was exceptionally irritated with Isaac Lubbe's acts of sloppy, unnecessary violence. He was determined that Isaac should be apprehended. He was certain that his other followers would easily work out that The Dark had assisted in Isaac's seizure. It would reinforce the message that there were consequences for anyone ignoring The Dark's wishes.]***

'He has the jewels in his hand,' said Brass. 'See if you can prise them free.'

It took both PCs, with the help of several volunteers, to recover the jewellery.

'That's mine,' grunted the thief, punching Sergeant Button in the stomach.

Brekkie studied the labels that were still attached.

'Your name Howte, is it?' she asked.

***

When Sergeant Button, PC Rawle and PC Woantee returned to police headquarters, with the offending large elf, he was quickly identified by Chief Inspector March Doubletime as Isaac Lubbe.

'Mr Lubbe,' he said. 'Haven't seen you for some time but I see you have been remarkably busy recently. With the offences you have committed, I think you may need a lawyer. If you do not have a lawyer, we can provide one for you.'

'I don't need any lawyer,' stated Isaac with unexpected bravado. 'I'm innocent. You can't prove I've done anything wrong.'

The list of charges against Isaac Lubbe was impressive.

'Innocent, eh?' asked March. 'Let me read the charges we are bringing against you, Isaac. We have murder and attempted murder. For both of these crimes, we have an eyewitness. That same witness saw you leaving the scene of the crime, which is another offence. You were clearly observed in an act of robbery with your partner, Morty Vicker, who you murdered after an argument. You were then seen to attack Mr Howte, a local jeweller. Fortunately for you, he is still alive and recovering in hospital. Subsequently, you were caught attempting to sell the jewellery you stole from Mr Howte, fraudulently passing it off as yours. When you were challenged by a group of decent, honest elves who were shopping in the mall, you attempted to attack them but were restrained by weight of numbers. That is attempted assault. When our officers apprehended you, you punched our Sergeant twice, which is actual assault, and, of course, you were also resisting arrest. I think you will be spending many years in custody for these crimes. Have you anything to say?'

'Yes,' said Isaac. 'I've changed my mind. I want a lawyer.'

CHAPTER TWENTY-FOUR
Benny travels to Hollow Earth

M ary and Mark were just finishing breakfast when Benny arrived.

'Want some breakfast?' asked Mary. 'They're still taking orders.'

'No, I'm fine. I had some toast earlier. I'd love a cup of tea if there's any going.'

'You're in luck, Benny. We've more tea than we know what to do with,' said Mark, gesturing to an extremely large teapot, taking centre stage on the table.

Once everyone had finished and the table cleared, by the server (the very friendly, rather attractive waitress, Benny noted), Mary stood up. 'Time we were on our way,' she announced.

'Follow us, Benny, and we'll take you to our vehicle. It's just a short walk from here.'

("Vehicle?" thought Benny. "What an unusual way to describe your car.")

After a short walk along the busy London road, Mark and Mary turned right into a smaller side road. After approximately fifty yards, Mark and Mary stepped into a small alley.

'Not much further now,' said Mary reassuringly.

Mark and Mary stopped in front of a white door, which was blank, apart from a sign stating "Warning. Police Notice. No admittance, at any time".

Mark produced a set of keys, unlocking the door.

Benny hesitated. 'That sign said "No admittance", so should we be going in, Mark?'

'Oh, don't worry,' said Mark. 'That's just to warn people off. It doesn't apply to us. 'Besides,' he added with a smile, 'I'm the one who put the sign up.'

They walked down two flights of stairs. They came to another door. Once again, Mark produced his set of keys, letting them through into what appeared, at first glance, to be an empty, dimly lit car park. As their eyes adjusted, Benny could see a moderately-sized, shabby-looking van parked near a wall.

'Here we are,' declared Mary. 'Hop in.' She hit a switch on the wall of the van, lighting its interior. This was in sharp contrast to the van's exterior. It was bright, modern, and well-equipped.

Mary settled into the driver's seat, while Mark took the passenger seat. 'Make sure you're well strapped in,' Mark called over his shoulder to Benny.

Mary reversed the van, turning until they faced a side wall. Mary drove straight at the wall. Benny gasped loudly. Just before they hit the wall, a concealed entrance opened, allowing them to proceed into the tunnel beyond.

'You can breathe again now, Benny,' said Mary, with a small chuckle.

Mary steered the van forward, slowly, until they were a few feet short of another apparent dead end. There were several loud clunks, as a metal cage rose from the floor to surround the vehicle.

'For our safety,' Mark explained to Benny.

On both sides of them, the walls appeared to be rising. Benny realised that, in fact, they were now descending. This descent continued for approximately one minute. They were now sitting at the entrance to an unusual circular tunnel, which sloped downwards. The metal cage was raised on some kind of pulley system, taking it back up and out of sight.

[No, I have no idea how this works. I am an author, not an engineer.]

'We're about to travel exceedingly fast down the tunnel ahead, Benny. Your ears will probably pop. This may help,' said Mark, passing a boiled sweet to Benny.

Mary moved them forward into the tunnel. Benny was aware that there was something peculiar about the movement of the van. Its tyres did not appear to make any noise as they advanced. The van's suspension also seemed exceptionally good, for such an old vehicle. If he did not know better, he would swear that they were floating. He placed the boiled sweet in his mouth, just as the van shot forward, descending at an alarming rate. Benny could not know that he was travelling inside an elvish vacuum tube. Equally, Benny could not know how deep the tunnel was or its final destination.

Eventually, they shot out of the end of the tube, slowing as rapidly as they had travelled. They were in a large hangar, very deep beneath the city. Unknown to Benny, their van could now be seen to be a saucer-shaped, metallic craft with the number twenty-three on its side, hovering approximately twenty feet off the floor. The holographic image of the van had disappeared.

'Craft 23, proceed to Bay 76. Craft 23 to Bay 76,' said a loud voice from a hidden loudspeaker.

As they descended, Benny was lost for words. All he could see were rows of metallic saucers. "Where am I," he wondered. "Area 51?"

Benny had been expecting to exit through the van door. He was taken aback when the roof of the van slid open.

'Everyone out,' said Mary, helping Benny onto some steps down to the floor.

'What is going on? Where exactly are we?' he asked.

'This,' said Mark gesturing around, 'is our destination. Hollow Earth. Just over there are the lifts back up to street level.'

"Street level" was not quite what Benny expected. These streets were not the crowded streets of London.

To Benny's left, he could see a large building, which he felt might be a railway station. On its frontage the words "Hollow Earth Central" were displayed in silver letters on a dark, green background. There were several rail or tram lines exiting on the right-hand side of the building, with occasional sheltered buildings, along the tracks. As these were marked "Tram stop", Benny quickly realised they were not train lines. To the left of the building was a fence. Beyond this, Benny could see a bridlepath and what appeared to be a wide cycle way with a footpath beside it. Beyond the cycle way was another fence with a six-lane motorway. The outer two lanes were clearly marked, with the words "Cab lane". Periodically, there were run-offs from the road to small buildings, marked "Cab stop". Benny could also see a pedestrian bridge. This started at an exit on the right of the building and spanned the tram lines, the bridlepath, and the cycle way, linking onto the footpath. On both sides of this built-up transport area, Benny could see wide, green vistas with rivers, lakes, trees, and shrubs. Small villages were just visible in the distance. In one, he was convinced he could see a cricket game being played.

Benny was astonished. He felt he had entered a film set, from some futuristic science fiction movie. As he watched,

Benny realised how few vehicles were on the motorway. It was busy but quiet by the standard of a typical motorway or freeway on Earth. He could see individuals strolling along the footpath. The bridlepath was currently occupied by a horse and carriage, followed closely by two riders on horseback. Six or seven cyclists could be seen heading for or just leaving the station.

Slowly, Benny realised that the individuals he was seeing were unusual. The predominant colour of the individuals was brown but brown in every conceivable shade from light yellowish-brown through to a brown that was so dark as to appear virtually coal black. It was as though a paint chart had been utilised for their skin tones. Their hair colours also ranged across the colour chart from white to black and every shade between. Additionally, he noted two blue beings, chatting to a purple one, as they walked along the footpath. This was something else for him to ask Mary and Mark.

Mark and Mary guided Benny to a nearby "Tram stop" just as a tram arrived. Once again, Benny noted some unusually coloured characters amongst the disembarking passengers. One was vivid green with striking red hair. Another was light orange with green hair. "Just like a carrot," thought Benny.

On the side of the tram were the letters H.E.T.T. 'This is ours,' declared Mark.

As they entered, Benny realised that the tram driver (a light brown individual with striking silver eyebrows) was wearing a smart, dark green uniform with the same letters picked out on the front of his peaked cap.

'H.E.T.T. – Hollow Earth Train and Tram Corporation,' explained Mary, correctly anticipating the question already forming in Benny's brain. 'It's only five minutes or so and we'll be at the Memorial Hall,' she said. 'We'll take you to see your father's memorial.'

Benny was lost for words.

'Don't worry,' said Mark. 'Hollow Earth is our capital city. We're used to it, but it is a lot to take in for a stranger.'

"Our capital city?" thought Benny. "What does he mean by *our* capital city?"

CHAPTER TWENTY-FIVE
A visit to Memorial Hall

'This is our stop,' stated Mary.

As he stepped off the tram, Benny looked up. He half expected to see futuristic aircraft passing overhead. He did not expect to see that they were fully enclosed in rock. Flying any kind of aircraft here would be suicidal.

'What is this place?' he asked. 'Where on earth are we?'

'We're not anywhere *on* earth,' said Mary. 'Hollow Earth is *in* earth, not *on* earth and we are in one of the largest underground cave complexes. I saw you looking up just now. What you were looking at is the cave roof. Now right in front of us is the building you need to visit.'

The structure had a strange, formidable appearance. It was clear that parts of the building were incredibly old, but it was equally clear that, over time, many additions had been made. To Benny, it felt like a building Dr Frankenstein might construct. The sign above the entrance proudly confirmed the edifice as Hollow Earth Memorial Hall.

'Come on in,' said Mary. 'There's no charge.'

Stepping inside, Benny was surprised again. In contrast to its odd exterior, the interior of the Hall was modern, warm, and welcoming, although extremely and unexpectedly vast.

Immediately in front of them were two doors with the word "Crematorium" displayed above.

To their left was an open area. A sign suspended from the ceiling read "Memorial Gardens".

'Through here,' said Mary, directing Benny into the Memorial Gardens. 'We need to look for the row marked with the letter U.'

'The letter U?' asked Benny.

'Yes, don't forget your father's surname was Upbowes not Bowes.'

After a few minutes walking, with Mary leading the way, they turned into the row marked U. 'Just up here,' said Mary.

She stopped in front of a plinth with a medium-sized marble cube on top.

The inscription on the cube read "In memory of Ty Upbowes, loving husband of Teidi Upbowes and loving father to Archer Upbowes. A well-liked and respected elf, taken before his time."

Benny's head was spinning. He was still attempting to process the idea that he had travelled underground into a secret society. Now on this memorial stone his father was described as an elf. He looked at the dates of his father's birth and death.

'Hold on, not only was my father an elf but according to these dates, he was two hundred and eighty-two years old when he died!'

'Yes, terribly tragic,' agreed Mark. 'To be taken so young. He had most of his life in front of him.'

'Most of his life? You're joking, right? Surely at two hundred and eighty-two, he was some kind of miraculous record-setter?' said Benny.

'No, not at all,' Mark replied. 'For a human, that would be a ridiculous, unbelievable age, but you father was an elf. Like all of us elves, he might have expected to reach anything between seven hundred and nine hundred years, even a thousand.'

'Hang on, hang on! This is too much,' declared Benny. 'So, you and Mary are both elves as well and I'm supposed to believe all elves live for hundreds of years? This is the best scam I've ever heard!'

'We're not trying to trick you, Benny,' said Mary. 'Look around you at these memorials. Look at the ages on each of them.'

Benny did just as she suggested. 'Nine hundred and forty-three, eight hundred and fifty-six, seven hundred and seventy-seven, one thousand and five,' he read aloud. 'I can't believe this! It can't be true!'

'It is all true, Benny. Everything we've told you,' said Mark. 'Why would we lie to you? We've nothing to gain.'

'I need to sit,' said Benny, plonking himself down on a flat memorial stone.

'Take a few deep breaths,' suggested Mary. 'Calm yourself.'

After a couple of minutes, Mary spoke again. 'How old do you think we are?'

'I'm not sure,' said Benny. 'I'm not good with people's ages. Late thirties, early forties?' he hazarded, hoping not to offend.

'Not even close, Benny,' said Mark. 'I am four hundred and fifty-four years old. I am sure Mary won't mind me sharing her age with you. She is four hundred and twelve years old.'

'How old? That is amazing!' said Benny. 'So, elves are very long-lived, and my father was an elf. What about my mother?'

'No, your mother is human which makes you quite unusual. Part human, part elf,' said Mark.

'So,' said Benny thoughtfully, 'will I live to be really old, like my father or will I just live a normal, human lifespan?'

'It really depends more on *where* you live,' said Mary. 'Elves have an extended lifespan, because of our daily exposure to the dust in the air of Hollow Earth. In fact, not just in Hollow Earth. Throughout all areas of Underside that we inhabit.'

'Underside?' asked Benny.

'Yes, Underside. Hollow Earth is our capital city, the capital of those parts of Underside that we elves control. Other parts are controlled by the fairies or the goblins.'

'Now I know you are joking. Fairies! Goblins!'

'They exist, Benny, and both are sworn enemies of the elves Most of the creatures you would consider to be mythical, or just characters in children's stories, do exist either here in Underside or in remote areas of Earth,' stated Mary.

'This really, really is too much, now,' he replied. 'I don't know whether to just go with it and believe you, laugh at the absurdity of everything you've told me, or sit in a corner somewhere to have a complete breakdown.'

'Completely understandable,' said Mark. 'We have thrown a lot at you, very quickly. Tell you what. Let's see your father's memorial and then we can have lunch.'

By now, Benny was totally confused. 'I've seen his memorial, just now.'

'That's just his memorial stone. Do you see that small button on the top? Press that and step back,' directed Mark.

Benny stood and pressed the button. He stepped back.

After a couple of moments, a life-size holographic figure appeared on top of the memorial stone.

'That's my father!' gasped Benny. 'I've seen him in photographs.'

As he spoke these words, Benny realised that those photographs must have been doctored in some way by his mother. Where the photographs he had been shown by his mother showed his father appearing as a heavily tanned figure with deep, brown hair, his father's hologram depicted him as dusky orange with jet black hair. It explained Benny's own hair colour and skin tone. He had often wondered in the past at his mahogany brown hair and why he looked tanned all year round when, in contrast, his mother was so pale with insipid, pastel-pink skin and mousy fair hair.

The holograph began to speak.

'If you are watching this image, then I must be dead and must have died before I could update this with anything more recent. Obviously, I do not know who is watching this recording. If I am speaking to my dear wife Teidi, I am sorry I cannot be there with you. You were the love of my life, and I cherish the time we had together. I will always love you and I hope you have found happiness in your life, without me. If I am talking to my son, Archer, I am sorry I was not there to see you grow up, but I hope that you have also found happiness. My love to you both always.'

The holograph faded. Mary walked over to Benny, who had sat back down on the memorial stone he had previously occupied. He was sobbing inconsolably. Mary sat next to him, putting her arm round him. After two or three minutes, Benny's crying subsided. He raised his head, wiping his face.

'Sorry, it's the shock, I think. I just wish I'd had the chance to meet him. Get to know him, but that wasn't to be. This is an enormous amount for me to process. I know some people recommend sweet tea for shock, but I've always found that when I'm anxious, I get hungry.' He managed a small smile. 'You mentioned lunch, Mark.'

'Yes, I did. We can go next door to The Charcoal Chimney. It's an excellent restaurant.'

Benny laughed. 'Why not? Of course, you have a restaurant right next door to the Crematorium, called The Charcoal Chimney. After everything you've shown me today, I cannot be surprised at anything!'

None of them noticed an elf, called Cornflower Blue, who was standing nearby, at another memorial stone. The violet-eyed, blue-skinned elf with deeper blue hair who happened to be just within earshot of their conversations. The elf watched them as they departed but did not attempt to follow them. Eventually, he headed for the exit.

'Very interesting,' whispered The Dark to himself. In the guise of his alter ego, Cornflower Blue, The Dark was merely another elf attending Hollow Earth Memorial Hall. Elves tend to favour bright, cheerful colours. As a result, Cornflower Blue's red top with golden yellow trousers and scarlet boots, did not draw attention to him. On his way out, he could afford himself the luxury of a cheerful greeting to two elves passing by.

'Lovely day, isn't it? Perfect for a walk,' he said, with a beaming smile.

'Oh yes, it certainly is,' replied one of the elves, with an equally large smile.

As The Dark, still wearing his personality disguise of Cornflower, wandered off, the other elf commented 'What a pleasant, friendly fellow.'

CHAPTER TWENTY-SIX
Lunch at The Charcoal Chimney

B enny began to relax during lunch. The Charcoal Chimney was just as excellent as Mark had promised. Benny's only problem was choosing which food to have from the extensive menu.

During lunch, Mary and Mark gently quizzed Benny, asking if he was satisfied with his current life.

'Do you enjoy entertaining people?' asked Mary.

Benny shrugged noncommittedly.

'What about your current job?' Mark queried. 'Do you enjoy working as a stand-up comedian? Are you happy playing SoSo the clown?'

Eventually, Benny smiled, pushing away his now, empty plate.

'OK, what's this really all about? You obviously came to find me. Then you brought me here to Hollow Earth and showed me my father's memorial, for which I am truly grateful. Then you told me that my father was an elf, that elves live for hundreds of years, and I am unique as I am part human and part elf. Now you want to know if I am happy in what I do. I am not stupid. Clearly you want something from me. So, I'll ask again. What is this about?'

Mark and Mary looked each other. Mark broke the silence.

'You are absolutely correct, Benny. We do want something from you but also, we want to offer you something. A way forward. A new start. A new life. One which we hope you would find fulfilling.'

'Alright, you have my interest. I'm listening.'

'We want you to be our next Santa Claus.'

For ten seconds or slightly more, Benny said nothing. Then he started to laugh. His laughter did not subside until at least thirty seconds later.

'Really?' he exclaimed. 'All this, just so you could persuade me to take on the role of a department store Santa Claus. That's my new start? Fulfilling? I've worked as a Santa in a department store before. I like children but sitting them next to me and asking them what they want for Christmas, while their parent whispers instructions in your ear? That's a new life I can happily do without. The answer is no. It's not for me.'

'No, Benny, that's not the job we are offering to you at all,' said Mary.

'This will take some explaining,' said Mark. 'Please, just allow us a few minutes. Firstly, I need to make one thing absolutely clear. There is, and always has been an actual Santa Claus.'

'A real Santa Claus?' asked Benny.

'Yes, a real Santa Claus.'

'A real person?'

'Yes. It started,' said Mark, 'with Saint Nicholas giving out a few gifts one Christmas.'

'Saint Nicholas? Well obviously, I've heard of Saint Nicholas, and I know that the name Santa Claus is a corruption of his name but a real Santa Claus. Surely, he's just a mythical figure. An idea. Something for children to believe in. Nothing more.'

'Yes and no,' Mark replied. 'The giving of presents at Christmas soon escalated. Before long, various cultures developed Christmas beliefs. Christmas traditions. When it became clear that these traditions would continue each year, it was inevitable that the concept of a friendly individual giving presents to children each year would arise. This individual is known by many names around the world. Santa Claus, Sinterklaas, Father Christmas, Kris Kringle, Pere Noel, Papa Noel, Babbo Natale, many more. The names are less important than the character.'

'But surely,' said Benny, 'these *are* just names for a mythical person. Not a real person.'

'Yes, that's true,' agreed Mark, 'but the traditions and beliefs grew to be so strong, particularly amongst children, that a representation, an embodiment of these beliefs was needed. An individual was needed to replace Saint Nicholas. I won't waste time explaining why now, but the elves agreed to take on this role. Santa Claus, as you know him, was born. An elf was nominated to *be* Santa Claus. When this elf had served his time, another elf was nominated to take his place. I was the elf nominated most recently.'

'Sorry, you're Santa Claus?' exclaimed Benny.

'He was,' stated Mary, 'but after hundreds of years of service, it is time for him to retire.'

'I need to find my replacement,' said Mark. 'A new individual with a fresh approach and new ideas is needed.'

'That's why we sought you out. We hoped that you might agree to be the next nominee, Benny,' added Mary.

'Me? After everything I've told you about my previous experience as a department store Santa Claus. You have to be joking!'

'No joke, Benny,' said Mary. 'As the real Santa Claus, you would not be expected to hand out presents in a department store,' Mary explained. 'There are countless stand-ins who take on that role. You might decide to take part occasionally but if you did it would be only to demonstrate to a stand-in how the job should be done. You would be more involved in the management of Christmas. Making Christmas happen.'

'I don't understand,' said Benny.

'I am not surprised,' said Mark. 'Do you remember that hangar you saw when we first arrived?'

'Area 51, you mean?'

'Not exactly but that hangar is one of twelve such hangars around the world. All those craft have holographic ability, allowing them to look and sound like Santa Claus in a sleigh. Each one is flown by a trained pilot who delivers an allocated number of Christmas presents. Santa's job is to ensure that those craft all deliver those presents correctly, on time. You may wish, as I did, to fly one craft yourself, but that will be your choice entirely.'

'So really a figurehead co-ordinating everything?' asked Benny.

'Yes,' agreed Mark, 'that is the most important part of the job. There are many other aspects but if you agree to take on the role, I will give you full training and accompany you throughout your first Christmas.'

'It is very tempting,' admitted Benny. 'If I'm honest, I'm not really going anywhere with my life at present. I've very little money, no career plans, and no real prospects whatsoever. Right Decision made. I am willing to give it a try on one condition.'

'What's that?' asked Mark.

'I want to know my mother will be looked after.'

'Of course,' said Mary. 'We will organise that for you. Naturally, you will be living here in Underside, but you can visit your mother as often as you like.'

'Living in Underside?'

'Essential, I'm afraid,' said Mark 'but the job is well paid, with a car, accommodation of your choosing and a clothing allowance included in the package.'

'Sounds perfect.'

'One last thing,' said Mark. 'There is a council meeting in two days. We would like you to attend with us, so we can introduce you as the new Santa. We can discuss all the details over dessert. What takes your fancy on the menu?'

CHAPTER TWENTY-SEVEN
Flaky meets Cornflower

Flaky Pastry was distracted. This was not unusual. Flaky was often distracted. Today, Flaky had a particular reason for being distracted. This was the day he would be attending his first ever council meeting to receive his Citizen of the Month medal.

That morning, he was so excited that Onion Gravy had difficulty keeping him calm. Usually, Flaky would have been busy dog-walking, but Potter had arranged for members of the Elite to walk the dogs so that Flaky could attend the meeting. Onion decided the best course of action was to keep Flaky occupied with other tasks.

'Flaky, I need supplies from Hollow Earth. Can you collect them for me with your tricycle and cart? Here's a list of everything I need and where to get them.'

'I'll get them straightaway, Onion. I'll be as quick as I can.'

Flaky set off on the cycle pathway, cycling as fast as he was able. He departed so quickly that when Onion remembered an additional item he wanted Flaky to obtain, he had to shout after him.

'Flaky, can you speak with Lottie. I need a couple of those small lights to fit in my toolbox. Lottie will know which ones I mean.'

'OK, Onion,' yelled Flaky as he disappeared.

Onion needed to fit some small lights into his toolbox for those occasions where he was working in poor light and could not see his tools clearly. He hoped Lottie would ensure Flaky was given the correct ones.

On his way to Hollow Earth, Flaky's attention was taken by some rabbits in a nearby field. He stood to watch them for ten minutes, fascinated by the amusing way they hopped about. As he continued on his way, Flaky began to worry.

'What were those extra items Onion wanted?' he said aloud. 'Oh yes, I remember!'

As Flaky neared the station, he stopped to watch the massive building works that were underway to construct new tunnels and new flitrails. This was to provide an improved service between Hollow Earth and the other major cities of Underside. Peak Rise in the north, River End in the west and Wind Stop in the east. Each of the cities were almost as large as Hollow Earth and the residents of each of these cities thought that their city should be the capital rather than Hollow Earth.

'A marvellous feat of engineering, isn't it?' said a quiet voice next to Flaky.

Flaky turned to look at the owner of the voice, a friendly-looking blue elf standing just to his left. He smiled at Flaky.

Flaky smiled back. 'Oh, yes. I think it's amazing,' he said.

'Sorry, I should introduce myself,' said the newcomer. 'I'm Cornflower Blue. Pleased to meet you.'

'Oh, pleased to meet you too, Mr ...Blue. I'm Flaky Pastry.'

'Please call me Cornflower. May I call you Flaky? Much more friendly, I think.'

'Yes, it is,' said Flaky, who was not used to making casual conversation and was not entirely sure what to say.

'I come here quite often to see what progress we are making,' stated Cornflower. 'I work for H.E.T.T. as an engineer but most of my work is in the tunnels. When I'm working on a piece of wiring in a dark bend of a tunnel, it's tricky to see how we are advancing overall. I like to visit this spot so that I can appreciate the incredible work being carried out by my colleagues.'

'Oh yes, it is incredible.'

'Will you use the new flitrail links once they are completed, Flaky?'

'I'd love to.'

'I have relatives in Peak Rise and Wind Stop that I don't see very often,' stated Cornflower. 'I'm looking forward to the new, improved services. It will be far easier for me to visit my cousin Denim Blue in Wind Stop and his daughter Skye. Also, my cousin Andy Manne in Peak Rise. How about you, Flaky?'

'No, I don't have any relatives to visit. I've never been to any of those other places. I just come here to collect supplies, but I like to watch the trams, the cars, and the workmen. Workmen! Oh no, I forgot I'm supposed to be working! Onion will be so cross. If he was here, he'd tell me to hurry up and get to the suppliers. Right now!'

'Onion?' queried Cornflower.

'Yes, I work for my friend, Onion Gravy but he gets annoyed with me if I "dawdle about" when I should be working. I must go. Nice to meet you, Cornflower.'

Flaky leapt onto his tricycle and sped off to the suppliers, pleased to have made a new friend. Flaky did not have many friends, as he found it difficult to make new ones or keep those friends he had.

[Unfortunately, most elves found Flaky's astonishing stupidity too annoying to tolerate.]

One and a half hours later, Flaky was making his way back to Little Merritiddle, feeling exceedingly pleased with himself. He had collected everything on Onion's list. He had even remembered the extras Onion had asked him to buy, although he was confused. He could not imagine why Onion might want them for his toolbox.

Onion was waiting for him on his return.

'Did you get everything?' he asked.

'Yes, it's in the cart and your extra items.'

'Good. Well done, Flaky. Let me just check.'

As he was checking the contents of the cart, Onion stopped.

'What's this?' he said, opening a small bag.

'I bought two like you asked. I got one for me as well. Out of my own money, Onion. It works really well when I cycle along.'

Flaky cycled around the yard, proudly pointing at his handlebars, from which an incredibly small red item was fluttering.

Onion was incredulous. 'You thought I wanted two of those?'

'Yes.' Flaky looked at the expression on his friend's face. 'Did I get something wrong, Onion?'

'Just a bit, Flaky. Why would I want two small kites for my toolbox?'

CHAPTER TWENTY-EIGHT
An update meeting

F ollowing their previous briefing meeting Potter had asked Ena to organise an update meeting. He decided that this meeting should be held in the same secure briefing room at the Southern border outpost, with the same personnel attending, with the addition of their new Chief of Police, Kuppa Broth. The only exceptions to this were two "guests" who would join at the end of the meeting and the new Santa if Mark and Mary's topside trip had been successful.

'Welcome, everyone,' said Potter. As was becoming customary, he placed a bag of barley twist sweets in the centre of the table. 'Please help yourselves.'

Potter turned to Ena Minnit.

'It looks like everyone is here, Ena, apart from Mark and Mary and our two guests who will be attending at the end of the meeting. Do we know when we can expect Mark and Mary to arrive?'

'Yes, Mary contacted me a few minutes back. They will be approximately quarter of an hour. You will be pleased to hear that they are bringing our new Santa Claus and a selection of cakes.'

Potter gave Ena a questioning look. 'Cakes?'

'Not everyone shares your and Wendy's enthusiasm for barley twist sweets,' said Ena.

Potter laughed. 'I cannot argue with that. It will be pleasant to have a relaxed few moments to have a drink and a cake anyway.' He glanced around the room. 'Right, we have the same item one on the agenda as last time. The Great Non-War. We had a summary at the last meeting with an indication of the physical and mental after-effects.'

Hazel Nutt was the first to speak on that subject.

'We have observed changes since the last meeting, Potter. Physically, the majority of our regular troops are recovered and have reported for duty. In my opinion, some of those troops remain mentally fragile but the medical and religious staff caring for them have reported a decrease in nightmares, bad dreams, or other sleep disorders.'

'That is reassuring news, Hazel,' Potter remarked.

'Yes, it is, but there are troops who may never recover from the trauma. I have asked our most experienced psychologists to draft an advisory report on those patients with a plan for their ongoing treatment.'

'Hmm, that is worrying,' said Potter. 'We cannot expect those troops to resume active service.'

'No, they will need alternative occupations in the future.'

'If I know our troops as well as I do,' said General Zingor, 'they will not accept being side-lined. Becoming civilians. I can guarantee they will wish to continue serving in whatever way they can. I am certain we can find them all ancillary roles. Captains Aird, Ponsonby-Smyth, and Carruthers, I will leave that in your capable hands. Report back to me as soon as you can.'

'Yes, General,' the three Captains answered, virtually in unison. General Zingor was the kind of General that inspired both respect and awe in the officers serving under her.

'Excellent. Thank you, all. Can you pass me a copy of the report, General, once you have it?'

'Absolutely, Mr Teasready.'

'Good. Now, how are those volunteers faring? I feel guilty about the suffering our regular troops underwent but I feel most guilty about those volunteers, suddenly and unexpectantly being thrown into battle.'

'You must stop feeling guilty, Potter,' said Wendy. 'You did what was necessary to save everyone as best you could. Anyway, let me put your mind at rest. Based on everything Hazel and I have been told or have seen for ourselves, the volunteers are recovering well. As you know, few of them suffered physical harm, as the regular troops protected them. Preparations for Christmas have helped greatly with most of their mental problems. They have been able to focus their minds on something positive.'

'That is a relief,' admitted Potter, popping a barley twist into his mouth, with a small smile. 'Hopefully, I will sleep better tonight. I have to confess that my nights have been troubled recently.'

'Potter, there is another related item we should discuss,' said Wendy. 'Merlin correctly predicted that the number of time leaks would reduce, which they have. But there is still a problem. Most elves do not understand what is happening. I will give you an example. An elf spoke to me yesterday. He told me that he was standing outside his house when his son walked past him four times, saying "Hello, Father" each time. When he looked inside, his son was not there. When he stepped outside, his son arrived yet again, saying "Hello, Father". He followed his son inside, saying "What's going on, son? You keep arriving. Is this some kind of joke you're playing on me? Are you staying this time?" and the son replied with "What do you mean, Father. I've only just got here!" – everyone is very confused.'

'I see. Yes, I understand, Wendy. I should have addressed this earlier. I will make a public announcement explaining our current difficulties with time leaks.'

Potter glanced down at the meeting agenda.

'Right, next we have our updates on the fairies and goblins from Merlin and Arthur.'

'When we were observing the conflict amongst the fairy factions, we noted an unexpected complication had arisen. It will require time to explain it correctly,' stated Merlin.

'Yes, we should update you on the goblins first,' said Arthur. 'There have been developments, but these are more readily explained. Amazingly, the two armies stopped fighting each other when the two goblin queens interceded. They persuaded the two goblin kings to negotiate a ceasefire. Our agents say this centres around an agreement to exchange thrones. They do not have details on what this involves but, most importantly it means the two sides are at peace. Our agents have also discovered that the two goblin factions are banding together to attack the fairies.'

'That is a strangely unexpected outcome but extremely good news for us,' Potter remarked. 'If the goblins are intending to attack the fairies, both sides will be distracted. We will no longer be their main target.'

CHAPTER TWENTY-NINE
Hammer's new throne

Queen Avalanche smiled as she approached her husband King Hammer. He was pretending not to fidget on his bone throne.

'Hammer, King Mountain is here with Queen Snowstorm and six north goblins,' she announced.

'WOT DEY WANT?' grumbled Hammer quietly.

'They have your new throne to swap for that uncomfortable bone throne, dear.'

'NOT UNCUMFY! DER KING SIT WHERE DER KING WANT!'

'I know, darling,' said the queen soothingly, 'but at least look at what they have brought.'

'RIGHT, WE DO DAT. SEE DER NEW FRONE. SEE IF LIKE.'

Avalanche escorted in King Mountain, Queen Snowstorm and six other north goblins, four of whom were carrying an exceptionally huge throne.

'Can you put the new throne just there, please?' asked Avalanche, pointing to a vacant area to Hammer's left.

'YEAH, PUT DER FRONE DERE,' agreed Hammer, with a whisper.

The throne was at least half again as large as Hammer's existing throne. It was constructed from rich, dark wood with brown leather upholstery. The chair arms and back were additionally covered in thick, black animal fur. The throne radiated luxury with comfort. Hammer stood to look at the new throne.

Stonebasher Clubface and his brother Knifecut Clubface together with Headsplitter Treetrunk and Boulder Daggerthrust proceeded to manoeuvre the throne into position. This took longer than it should as all four goblins attempted to pull in different directions. The team was supervised by Cutslash Bladegrinder and OneEye Hookhand. Eventually, they placed the new throne next to the older throne.

It was debatable how much help OneEye was. 'Put der frone down,' he advised.

'It down already,' said Cutslash.

'Yeah, fort so,' said OneEye.

'Turn round. It wrong way,' instructed Cutslash. He was correct as the new throne was facing to the left at a right angle to Hammer's existing throne. "Helpfully", the goblins turned the throne through one hundred and eighty degrees. It was now facing to the right, at a right angle to the old throne.

'Frone moved,' stated Headsplitter triumphantly.

Queen Snowstorm stepped forward. 'No, that is not right, is it?' she growled.

'See this? This is the front of the throne we brought. This is the front of King Hammer's throne. The front of both thrones should be facing the same way. Understand, Cutslash?'

'Yeah, me understand, your Queenness.' Hastily, Cutslash hissed orders to the other goblins. After lengthy arguing, they finally rearranged the thrones. Both thrones were now facing to the right.

'No!' yelled Snowstorm. No amount of explanation or gesturing helped. The goblins did not understand what was wrong or what the queen wanted.

'Maybe a picture would be useful,' suggested Avalanche.

'Yes, good idea,' said Snowstorm. Quickly she drew a selection of pictures showing the two thrones in every conceivable configuration. She placed a large X below all of the pictures except the one showing the two thrones correctly aligned.

Snowstorm called over Cutslash and OneEye.

'Look at these drawings,' she commanded.

'Yeah, see dem, Queenness,' said Cutslash.

'Wot drawins?' asked OneEye, looking through his eye patch.

Snowstorm sighed and grabbing OneEye by the shoulders, moved him until he was looking with his one eye.

'Oh, yeah, see dem now. Why hide dem so me no see dem, your magictree?'

Snowstorm's exasperation was growing as each second passed.

'They were not hidden, OneEye! You were trying to look through your patch. Now just be quiet and look at the drawings. With your good eye!'

'Yeah, do dat den, magictree queenness.'

'Good. Both of you look closely.'

Both goblins pressed their noses to the drawings.

'Not *that* close!'

When Cutslash and OneEye had withdrawn their heads to a reasonable distance, the queen continued.

'Do you see all these drawings with a large X? Do *not* put the thrones like any of those.'

'No, not do dem,' said OneEye.

'Wot do den, queenness?' asked Cutslash.

'Do you see the drawing without a large X?' said Snowtorm, repositioning OneEye as she spoke.

'See dat, magictree,' confirmed OneEye.

'Yeah, me see dat too, queenness,' declared Cutslash.

'Good. Put the thrones like that.'

That worked. At last, the thrones were in place.

'It would be best to sit in one throne after another, your Majesty,' Avalanche stated, 'so you can decide if the new throne is acceptable.' Avalanche knew she needed to address Hammer formally in front of guests.

Hammer returned to his seat on his bone throne. He fidgeted for a couple of minutes, before settling on an acceptable position. It was apparent to Avalanche that his existing throne was becoming increasingly difficult for Hammer to sit on, but she knew that being a proud goblin monarch, he would never admit this.

'Would you care to try the new throne, your Majesty?' queried Snowstorm.

Hammer sat on the new throne.

He wriggled for a minute or so and said calmly, 'YEAH, DIS DO. TAKE DER OLD BONE FING.'

Hammer relaxed into the comfort of his new throne. He looked at Avalanche.

'ME HAPPY. GIVE BIG FEAST FOR NEW FRIENDS.'

Hammer leaned forward. Unexpectedly, he smiled at Drumnail Rockfall and Gravel Blackhead.

'GET DER TABLES FOR FEAST,' he ordered in one of his softest voices.

'We do dat, your Majesty,' said Gravel, a goblin who knew not to say "magictree" or "kingness" to his king.

Hammer beckoned to Earthquake Mallethand.

'GET DER FOOD FOR DER FEAST,' he commanded gently.

'Yes, my Kingness,' Earthquake replied.

Hammer waved a hand in the direction of Axecutter Gravelface.

'GET DER DRINKS FOR DER FEAST,' he directed. Once again, Hammer employed his "inside" voice.

'Will do dat, Sire,' said Axecutter.

Feasting was a regular goblin pastime. When it came to sheer extravagance, a goblin feast was rarely bettered but this one surpassed most that had proceeded it.

At the end of the feast, Hammer slammed his four-foot sword on the table to obtain silence. He placed an inebriated arm around King Mountain's shoulders affectionately.

'NOW WE GO. MAKE DER PLAN FOR DER WAR WID DER FAIRIES.'

CHAPTER THIRTY
The Seven

M erlin attracted Potter's attention with a subtle wave of his hand.

'We will need to continue to monitor the activities of the goblins, Potter. I accept that their desire to war with the fairies is beneficial but, it is conceivable that the goblins will not wish to cease hostilities. As we all know, goblins are an aggressive, bloodthirsty species, who enjoy fighting. Should they defeat the fairies, their attention may return to us.'

'I agree entirely, Merlin, but I suggest our best policy at present is to wait. It is entirely feasible that the fairies may win any war with the goblins or that the two sides might not fight at all. We need to see what happens.'

'Yes, certainly. That brings us succinctly to the fairies and the complication that has arisen. The attacks on King Elderberry's castle by Queen Parsnip Mash and her sister Lady Butternut Risotto have been rebuffed. Their forces are defeated.'

'Surely that is not a concern for us, Merlin,' Potter contended. 'Obviously, that means the fairies are now better placed to defend themselves against the goblins. Yes, it makes a war between them more likely, but I do not understand why that is a problem for us. Is there something else?'

'Indeed, there is, my friend,' Merlin replied. 'The defeat of the queen and her sister is where the difficulty started. King Elderberry was infuriated by the treason of his wife and her sister. In the past, Elderberry's father would have beheaded them both, without trial, but Elderberry chose an alternative punishment. He took the unprecedented action of contacting The Seven, led by Lavender Bushel. He asked them to cast an expulsion spell on the sisters.'

✳✳✳

Parsnip Mash strained ineffectively against her chains, attempting to free herself.

'DO YOU KNOW WHO YOU ARE DEALING WITH?' she demanded of the commander.

Butternut stood beside her, forlornly weeping her fate, and rattling her chains together like a demented spectre.

'Why did we do it, Parsnip? We were so stupid.'

'OH, DO SHUT UP AND STOP CRYING!' bawled Parsnip.

Butternut wrenched her body round in the chains until she was facing Parsnip. 'DON'T YOU SHOUT AT ME. IT'S YOUR FAULT THIS HAS HAPPENED!' she screamed.

'MY FAULT? NOBODY ORDERED YOU TO JOIN IN.'

'Silence, please,' said an authoritative voice.

Lavender Bushel and the others of The Seven had arrived. Lavender gestured towards the captives. Suddenly, their mouths closed. They were unable to speak.

Lavender stepped forward.

'His Majesty has given me a message to read aloud. It reads as follows:

"'Lavender, these two fairies have committed treason against their king. I request that The Seven cast a spell on them to last for fifty years. It must exclude them from all fairy realms throughout Underside. Further, it must exclude them from contact with any other fairy. Should they attempt to break through the spell, they will experience excruciating, unbearable pain."

'As loyal subjects of his Majesty, we will pass his sentence once the commander has read the message, he received from the king.'

The commander moved forward, next to Lavender.

'His Majesty's message to me reads as follows:

"'Henceforward, by my royal decree, the marriages that were made by the prisoners are annulled. All their titles, lands, rights, and privileges are hereby removed. They shall be known merely as fairy Parsnip Mash and fairy Butternut Risotto. Commander, you may offer them the alternative of beheading. If they choose banishment, The Seven will cast the spell as requested. Following that, commander, take them to the farthest edge of the fairy realms. There the Seven can release them from their chains and you must ensure they depart into the hinterlands."

'That concludes his Majesty's message to me. Lavender, the prisoners have already declined the offer of beheading.'

Lavender beckoned to the other members of The Seven. 'Step well back, commander.'

The commander retreated as instructed. The Seven encircled Parsnip and Butternut. Lavender began chanting, invoking the magic to create the spell. He was soon joined by the others. Bright sparkling fire burst out of their fingers, engulfing the sisters. They writhed in agony as the spell took hold. Finally, the cascade of magical fire subsided. Parsnip and Butternut collapsed to the floor.

'The spell is cast, commander. We will take them to the outskirts of fairy realms. They will be too weak to resist.'

The sisters did not struggle on their journey. Any desire to fight their fate had deserted them. Lavender freed them from their imposed silence. They were released into the wastelands with a meagre supply of food and drink. As they departed, the commander said, 'The supplies are just to allow you to survive in the short term. Once they are gone, you must find food and water as best you can.'

As the outcasts stumbled across the rocky wilderness, Parsnip found her voice.

'This is not over, sister. They have forgotten that we still have our magic powers.'

'What use are they here, Parsnip?'

'They will allow us to start a new life. Finding food and water will not be an issue for us. We can create a realm for ourselves here.'

'Here? There are no fairies we can control. You heard for yourself. We dare not approach them.'

'Do not despair, Butternut. There are other creatures in Underside that we *can* control.'

CHAPTER THIRTY-ONE
Meet the new Santa Claus

'What exactly is an expulsion spell, Merlin?' queried Lottie. 'I have never heard of such a spell. What does it do?'

'This spell excludes them for fifty years from every fairy realm,' explained Merlin. 'For any fairy this is a terrible fate.'

'Unpleasant maybe,' noted Lottie, 'but is it such a terrible fate? After fifty years they can return and continue with their lives.'

'Unfortunately for them both, that is highly unlikely,' stated Merlin. 'Neither Parsnip nor Butternut are young. Effectively, this is a dreadful life sentence. Unlike elves, fairies do not have lengthy lifespans. If they survive their banishment, they will be quite elderly after fifty years have passed but that is the least of their worries. As exiles, where will they go? The expulsion spell prohibits them from approaching any fairy. The goblins are readying for war against the fairies so they will kill any fairy on sight, even exiled fairies. Naturally, they will be unwelcome pariahs in elvish regions. I cannot think of any race that will take them in. Their only recourse will be to retreat to a sparsely populated region, living a reclusive life as outsiders. Should they decide to return to the fairy realms after fifty years, they will remain outcasts with no standing in fairy society. An appalling destiny.'

'I see what you mean, Merlin,' said Lottie. 'I failed to understand how awful their circumstances are. King Elderberry must truly hate his wife and her sister to subject them to such a ghastly sentence.'

'I don't wish to be rude,' said Carruthers, 'but who are The Seven and who is this Lavender Bushel chap?'

Potter had helped himself to another barley twist and was sucking on this thoughtfully.

'Sorry, captain. You would not be aware of them. They are the seven most powerful fairies that exist. Their leader, Lavender Bushel, is an extremely potent magician. Second only to yourself, Merlin, would you say?'

'Indeed,' Merlin answered.

'You must have more to tell us,' Potter said to Merlin. 'What is the impact of this for elvish society?'

'Immediately, there is no concern but The Seven rarely involve themselves in everyday fairy life. They might continue to remain outside fairy society but by contacting them in this matter, Elderberry has introduced a dangerous factor into our lives. If The Seven were ever to lead the fairies against us, the elves would be defeated. I could fight off Lavender but not all The Seven. That is the complication I mentioned earlier.'

'Yes, I see,' said Potter. 'I understand why you are worried, Merlin. We must discuss this further. Hopefully, it presents us with a problem that will never arise.'

As Potter finished speaking, three figures entered.

'I apologise for our late arrival, everyone,' declared Mary Tyme. 'We have just returned from Topside.'

'Yes, and we are pleased to introduce you all to the gentleman we hope will become our new Santa Claus,' announced Mark Tyme. 'Everyone, this is Benny Bowes.'

'As promised,' added Mary, 'We have brought refreshments.'

'Excellent,' said Potter. 'Let's take a break. It will also afford an opportunity for you all to meet Benny,' concluded Potter.

Mary and Mark escorted Benny around, introducing him to the council members. Benny was surprised how comfortable he was, taking on this new, daunting but exciting role. He realised that he felt "at home" for the first time in his life.

After the elves had consumed all the refreshments (with immense pleasure), they continued with the remaining agenda items.

'Establishing Benny as our new Santa Claus will require substantial effort from us all. We must provide him with all the support we are able to give,' stated Potter.

'I concur,' said Mark. 'As the outgoing representative, I intend, not only to train Benny in every aspect of the work but also, to accompany him throughout his first Christmas. As a temporary arrangement, Mary has arranged accommodation for Benny in an unused council room, but tomorrow, we intend to help him find somewhere more suitable to live.'

'Arthur and I will ease you through the necessary Santa paperwork,' added Ena, 'including a bank account with your first payment. Lottie and Bingo, when he returns from Topside, will help with your provisions.'

'Bingo?' queried Benny.

'Sorry, you know him as Franklin Houzey, but his real name is Bingo,' explained Lottie.

'I expect that we have given you more than enough to think about for today, Benny,' said Mary. 'Do you have any immediate concerns?'

'No, not at all,' said Benny, 'but can I ask Mark just one thing?'

'Certainly, Benny,' replied Mary.

'It is this. My given elf name is Archer Upbowes. As I will be living and working with elves, I would like to be known by that name. It was my mother who decided to call me Benny Bowes, but it is a name I have never liked.'

'Of course. That's excellent!' Mark exclaimed, smiling broadly.

Potter perused the agenda. 'That is the last item on our agenda. Are there any other items to discuss before we bring in our special guests?'

Mary smiled at Kuppa. 'How is the creation of your new police department progressing, Kuppa?'

'Slowly but successfully, so far,' said Kuppa. 'It is stimulating but testing at times. For example, after the war we gained three goblins, who had been taken prisoner. Their training is "progressing" and their arrest rate is outstanding, but we have to release most of their prisoners without charge.'

'Why is that?' queried Potter.

Kuppa grinned. 'Would you be happy to be arrested because a police officer thought you had looked at him? Not strangely, just looked at him. I would not be happy nor was the innocent citizen concerned. It took me ten minutes to convince her not to take us to court. All our goblins are keen to uphold the law, but their grasp of the law is astonishingly poor. The worst of the three is PC Wallbreaker. He is eager but, truly, he is over-eager. He will arrest someone for anything. Yesterday, he arrested an elf who was window shopping in the mall. He arrested him for, and I quote, "finking of der jewels taking". I need to keep a close eye on all our goblin officers.

'However, we have two other excellent officers who have taken most of the administrative load from my shoulders. Our new scientific officers are busy establishing the forensic and

DNA facilities. For a while, we struggled with the vast numbers of petty crimes, but we are beginning to cope with the workload. I know you are aware of the crocodile incident…'

'Yes, and still enjoying the sandwiches,' said Potter, laughing.

'Yes, indeed,' chuckled Kuppa. 'I expect we will never live it down, but it has been a useful first exercise for everyone. On a more serious note, we have now arrested a suspect, accused of theft and murder, but I believe we will be covering that at the end of the meeting.'

'Yes, that is right. We will.'

'May I just update you on one last item before we proceed, Potter?'

'By all means.'

'We now have four constables with dogs trained by Bingo, Lottie and their dog, Banger. They are all capable of detecting potentially explosive devices.'

'Marvellous news.'

'Sorry, everyone, but trained police dogs?' said Ena. 'How much is that costing the council?'

'Not a thing!' declared Kuppa. 'These were dogs owned by the constables. The officers volunteered for this additional duty. The training was carried out in their own time. As for the animals, the dogs all love the work.'

'I apologise, Kuppa. I did not mean to be so sharp. I must agree with Potter. This is marvellous news. I am certain we can find funds to compensate the constables for their time. Perhaps we could furnish the dogs with smart coats with the words "Police Dog" on each side.'

'I will speak to Bingo about the coats, He has been Topside recently but he's due back next week. I am sure he will know someone who can supply us with smart dog coats.'

CHAPTER THIRTY-TWO
Any other business?

'Excellent. Thank you for that very useful briefing, Kuppa. Are there any other matters anyone wishes to raise before Kuppa updates us on the outcome of her first serious crime case?' asked Potter with a smile and a small shrug of his shoulders, before inserting yet another barley twist sweet into his mouth.

'I have four, Potter,' said Ena. 'All of them important but not very exciting.'

'Of course, we must deal with anything important. Still, I don't know about anyone else but, I am happy if these items are not very exciting, Ena. Recently, I've had more than enough excitement,' said Potter with a grin. 'What's the first item?'

'The financial report is the first item. I was worried,' said Ena, 'that council funds might be showing a deficit, following the expenditure during the Great Non-War. In fact, they are better than I expected. I have concluded that as less was spent on matters not related to the war effort, this acted as a balancing factor.' Ena distributed a sheet of figures to the group.

'I'm a military man, Ena. Never much good with figures,' declared Carruthers. 'Can you spell out what it means to an old soldier?'

'Naturally, I can, captain. It means we have a healthy surplus.'

'Oh, that is good news!' exclaimed Potter. 'I must admit I have been concerned that we were in financial difficulties. Have you any suggestions for spending this unexpected bonus?'

'Yes, my remaining three items require expenditure, which can be covered by this surplus. The second item on my list is the state of the roads between Hollow Earth and the surrounding small towns and villages. Frankly, they are in a shocking condition. They are poorly maintained with irregular, patchy surfaces and countless potholes. Some are extremely dangerous. They need resurfacing urgently before someone has a severe accident.'

[At this juncture, for reasons that were self-evident, most of the meeting members thought of Flaky Pastry, cycling these roads on his tricycle, like an elf possessed.]

'That is a serious consideration. Please allocate what is needed immediately, Ena.'

'Thank you, Potter. The next item is the new rail development, which will improve links with our sister cities. The companies involved have offered two alternatives for the new rail and tram terminus. One is functional but, truthfully, dreadfully basic. The other will allow us to modernise Hollow Earth Central entirely. The majority of the outlay will be by the development companies. With a small investment by the council, there will be abundant funds to create a brand-new terminus, which will be the envy of Underside.'

Potter was impressed. 'Please pass me all the details, Ena. We must discuss this, but it needs a separate meeting.'

'There is one further item, Potter. The most important of all. Hazel and Wendy have suggested a Spring dance to cheer everyone up. We will have quite enough funds to cover this.'

'Sounds like a wonderful idea,' said Potter. 'However, I have one condition.'

'What is that, Potter?' Ena asked.

'I agree to it, but only if you book that marvellous square dance band from Little Merritiddle again,' said Potter, beaming widely.

Potter now directed his gaze once more, at Kuppa.

'Kuppa, what is the progress with this elf you have arrested for theft and murder?'

'Well, Potter, let me clarify a few points of law as I update the meeting. It is true that we have an individual held in our custody. We have charged that elf with several offences. Robbery with violence, handling stolen goods, murder, attempted murder and attempting to evade arrest. I have been advised by our lawyers that he must not be considered guilty of any of these charges until he has faced trial for the stated offences and found guilty. Until then he remains a suspect only. A date for trial of this elf has not been set. As we do not have the appropriate facilities, we have arranged for the suspect's transfer to a prison cell controlled by the Elite. The suspect will be held there for whatever period of time is required for evidence to be collected.'

Kuppa smiled wryly. 'I'm sorry if that all sounds a bit dry but that's police work for you! On a more positive note, I believe you have two special guests waiting outside for our attention.'

'That is true, Kuppa. Would you like to call them in?'

✳✳✳

Flaky and Onion had arrived and were waiting outside the meeting room. Flaky's excitement had changed into nervous tension. He had visited the toilets three times in the last hour.

When Kuppa Broth eventually summoned Onion and Flaky, Flaky rushed to the door. In his eagerness, he ran into the edge of the door she was holding open, yet no sooner had he hit the floor, then he bounced back to his feet. It was typical Flaky behaviour. He fell over so regularly that he was practised in swift recoveries, always leaping up as quickly as he could, hoping no-one had noticed.

'Are you alright, Flaky?' asked Kuppa, looking at him with concern.

Flaky blurted out a hurried response. 'Yes, thank you Mist Kuppa, I did not hurt myself. Err, sorry I mean thank you Mist Broth, police chief of the office.'

'Flaky, it's Mist Broth, Chief of Police,' murmured Onion from the corner of his mouth. He smiled sheepishly at the meeting attendees, as if to say, "he cannot help it".

Potter gave Onion and Flaky a friendly wave.

'Ah, I see our guests of honour are here. Welcome, gentlemen. Please, take a seat.'

Potter gestured to two chairs set out to one side of the meeting room. As they walked over to them, Flaky whispered to his friend, 'Where have I got to take the seat, Onion?'

'Give me strength,' sighed Onion. 'You do not need to take the seat anywhere, Flaky. Just sit on it.'

Unfortunately, Flaky reached the chairs ahead of Onion. He sat down quickly. So quickly that he tumbled off the side, onto the floor, taking the chair with him as he fell. Flaky jumped up. In his eagerness to right the chair he stumbled, knocking both chairs to the floor. The following two minutes were a typical, accidental Flaky comedy routine as he attempted to return the seats to where they had been sited. Onion stood by quietly, waiting for Flaky to finish.

At last, Flaky sat down. Slowly. Onion joined him, with a further sigh.

Potter bit his lower lip to stifle his laughter. With his composure regained, he started the award ceremony.

'Onion, Flaky, I asked you to attend this meeting so that we might present you both with awards.' As he announced this, two guards placed a table in front of the two, on which they placed two boxes. Potter walked around behind the table.

'I know you were not expecting any award today, Onion, but everyone on the council felt that we should acknowledge your recent rebuilding work, following the war. Although many elves were involved in that activity, your efforts were excellent. Quite exemplary. For that reason, we are presenting you with this "Certificate of Merit".

Potter passed Onion a scroll, tied with a gold-coloured ribbon. Onion was surprised and clearly embarrassed by this unforeseen honour.

'Thank you, Mr Teasready,' he mumbled faintly, bowing slightly.

'My pleasure,' said Potter. He waved Flaky towards him.

'Now, we come to the main award of the day. Kuppa, will you present Flaky with his medal?'

'Bend forward when Kuppa gives you the medal,' Onion hissed to Flaky.

Kuppa stepped forward. 'It gives me incredible pleasure to present you with the "Citizen of the Month" medal, for your recent bravery and assistance to my officers. This allowed us to catch our suspect, who may possibly be proved to be a dangerous criminal. Well done, Flaky.'

As Kuppa endeavoured to place the medal over Flaky's head, he bent forward. So far that his nose almost touched the floor.

'Too far!' whispered Onion, urgently straightening Flaky to an upright position. Eventually, Kuppa was able to place the medal over Flaky's neck.

Flaky was elated. He stood, proudly looking down at his award.

'Thank you, thank you, Mist Chief of Broth Police,' he stammered.

CHAPTER THIRTY-THREE
The goblins prepare
for war (again!)

The goblins had continued their preparations for war with the fairies. Two of the goblins had chosen to rest propped against a huge boulder, while they sharpened their weapons. As they sat there, an enormous, hairy figure walked by.

'Wot dat?' asked Smashface Stonebreaker.

'Wot?' replied Drumnail Rockfall.

'Dat fing,' said Smashface.

'Wot fing?' queried Drumnail, who had been looking the other way.

'Dat hairy fing,' said Smashface.

'Not see der hairy fing,' answered Drumnail.

The massive, hairy creature returned, striding past in the opposite direction.

'See? Dat hairy fing,' stated Smashface, pointing.

'Yeah, see dat fing,' agreed Drumnail, who was now looking the right way.

'Wot is der hairy fing?' questioned Smashface.

'Dunno, Axecutter Gravelface in der big, furry coat?' wondered Drumnail.

[This explanation was unexpectedly plausible, as Axecutter was an enormously large, exceptionally hairy goblin.]

'Yeah, it Axecutter in der big, hairy coat. Hur, Hur!' said Smashface.

'Hur, Hur! Yeah, Axecutter!' laughed Drumnail.

Stabber Thunderfoot, a hobgoblin with a hobgoblin's increased intelligence, had listened with amusement to this exchange. As he walked across to them, he was greeted by Smashface.

'Stabber. See Axecutter in der big coat?'

'That was not Axecutter,' Stabber explained. 'That was a Sasquatch or Yeti, as they are also known.'

The goblins looked mystified.

'Slash watch or jelly?' questioned Drumnail.

'No, Sasquatch or Yeti,' corrected Stabber. 'You know, Bigfoot.'

Both goblins looked down.

'Not got der big foot!' declared Smashface.

'No, me not got der big foot,' added Drumnail.

'Not you two,' said Stabber. 'The creature you saw was a Bigfoot.'

'So, not Axecutter in der big coat?' asked Smashface.

'No.'

Stabber wandered off, his expression a mixture of hilarity bound together with reluctant acceptance of the fact that his hobgoblin brainpower was wasted in the company of goblins.

✿✿✿

The two goblin kings, Hammer Legbreaker, King of the South goblins and Mountain Stonewall, King of the North goblins were planning their campaign against the fairies.

[In reality goblins, even goblin Kings, do not understand words like planning or campaign. As a result, there was no planning involved in this discussion between the Kings. It consisted primarily with stating how hard they would whack each of the fairies.]

Their wives, Queen Avalanche Jawcrusher and Queen Snowstorm Headbreaker sat quietly to one side, sipping glasses of wine while listening with some concern to the aggressive posturing of the two monarchs.

'Hammer dear, have you decided when you and your army will leave or how you will find King Elderberry's castle?' asked Avalanche.

'KING GO, ARMY GO' was Hammer's quietly spoken and less than helpful reply.

'YEAH, KING GO, ARMY GO,' agreed Mountain, equally quietly.

'But when will that be, your Majesties? Tomorrow, three days' time, next week?' queried Snowstorm.

'GO MORNIN?' whispered Hammer directing his query to Mountain.

'YEAH, GO MORNIN,' muttered Mountain.

'GO MORNIN,' murmured Hammer, in confirmation to the two queens.

'Fine, so you will leave tomorrow. How will you find the fairies?' wondered Avalanche.

'DAT EASY. FOLLOW DER SIGNS,' stated Mountain, quietly but triumphantly.

'YEAH, DO DAT,' agreed Hammer, with the slightly grumbly mumble of a goblin king who wished he had thought of it first.

'Shall I make an announcement to all your warriors, telling them that you leave to battle the fairies tomorrow?' asked Avalanche.

'YEAH, DO DAT FING,' said Hammer.

'ALL GOBLINS GO. BRING ALL DER WEAPONS,' commanded Mountain, in the most "polite company", understated voice he could manage.

CHAPTER THIRTY-FOUR
The fairies prepare their defence

From the moment he had met with Cornflower Blue and learnt of the intention by the goblins to attack the fairies, King Elderberry had begun to prepare the defence of his domain. Elderberry was aware that the fairies could not defeat the goblins in straightforward combat. The goblins were more aggressive, more violent than the fairies. He knew that the goblins considered fighting to be a normal, everyday activity. The fairies did not. Further, he was aware that, with the arrival of the north goblins, the goblin army was effectively doubled in size. The fairies could only defeat the goblins by using their particular range of skills: magic combined with typical devious, cunning, sneaky, fairy subterfuge and nastiness.

King Elderberry had summoned his son, Prince Dandelion. He was addressing the prince in his usual, slow, languorous style. The king's delivery was so inordinately monotonous, that Dandelion had barely heard a word his father had uttered. He was happily falling into gentle, dreamy sleep when he stirred suddenly, with the realisation that his father was still talking and he really ought to be listening. More importantly he recognised that his father was using the royal "we". He needed to pay attention.

'Dandelion, we will not tolerate a goblin invasion. We are the monarch, the absolute ruler of this kingdom. We will not surrender our realm to those savages. Our father would never have permitted such an intrusion. Such an incursion remains unthinkable. We will not allow defeat by the goblins. We find that unacceptable. It is imperative that we use all our resources against them. We believe the goblins do not know where our castle is located. We are certain that they are too foolish to admit this or ask anyone for directions. This we can use to our advantage; their disadvantage.'

'How will we achieve that, your majesty?'

'We need you to construct some signs. If the goblins follow these, as we are sure they will, our success will be guaranteed. This is what we have in mind.'

Elderberry passed several sheets of instructions to his son, which included numerous diagrams and pictures.

Dandelion read these through before grinning widely at the king.

'Brilliant, father. I almost feel sorry for the goblins. They will have no understanding of what has transpired.'

During the next few days, Dandelion employed the best fairy woodworkers in the land, to create a series of road signs.

✿✿✿

When the rampaging goblin army, led by their two kings, reached the borders of King Elderberry's territory, they came across forks in the road ahead of them. There were a variety of roads the goblins might follow. Goblins were not adept at making choices. Fortunately, they could see a signpost ahead that could assist them. Unfortunately, few goblins can read.

Fortunately, they had one goblin, OneEye Hookhand, who had been trained in the basics by his mother, who was a hobgoblin. (Regrettably, he had not inherited any of her intelligence.) Equally helpfully, the arms of the signpost included drawings to provide additional clarity.

[The goblins had travelled this way previously when they attacked the elves in The Great Non-War. They did not recall seeing any signs but then goblins are notoriously poor at remembering anything. None of them questioned why there was a sign in the road that was not there before. This was exactly what King Elderberry had anticipated.]

'WHAT DER SIGNS SAY,' wondered Hammer, almost inaudibly. A goblin king never admits willingly to any shortcoming.

'Magictree kingness, me read der signs,' offered OneEye.

'YEAH, READ DER SIGNS DEN.'

OneEye's colleague, Cutslash Bladegrinder moved OneEye so that he was facing the signpost. Strangely, OneEye held his hand over his good eye as he attempted to read the signpost.

'It gone dark,' he complained. Cutslash (who had known OneEye long enough to anticipate certain difficulties) repositioned OneEye's hand so that it now covered his eyepatch, while he read.

'Dat better,' said OneEye.

Pointing to the sign that indicated the direction they had journeyed from, which displayed a passable image of a goblin, he read, 'Dat say goblins.'

'Dat us,' declared a voice helpfully from the midst of the massed ranks of goblins.

Offset to the right on the signpost was a sign with a picture of two individuals in pointy hats.

'Dat say der wizzies and der witchers,' OneEye proclaimed.

Cutslash took hold of OneEye's shoulders, shifting him to the left.

'An dat say der Elves,' OneEye announced confidently, as he waved his hook-embellished arm in the general direction of the sign to the left. This had a depiction of an unpleasant, evil, distorted red face. It looked nothing like an elf but there was no surprise in this. Both fairies and goblins hated elves with a passion. Any illustration of an elf reflected the artist's bias. Their absolute loathing of elves.

Conversely, the final sign, which pointed forwards, showed a remarkably, but quite unbelievably, handsome fairy.

'Dat say fairies,' confirmed OneEye.

'DIS WAY,' yelled Hammer so loudly that he set off a short-lived but impressive earth tremor.

CHAPTER THIRTY-FIVE
Lost in fairy lands

Following Hammer's command, the goblins raced off, without a second thought.

[Of course, the goblins had not managed a first thought for this second thought to follow, but I imagine you guessed that.]

After just over half an hour, the goblins began to tire. They stopped running.

Hammer caught up with the goblin troops that were ahead of the main army. Almost soundlessly, for a goblin king, he asked 'WHY STOP?'

'No see der fairies,' said Drumnail Rockfall.

King Mountain was a few yards behind Hammer. Predictably, as he drew level, he asked, virtually inaudibly, for a goblin king, 'WHY STOP?'

'No fairies,' explained Gravel Blackhead.

OneEye, who had appointed himself scout as well as sign reader, had ventured around a bend in the road. Excitedly, he returned calling out 'Nuvver sign'.

Two goblins attempted to attack him, thinking he was an enemy.

'It me, OneEye,' he shouted.

'Magictrees,' he continued, struggling to free himself. 'Nuvver sign in road.' He gestured around the bend with his hook.

This signpost had two arms. (Cutslash's assistance was not required on this occasion.)

'Dat say der Steaming Mound,' said OneEye looking at the sign on the left, which had a basic sketch of a mountain with wavy lines above it.

'Dat say der Castle,' said OneEye, indicating the sign on the right, with a helpful picture of an attractive castle.

'GO CASTLE!' stated Mountain gently but firmly.

Not wishing to be left out, Hammer concurred with Mountain's suggestion.

'YEAH, DO DAT!' Adding, 'NOT DO DER STINKY, SMELLY, STEAMY FING.'

[No-one had suggested that Steaming Mound was stinky or smelly, but Hammer's assumption was accurate. Steaming Mound was an abnormally foul, unpleasantly fetid, plateau-topped hill originally created by magma outflow from an ancient volcano.]

Unbeknownst to the goblins, the fairies had positioned the signpost with the arms pointing in the wrong direction. The sign stating Castle actually directed the goblins towards Steaming Mound.

The goblins raced excitedly in the direction of the castle. After an hour or so of running, jogging, sprinting, loping or eventually plodding along at a slow walking pace, the lead goblins began sniffing the air.

'Wot der smell?'

'Dunno. Stinky. Dat you?'

'Not me. Me no smell. Must be Ratboner.'

'Yeah, Ratboner be whiffy old ponger.'

*[Ratboner Nailbeater was a particularly reeking example
of goblin manhood (or possibly womanhood. It's difficult
to tell!). Most goblins have a tendency towards a natural,
powerful stench but Ratboner's was so disgusting that few
goblins were able to stand near him without their eyes
streaming. This was usually followed by extreme bouts of
choking, coughing, or sneezing and observations such as
"take der bath, Ratboner".]*

'Fink not Ratboner.'

'Yeah?'

'Yeah, see him back dere.'

'Sure?'

'Yeah, big space round him.'

'Fink it dat,' said the lead goblin, indicating something ahead
of them. The something was Steaming Mound.

Steaming Mound was a very wide hill with a flat summit,
but the fairies had cast a spell, giving the mound the appearance
of a gigantic mountain, so tall that its crest projected at least a
mile out of Underside into Topside. Its base was surrounded by
a murky, hazy pall which was providing the rotten odour being
experienced by the goblins. Its illusory pinnacle was cloaked in
drifting clouds.

'Dat der big hill! Fink castle uvver side?'

'Dunno. Too big to climb.'

'Go round?'

'Yeah, go round.'

The decision to advance around Steaming Mound in order
to locate King Elderberry's castle was, for goblins, unexpectedly
intelligent. Then again, the goblins could not know that the
king's castle was not sited next to Steaming Mound. Naturally,

a brighter individual would have instinctively recognised how unlikely that was. Why would any king place his castle adjacent to such an awful, putrid, stinking pile?

Moreover, there was no way that the goblins could be aware that the fairies had cast an obscuring spell on the path around Steaming Mound. This spell ensured that the goblins were unable to detect any details whatsoever as they progressed along the path.

Without knowing, the goblins circled the mound eight times. Effectively, the goblin army was in fixed orbit around the hill. Eventually, two or three neurons fired in the brain of one of the goblins.

'Fink dis path not dis long. Fink go round in der big circle fing.'

'Dat right! Need go back.'

'Find der path.'

As the goblins could not see any discernible features on this enchanted path, finding the way back was both difficult and time consuming.

Finally, a goblin yelled, 'Me find der path.' Almost simultaneously, a second goblin shouted 'No, me find der path.' Such a conundrum was a nightmare for the limited brain power of the goblins. The presence of the two kings proved fortuitous. King Mountain was close to the first path discoverer. King Hammer was close to the second.

'MOUNTAIN GO DIS PATH,' Mountain said in a voice barely audible to the other goblins.

'HAMMER GO DIS PATH,' declared Hammer in a similarly inaudible whisper.

Instinctively, the north goblins followed Mountain while the south goblins trailed after Hammer.

Hammer's party were fortunate. They soon found themselves on the path back. They settled down to wait.

Mountain's party came upon another fork in the road. This had no helpful signpost.

Mountain took the decision that any brave king would make in this situation. He sent others to "do the dirty work". Pointing at about half of the goblins, he murmured, 'GO DAT WAY', waving an arm to his left. Gesturing to the remaining goblins while indicating the path to the right, he muttered, 'GO DAT WAY.' Mountain sat on a nearby rock to await the return of his soldiers.

The goblin party that ventured left had not journeyed far when they began to sniff the air worriedly. The goblins were unaware of the concept of déjà vu, although that was exactly what they were experiencing.

'Wot der stink?'

'Dat like der smelly mountain.'

'Not same.'

'No, not same but big pong.'

'Like Ratboner but more stinky.'

'Yeah, more whiffy pong.'

Finally, the source of the abominable odour became clear. The goblins stumbled upon a reeking swamp. More accurately, the first twelve stumbled headfirst *into* the swamp. Within minutes a dozen, slime-covered figures, plastered in brown, muddy vegetation, and assorted sludgy deposits exited the swamp.

'Monsters!' yelled a goblin. Panic is common amongst goblins. Within seconds the other goblins were rushing back along the path pursued by the slurry-coated "monsters".

'It us. Not der monsters!' the "monsters" called out.

At last, as pieces of the filthy grime fell away, the panicking goblins could see that the "monsters" were merely their unlucky comrades. 'Why got der mud on?' asked one.

'Fell in der muck,' one replied. It was ten minutes before the dry goblins ceased laughing at their unfortunate wet friends. Finally, they all traipsed back to Mountain. 'Dat way der pongy bog fing,' they explained.

Mountain's other goblin horde, which had trekked to the right, soon reached yet another signpost. Fortuitously, this group contained OneEye Hookhand.

Signalling with his good hand, he declared, 'Der Castle dis way.'

The goblins ran excitedly along this pathway, whooping with joy. Before long they saw two enormous gates. Beyond the gates, the goblins were unable to see anything other than darkness. Thinking they were entering the castle, they charged forward, leaving behind only the more exhausted members of the party. These weary few were able to watch, with surprise, as two huge metallic gates clanged shut behind their comrades.

Inside the gates, the area was suddenly illuminated. A powerful, sarcastic voice reverberated around the walls. 'Welcome to the King's dungeons. You are now our prisoners. We hope you enjoy your stay.'

The goblins still outside the gates looked at each other.

'Go back to der king?'

'Yeah, fink go back.'

When this miniscule group staggered back tiredly to their king, he was confused.

Almost soundlessly, he asked, 'WOT DUN WID UVVERS?'

'Dey in der prison, Magictree.'

King Mountain's strange collection of goblins wandered lethargically along the path to where Hammer and the others were waiting. Included in this company were the tiny faction of goblins not taken prisoner at the gates, who had the decency to look guilty as well as relieved, the twelve, sodden swamp monsters and a clutch of their dry, still chortling comrades.

King Hammer's goblin horde were sitting happily, by the side of the road, munching on food from an exceptionally large container. Queen Avalanche never allowed her husband to go to war, without provisions.

'WANT DER FOOD?' asked Hammer with a quiet, regal smile, biting off an enormous chunk of meat.

Usually, such a provocative development would have led to a typical outbreak of uncontrolled, goblin rage from King Mountain and his crowd of disgruntled warriors. In this instance, they were so fatigued they simply slumped to the floor.

'GOT DER HORN MEAT?' was all that Mountain could manage.

[Unlike elves, goblins rarely venture Topside. Subtleties of meat classification such as beef, lamb, pork, chicken, duck, turkey, or venison were unknown to them. To any average goblin, there was only "der horn meat" (from cows, deer or goats), "der fluffy meat" (from sheep), "der grunt meat" (from pigs and boars), "der flappy meat" (from chickens, duck or turkeys), "der clip clop meat" (from horses or ponies) or "der splashy meat" (from fish).]

CHAPTER THIRTY-SIX
Leaflets for the Spring Dance

F laky was inordinately proud of his medal. He kept polishing it against his tunic and staring at it. Whenever Onion came near, he proudly held up the medal inches from his employer's face with a wide, beaming smile. Any caller to Onion's workshop was shown Flaky's medal in a similar fashion, accompanied unnecessarily by the words 'I got this medal'.

Potter had asked Onion to construct extra tables for the Spring Dance, to cater for the expected additional village guests.

Flaky was "helping". As he lifted a long plank of wood, he was distracted by the glitter of his medal. Within moments, he had succeeded in pushing the plank through the loop of ribbon that held the medal around his neck. He tried to free himself, frantically swinging the plank in circles. His first attempt was in a clockwise arc which was swiftly followed by an anti-clockwise sweep.

Onion's past experiences with such "Flaky induced" incidents saved him from significant injury. He leant back as the plank's first swing missed his face by inches. Immediately, he bent forward as the plank returned, passing just over his head.

'Flaky, stop! Don't move again. I'll free you,' yelled Onion.

Carefully, he extricated Flaky, putting the plank on the floor.

'Do you remember that presentation box Kuppa gave you to keep your medal safe?' he asked.

'Oh yes, it looks really shiny and important in the box,' agreed Flaky.

'Well, why don't you put your medal in that box and place it somewhere safe? You don't want to lose it.'

'No, I've never been given a medal before and it's so big and shiny. I'll put it away right now, Onion.'

Flaky hurried forward and placed the medal box on the top shelf above Onion's desk, knocking against a large wood-working book. Like a row of dominoes, the books on the shelf all toppled into each other, leaving a heavy plumbing book teetering on the end of the shelf.

Onion waited in horrified fascination for the inevitable thump of the book falling onto Flaky's head, but nothing happened. Amazingly, Flaky walked away unharmed.

Onion walked over to his desk, as his phone rang. The vibration was just enough to move the quivering plumbing book a further inch. It wobbled momentarily before tumbling down onto Onion's head. He fell down behind his desk. Flaky spun around as he heard the noise behind him. He could not see his employer.

'Onion?'

'Behind the desk, Flaky. Just dusting off this plumbing book. It fell onto the floor. Fortunately, my head broke its fall.'

As usual, Onion's sarcasm was wasted on Flaky. Onion rubbed his head cautiously, allowing himself a small groan.

'Don't worry about this mess, Flaky. I'll tidy it up.'

The remainder of the morning passed without any other significant disasters.

The chief reason for this was Flaky's continuing excitement, which meant he had completely forgotten about work.

'I can't wait to show everyone my medal,' he declared every few minutes.

Eventually, Onion could no longer stand any more of Flaky's enthusiasm.

'Shouldn't you be walking the dogs about now?' he asked hopefully.

'No, Onion, I walked them earlier. I won't be walking them again until this evening.'

Luckily for Onion, he spotted a large pile of papers on the edge of one of the tables. It was the leaflets advertising the Spring Dance, which Ena had asked him to circulate around the villages.

'Flaky,' he said, 'I have an important job for you. Do you see these leaflets?' he asked, placing his hand on the top of the pile. 'Mistress Minnit has asked us to deliver these to all of the surrounding villages. They need to be displayed on their Village notice boards or in their shop windows, so that everyone will know about the Dance. Do you think you can do that for her?'

'Yes, Onion, I will leave right now.' Flaky dashed across to his tricycle and cart.

Onion stopped him just as he was about to leave.

'Did you forget something, Flaky?'

No, Onion, I don't think so. I have the cart and my tricycle. I'm ready to leave.'

'Where are the leaflets you are delivering?'

'They're on the table just there, Onion.'

Onion stared at Flaky in disbelief. 'Do you think it might be better if you loaded them into your cart?'

'Oh yes. Sorry, Onion.'

For the next three hours Flaky dashed busily from village to village with the leaflets. Before he left, Onion had told him what to say at each village he visited.

'Can you pin one of these leaflets on your village noticeboard and stick some up in your shop or house windows for Mistress Minnit, please?'

At first, Flaky had difficulty remembering what he had to say to the residents of each village, which led to more than a little confusion and amusement for each villager he met.

'Can you stick one of these leaflets up your noticeboard?' he asked one villager.

'Can you pin this noticeboard to your window?' he asked another.

'Can you put Mistress Minnit in your shop window?' he asked a third.

After several of these false starts, Flaky sat down for five minutes to remember what Onion had said. Eventually, he began to deliver his message correctly.

Flaky was delayed for almost ten minutes at Babbsley Reach, when he stopped to talk with Lemon Puff. In many ways, she was similar to Flaky. She was not gifted with noticeably excessive intellectual abilities. Her brainpower was superior to Flaky's but, in reality, the difference was not huge. Both of the elves were young. Lemon was a mere sixty-nine years of age, while Flaky was barely older at seventy.

Whilst the two were similar in age and intellectual ability, Lemon did not share Flaky's scrawny build or untidy, dishevelled appearance. She was of average build for a female elf and at five feet nine (and a half!) inches she was of typical height. Invariably, Lemon was smartly dressed with her light tangerine-toned, mid-length hair always neatly styled, atop her smiling, golden sandy face. Her natural cheerful demeanour was reflected in her ruby coloured eyes, which were usually described as sparkling.

The most significant difference between the two was in the way they were perceived. Where Flaky was seen as stupid, irritating, and clumsy, Lemon was not. She was an extremely cheerful, charming, friendly elf. The other villagers excused her lack of intelligence, with phrases such as "I know she's not the brightest but she's so nice and helpful" or "She's just a bit scatty. She can't help it".

Everyone liked Lemon and Lemon liked everyone. Lemon and Flaky had met at the fireworks celebration in Little Merritiddle the previous year. Although Lemon liked everyone, she *really* liked Flaky. Flaky also *really* liked Lemon. He was delighted when, by accident, he almost run her over with his tricycle. Lemon glanced at the leaflets.

'Spring Dance? That sounds exciting! Are you going, Flaky?'

Flaky turned an interesting shade of pink. 'Yes, Lemon. Onion's taking me.'

'That's lovely! We could be dance partners!'

'Dance partners? That would be nice, but I don't know much dancing.'

'Nor do I but we can try. Please say you will.'

Flaky was experiencing panic combined with excitement with a further very pleasant emotion he had never experienced before.

'I...I...I... will be lovely to be your dance partner,' he stammered. 'Sorry, no I mean, I will love to dance with you, Lemony. No, I mean Lemon.' Flaky gave Lemon a weak, embarrassed smile.

'That is wonderful, Flaky. I can hardly wait! Can I take a handful of these leaflets? I will pass them to Minnie Peppers. She's clever. She will know what to do with them.'

Lemon blew Flaky a kiss as he left. Flaky was so surprised, he fell off his tricycle. He was soon back on his feet, grabbing hold of his trike. He was not sure what to do so he smiled and waved. Lemon giggled then waved back.

As Flaky approached Lower Tinkerton, he spotted Carr Pette, a well-respected, serious but friendly villager. Carr's appearance was often described as the embodiment of autumn. Her caramel tinted eyes looked out at the world from her honey hued face. A face which was framed by her mid-length cinnamon shaded hair. Carr's distinctive appearance meant she was easy to spot, even for Flaky. He was just going to stop to ask her if she could pass round some leaflets when a voice called out to him.

'Hello Flaky, I thought that was you,' said Cornflower Blue as he strolled towards him, carrying a large bunch of flowers, 'you look busy. Oh, and a very good morning to you, Carr. How are you today?'

Carr Pette smiled broadly at Cornflower, blushing slightly. Secretly, she had always had a crush on Cornflower. 'Cornflower, how lovely to see you. Are those flowers for me?' she enquired teasingly.

Cornflower returned her smile. 'Sorry to disappoint you, Carr, but I'm on my way to the Crematorium to put these on the memorial for my parents. I will make sure to buy you a bunch next time I wander into the village. So, Flaky, what are you up to today?'

'I have to deliver these leaflets about the Spring Dance to all the villages, Cornflower.'

'Sounds like challenging work. I could help you to deliver them when I return from the Crematorium. Actually, do you want to come with me, Flaky? I'll buy you lunch at The Chimney and then we can finish delivering these leaflets. How does that sound?'

'Oh, that sounds very nice. Thank you.'

As they left with Flaky cycling slowly and Cornflower walking beside him, Carr sighed gently. 'What a nice elf!'

When they reached the Hollow Earth Crematorium, Cornflower led Flaky to the memorials for his parents. Cornflower had arranged for the two memorials, for his mother Ocean and his father Peacock, to be combined. Cornflower removed wilting flowers from the two memorial vessels.

He handed the old flowers to Flaky.

'Flaky, could you put these in that large bin over there labelled "Composter" please?'

'Of course, Cornflower.'

Cornflower emptied the old water into a sloping trough, which served all the memorials. He then walked over to a large sink where he washed out the vessels and filled them with fresh water from the tap.

He crossed back to the memorial where Flaky was waiting for him, staring at the water gushing down the trough.

'Where does all that water go?' he asked.

'It runs into a filtering machine,' answered Cornflower, 'the clean water is fed into the river. The residue is fed back into the main composting process. Now, would you like to help me arrange the flowers, Flaky? I put half in each vase.'

'Oh, can I? Yes, please.'

After a few minutes, they stopped. Cornflower stood back.

'Perfect! Thank you, Flaky. Let's get lunch.' He gave a small bow to the memorial. 'See you next week, Mum and Dad.'

Cornflower inclined his head towards Flaky with a twinkling grin on his face. 'I like to pay my respects to my parents each week but now it is time for something happier. Lunch. Have you been to The Charcoal Chimney before, Flaky?'

'No, I've never been.'

'In that case you are in for a treat. The food is delicious. I often pop in after I've been here, but it will be more pleasant with you for company.'

Flaky hesitated. 'Do you think they would allow me to leave some leaflets about the Spring Dance here, Cornflower?'

'I'm sure it won't be a problem. As I am a regular visitor, the staff knows me. I'll speak to them. I expect they will be happy to take some leaflets and put them up on their notice boards.'

CHAPTER THIRTY-SEVEN
Flaky and Cornflower

Flaky could not believe the incredible selection of food on the menu at the restaurant. He was also impressed by the fact that everyone seemed to know Cornflower. He particularly enjoyed being introduced to them as "my very good friend, Flaky Pastry".

Over lunch they discussed the upcoming dance.

Flaky admitted, 'I have never been to a posh dance.'

'Neither have I,' said Cornflower. 'Perhaps we can keep each other company, as friends should?'

'Oh yes, I would like that. I expect Onion will bring us in his van, but it will be nice to have someone else to talk to.'

'Isn't Onion your friend, as well as your employer?' inquired Cornflower.

'He is, but he's quite bossy. He gets cross with me because I am stupid and clumsy, which I am, and because I get everything wrong, which I do. I can't talk to Onion like I do with you.'

'That is a shame, Flaky. We cannot all be clever, and everyone makes mistakes sometimes. As for clumsiness, surely that is something you cannot help.'

'I wish Onion thought that. Onion thinks I am the stupidest, clumsiest person he knows.'

'I see. Why do you still work for him if he thinks you are so bad?'

Flaky looked down at the floor. He was clearly embarrassed.

'Onion watches out for me,' he muttered. 'When my mum left, Onion promised her he would take me in and look after me. Most elves can't put up with me for long, but Onion is different. Even though he gets frost…thrush…frusticated…'

'Frustrated?'

'Yes, he gets frustrated, but he puts up with me and lets me work for him. He is my only friend.'

'Your only friend? That is sad.'

'Well, he was my only friend until I met you, Cornflower.'

'I am very glad we are friends, Flaky.'

Cornflower realised that he meant everything he said. He genuinely enjoyed Flaky's company. He found his innocence refreshing. His found his enthusiasm for life stimulating.

However, at times, Cornflower was perplexed by his own nature. For many months, he had suffered unexplained blanks in his memory. Repeatedly, he woke in his bed, his living room or even occasionally in the middle of the street with no recollection of how he came to be there.

As the ever-present magic dust in the atmosphere ensured that elves rarely became ill, Underside's medical profession was accustomed, primarily, to treating minor ailments. This problem was beyond their experience. As injuries were dealt with by the Hospital, Cornflower's case was referred there, in case he had suffered a mysterious trauma, in the past. Countless tests proved that he had no physical concerns.

Finally, Cornflower was referred to a psychologist called Dr Annie Payne.

[Yes, even serious doctors have dubious names in Underside!]

Psychiatry and psychology were new disciplines for elvish doctors. Despite this, a few keen professionals had decided that a study of these new specialities was worthwhile. One such medical practitioner was Annie Payne. Annie spent months in dedicated self-education. She became a remarkably proficient psychologist through the practical application of her newly acquired skills. In particular, dealing with elves affected by The Great Non-War provided her with an enormous wealth of opportunities for investigative research. Annie became so experienced that she was considered the foremost psychologist in Underside.

Cornflower Blue's case was a challenge for her new abilities, but in due course, Dr Payne had a diagnosis. An answer to Cornflower's concerns. She identified Cornflower's blackouts as the results of a split personality.

'Split personality? What does that mean, Doctor?'

'All elves have several sides to their personality. For example, how an elf presents themselves to their parents, their child, their friends, their work colleagues will all differ, even if those personality variations are minor. Many of us are unaware that we act this way, until this is pointed out by another elf.'

'Even you, Doctor?'

'Of course, Cornflower. For instance, I have been told, by my colleagues, that I adopt a serious, professional demeanour when I am with a client, which is quite at odds with my usual self. Oh, and Cornflower, please call me Annie. Doctor is so formal!'

'Oh right. I will, Annie, but I am still not sure I understand. Where does this split personality fit into the picture?'

'An understandable question, Cornflower. I need to explain myself more fully. A split personality is quite rare. It occurs when two or more of the alternative aspects, which make up an elf's personality, take control of that individual and function as separate entities, in their own right. In the majority of cases of split personality, two distinct personalities are manifested. In some incredibly rare situations, a person creates more than two discrete versions of themselves. Psychologists refer to this as multiple personalities.'

'I see. So, you believe I have two versions of myself, but why do I have these blackouts, Annie?'

'When your other self is in control, you have no recollection of what your alter ego has done. It is possible that the same is true for them, but it is likely that they are the dominant personality,' she told him.

'What does that mean?' asked Cornflower.

'I suspect your alternative personality is aware of everything *you* do but chooses to keep their presence hidden in the depths of your mind. This allows them to control everything *they* do but also watch or direct *your* actions, as they desire.'

'Good grief. That is extremely troubling. What can I do to resolve this?'

'Nothing immediately, as unfortunately we are out of time, Cornflower. We need further sessions if you wish to examine your condition in greater detail. It is unlikely that a quick solution can be found, but such a personality fracture will have resulted from either a physical or mental trauma in your past. If you decide to attend further sessions, you can prepare by considering where and when such a trauma might have occurred.'

'Thank you, Annie. I will book my next session with your secretary and see if I can recall any damaging trauma in my past before I attend.'

'Good. Until next time, Cornflower.'

When her secretary, an avid reader accurately named Paige Turner, came in to confirm that Cornflower had booked another meeting, Dr Payne smiled thoughtfully.

'Interesting case, Paige.'

Cornflower was, in fact, kept completely in the dark by The Dark.

Over time, Cornflower began to suspect the identity of his other self. He guessed, based on the timings of the gaps in his memory and the activities of a certain notorious individual that no-one could find, that in fact, *he* might be the criminal who called himself The Dark. It was most disturbing. Regrettably, there was nothing Cornflower could do. Whenever he resolved to hand himself over to the authorities, The Dark took control, preventing any such action. When Cornflower "came to" a day or so later, he invariably struggled to recall what he had been about to undertake.

Even when Cornflower's personality was predominant, The Dark was never fully excluded. He was always completely aware of Cornflower's actions although he could not always control them. This provided The Dark with a significant advantage. He could accomplish some of his nefarious activities, whilst "disguised" as Cornflower Blue. As The Dark experienced everything Cornflower thought, every action he carried out and every utterance he made, pretending to be him was not difficult for The Dark.

Sometimes, Cornflower was conscious of a conflict within himself, as though "something" was striving to break through.

Something hostile and unpleasant. When this occurred, he could only wait until the sensation passed. He could not realise that these occasions resulted from The Dark's disappointment at or dislike of one of Cornflower's actions, such as his friendship with Flaky. The Dark did not share Cornflower's view of Flaky. The Dark considered Flaky an irritating irrelevance, of which he would happily rid himself.

Cornflower inhaled deeply, calming himself. He became aware that Flaky had spoken to him.

'I'm terribly sorry, Flaky. I was daydreaming. I didn't catch what you said.'

'That's alright, Cornflower. I'm used to no-one listening to me. Most elves think I am so silly that I have nothing to say, anyway.'

'Well, I did not mean to ignore you, and I think it is the other elves who are silly not to listen to you. Now, what was it you said?'

'I was just saying that I need to deliver the rest of the leaflets and get back home to do my evening dog walking.'

'Good point, Flaky. I will just pay up and then we can crack on. Where are we delivering next?'

By sharing the delivery duties, the leaflets were soon reduced, leaving just one small pile.

'I think I need to go now, Cornflower. Onion will be worried. I'll do the rest tomorrow.'

'Where are these for?' asked Cornflower.

'Lower Tinkerton. It's where I was going when I met you. It's the only village we haven't been to,' Flaky replied.

'Lower Tinkerton? I can take them. I live near to the village. That way, you won't be late. I'll speak with Carr Pette, their village elder. She will be happy to help, I am sure.'

'Really? Thanks, Cornflower. Onion will be pleased they are all done but I really must leave now, otherwise Onion will be cross. Bye.'

Depositing the leaflets with Cornflower, Flaky leapt on his trike and dashed off, leaving a smiling Cornflower in his wake.

As expected, Onion was waiting anxiously for Flaky, holding the leads of six dogs.

'Ah, there you are, Flaky. I was beginning to wonder where you were. As you can see, you are late for your evening dog walking. Where are all the leaflets? You didn't lose them, did you?'

'No, Onion. They're all delivered. My friend Cornflower helped me.'

'Really? I am impressed. I must meet Cornflower. He sounds a very good friend indeed. Do you want to clean yourself up quickly? Then you can take these poor animals out. Some of them have been waiting for about quarter of an hour.'

Flaky dashed inside, falling over the threshold on the way. In the bathroom, as he rushed to get ready, he dropped the soap from the sink onto the floor. Twice. As he attempted to retrieve the soap the second time, he inadvertently stepped on it, falling headlong into the bath. He climbed out of the bath. 'I'm fine,' he declared to the empty room.

Onion, who was waiting outside, was unaware of Flaky's most recent clumsy misfortune. He was genuinely impressed that Flaky had delivered all the leaflets. He was delighted that Cornflower had helped him. Onion knew that Flaky had very few friends. He was pleased that Flaky had found such a good friend. It was a small, magic moment in Flaky's life, Onion mused to himself.

Flaky sprinted out of the house. In his urgency, he ran straight into the dog leads that Onion was holding. Within seconds, Flaky was floored again, wrapped in a messy tangle of dogs and leads. "Well, that magic moment didn't last long," thought Onion.

'I'm alright,' stated a voice from the floor.

CHAPTER THIRTY-EIGHT
Cornflower Blue's cottage

It was true that Cornflower did live just outside Lower Tinkerton, in a small, cosy cottage, completely removed both in physical location and appearance from the dank, dreary cave inhabited by The Dark. Or so it seemed.

In reality, the quaint, homely exterior of the cottage concealed a masterpiece of engineering, which was contained within. Cornflower was a qualified electrician and builder. The Dark, working through Cornflower, altered his cottage so that Cornflower's absences, as The Dark, would not draw unwanted attention. The Dark had Cornflower rig electronic devices inside the cottage to periodically turn lights, music, television, and audio equipment on and off. He had recorded sounds of him moving about, showering, cleaning his teeth, even using the toilet. All this apparent activity was designed to make other elves assume Cornflower was inside the cottage when, in fact, he was out.

Naturally, these electronic devices were not obvious to anyone Cornflower might invite into the cottage. The Dark had ensured that Cornflower had made these virtually invisible, as well as making certain that the Cornflower side of his mind remained unaware of their existence.

The Dark also had Cornflower construct a secret tunnel into the cellar of the cottage. Its entrance was approximately a mile from the property. This tunnel allowed him to access the property without being seen. By entering through the tunnel, he could exit through the front door of the cottage, adding to the illusion that he had been inside. The Dark, in his Cornflower disguise, usually delayed his exit deliberately until he spotted another elf passing by. He always greeted them with his customary friendly manner, guaranteeing that they would remember seeing him leave. From time to time, The Dark ensured Cornflower was spotted entering through his front door, to avoid arousing suspicion.

In the recesses of Cornflower's mind, the lurking personality of The Dark gradually absorbed many of Cornflower's engineering abilities. Ultimately, he decided he must create a similar secret entrance tunnel to his cave, using what he had learnt. The remoteness of its location meant that The Dark was unconcerned about prying eyes. Nonetheless, he was aware that his normal approach to his cave made it possible, albeit it unlikely, for him to be seen arriving and changing from Cornflower's clothes into the attire of The Dark.

Before long, The Dark had created a secret entrance to his cave.

The Dark utilised a large tree at the end of a long, meandering lane leading nowhere, to obscure this new entrance. Concealed behind this large tree, where he had habitually left a rucksack containing The Dark's "outfit", he had constructed a trapdoor camouflaged with fake grass, moss, and soil. Beneath this he had built a few steps, which led down to a new pathway. This he had fashioned as a gentle, curving slope which joined with an existing corridor. The Dark was overjoyed with his handiwork. He was now able to enter or leave his cave undetected.

***

For most of his life, Cornflower Blue was a typical elf. He was pleasant, cheerful, and hard-working. The principal, singular focus of his existence was Christmas. This obsession, shared by most elves, kept him happy with whatever work he tackled. As long as it was involved with Christmas, Cornflower did not mind. As a young elf, Cornflower trained initially as a designer but soon transferred his interest to building, specialising in electrical work. He soon became a skilled builder and electrician.

When a vacancy occurred in the Teddy Bear Stuffing factory for a maintenance engineer, Cornflower successfully applied for the position. His skills were perfect for this appointment.

[In case it crosses your mind, the elves do not manufacture every teddy bear that is sold. This would be totally impractical, if not actually impossible. Still, the elves do like to "keep their hand in" by producing a few thousand, reasonably priced bears each month. The elves pride themselves on their success in making such bears to high quality standards. They are mortified whenever they hear that one of their bears is travelling around Topside, in all weathers, strapped to the front grille of a commercial vehicle.]

After two years, Cornflower was promoted to senior maintenance engineer. He was responsible for three stuffing machines together with their associated conveyor belts. Further, he was assigned the additional role of quality control. Cornflower considered quality control to be the most vital function he undertook. He felt fulfilled carrying out such significant, satisfying work. There could be no doubt that he was an extremely happy elf.

Until the fateful day that Henny Minnit volunteered to help at the factory.

There was a major accident on the road leading to the factory, which was caused, according to witnesses, by an elf, on a poorly maintained tricycle, who veered across two traffic lanes without warning. Witnesses claimed that the elf apologised profusely countless times, explaining that he was trying to avoid all the potholes. He then sped away, completely oblivious to the turmoil and disarray left in his wake. No-one thought to find out the elf's name, although one witness was sure that he mumbled something about an onion.

The delays occasioned by the accident led to an unanticipated late arrival by Cornflower's colleague, Brandy Snappe. She oversaw the three stuffing machines adjacent to Cornflower's. Making matters worse was the additional problem caused by Arthur Chance being taken ill. Although minor health issues do arise in Underside, most elves maintain excellent health throughout their long lives. Arthur's illness was a very rare occurrence and, as it turned out, an ill-fated, unfortunately timed incident. Arthur worked as a supervisor on one of the production lines. The manager asked Cornflower to look after Brandy's machines as well as his own. This seemed to be an obvious, sensible decision. Sadly, this decision gave rise to an unlucky series of unforeseen consequences.

His manager recognised that he risked overloading Cornflower by asking him to oversee an additional three machines. The absence of Arthur Chance, a trained supervisor, was a further concern. The manager decided to request a volunteer, from the elvish community, to provide additional assistance by operating one of the conveyor belt machines.

Henny Minnit, Arthur Chance's nephew, was the first to arrive. For the safe running of a conveyor belt, Henny was not an ideal choice. He had not worked at the factory previously, knew absolutely nothing about the safety rules and would have taken scant notice of them anyway.

Henny's appearance gave little indication of his true nature. Elves noting his pale skin, blue eyes, and blond hair, could be forgiven for imagining that here, in front of them, was a quiet, unassuming individual. He did not have the obvious appearance of a risk taker. In truth, Henny was a relaxed, carefree elf who enjoyed life, taking it as he found it. To put it another way, he gave no thought whatsoever to risks, danger or safety for himself or others.

On this particular day, Henny was wearing a jolly Christmas tie, which suited his humorous but flippant nature. Cornflower knew this was a hazard. He instructed Henny, that to be safe, he should remove the tie or tuck it into his shirt. Henny smiled and nodded as if agreeing but, as he wanted to show off his new tie, he did not remove it or tuck it into his shirt. Henny had many positive, admirable traits. Regrettably, complying with sensible safety suggestions was not among them.

When Cornflower was called away to fix a problem on Brandy's production line, Henny was left unsupervised temporarily. Cornflower's parting words to Henny were,

'I shan't be long. If anything happens, call me back over. I'm only a couple of yards away. Don't try to sort anything out yourself and don't touch anything. It's too dangerous!'

In the two to three minutes that Cornflower was absent, Henny noticed something on the conveyor. This was merely a piece of surplus stuffing fabric that would cause no problems. Henny did not appreciate its insignificance, but he was keen to help. Knowing that Cornflower was busy, Henny decided that he could just dust it off, without troubling Cornflower. Unfortunately, this was a poor decision and proved to be Henny's last. The floating end of his colourful tie became entangled in one of the conveyor belt rollers. Henny was unable to free the tie or himself. Lamentably, he was strangled by the machinery before the automatic safety cut in or Cornflower could rush back to free him.

It was a tragic accident but, as with most tragic accidents, investigations have to be carried out. The review exonerated Cornflower absolutely, stating not only that he had acted correctly throughout, but that he was clearly not at fault for the accident.

Cornflower was distraught but his distress was minimal when compared to that of Henny's relatives and friends. They struggled to accept that sometimes an accident is just that. An accident. Inevitably, they felt they needed to determine who or what was to blame. Unluckily for Cornflower, he was the obvious scapegoat.

Mark Tyme, as leader of the council, could see that this blame was unfair, but he also understood that Cornflower's reputation was tarnished. No-one would trust him now. To protect him, he needed to "take Cornflower out of the firing line". He resolved to move him to a "safer job".

Cornflower had loved working at the Teddy Bear Stuffing factory. He was truly contented. He could not conceive of any better employment for an elf. The loss of both his occupation and career added further misery to the anguish he already felt at Henny's death. His life was changed forever.

Mark arranged for Cornflower to be employed in Cole Black's Alternative Christmas Gift factory. This factory catered for those humans that most elves thought "strange". Humans who did not enjoy Christmas. The factory produced "non-Christmassy" cards, ties, and jumpers. They also produced some items that although originally targeted at non-celebrants were adopted by humans that did celebrate Christmas. Notably, these included black and white Santa hats, which were immensely popular with fans of football teams that played in those colours. Another of Cole's popular ranges was the black artificial Christmas trees, which were considered by some as "more stylish" than traditional green trees.

Cornflower found the factory's output depressing. It was vastly removed from the cheerful, seasonal happiness of the output from the Teddy Bear Stuffing factory. Initially, Cornflower attempted to embrace the work at Black's. He even designed a range of crackers called Christmas Blackers, with black party hats, downbeat jokes and negative, discouraging mottos. They sold surprisingly well. Cole Black was thrilled with them, but Cornflower remained unhappy.

Cornflower grew increasingly discontent. Not only had he lost his responsible role, but he was no longer contributing positively to Christmas. Additionally, his skills, for which he had trained so diligently, were no longer being utilised. He grew to hate his new work.

Cornflower started to turn his now, black, hate-filled thoughts against all elves, particularly Mark Tyme and the council, who he felt had blamed him unfairly for Henny's terrible demise. He could not see Mark's decision as a protective one.

When he placed Cornflower in this "safer job", Mark could not know how disastrous his judgement was. He could not anticipate that this decision would lead to severe, mental health problems for Cornflower, or that it marked the beginning of Cornflower's split personality.

Mark would never know that this was the moment that marked the dawn of Cornflower's alter ego. This was the beginning. The birth of The Dark.

✵✵✵

After three years, Cornflower could not stand working at Cole Black's factory any longer. His frustration, anger, and sense of vexed irritation at how badly he felt he had been treated began to sour his personality. He began to fall into dark, irrational moods where he imagined wreaking revenge on all those he held to blame for his current misfortune.

Cornflower's abilities meant that obtaining employment elsewhere was not difficult for him. He applied for a position as an electrician with H.E.T.T. Their management were thrilled to have such a skilled engineer at their disposal. After six months they considered him so indispensable that they were content to assign tasks to Cornflower, leaving him completely unsupervised. They were unconcerned. They knew Cornflower always completed his work effectively and on time.

It was true that Cornflower completed his tasks to a high standard, usually finishing them very quickly, but working on his own created unanticipated complications. The extra time afforded him by his speedy completion of every assignment, additionally gave him too much time to brood. Gradually, without any forethought on his part, Cornflower's brooding began to alter his personality. At times, it was clear to him that he no longer desired happiness or contentment. He looked for ways to satisfy his forlorn despondency. Rather than his usual bright attire, he started buying black clothes. Soon he had accumulated an impressive collection of alternative clothing

He possessed multiple hats, shirts, jackets, trousers, socks, shoes, boots. All in imposing shades of black. Over time, he purchased numerous "jolly" masks from Bingo's shop, which he secretly painted black. His costume was now complete. His black double had arrived. He gave his alternate self a name, The Dark.

Cornflower explored the remote tunnels and passageways that were within walking distance of his house. Finally, he discovered a large, undetected cavern. This would become The Dark's lair. The Dark's hidden hideout soon felt more like home than Cornflower's cottage. As his alter ego became increasingly active, the split in Cornflower's personality was fully established, with The Dark as the dominant personality. As an electrician, Cornflower had access to TV screens and computers that were no longer working properly. To avoid suspicion, The Dark, working through Cornflower, renovated some of these but reported back to his managers that others were beyond repair. These, he stated, had been scrapped. Naturally, The Dark had, in fact, repaired them. They now resided in his lair.

CHAPTER THIRTY-NINE

Let's have a barbecue
and karaoke

P otter had decided that in addition to the Spring Dance, he would ask Ena and Arthur to organise a barbecue with a karaoke night, to occur the week before the Dance.

'A barbecue with karaoke, Potter! That sounds wonderful,' remarked Wendy when he told her what he had in mind.

'It will cheer everyone up. Ensure they're all in a good mood for the dance,' he clarified.

Unfortunately, some of this conversation was overheard by Flaky Pastry when he was delivering leaflets for the Spring Dance. As you might expect, Flaky misheard this conversation as well as misunderstanding what Potter and Wendy had discussed.

On his return to Little Merritiddle, Flaky sought out Onion Gravy. Onion was easy to locate. It was lunchtime, so as usual he was sitting in The Flooded Meadow with Helen and Ewan Earth. They had just finished their meals when Flaky rushed in to join them. Flaky made his customary noisy entrance. In his enthusiasm to impart his news, he tripped over a chair, stood up, tripped over a stool, stood up again and finally sat down abruptly. He was caught by Onion as he was about to fall off the chair that he had just sat on.

'How many carrots will we need, Onion?' he asked breathlessly.

The others stared at him. Flaky often spoke in riddles but even for Flaky this was an unusual conversation starter.

'I have no idea what you mean, Flaky,' said Onion. 'Do you want to order some lunch from the menu? Then you can take a deep breath and explain yourself calmly.'

'Yes, Onion,' agreed Flaky. Onion could guess what his friend would order but he also knew that as a notoriously slow reader, reading the menu would compel Flaky to refocus his mind.

Finally, Flaky looked up from the menu.

'I'll have a croc burger and chips with a pint of Hollow Earth IPA, please, Onion.'

'I'll get those for you,' said Pearly Wisdom, who was collecting glasses from an adjacent table.

'Right,' said Onion, 'now why do you think we need carrots, Flaky?'

'For the Carrot Cookie night next Saturday. I heard people talking about it, but I've never made those before, so I don't know how many carrots we need, how much flour, sugar, or butter.'

Onion sighed. 'Carrot cookies? Why would anyone wish to make cookies with carrots in?'

[I will hazard a guess what you might be thinking. Undoubtedly, there are some Chefs that consider carrots in cookies to be quite acceptable. The same chefs that might consider full English breakfast flavour ice cream to be quite normal. To them, carrots in cookies would be unusual perhaps but acceptable, nonetheless. Then again, none of these Chefs live in Underside!]

At this point Helen Earth joined in the discussion.

'I've heard that Mr Teasready has arranged some evening entertainment. It's karaoke, Flaky, not Carrot Cookie.'

'Yes, that's what I heard as well,' added Ewan.

Flaky was baffled. Whenever Flaky was confused, as he often was, he turned to his friend for enlightenment.

'What's that then, Onion?'

'Singing.'

'Not a cooking contest, then?'

'No, Flaky.'

'I won't need to bring the peeler then, Onion?'

'No, Flaky.'

'So, what is this thing that Carrie Hokey does then, Onion?'

Onion decided to forego correcting Flaky at this point.

'Well, as I said it's singing. It's one of those human events that Bingo showed us. It often follows a barbecue.'

'What, a queue for a dolly?' asked Flaky, with surprise.

[Sorry. Of course, other doll brands are available.]

'No, it's nothing to do with dolls. It's when humans sit outside in their garden, put food on a grill and set fire to it until it is burnt black. They seem to like their food like a cinder on the outside but uncooked in the middle,' explained Onion.

'For some reason,' he continued, 'the cook is nearly always a man wearing an apron with a rude picture or a terrible joke on it. He always gets smoke in his eyes, while his friends make jokes at his expense. Sometimes the cook will hit one of his friends with a cloth or try to stick him with a fork. I don't know why. They all drink a lot and talk very loudly.'

'So, is that the start of the Harry Cokey then?' said Flaky. 'I've seen that when I was taken Topside. It's where they all shake bits of themselves about and then run at each other, yelling.'

'No, that's the Hokey Cokey. The karaoke is a competition where they play a song everyone knows but without the words.'

'Without the words, Onion?'

'Yes, they show them on a screen and people have to sing along with that. The winner is the human that sings the most wrong notes, gets the words wrong or forgets the words completely.'

'How is it that they're the winner, Onion? When I joined in the sing song at The Meadow the other night and did all of that, I didn't win anything. You told me I was making a terrible racket and should stop singing.'

'Yes, because there wasn't a karaoke competition that night.'

'Oh, I see, so it doesn't count unless it is a proper Carrie Hokey competition then?'

'Yes, Flaky.'

'She must be very busy.'

'Who?'

'Carrie Hokey. Setting all those competitions.'

Onion thought about explaining but decided it was too much effort.

'Yes, Flaky, she must be.'

CHAPTER FORTY
Incident at the barbecue

E na and Arthur had decided to hold the barbecue outside the council building. There was a large area of green, with plenty of room for tables and chairs.

Once again Flaky delivered the leaflets advertising the event. His recent experience distributing the Spring Dance leaflets meant he did not repeat his previous mistakes. Flaky made all new ones.

Flaky's new mistakes did not impact his own village of Little Merritiddle. Onion, in anticipation of Flaky-related problems or confusion, decided to retain the leaflets for their village and distribute them himself.

Flaky was still struggling to understand why there was a barbers' queue or in what way Carrie Hokey was involved. Shortly after departing his village, he stopped to read one of the leaflets. This did not help. Flaky's reading skills were limited, at best. As a result, he regularly misunderstood anything he read, muddling the meaning.

As he cycled to the first place on his delivery list, Flaky puzzled over the sentence "barbecue on the green". He was baffled. "The green what?", he wondered.

The first destination on Flaky's list was the Elite headquarters He was stopped at the entrance by Private Tommie Gunne.

'Who goes there?' demanded Tommie.

'It's me, Flaky Pastry. I goes there. Got these leaflets. Can you tell everyone there's a queue at the barbers?'

Tommie looked across to his colleague, Private Lodge Quarters. Both privates were mystified.

'A queue at the barbers?' asked Lodge.

'Yes, it's this Saturday,' Flaky confirmed. He sped off before the soldiers could ask him to clarify.

At Lower Tinkerton, Flaky passed the leaflets to Carr Pette.

'These are for Barbara Kew on Saturday,' he assured her confidently. Once again, Flaky dashed away leaving the recipient of his delivery in complete confusion.

Carr scratched her head in bewilderment. 'Barbara Kew? There's no-one in the village with that name.'

Minnie Peppers was the unlucky beneficiary of Flaky's next incomprehensible message at Babbsley Reach.

'Can you pass these to Cara?' he asked.

'Cara who?' queried Minnie, understandably.

'Oh, sorry. They're for Cara Hockey.'

"Who is Cara Hockey?" Minnie pondered, as Flaky left. "I don't know anyone of that name." She looked at the leaflet and laughed aloud. 'Ah, now I see.'

Flaky continued on his way, leaving a trail of baffled villagers in his wake.

✵✵✵

Elves were milling around the green, setting up tables and chairs when Onion arrived in his delivery van, together with Bingo.

'I've got four very large barbecue grills in the back of Onion's van,' Bingo called out as he climbed down from the cab. 'I need some volunteers with strong arms and backs to help unload them and put them in place.' Spotting her as he spoke, Bingo asked, 'Where do you want these, Ena?'

The mass of enthusiastically helpful Elves made short work of unloading and unpacking the grills. Bingo soon found additional employment for them.

'There are eight sacks of charcoal in the van. Can you place two sacks next to each barbecue grill? Please be careful they are very heavy. When you lift them, make sure there are two of you to each sack. I don't want anyone hurting their back,' Bingo instructed. Quietly he added, almost to himself, 'Or complaining about it to me, if you do.'

Arthur had been inside the Council Hall. Hearing the sound of busy elves, he sauntered over.

'This looks terrific, Bingo.'

'Thanks, Arthur. I'll bring the food along later. The karaoke equipment is still in the van. We need some trustworthy, careful elves to bring it into the hall. Have you set up some tables for it to go on?'

'Yes, all ready, waiting, and safe. You've probably noticed that Kuppa has sent some of her constables across for security. The Dark will receive a warm welcome if he decides to show himself at the barbecue.'

Despite the heightened police presence, nobody noticed the elf that casually dropped something into one of the barbecue grills, as he ambled past. The Dark's confederates were well practised in the art of subterfuge.

Ena had asked Potter to officially "open" the barbecue. Potter was not used to operating a microphone. As a result, his microphone technique was the typical, uncertain, hesitant approach of the amateur. He created a gloriously loud feedback as he picked it up.

'Is this on?' he bellowed inadvertently but predictably. 'Can you all hear me?' he yelled.

'Yes, loud and clear, Pottsie,' called Wendy.

'They probably heard you in Peak Rise, River End and Wind Stop,' added Bingo with a smile.

'Oh right, in that case, I declare this Spring Barbecue and Karaoke officially open.'

Just as the four self-appointed barbecue chefs were about to light the grills and commence cooking, there was a loud buzzing sound from the Tannoy system. The croaky, distorted voice of The Dark rang out.

'Greetings, everyone. Sorry to temporarily disturb your fun. In particular, hello to you, Kuppa. What a wonderful display of police officers here. Makes you feel proud, doesn't it? I hope I haven't kept you and your new police force too busy solving all those minor crimes I organised. I was delighted that you caught Mr Lubbe with a little prompting by some of my associates. Cannot have thugs like him around now, can we?

'I'm sure you'll be pleased to hear that I am not ignoring all your planned events this year. I have a delightful surprise for your barbecue, which I'm afraid your officers must have missed. I've prepared my own little recipe. Just remember that it's important that the barbecue chef cooks the sausages thoroughly, but you all need to beware the sizzling sausage that aims to cook the chef.'

Kuppa sprinted towards the barbecue grills. The last time Kuppa had moved this fast it was to prevent a possible explosion at the entrance to the Council Hall. That attempt had also been the handiwork of The Dark. As she ran, she yelled to the chefs.

'Don't light those fires! For your own sakes, whatever you do don't light them!'

Two of the chefs were poised over the grills with lighted tapers in their hands. One quickly doused his taper in a bucket of water, which he had with him in case he needed to control the fire on the grill. The other extinguished his flame between his fingers and thumb with a small yelp. *[Painful but effective.]*

Despite the fact that she had been the furthest away, Kuppa arrived at the grills seconds before Bingo. They quickly lifted the lids on the barbecue grills. In the third one they came to, they discovered something that most definitely did not belong – a stick of dynamite with a long fuse. Bingo cautiously lifted the stick, carefully removing the fuse.

'The fuse would have been unnecessary had the grill been lit. The flames would have ensured detonation anyway, but I expect The Dark knew that.'

'Adding the fuse was just another of his theatrical touches. He does like to be dramatic,' reflected Kuppa.

'I'll be right back,' said Bingo, as he left still holding the dynamite. When he returned a few minutes later, the dynamite was gone.

Pointing to the bucket by the grill, Bingo said, 'This elf gave me an idea. I've put that dynamite in a bucket of water for safety until I can dispose of it properly. The fuse I've put into my stores.'

The Dark had watched the proceedings with glee. The Tannoy crackled back into life with his less than dulcet tones.

'Bravo, both of you,' he rasped. 'Did you enjoy my little prank? I expect it added a spark to the proceedings,' he sniggered. 'I knew you would find my jolly little banger in time. I just wanted to be part of the fun. I can promise there will be no more shocks from me today. I shan't join you for all the merriment, but I will be watching. Naturally, I will also be listening to the expected caterwauling you will all make at the karaoke. Are you supplying ear plugs? I expect you could put some aside for me,' he chortled, 'but I may forget to collect them.'

There was a loud click as the Tannoy went silent.

There was an edgy wariness in the crowd for the following hour, but in the end, they decided that The Dark had not arranged any additional, unwanted diversions. The elves relaxed noticeably. They began to enjoy themselves.

Dusty Baker had provided a veritable feast of barbecue food. Inevitably, there were various crocodile products, pork, beef, fish and naturally two vegetarian options. Dusty was a butcher who prided himself on the variety of foodstuffs he produced. One of his most popular offerings was the pork with elfberry sausage. Of the two vegetarian dishes the most successful was the Dusty vegeburger. The ingredients were a Dusty trade secret, but the elves suspected that cheese, tomatoes, carrots, lentils, cauliflower, and broccoli were involved.

Most of the food had been consumed by the time Potter announced that the karaoke was due to start in the Great Hall of the Council chambers in one hour.

[It is worth noting that Flaky Pastry had eaten a significant proportion of the food. Some of the barbecued burgers, steaks, or sausages were left over. It was clear that Flaky thought it was his duty to rectify this by consuming any surplus fare. This was quite normal for Flaky. He had always been able to devour vast quantities of food while remaining as thin as a rake. The question "Where does he put it all?" was asked regularly.]

Kuppa felt duty bound to perform a thorough check of the building beforehand. It was also a chance for her to see how her new police dogs would perform. She was impressed with the efficiency and thoroughness of the dogs and their handlers, but immensely relieved that the dogs found nothing.

CHAPTER FORTY-ONE
The karaoke evening

K araoke was quite a recent form of entertainment for the elves. The elves listened intently while Potter explained how it operated.

'The music of a well-known song will be played. The words will be displayed on this screen here, so that you can sing along with the tune.'

As you might expect, the elves spotted a golden opportunity for a debate.

[No, not an argument. As we know, elves never argue. They may contend, dispute, disagree, squabble, maintain, claim, even quarrel or bicker, but they never ever argue. Or so they tell me!]

'Why not just listen to the song with the words?' asked Helen Earth.

'Yes, makes far more sense. If someone has gone to all that trouble to create a song with words, surely anything we do, won't be so good,' agreed Ewan Earth.

'Can't be. Couldn't possibly!' stated Minnie Peppers.

'That's just the point!' explained Potter, who had been involved in this kind of discussion before. He took a deep breath, then inserted a barley twist sweet in his mouth to calm himself. 'When you sing along, it's just for fun. You're not expected to be as good as the original. I went to a karaoke when I was Topside. The humans who attended had consumed vast quantities of alcohol. Very few of them sang anything like the original song. In fact, most of the singing was, at best, a bit strained.'

'Maybe we should just give it a try? See how we get on,' suggested Onion Gravy.

'Thank you, Onion. Excellent idea,' said Potter.

In fact, Onion was drafted into action for the first song. All the elves agreed that his rendition of "Twice around the elfberry tree" was really "quite good" and actually sounded practically the same as the original recording.

'Almost like hearing the real thing,' commented Bingo, albeit with just the hint of a sardonic smile.

After that, the elves were falling over each other to "have a go".

First to wrestle their way to the microphone were the Earths. The assembled elvish audience were impressed not only with their singing but also their well-staged harmonising during their rendition of "All along the bank". The few regulars from The Meadow in Little Merritiddle, who were present, had heard the Earths sing this previously. Most of this audience had not, so the Earths received resounding applause.

Next to the microphone was Doris Aupen who belted out the well-known drinking song "Fill your glass, drink it down, fill it again" with great vigour and gusto. This was a guaranteed crowd-pleaser. They clapped along or stamped their feet in time to the music.

Derrie Farmer accompanied by Frank Leigh changed the mood with a faithful but slushy rendering of "It's all in your smile". For the next song they were joined by Redd Shooz partnered by Kuppa Broth. The quartet performed a sentimental but not overly schmaltzy interpretation of "When we walk by the stream".

Flaky, due to the enormous volume of food he had munched his way through, had dozed throughout all the early singing acts. Onion gave him a friendly kick to wake him.

'Come on, Flaky, you're missing the fun. This can be your big chance to show everyone what you can do.'

'I'm not sure, Onion. I've only ever sung in The Meadow when I've had too much to drink. People will think I'm stupid and laugh at me.'

'What you need is a couple of pints to steady your nerves. Don't worry, I'm not drinking so I'll make sure you get home.'

Four hastily downed pints later, Flaky was ready.

What followed was a masterclass in the recent "tradition" of awful karaoke singing. Flaky staggered to his feet, commencing with his attempt at "The old haycart". Initially, he sang the wrong words to the right tune. Then he sang the right (well, almost right) words to the wrong tune. He even contrived finally to sing both the wrong words and the wrong tune.

Flaky accidentally changed the title of the next song. In Flaky's hands, the lovely old ballad "The Weaver and his rug" became "The Beaver and his jug".

Flaky's new friend Lemon Puff joined him for "Drown your sorrows", although most of the audience suspected Flaky sang "Drown your swallows". The duo further tackled the difficult "The Wizard and the Witch". Flaky seemed convinced that the words were "The Wizzie and the Whiff".

Lemon tried to save the day by persuading Flaky to sing another popular drinking song, "Ride your donkey home".

Flaky was particularly keen to sing this, as it was one of his favourite songs. Unfortunately, his alcoholic consumption affected his memory. Flaky happily sang ten verses of the song, roaring out the chorus each time as "Ride your monkey home".

Flaky tried another drinking song, "The old, dry tavern", which in Flaky's version became "The mouldy, sly salmon". Finally (and thankfully in the minds of some elves), Flaky's singing croaked to a halt. Lemon guided him to a seat, where he promptly fell asleep.

The karaoke concluded with a rousing singalong. Flaky stirred from his impromptu nap just in time to join in, happily disrupting the crowd's rendition of "The leaves are green, and the trees are brown" with his own unique interpretation. "My knees are green, and the trees fall down."

Potter announced that the karaoke evening had now ended but passed out forms to allow everyone to vote for their favourite singer.

It was universally agreed that Flaky was the unexpected "star" of the evening. Absolutely the worst karaoke singer anyone had ever heard but inexplicably so bad that he was genuinely good entertainment. It was no surprise that he won the vote easily.

Potter called Flaky over, announcing that he had been voted "The karaoke singer of the evening". He presented him with a small, meaningless trophy. This did not matter to Flaky. To him the trophy was every bit as exciting as his medal.

He showed off the trophy to anyone and everyone.

'Look, I got this trophy!' he declared.

Lemon was the only elf that seemed as overjoyed as Flaky. 'Flaky won a trophy,' she called out.

Onion was less than ecstatic as he drove them home, dropping Lemon off on the way.

"I expect I will never hear the end of this," he reflected.

CHAPTER FORTY-TWO
Police preparations for
the Spring Dance

For Chief of Police, Kuppa Broth, the following week's Spring Dance was not only an event to look forward to but also an important security exercise. No one had heard anything further from The Dark, which she found worrying as well as irksome. The Dark's silence was strange, but it meant that she could only surmise what his next activity might be or his likely target. Nothing was certain other than her expectation that he was not idle. She knew that somewhere he was busy, plotting his next criminal act. The Spring Dance suggested itself as an obvious target.

Kuppa decided that this provided her with a second opportunity to use her newly trained police dogs. On the day before the dance, she ordered the dog handlers to sweep the hall to ensure that there were no hidden devices. She was relieved when the dogs were unable to locate anything suspicious. Kuppa was determined that the Dance should not be interrupted by The Dark. She decided that the dogs would examine the building again, just before the guests arrived. She was unaware that The Dark had no intention of leaving any bombs at the Spring Dance, as he would be attending the Dance himself, in the person of

Cornflower Blue. The Dark was mentally unstable, but he was not so unbalanced that he would risk blowing himself up.

Kuppa had asked Chief Inspector March Doubletime to coordinate security for the Spring Dance between the police and the elite. Sergeant Cotten Shirt, who was still recovering from injuries in The Great Non-War, was on "light duties" and was organising the Elite's efforts. Kuppa was secretly delighted that her boyfriend, Private Redd Shooz, had been assigned to work with Sergeant Shirt.

Chief Inspector Doubletime had allocated Sally Forth to door security duties. Since her involvement in resolving the recent robbery and murder at Howte's, PC Forth had continued to perform her policing duties in an exemplary fashion. Kuppa had kept her promise to Sally. In recognition of Sally's efforts, PC Forth had been promoted to Sergeant Forth.

The downside of Sergeant Forth's successes was that she had proved to be the only officer with the patience and intelligence to achieve positive results working with the goblin constables. More accurately, she was the only officer who had been able to achieve positive results *despite* working with the goblin constables.

So it was that the Sergeant was currently "looking after the goblins" again, as no other police officers would work with them. Sally was not happy with this state of affairs, but Kuppa had succeeded in placating her. Kuppa assured Sally that the present situation was merely a short-term solution. Kuppa was determined to establish procedures that would be followed by all officers when dealing with the goblins, removing the need for a specialist goblin minder.

Sally looked forward expectantly to that future date. She did not appreciate the jokey references of her colleagues. "Watch out, here comes the goblin trainer", "here she is, the queen of the goblins" or "Sergeant Forth, mistress of the idiots".

As the goblin PCs were to be on door guarding duty, there was little for them to do apart from looking menacing, which was straightforward for any goblin, and checking the tickets of the guests as they arrived.

'All you have to do is stand there and check tickets,' explained Sally to PCs Mountain Boncebasher, Granite Rockearth and Cliff Wallbreaker.

'Let in anyone with tickets. If they do not have a ticket, direct them to the table over there so they can buy a ticket.'

'Di Reck? Who dat?' asked Granite.

'Just point at that table and say you can buy a ticket there.'

'Right. From Di Reck?' questioned Mountain.

'Forget Di Reck. Just point at the table,' said the Sergeant.

'OK, do dat den, Sarge,' agreed Granite.

'Now the tickets are in two parts. One blue part and one white. If they have a ticket, you take the blue part, put it in the red container there and let them keep the white part.'

'Why? Wot do wid white bit?' wondered Mountain.

'If they go outside for a breath of air, they can show you the white part and you let them back in. Understand?'

'Fink so,' said Boncebasher. Granite and Cliff nodded.

'Let's practise,' said Sally. She produced a spare ticket.

'Now what do you do when I walk up?'

The goblins looked at each other. 'Dunno,' said Granite.

'Ask to see my ticket.'

'Oh yeah, check der ticket,' said Mountain.

'So, what do you say?' queried Sally with quite admirable calm.

'Hands up?' offered Cliff.

'Yeah, dat good idea,' ventured Granite.

'No, Cliff. Dat wrong. Fink say got der tickets?' corrected Mountain.

'Good.' Sally handed the two-part ticket to Mountain.

'Yeah, dey tickets,' said Mountain. He put both the blue and white parts into the red container.

'No, Mountain,' said Sally, 'you only put the blue part in the container. Let's try again.'

Sally walked up again with tickets in her hand.

Granite checked the tickets. 'Yeah, dey der tickets.' He took the white part from Sally, put it into the container, returning the blue part to her.

Sally heaved a sigh. 'No, Granite, that's the wrong way round.'

After many, many, wearying attempts, each of the goblin PCs successfully took the blue ticket, placed it into the container and returned the white ticket to the Sergeant.

Having achieved this result, Sally attempted to enter once more, displaying her white ticket.

Mountain stopped her. 'Show both der tickets.'

Sally explained everything again until she was as blue in the face as the blue ticket she no longer possessed.

'OK, now let's pretend I don't have a ticket,' said Sally. She walked up.

'Show der tickets,' demanded Granite.

'I don't have a ticket.'

'No ticket, no get in,' stated Mountain.

Cliff attempted to arrest her. 'No ticket, go to der jail.'

'No, no, no! You don't arrest anyone!' declared the exasperated Sergeant.

'Remember? You point them to the table where they can buy a ticket.'

'Oh yeah. Got it!' said Granite.

'Again, I walk up with no ticket. What do you do?'

'No ticket, no get in. See der table? Buy der tickets dere,' pronounced Mountain triumphantly.

After fifty attempts, the goblins appeared to finally understand but Sally decided to stay to supervise, while the first few guests arrived.

CHAPTER FORTY-THREE
Cyan and Cornflower

Dustee Ashe, the Senior Crematorium Supervisor, was training up Cyan Hope, a new member of staff at the Hollow Earth Crematorium. With her serious nature, naturally ash grey hair, black eyes and "pebble beach" toned skin, Dustee suited both her name and her occupation. Dustee was finding this training both onerous and irksome, as Cyan was so easily distracted.

There was a reason for Cyan's lack of attention. Although this was her third work position, Cyan had yet to find employment which genuinely suited her aspirations or inspired her. Unlike Dustee, who had, very happily, worked her way up to her current position from the "bottom rung of the ladder", Cyan was not convinced that Junior Crematorium Administrator was that "one job" she was seeking.

Cyan had noted there was a vacancy for an experienced chef next door at The Charcoal Chimney. She was energetically discovering what was demanded of a top chef. This was a position for which she had no training, but she began to wonder if it was a profession she might enjoy. At two hundred and thirty-six years of age, she was still a young elf. She had plenty of time to retrain.

As Cyan was dreaming about her potential new career, she spotted a remarkably attractive blue elf walking into the Crematorium.

'Who's that handsome fellow?' asked Cyan. 'He looks very pleasant.'

'Oh, that's Mr Blue. Cornflower Blue,' replied Dustee. 'Lovely fellow. Calls in regularly to visit his parents' memorial.'

Dustee took a deep, calming breath. 'Now if you have finished checking vacancies or admiring our customers, can we get on, Mist Hope? We have an enormous amount of training to get through today.' Dustee did not mention her own interest in Cornflower, a client with whom she was more than a little smitten. She realised that even at four hundred and eighty-five years of age, she had a "girlish crush" on Cornflower and did not want to compete with a younger, slender, attractive elf, who might prove a tempting distraction to him.

'Is it just coincidence that he is called Mr Blue, and he is in fact a blue elf?' asked Cyan.

Dustee decided a detailed answer may satisfy Cyan. By providing the fairly uninteresting facts of his family, she hoped to deflect Cyan's interest away from Cornflower. She hoped to change the subject and refocus Cyan on the instructions she was attempting to impart. Aside from that, she did not want Cyan stealing Cornflower from her. "I saw him first," she thought to herself.

'Oh no,' Dustee responded to Cyan's query. 'As far as I am aware the whole family are various shades of blue. As a result, it seems to have become a tradition to name each child by their shade of blue. Mr Blue's parents were called Peacock and Ocean. Apparently, Peacock was first attracted to Ocean Waive by her unusual marine-blue tone. In turn, she was so besotted with him that, when they wed, she could hardly wait to alter her last name from Waive to Blue. I believe Mr Blue also has a cousin called Denim Blue with a daughter named Skye. I imagine they are both blue individuals.'

All this made perfect sense to Cyan. Her parents had named her Cyan because of her blue-green skin and pale blue hair.

"Perhaps my colour might appeal to Mr Blue," she wondered dreamily to herself, unconsciously flicking her hair back, as she pondered.

***

Cornflower was experiencing a perplexing afternoon. One of many he had suffered recently. As it was Saturday, Cornflower was only scheduled for work that morning. He remembered travelling to the new railway tunnels being constructed at Hollow Earth Central. He also recalled successfully completing all the wiring tasks, which he had allocated himself. He did not recollect how he had journeyed here. To the Crematorium.

What Cornflower did not know; indeed, could not know, was that The Dark had taken control of his actions. Cornflower was unaware that before departing Hollow Earth, he had completed some additional tasks in the tunnels on behalf of his alter ego. It was The Dark who caught the tram to the Crematorium, returning control to Cornflower when he arrived.

When Cornflower "woke up" he knew that he had intended to visit his parents' memorial even though he was unsure how he had travelled there. It was Cornflower's practice to purchase flowers to bring with him. He looked down. He had no flowers in his hands. It was most strange. Fortunately, he knew there were always flowers for sale at the reception desk.

Cornflower walked across to the desk but did not recognise the elf behind the counter. Dustee had left Cyan in charge while she assisted some elves who were seeking the final resting place of a relative they had not previously visited.

Cyan looked up as Cornflower approached. The two elves stared at each other for about fifteen seconds. Both were transfixed momentarily. Cyan was the first to break the stare. She blinked, shaking her head slightly and smiling up at the guest at her desk.

'I'm so sorry for staring but it's just your eyes are such a vivid shade of violet. Quite startling against the blue of your skin. For a moment, I was entirely distracted. Very rude and unprofessional of me. Please accept my apologies. Can I help you with something?'

'Yes, you can but I should also apologise for staring,' said Cornflower, returning Cyan's smile. 'I was equally mesmerised by the colour of your eyes. That combination of dark blue with green is astonishing. So, if you were rude, I was also rude to gaze at you as I did.' He paused. 'Perhaps we should start this conversation again?' He held out his hand. 'I'm Cornflower Blue. Pleased to meet you.'

'Cyan Hope. Pleased to meet you, Mr Blue. What can I do for you?'

'To begin with, please call me Cornflower. I'd like two bunches of flowers, please. Those two there look perfect, Cyan. Sorry, very presumptive of me. May I call you Cyan?'

'Oh, please do. Cornflower, I am on my lunch break in ten minutes. I don't suppose...'

'I would love to join you. I'll just visit my parents' memorial. I'll be right back. Don't go anywhere.'

Cyan felt that, at this juncture, she would avoid mentioning to Cornflower that she already knew who he was or how that came to be. "Plenty of time for that at a later date," she thought.

True to his word, Cornflower came back about ten minutes later just as Dustee Ashe returned.

'I'm off to lunch, Dustee,' Cyan announced. 'Back in an hour.'

Dustee stood gawping, with her mouth wide open, as her trainee departed towards The Charcoal Chimney.

'How did that happen?' she mumbled to herself. 'I was only away for twenty minutes and in that time, she managed to arrange a lunch date with Cornflower Blue. I've been trying to speak to him for weeks.'

Some relationships happen and outside observers will comment "it was meant to be". Between Cyan and Cornflower this was exactly what occurred. They felt relaxed and comfortable in each other's company. Their conversation flowed easily during lunch. By the end of the hour, they had agreed to attend the Spring Dance together.

The Dark rested behind Cornflower's eyes, watching quietly. He did not care about this budding relationship. For The Dark it was merely a convenience. Someone to accompany him to the Spring Dance other than Flaky Pastry. He had no regard for anything or anyone other than himself and, of course, his hatred of all elves. Especially, his hatred of Mark Tyme but now additionally, his newly acquired targets: Potter Teasready and Kuppa Broth. Nothing else mattered to him.

CHAPTER FORTY-FOUR
Onion prepares for
the Spring Dance

Onion Gravy had been working in Lower Tinkerton that morning, building an extension to the Village Hall. As the most senior member of the village, Carr Pette deemed it her duty to oversee the work, offering whatever help she could. Onion soon recognised that Carr possessed some unexpected skills. Her assistance went far beyond basic fetching and carrying. It was clear to him that she was an accomplished wood worker. When Carr fetched him a mid-morning drink, Onion felt compelled to ask her how this came to be.

'Mistress Pette, if you don't object to me asking, where did you learn your carpentry craft? It is rare for an untrained elf to show such mastery.'

'Onion, please call me Carr. We know each other well enough by now. As for my abilities in carpentry, I have my father to thank. He taught me everything I know.'

'What, Tapp? I thought he was an engineer. Machines and so on.'

'He is but Tapp is my stepfather not my actual father. My father was a master carpenter called Carver Ree. My mother and father separated after many happy years together. I was never sure why. My mother's second marriage was to Tapp Pette. When they married, I took his last name.'

Onion scratched his head, a habit of his when he was thinking.

'So, you are really Carr Ree?' he queried.

Carr smiled. 'Not exactly, Onion. I was named after my father. My original name was the same as his but spelt KARVA. So, I was called Karva Ree and really, I should be known as Karva Pette, but I allow everyone to call me Carr Pette. It's easier.'

'I think Karva is a lovely name. I prefer it to Carr. Might I call you that in future?'

Although Carr had always been taken with Cornflower Blue, she had long admired Onion Gravy. She respected anyone who worked with their hands. Moreover, she knew Onion was a kind, hard-working elf. She liked him greatly. Carr decided to take a chance.

'I am very happy for you to call me Karva. Now, changing the subject slightly – are you going to the Spring Dance tonight, Onion?'

'Yes, I'm taking Flaky.'

'Do you think you might be able to pick me up on your way? I would be delighted to have you as my dance partner if you agree.'

Onion was more experienced than Flaky, in matters of the heart, but despite this he was every bit as flustered as Flaky might have been. He took a couple of breaths to calm himself.

'I do not know what to say. This is really unexpected but … in a very pleasant way. I would be honoured to have you as my dance partner tonight, Karva. I will pick you up at six, if that's alright?'

'That's lovely. Thank you. See you later, Onion.'

***

When Onion arrived back at his yard, he was met by an extremely over-stimulated Flaky, who was dancing on the spot with excitement.

'It's the Spring Dance tonight, Onion. I can hardly wait! I'm going with Lemons!'

'You're going with lemons? Food and drinks are being provided, Flaky. You don't need to take anything.'

'No, sorry, Onion. I don't mean I want to take lemons. I mean I do want to take Lemon.'

'Flaky you're not making much sense. You don't want to take lemons, but you do want to take lemons. Which is it?'

'Sorry, Onion. I wish I wasn't so stupid. I mean I want to take Lemon Puff to the Dance.'

Onion scratched his head.

'So now, you don't want to take any fruit, but you do want to take biscuits?'

It was Flaky's turn to feel confused. He stared at Onion blankly.

'Let's start again,' suggested Onion. 'What do you want to take to the Dance?'

'It's not a what, Onion. It's a who.'

'I see,' said Onion, who didn't see at all. 'What do you mean?'

'I want to take Lemon Puff. You know that lovely elf from Babbsley Reach.'

'Ah!' said Onion, who finally did see.

Onion executed a speedy calculation in his head.

'One van, two seats, four elves. That won't work,' he whispered.

'Have I got it wrong again, Onion?' asked Flaky.

'No, not at all, Flaky. Everything will be fine. I just need to get on with something while you are out on your evening dog walk.'

As soon as Flaky departed, Onion moved into overdrive.

Onion had been keeping an old, dilapidated car, from which he was hoping to retrieve spare parts. To begin with, he removed three seats together with their seat belts. In a remarkably short time, he fitted two of the seats against one wall in the back of his van. He fitted the other seat into Flaky's cart. He salvaged a strip light from his stores which he installed in the inside roof of his van, wiring it to the van's battery. Finally, he constructed a ramp onto the rear of the van and two safety straps that ran along the length of the wall facing the new seats.

On his return, Flaky searched around the yard for several minutes. His tricycle and cart were nowhere to be seen.

'Onion, I've lost my trike and my cart. I thought I left them here in the yard, but I must have been silly again and left them somewhere. Can you help me find them?'

Onion laughed.

'Look inside the back of the van,' he stated, as he opened the door. 'Hold on, I'll start the engine so you can see.'

As the engine fired into life the overhead strip light shone down on the new seats with Flaky's tricycle and cart securely fastened on the other wall.

'My partner for the Dance is Carr Pette from Lower Tinkerton, although I have found out that her real name is Karva,' Onion declared. 'When we go to the Dance tonight, we will pick up Karva who can sit up front with me. You can travel in one of the seats in the back. When we reach Babbsley Reach, you can hop out and help Lemon Puff into the other seat. When the Dance finishes and we all leave, you can either come back with me in the van or if you prefer, we can unload your tricycle and cart so that you can take Lemon home on that. Might be a bit more … romantic.'

As was often the case, Onion was totally astounded by Flaky's reaction. Flaky ran up to Onion, giving him a huge hug.

'Thank you, Thank you, Onion.' He leapt into the van to try out one of the seats. Amazingly, Flaky did not trip over, bang his head, or miss the seat, though Onion had to spend five minutes disentangling Flaky from a seat belt. Not even the belt for the seat that he was seated in. Somehow, Flaky had contrived to place one of his feet through the seat belt as well as wrapping the belt around his neck. Onion could not imagine how he had accomplished this.

CHAPTER FORTY-FIVE
A caller for the Spring Dance

As Potter had requested, Ena had successfully booked the Little Merritiddle Square Dance Sextet to provide the music for the Dance. There was just one small problem. Every square or barn dance requires a caller to instruct the dancers on which dance moves to follow. The band's regular caller was Caulder Merrydance, who was also the regular caller for Greater Dingleberry Folk Music Troupe. Regrettably, Caulder was not available as he had promised to act as caller at a wedding reception in Greater Dingleberry.

[In case you're wondering, as I did, how it is that Caulder has a name so befitting his favourite pastime? Wonder no longer. This is no fortuitous coincidence. When Caulder Shotz served as a Sergeant in the Elvish Elite with his father Major Shotgunne Shotz and his mother Captain Annie Shotz, they dreamt of him having a long, illustrious military career. Caulder's only dream was to create a future for himself in music. He learnt to play piano and violin. Soon he was composing his own tunes, some of which sold well, as well as teaching younger elves to play piano. Before long, he was a part-time member of both the Little Merritiddle Square Dance Sextet and

Greater Dingleberry Folk Music Troupe. He taught
himself how to become a dance caller and left the Elite,
much to the disappointment of his parents. Before long,
he met Dainty Merrydance, the banjo player for Greater
Dingleberry. It was love at first sight (or first note). When
they married, it made perfect sense to Caulder to take
Dainty's surname.]

Faced with the dilemma of having to cancel the Spring
Dance (no caller, no Dance!) or revert to pre-recorded music,
Ena, Wendy, and Kuppa held an emergency meeting.

Luckily, Kuppa was confident that she had a solution. She
smiled broadly at her two colleagues.

'I know someone who not only has experience of calling at
a Dance but who will also be free to attend,' she announced.

'Who's that?' asked Wendy.

'My father.'

'What, Beef? How do you know he is available?'
queried Wendy.

'He's just recently joined our police force as a constable.
He insisted he wanted no special treatment, so this is the
perfect chance for me to show that I am taking him at his
word. He may be my dad but as his commanding officer, I'll
tell him he has to attend the Dance as our caller. Actually,
he'll be thrilled. He loves anything like this. He's an excellent
caller, but he will really enjoy having an audience for his
terrible jokes.'

'That's settled then. What a relief. I'll leave everything in
your capable hands, Kuppa,' said Ena.

***

267

There was little doubt that Beef Broth had all the attributes required to be a first-rate dance caller. At first glance, other elves could be forgiven for seeing this large figure with the booming voice as extremely discouraging. With his oatmeal face contrasted with a bushy chestnut beard and matching thick, tangled chestnut hair, Beef appeared intimidating. However, this impression was misleading. His twinkling, laughing, green eyes showed his true character. His actual cheerful, happy personality was displayed clearly on his face. From the outset, Beef put everyone at their ease.

'I know some of you will be unfamiliar with the dance moves in a barn or square dance but please don't worry,' he declared. 'I will go through the steps with you beforehand and it doesn't matter too much if you get the steps wrong. The main thing is to have fun. Enjoy yourselves. Let's practise the moves for the first dance while the band tries to remember how to play their instruments.'

There were a few muttered, light-hearted comments from behind Beef.

'My mistake, everyone. They do know how to play them. Apparently, they're just tuning up. That explains why I didn't recognise the song!'

Once the dancing commenced, it was clear that Beef knew all the moves and his friendly bellow was easily audible above the noise of the dancers.

Watching on were the three goblin constables, Mountain Boncebasher, Granite Rockearth and Cliff Wallbreaker.

Kuppa had asked Sergeant Sally Forth if the goblins might be left unattended.

'I think they finally understand the ticket process, but I can position myself nearby to keep an eye on them, Chief. Particularly,

PC Wallbreaker. He is probably the least intelligent of the three. Extremely enthusiastic but, well, how can I put this politely?'

'A bit dense?' ventured Kuppa, who worried rather less than Sally over the comments she made about her goblin PCs. Since she knew they did not understand much of what was said to them, or about them, she knew they were highly unlikely to be offended.

'Yes, definitely somewhat slow. He is very keen to arrest elves but the offences for which he arrests them often make little or no sense. So, I need to keep a wary eye on him.'

'I see. That doesn't sound like you will have much time available to enjoy yourself,' remarked Kuppa. 'Perhaps we can share the burden? We'll stand back a bit. See how they get on and I'll also watch out for any difficulties that arise.'

As it happened, the goblins caused remarkably few setbacks. At last, they seemed to have mastered the idea of the white ticket, although Kuppa needed to intervene when Cliff attempted to arrest two elves for "leaving too early" when all they needed was a "comfort break".

Goblins do not have a cultural history of music or dance, apart from the occasional war dance or battle chant taught to goblins when they are very young.

[These battle chants are regularly used by goblin parents as a substitute to lullabies for their infants. Consequently, these chants are ingrained from such an early age that they are known by all goblins – even the truly, stupendously, vacant ones.]

As a result, the goblins did not understand what they were listening to or watching.

'Wot all der noise?' asked Cliff.

'Dunno,' replied Mountain helpfully. 'Fink, it called der music.'

'Dey not hurt den?'

'No, fink dat der dancing,' added Granite.

'Wot all dat jumping and fings?' said Cliff.

'Fink it der war dance,' stated Granite, following a long, painful pause while he endeavoured to decide.

'Who dat big elf?' Cliff enquired.

'Wot big elf?' said Mountain.

'Der big, shouty elf,' stated Cliff, waving a finger in the general direction of Beef Broth.

Mountain looked across at Beef.

'Dunno,' he managed after a lengthy, agonising think.

'Me, neiver,' said Granite, after an equally long, excruciating ponder.

'Mountain,' wondered Cliff, 'why der big elf do der shouty fing at dat uvver elf?'

'Wot uvver elf?

'Der uvver elf. Der elf wot doing der war dance fing,' said Cliff, waving at the elves on the dance floor.

'Wot elf, Cliff? Lotta elves do der dance fing.'

'Dat elf. Dat Dozy Joe.'

The goblins listened carefully while Beef was calling out the next dance move.

'Take your partner. Do-Si-Do,' he called.

'Dunno wot elf is der Dozy Joe,' declared Mountain finally, after fully a minute of agonising consideration.

CHAPTER FORTY-SIX
The Spring Dance commences

Cornflower had arrived in time for the dance, but only just. The reason for his delay was confusing. He had found himself at home, standing in front of his cellar door, with no idea of how he had got there. A recurring incidence, which he did not enjoy. He had rushed to get himself ready for the Dance.

'Another blackout,' he murmured, while changing into his smart clothes. As on previous occasions, The Dark was fully aware of Cornflower's recent activities. The Dark had been actively composing his latest communication to Kuppa. One which, for reasons known only to himself, he did not intend to send. Yet.

The band were just preparing to start when Cornflower entered the dance hall.

Cyan had just deposited her coat in the cloakroom. She greeted Cornflower with a cheerful wave. Cornflower wandered over to join her. As he did, he found himself puzzling over these empty, blank periods in his memory. He knew, through his sessions with Annie Payne, that they were taking place whenever his alter ego took control, but he still did not understand why he could never recall anything. Surely, he thought, he ought to be able to remember something. Maybe even take back some degree of control of his mind and body. He decided he must address this at his next session with Annie.

When Cornflower reached Cyan, he was frowning, having completely forgotten to return her smile. Cyan took both his hands, presenting him with a further smile.

'What's the matter, Cornflower? I've never seen you look so sad.'

At that precise moment, Beef Broth began his introductory routine. When he asked dancers to take to the floor, Cornflower finally managed to grin.

'Shall we? I'll explain everything later but let's dance first. It will cheer me up.'

'Cornflower, I'm so pleased you're here,' said a quiet voice beside him.

'Flaky! How delightful. Flaky, this is my friend Cyan Hope. Cyan, this is my good friend Flaky Pastry that I have told you about and …'

Flaky stood staring at Cornflower for several seconds.

'… and Flaky, your friend is?' prompted Cornflower.

'Oh, sorry. Cornflower and Stan, this my dance partner, Lemon Puff.'

'Delighted to meet you, Lemon,' said Cornflower.

Cyan was giggling. 'Yes, it's very good to meet you both. Oh, and it's Cyan, Flaky. Not Stan.'

'Sorry, Cyan. I am silly. I'm not very good with names.'

"Or much else," thought Onion as he walked up to them, arm in arm with Karva.

Onion stepped forward. 'You must be Cornflower Blue. I'm Onion Gravy. Flaky has told me a great deal about you and your friendship. This is my friend who Flaky knows as Carr Pette, although I have recently discovered that her full name is Karva.'

The goblins overheard this exchange. Granite leant across to Mountain.

'Dat elf got der funny name,' observed Granite.

'Der funny name?'

'Yeah, car door.'

'Wot der car?' asked Cliff.

'Like cart but no horse,' stated Mountain with a short burst of unexpected intellectual clarity. 'Spec dey eat der horse,' he concluded.

'Delighted to finally meet you, Onion,' declared Cornflower. 'Flaky is always talking about his best friend, Onion Gravy… and Carr, I didn't know your real name was Karva. What a beautiful name. Everyone, this is my friend Cyan Hope who has agreed to be my dance partner.'

'Can you all form up into dance teams of eight?' called Beef. 'I'll run through the steps before the music starts. By the way, why did the chicken cross the road?'

'To get to the other side,' yelled all the elves.

'No, he's a chicken. It was just in-grained!' said Beef, laughing loudly.

There were smiles and groans all round.

'We have six already,' said Cyan. 'We just need two more.'

'I'm not much for dancing,' said Onion. 'I don't mind watching.'

'Don't be silly,' goaded Karva. 'You'll probably enjoy it.'

'Please, Onion!' insisted Flaky. 'You know you can dance. Remember how you jumped up and down yesterday when I dropped that bag of nails on your foot?'

'Oh, I *do* remember, Flaky. So does my big toe! Well, I suppose I could attempt a dance or two. If I must. If it keeps everyone happy but we need two more.'

He spotted Candy Panboil and Baton Burg standing to one side. Onion knew them well from when he had carried out work at the school and the barracks. He waved at them.

'Do you want to come and join us? Make up our eight?' he queried.

'Yes, please. Should be fun!' exclaimed Candy.

'Perhaps we can make the remaining introductions after this first dance,' Onion suggested.

CHAPTER FORTY-SEVEN
The dancers prepare

T he dancers waited patiently as Beef Broth explained the three moves involved in the first dance of the evening. There was little doubt that Beef commanded attention when he spoke. All the elves listened without querying anything or bickering amongst themselves.

[A singularly exceptional occurrence amongst any collection of elves!]

Beef had already told the dancers to form groups of eight. Now he advised them, that if they wished, they could stick to these teams for any future such dance.

'I'll call you set one,' he informed the team consisting of Cotten Shirt, Hazel Nutt, Potter Teasready, Wendy Panboil, Ena Minnit, Arthur Moe, Kuppa Broth and Redd Shooz. Beef sized up each set in turn. He expected no problems with set one, a group of intelligent, sensible elves.

Beef was totally content with the dancers in set two. This set consisted of eight dworfs on a "wind down" evening out. Currently, they were assisting the elves in the new railway tunnels, adding their considerable knowledge as master craft workers. Dworfs are a logical, meticulous, organised race. Beef knew they would take the evening's dance routines seriously. Very seriously!

There were two married couples in this set. Circe Wainwright who had persuaded her husband Horatio to take part together with the Carpenters, Heracles and Diana, who were eager to "give this dancing a try". Additionally, Aphrodite Blacksmith was accompanied (reluctantly) by her brother Goliath while Venus Woodman was escorted for the evening by Achilles Weaver.

Set three was a disparate group of workers from businesses based in the Galaxy Mall. It appeared that they all knew each other and were determined to enjoy the night's entertainment. They were the last of the sets to assemble, giving Beef no time to find out anything about them but he was not concerned. It was clear that they were very happy with each other's company. No doubt they would make some mistakes, but unquestionably they would correct these as the dance progressed, with a significant deal of laughter.

Set four was a different proposition altogether.

It was an exceedingly mixed group. Quite difficult to predict. Beef was relaxed regarding the pairing of Candy Panboil with Baton Burg. He expected them to attempt to carry out the correct dance moves but to have fun if something went wrong.

Karva Pette who was paired with Onion Gravy seemed a sensible elf, but Onion Gravy did not strike him as a "joiner-in". Karva's encouragement might be required. As if to confirm Beef's assessment, he heard Karva whisper to Onion, as she took his hand.

'It's alright. Just relax, it'll be a bit of fun.'

"Fun? With Flaky taking part?" Onion thought to himself but, despite his reservations he offered Karva a small nod of agreement combined with an equally small and rather weak smile.

'I'll give it a go,' he said.

Beef Broth guessed that love had just arrived for the Cornflower Blue, Cyan Hope twosome, so he expected they might be somewhat distracted, drifting rather than dancing through the evening.

Most disturbing was the final duo in this set, Flaky Pastry with Lemon Puff.

If pressed for an opinion, Beef would have judged that the couple possessed marginally less than a single elf's intelligence between them. Undoubtedly, Lemon was the "smarter" of the two, embracing almost two-thirds of this limited, shared intellect, with Flaky owning about one-third.

First impressions can be misleading. Flaky might not be as stupid as he appeared. If he was, Beef could only cross his fingers and hope for an unexpected, positive outcome.

Similarly, Onion was concerned about Flaky's chances of mastering such complicated dance moves. Further, he was aware that, although Flaky had seemed to listen intently to Beef's instructions, it was unlikely that he had retained much. Experience told Onion that asking Flaky to remember three dance moves was more than a little ambitious. After all, he struggled with understanding just one simple instruction, but *three*?

Onion wondered how many minutes would pass before Flaky-induced chaos ensued.

The answer was approximately ten minutes.

At first, every set, bar one, went awry, muddling at least one of the moves or the order that they followed each other.

Beef stepped in, laughing loudly. 'Don't worry, anyone. This always happens at first. Let's try again.'

The solitary exception to this muddle were the dworfs, who had not only listened extremely carefully, but had even taken precise, detailed notes. From the outset, they were step perfect.

[I believe the dworfs would have been disappointed in themselves, had their dancing been anything other than flawless. It does not matter to dworfs if they are presented with something they have not encountered before. By nature, dworfs are fastidious. Whatever the task, a dworf will tackle it with great care. They are a proud race who take equal pride in the work they carry out. As any dworf will be only too pleased to tell you!]

After ten minutes, with some additional coaching by Beef, all the dancers settled into the routine with every set completing each dance step correctly (more or less). With the exclusion of one set. Set four.

Set four's only star pupils were Candy and Baton. Their dancing was almost as immaculate as the dworfs, but this was not the case with the other dancers in the set.

Cornflower danced wonderfully with Cyan. Cyan danced wonderfully with Cornflower. They had eyes for no-one else. They whispered loving "sweet nothings" to one another. They were oblivious to the rest of the set or Beef's instruction. They floated around to the music, casually inventing their own dance steps. The other elves in the set had seen this kind of "new love" before. They accepted the pair as merely another obstacle to avoid. When the music stopped, Cyan was locked together in a passionate kiss with Cornflower.

As Beef had anticipated, Onion needed more than a little prompting from Karva to take part. Once he did, his awkwardness and inabilities in the dance arena began to show. Onion was remarkably talented when working with his hands. Sadly, this talent had steadfastly refused to transfer itself to the rest of his body.

Some individuals are described as having "two left feet". Onion gave the impression of having three or four. Karva spent as much time grabbing Onion's arm to steady him as she did carrying out the dance steps. Despite this, they managed to complete all the dance moves somehow, with Karva's grace (and sense of humour) covering for most of Onion's clumsiness.

CHAPTER FORTY-EIGHT
Flaky disrupts the dancing

A ny problems the dancers in set four had experienced, were as nothing compared to the disarray or disorder introduced to the group, or indeed the dancefloor as a whole, by the dancing of Flaky with Lemon.

The problems began immediately Beef completed his ten-minute introduction.

'Take two steps away from your partners,' Beef instructed.

Had Beef known Flaky better, he might have been more specific with his instructions. While all the dancers, other than Flaky, took two small steps away from their partners, Flaky took two giant steps. Suddenly, he realised that he was stranded away from everyone else in the middle of the dancefloor. Panicking, as he realised now where he ought to be standing, Flaky attempted to dash forward. He succeeded only in tangling his legs together, falling on his face but rolling instantly upright.

'I'm fine!' he declared. Flaky was master of very few activities, but as he fell over so often, he was certainly a master of the speedy recovery. Lemon giggled, taking Flaky by the hands. Gently she led him back to the correct position.

Beef raised an eyebrow before continuing.

'Right. Everyone turn to face your partner and take a *small* step forward.'

(Beef Broth was a quick learner. He knew about Flaky Pastry. All of Underside was aware of Flaky's antics. Beef had listened but had not been completely convinced. "Surely, he cannot be so bad," he had thought, but his first impressions together with his first real encounter with Flaky had changed his view.)

Before Beef could say anything further, both Lemon and Flaky decided to bow to each other. They banged heads together, falling to the floor. Flaky leapt to his feet, as if nothing untoward had occurred. Lemon recommenced giggling.

'Can you help me up, Flaky?' she asked.

Flaky was unpractised in helping others. Turning an interesting shade of red, he bent down and helped Lemon to her feet.

'We are a couple of sillies,' she said, beaming at Flaky. Flaky's face changed into an even darker shade of red. Lemon smiled, kissing him on the cheek. This was unfamiliar territory for Flaky. He had no idea what to do or say next. The couple were rescued from any decision making by Beef calling out the next dance step.

Flaky heard, 'Right, swing your partner round.' As he had been recovering from his fall, he did not hear the preceding instruction to "cross your hands over and take your partner once round when I say swing your partner".

The result was Flaky swinging Lemon completely off her feet, nearly decapitating Onion and Karva.

"I knew this was a bad idea," Onion thought.

Lemon squealed with delight as she was swung around. She was deposited on the floor with Flaky tumbling beside her.

Once more, Lemon was giggling.

'You are such a silly, Flaky, but such fun!' she declared, hugging him tightly.

Flaky's face achieved an almost purple flush.

Beef waited while set four re-established itself.

Beef had shown the groups the Do-Si-Do move which involves dancers advancing towards one another, passing each other back-to-back; then returning to their start point while still back-to-back. It was a slightly tricky move but one that should be easy for all the elves. Onion had his doubts. How would Flaky manage that?

When Beef announced 'Do-Si-Do with your partner,' Onion expected the worst.

Flaky started well, advancing towards Lemon with ill-placed confidence. However, it was soon clear that Flaky had forgotten what to do next. He stood watching the other dancers to see what they were doing. Lemon was also unsure so while Flaky stood uncertainly, she copied the other elves, performing the first part of the Do-Si-Do without Flaky. Having observed the other dancers, Flaky attempted hastily to dance around Lemon, while she was endeavouring to complete the remainder of the Do-Si-Do. As she returned to her start place back-to-back with her invisible partner, Flaky joined in but dancing in front of Lemon, looking her straight in the face. She laughed, spinning him round into the correct position at precisely the moment Beef called the next instruction.

'Turn and face your partners once more.'

Obviously, Flaky turned the wrong way. When Lemon turned, she found herself looking at the back of Flaky's head. For a second, Flaky wondered where everyone had gone, before Lemon took hold of his shoulders, fondly rotating him round.

Flaky Pastry was very well known throughout Underside. Some elves found his clumsiness or stupidity irritating but most tolerated his accidental blunders. It was just how Flaky was –

inadvertently entertaining and amusing with his unplanned antics. He could not help himself. Most of the elves merely smiled while some politely hid their mirth behind their hands.

Beef was struggling not to burst out laughing, while thinking that he now understood the comments he had heard regarding Flaky. He decided that as everyone was so happy, it would be a good opportunity for one of his jokes.

'Why did the cow cross the road?' he asked.

'Because it was the chicken's day off?' Bingo ventured.

'No, it was because she wanted to get to the udder side!'

Beef laughed heartily. The majority of the elves groaned.

As the evening progressed, so did the Flaky-centred disasters. Beef cheerfully called out each new dance move. Flaky cheerfully succeeded in failing to complete any move correctly.

When instructed to dance down the middle and up the back, Flaky tried to dance up the back, then down the middle. As he battered his way through the other dancers, he could be heard loudly apologising: 'Sorry, sorry, my mistake. I've got it wrong again'.

In one of the dances, the couple at the top of the set created an arch with their arms for everyone to dance under. As Flaky took Lemon in the wrong direction, by the time he realised and turned round to head for the arch, the couple making the arch were about to move to the next steps. Flaky desperately rushed Lemon towards the top couple. He only achieved more confusion and disorder, as he crashed into the top couple, with Lemon in tow, just as they took their arms down. All four dancers fell to the floor. Candy and Baton, the unlucky recipients of Flaky's latest error, sat on the floor laughing almost as much as Lemon.

Beef took this opportunity to tell some more of his terrible jokes.

'How do you tell if a cow is in your fridge?' he asked.

'You can't shut the door,' answered most of the elves, in unison.

'OK, you know that one, but do you know the other way to tell?'

This time there was silence, except for a handful of elves who helpfully said 'No'.

'When you open the door, the mooing gets louder,' said Beef, laughing noisily.

There were groans all round once more.

The Flaky-generated disarray continued. Beef organised all the dancers into a large circle.

'Step to the right then step to the left,' he directed. Flaky stepped left then right. A confused Lemon endeavoured to follow Flaky's lead. Bumping into the other dancers, they caused a muddled ripple to pass round the circle.

'Your other left, Flaky and Lemon,' cried Beef.

Beef remained optimistic but realistic as he called the dance moves, declaring at one point to the gathered elves, 'I'm sure you'll find this easy. Well, most of you, anyway.' He smiled at Flaky and Lemon. Flaky turned red once more.

Eventually, Beef decided the dancers needed a break.

'I think it's time to get something to eat and drink, everyone. By the way, how do you know if a cow has been in your fridge? …Don't know? Hoofprints in the butter!'

Yet again, Beef burst out laughing. The elves groaned but they grinned as well. Beef was a popular elf. No-one minded his dreadful jokes or the fact that he liked them more than anyone else.

[You might feel you have heard dreadful jokes like these before, only involving elephants not cows. You would be

right. On a visit to Topside in the past, Beef had bought a joke book. This contained a multitude of elephant jokes which Beef felt he could use. Since there were no elephants in Underside, he adapted the awful elephant jokes into awful cow jokes. I'll let you judge whether it was worth the effort!]

As the dancing renewed, Flaky renewed his efforts to join in successfully. Regrettably, the dance moves changed too quickly for him to keep up. No matter how hard he tried he only succeeded in inventing more means of creating turmoil.

In a dance where everyone progressed round to a new partner, Flaky repeatedly finished at another male elf, while the female elf he should have reached stood to one side in bewilderment. In dances where he should step forward, he inevitably stepped backward. Right and left remained a consistent mystery for Flaky. Lemon followed Flaky's lead as he unvaryingly took her on yet another mystery tour around the floor. Lemon did not mind. Flaky's guidance might be overly confident and misjudged but it added to Lemon's fun.

CHAPTER FORTY-NINE
The Spring Dance concludes

Despite Flaky's vast collection of mistakes, everyone enjoyed themselves tremendously. There were regular outbreaks of barely contained merriment. Invariably the laughter centred around Flaky's (and to a lesser extent, Lemon's) accidentally entertaining antics. Virtually all of the other elves, even those that found Flaky irritating at times, were fond of him so there was no malice in their amusement.

As the evening drew to a close, Ena passed round forms for everyone to complete to nominate "The best dancers of the evening". The form also had a section to vote for "The most spirited dancers of the evening".

It came as no surprise to anyone when Ena announced that the dworf couple Venus Woodman and Achilles Weaver were voted the best dancers. It was agreed that the dworfs had been faultless, never getting a single step wrong and fully deserved the trophies they were presented. It was an equally unsurprising verdict when Ena declared Flaky and Lemon to be the most spirited dancers. As they received their medals, Flaky turned beaming to Onion, mouthing, 'I got a medal, Onion!'

Onion sighed. 'Another medal,' he murmured. "There will be no way to keep him quiet," he thought.

As everyone was preparing to leave, Candy encountered Lemon in the Ladies' cloakroom.

'Have you enjoyed yourself?' she asked.

'Oh yes. I had a lovely time with Flaky. He's a bit silly but that's why I like him. He's not clever but nor am I. I'm hoping he will ask me out again on a proper date.'

'I shouldn't wait too long for Flaky to make a move,' suggested Candy. 'I can see he really likes you as well, but he won't ever do anything. I don't think he knows how. He has never had a girlfriend before.'

'Never! I'm his first? How lovely.'

'Yes. If you want to see him again, you will have to ask him. I'm sure he won't say no.'

'Thanks for telling me, Candy. You are a real friend. I will ask him. Definitely!'

True to his word, Onion helped Flaky unload his tricycle from Onion's van so that Flaky could take Lemon home to Babbsley Reach. Conversation was slightly stilted and awkward with Lemon sitting behind Flaky, so he had to look over his shoulder to talk. When they arrived at her cottage, Lemon took Flaky's hand.

'I have really enjoyed myself tonight. I was wondering if I might see you again. If you would like to.'

Flaky flushed pink. An act he was becoming quite practised at. He rubbed one foot over the other in an embarrassed manner.

'I…I… I'd love to.' He stammered.

'I have every Wednesday off. Would you be able to join me? Perhaps we can have a picnic somewhere?'

'Oh yes. I'll speak to Onion. I am sure he won't mind. I often visit the station where they're building the new tunnels to watch the work.'

'Yes, there is a lovely park near the station. It takes no time at all to drive there.'

'Drive?' said a puzzled Flaky.

'Oh yes. I have a car. I didn't want to say anything to you or Onion. It was so nice of you to take me to the dance. I didn't want to spoil things.'

Lemon kissed Flaky on the cheek. Then, thinking again, she gently took him by the shoulders, kissing him firmly on the lips.

'Goodnight, Flaky. I'll come and collect you at 11:00 on Wednesday, if that's OK?'

'Oh yes, please. See you on Wednesday.'

Lemon waved to Flaky as he cycled away. Flaky waved back, narrowly avoiding falling off his trike.

As he cycled home, Flaky's mind was buzzing. He did not know what to think. He did not know what to do but, he was certain of one thing. He was very happy. Had Flaky been aware of the word "blissfully", he would have described himself as feeling blissfully happy. As blissfully was outside of Flaky's vocabulary, he settled on very happy.

When Flaky arrived home, he swiftly adopted his now familiar routine of walking up to Onion while holding his medal high under Onion's nose.

'I got a medal!' he stated cheerfully.

'Yes, I know. Do you want to put it on your special shelf?'

Recently, Onion had fixed a shelf on the wall to provide Flaky with a safe location for his medals. It had the added advantage that it stopped (or at least slowed) Flaky from greeting every new customer entering the workshop with the same 'I got a medal' routine.

Flaky proudly kept every certificate, badge, or medal he had ever received on his special shelf. These included his school attendance record ("acceptable but late on nine occasions, six of these when he became lost and was unable to locate the school"); his school reports (full of comments such as "not fully aware", "struggles to understand the subject", "lacks basic common sense and intelligence", or "tries but needs to try even harder"; his ten school "best behaved pupil" badges (given as an act of sympathy by certain teachers); his school graduation certificate (graduated on his fifth attempt); and his tricycle proficiency test certificate (passed on the eighth attempt).

In pride of place in the centre of the shelf, Flaky kept his recently awarded "Citizen of the Month" medal and his "Karaoke Singer of the Evening" trophy.

That night, Flaky was nervously excited. He had gained yet another medal but, more importantly, he had gained a girlfriend. As he had never had a girlfriend previously, he was not entirely sure what that meant. He knew boyfriends had girlfriends, but he had no idea what a boyfriend had to do. Onion was clever (compared to Flaky). He usually had answers for Flaky's questions. Even the difficult ones. Flaky hoped that Onion would explain to him what a boyfriend was supposed to do.

Flaky's brain seldom had room for worries. This occasion was an exception. It was an extremely long time before Flaky settled into sleep, but when he finally achieved slumber, he slept well with pink, fluffy dreams to keep him company.

CHAPTER FIFTY
The Dark emerges

F ollowing the dance, Cornflower escorted Cyan to her cottage, which was close to Hollow Earth Central station. Eventually, after an extended farewell to Cyan, he walked to the nearest tram stop.

[In truth, the farewell was a quite typical farewell by new lovers. You may have experience of such a farewell yourself, either as a participant or interested onlooker. When I say it was extended, I mean, of course, ridiculously, embarrassingly, lengthy. Two trains and four trams departed while they were embracing each other lovingly. Neither one of them noticed this fact.]

Eventually, Cornflower hopped onto the next tram to Lower Tinkerton. The journey afforded him essential thinking time. Having met Cyan, his future seemed clear. He could not imagine a life without her. Then again, if he were to have a sensible future with Cyan, he owed it to her to resolve his mental health issues. He determined to book another session with Dr Payne the next day.

Although she had no practical experience, Annie Payne had read widely on the subject of hypnosis. Annie had discovered that in order for someone to be hypnotised they needed to be relaxed using calming, peaceful images, or music. By repeating certain words or phrases a trance-like state could be induced that allowed the subject to better focus or concentrate. Annie was keen to see if hypnosis could assist Cornflower.

When he contacted her, Annie offered hypnotherapy to help investigate Cornflower's regular blackouts. She advised him that under hypnosis, she might help him to establish the cause of his memory blanks and time loss. She remained convinced that it was connected to his split personality.

Annie had decided that she would proceed slowly at their next session. She did not wish to hurry Cornflower into the hypnotherapy. She thought it was important to relax him naturally with a few straightforward questions. After a couple of minutes, she suggested that they might listen to music. Cornflower reacted immediately she turned the music on.

'Oh, I know this. One of my favourites. Very pleasant.'

As he began to relax noticeably, Annie started talking to him very gently, subtly repeating certain words. Before long, she noted that his head was dropping; his eyelids slowly closing.

'You now feel vey relaxed. If it is more comfortable, close your eyes. Just listen to the music and my voice. I want you to think back to the last occasion that you had a blackout. Can you recall where you were?'

'Yes, I was…I was…'

Annie was worried. Had she made a mistake in her approach? Had she pushed Cornflower too far, too fast?

'Just relax. Let the memory come,' she said reassuringly.

What Annie could not know was that The Dark was also attending her session. Sitting at the back of Cornflower's consciousness, he was watching carefully. Listening to her every word.

'I will try but it is hard. Something is blocking me. Stopping me from remembering,' whispered Cornflower.

Annie realised this was too traumatic for him.

'Alright, Cornflower. Count slowly back from five. When you reach one you will be fully awake.'

Cornflower started counting.

'Five, four, three, two, one.'

As he reached one, he was suddenly alert and conscious. There was a sudden change in the Cornflower that Dr Payne was accustomed to treating. His face altered, as the other half of his split personality stepped to the fore. It was as though Cornflower had abruptly donned the mask of an entirely separate individual. His customary pleasant demeanour had disappeared to be replaced with that of an aggressively angry, scowling face. The new face attempted an unconvincing smile. There was no genuine friendliness present in his unpleasant sneer.

'Who do you think you are, mistress, to summon me at your merest whim?' asked the face, with a hostile whisper.

Annie was taken aback. She was not sure how to manage this unexpected development.

'Dr Annie Payne but you know this, Cornflower.'

'No, No. I am not that pathetic drip, Cornflower,' said the face with a look of derisive scorn.

Initially, Annie was dumbfounded but she soon regained her control. It was obvious to her that placing Cornflower under hypnosis had resulted in an unforeseen outcome. Cornflower's other personality was now present.

Comprehending the situation she found herself in, Annie decided to continue, hoping to manage the remainder of the session.

'Please accept my apologies, sir, but if you are not Cornflower, who am I addressing?'

'I'm sure you know, if you only allow yourself to believe it,' stated the face, with a belligerent snarl.

His voice was a disagreeable, spiteful croak. 'I am The Dark,' he announced proudly. 'The Dark knows you, Doctor. The Dark watches you. The Dark watches everyone. The Dark is always watching you all.'

The Dark started to laugh. A guttural, nasty screech like the rasping caw of an unfriendly crow. But as quickly as The Dark had appeared, his guffawing cackle was cut short. The tenseness in his facial features diminished. His countenance softened, returning to Cornflower's normal, amiable, likeable appearance. Cornflower had woken fully from his hypnotic state.

He looked around the room, avoiding the stock predictable question of 'Where am I?'.

Instead, glancing across at his therapist, he asked, 'Dr Payne, what just happened?'

'That, Cornflower, is a particularly good question. I am afraid I am not too sure what happened. I need to review the recording of our session; consider what we do next to move forward. As I am stopping this session early, your next session will be free. I suggest you book with Mist Turner for about two weeks from now.'

Annie was unsure what her next course of action should be. She was aware her role as a psychologist had similar responsibilities to that of a medical doctor. Her patients, or clients as she liked to call them, expected her to respect their privacy. She promised all her clients full patient confidentiality. Annie felt obliged to abide by this promise. On the other hand, none of her other clients had ever confessed to being a wanted terrorist.

Annie was in a quandary. Should she break patient confidentiality by reporting Cornflower to the police? Legally, she knew that was the correct course of action. On the other hand, she felt that to inform them was morally incorrect. Moreover, Cornflower had been under hypnosis when he claimed to be The Dark. Annie knew from her detailed research into the subject that a hypnotised individual might indulge their personal fantasies by confessing to something that they desired to be real but which, actually, was not true. Was that all this was? Cornflower led an ordinary life. Did part of him seek infamy and notoriety?

Conversely, if Cornflower was secretly The Dark, was it not her duty to pass this information to the police? If he really was The Dark surely, she must tell them? If she did not, then she might be withholding vital evidence from them or even aiding a known criminal. Annie truly did not know what to do. Maybe she should make an appointment to see Cornflower more urgently. Seeing him again might allow her to decide.

Annie asked Paige to check her diary. She was delighted. She had one space available the following afternoon. She contacted Cornflower immediately.

'Cornflower? It's Dr Payne. An issue has arisen related to your hypnosis session.'

'Oh, is there a problem, Doctor?'

'No, nothing to worry about, but I wonder if you would be free to attend another session at three tomorrow so that we could carry out a follow-up hypnosis?'

'Yes, I'm free. Happy to oblige if you feel a further session is necessary.'

'Thank you, Cornflower. I will see you tomorrow.'

A wicked smile spread across Cornflower's face. The wicked smile of The Dark, who was no longer merely residing in the back of Cornflower's mind. Currently, he needed full control of his other self.

Cornflower was a trusted employee of H.E.T.T. Presently, he was working as a member of the team which was constructing the new rail tunnels. From the Dark's heinous perspective, this was an opportunity "too good to miss". To bring his plans to fruition, it was necessary for him to have unchallenged, unnoticed admittance to those tunnels. It was obvious, to his twisted mind, that Cornflower could afford him that access.

Nonetheless, his first priority was Annie Payne. The Dark had failed to anticipate anyone discovering his alternative identity. He was irritated at himself. Clearly, he should have allowed for such an eventuality. All the same, it was only a minor setback to his schedule.

As the Dark deliberated, a resolution presented itself. He had paid careful attention to the good doctor's hypnosis procedures. Surely, he could twist them to his own ends.

He had been wondering how he might inveigle himself into a further hypnosis session with Dr Payne. So he was overjoyed when she invited him, without any prompting. Annie Payne could not know that such an innocuous decision, on her part, would have such far-reaching, potentially fateful consequences.

✻✻✻

Annie had reviewed the troubling recording of her last session with Cornflower. Additionally, she had spent nearly three hours extensively reassessing both hypnosis and multiple personality syndrome. She felt fully prepared for any possible further encounter with The Dark.

Sadly, for Annie, The Dark had spent nearly four hours preparing for their next appointment. He had no intention of allowing the doctor to force his reappearance under hypnosis. She was unaware that he regularly spent time in the guise of Cornflower, controlling his other self's every thought or move. While the body of Cornflower would attend the next session, it would be The Dark's mind commanding that body.

At their next meeting, Annie was pleased to note that Cornflower had returned to his more usual, friendly self. During their introductory questions and answers, she could detect no sign of any residual malevolence. When she suggested they continue with the hypnotherapy that they had stopped last time so abruptly, Cornflower surprised her with a suggestion.

'Annie, might we use this recording during my hypnosis? It's something I purchased some months ago at Bingo's to help when I was having trouble sleeping. It combines soothing sounds such as birdsong, a breeze through the bushes or a gurgling stream with gentle music. I find it most relaxing.'

'Of course, Cornflower. It is always helpful to relax in hypnosis.'

When Annie bent to insert the recording, she did not notice the quick, furtive movement by Cornflower. As the music and sounds drifted across the room, Cornflower visibly relaxed.

'How are you feeling, Cornflower?'

'I'm fine, Annie. Very sleepy.'

'Just relax. Let the sleep wash over you.'

As she said this, she realised how tired *she* was feeling. She could barely keep awake. Within minutes, she slipped into a deep, peaceful, sleep.

The Dark removed his earplugs. He had still been able to hear the doctor and the recording, but the plugs had served one extremely useful purpose. He had not heard any of the subliminal messages he had recorded under the main soundtrack. The doctor had heard every subliminal message telling her how tired she was, how fatigued she felt, how much she needed to sleep.

Annie woke with a start. Had she dropped off while with a patient? How unprofessional! She deduced that it may have been just momentary. Cornflower showed every sign of remaining in his hypnotised state. She could recall no details of their encounter, but she was certain it had been productive. Gradually, she brought Cornflower back to consciousness. Immediately, he smiled at her.

'Thank you, Annie. That was very helpful. It has cleared up some worries for me.'

Annie was concerned that she could not recollect what had been discussed but most importantly her patient was happy. No doctor could hope for a better result.

Later, she discovered that not only had she forgotten to record this latest session but, additionally, she could not find any recording or notes of their previous meeting. It was as if they had been removed. Disturbingly, she had no memory of the topics they had examined.

For once, the statement made by The Dark was entirely truthful. By feigning his own hypnotic trance while placing Annie under hypnosis instead, he had ensured that all record or recollection of his accidental appearance was removed. Furthermore, he had added another valuable skill to his repertoire.

CHAPTER FIFTY-ONE
Defeated goblins

After their exceptionably unsuccessful campaign against the fairies, a completely embarrassed, dejected band of very depressed goblins stumbled into the goblin camp, where the two Queens greeted them.

'Better late than never,' observed Queen Avalanche with scarcely concealed condescension. 'If you two mighty kings have stopped your idiotic fighting now, you need to accept that the fairies beat you.'

'FAIRIES NOT BEAT US,' grumbled Hammer, almost to himself.

'NO, FAIRIES TRICK DER BRAVE GOBLINS,' said Mountain, under his breath.

'You lost,' growled Snowstorm.

'Yes, and they sent you a message,' Avalanche informed them. 'It arrived by arrow.'

'Nearly hit me,' added Snowstorm.

'We lost the battle. As losers, we need to meet the demands of the fairies,' said Avalanche.

'DEM ARMS?' whispered Hammer.

'No, demands.' Avalanche could see that Hammer remained baffled. 'Do what the fairies want,' she explained.

'WOT WANT?'

'An end to the fighting. They want us to be allies once more.'

'WHO DIS AL EYES?' murmured Mountain.

Snowstorm attempted clarification. 'It's not Al Eyes, it's allies in battle.'

Sensing continuing mystification, she continued, 'They want fairies and goblins to be friends once more.'

'FRIENDS?' questioned Hammer, quietly.

'Yes,' said Avalanche. 'If we stop fighting the fairies, they will be our friends again and they will give us back our prisoners.'

Hammer looked at Mountain. Mountain looked back at Hammer.

'S'POSE,' conceded Mountain softly.

'YEAH, DO DAT,' said Hammer unobtrusively.

Avalanche noted a remarkably pained expression on Hammer's face. She knew from experience that this meant she was observing the occurrence of an unusually rare phenomenon. Hammer was straining his brain as he attempted to think. Not merely to think but to think deeply. Finally, his expression changed as his overworked brain cells concluded their effort.

'WOT DO DEN IF NOT FIGHTING?' he asked gently.

Avalanche smiled and gave a small nod to Snowstorm. She pointed to an incredibly huge pile of dead goblins, with a cloud of surrounding insects.

'You need to bury these brave warriors killed when you two and your armies were fighting each other. They are becoming very smelly.'

Hammer nodded. 'YEAH, DER BIG STINKY,' he agreed mildly.

As he pointed at goblin bodies with brown or reddish skin, Hammer turned his gaze towards Mountain.

'DESE YOUR STINKERS,' he declared almost inaudibly.

'Yes, you are quite right, your Majesty,' said Queen Snowstorm. 'We will take our dead goblins away to bury them. Won't we, Mountain?' As she said this, she offered him a "don't you dare to argue" stare.

'WE TAKE DER NORTH GOBLIN STINKERS,' confirmed Mountain in a soft "not do der argue" voice.

After Mountain, Snowstorm and the other North goblins had departed, Hammer turned to Avalanche, looking at something she was holding.

'WOT DAT DERE?' he asked Avalanche unobtrusively.

'This is all the things you have to do, once you have buried those bodies,' she replied.

'FINGS?'

'Yes, lots of things.'

'AH, GOOD,' muttered Hammer, contriving to sound both unconvincing and unenthusiastic.

Standing nearby were four of Hammer's most trustworthy warriors, Gravel Blackhead, Earthquake Mallethand, Drumnail Rockfall and Axecutter Gravelface.

'GRAVEL, EARTHQUAKE, DRUMNAIL, AXECUTTER. QUEEN WANT DER STINKERS BURIED,' stated Hammer in his most agreeable voice. Seeing the look on Avalanche's face, he added, 'AND DER KING WANT DEM BURIED. GET LOTS WARRIORS. DIG DER BIG HOLE. BURY DER STINKERS NOW.'

Within an hour, the goblin warriors had excavated an enormous pit, into which only a few had accidentally fallen and had to be retrieved. Gravel and Earthquake reclaimed the weapons of their fallen comrades, before all the bodies were unceremoniously tipped into their final resting place. Goblins are not sentimental regarding death or burial. Consequently, no words were spoken as they filled in the hole. No monument was left on the impromptu grave. The gravediggers were unconcerned. If the goblins had given any thought to those goblins that had been killed, it might have been 'Dere fault dey got dead'.

'DEAD GOBLINS IN DER BIG HOLE, AVALANCHE,' stated Hammer softly but with quiet triumph. He started to pick up his battle sword. 'GO DO DER FIGHTING NOW?'

'No, as I have already said, there will be no more fighting, dearest. We need peace now,' said Avalanche, in a no-argument tone of voice.

Seeing that look, Hammer put the sword down.

'HAMMER NOT LIKE DER PEAS OR DER UDDER GREEN FINGS!' he muttered.

Queen Avalanche was a patient queen. She loved Hammer dearly but, at times, even she found it exasperating to deal with him.

'Not peas; peace,' she explained.

Noting that, clearly, Hammer was totally mystified, she tried again.

'When there is no war; no battles, we have peace.'

'DOAN LIKE DER PEAS,' groaned Hammer.

Seeing the persisting bewilderment in Hammer's face, Avalanche decided to attempt no further explanations.

'Never mind, darling, but please, no more fighting!'

'WOT DO DEN?' King Hammer asked, sighing gently when he spotted that, once more, Queen Avalanche was looking at *that* paper.

Avalanche bestowed Hammer with a generous smile. Hammer was rarely nervous, but he had seen this smile before. It said: "Doan do der fighting. Doan do der Hammer fings. Do der udder Avalanche fings."

301

Avalanche was determined to describe her next requirement as simply as possible. Every time Hammer looked puzzled, she reworded her explanation.

'Many buildings...Lots of buildings...Lots of houses were destroyed...Lots of houses were smashed in fighting. We need to rebuild.'

'DOAN NO REED BILL!' stated Hammer almost soundlessly.

Avalanche exhaled noisily.

'We need to *mend* the houses.'

'YEAH. DO DAT FING, AVALANCHE.'

Goblin warriors understand extraordinarily little, other than fighting. If the King does not order them to do something, they tend to slope off in a disinterested, uninvolved way. Unluckily, for him, Gravel Blackhead had been slow to slope off after the burial. He was sitting supported, albeit barely, by a small sapling which was bending, in a worrying manner, beneath his weight. When Hammer gestured for Gravel to join him, he sprang to his feet, reaching an upright position with impressive speed. The flattened sapling seemed beyond any hope of springing upright whatsoever.

'Majesty?'

'GRAVEL, GET LOTS GOBLINS. DO DER HOUSE MENDS FOR DER QUEEN...AND DER KING,' murmured Hammer.

'Yeah, do dat, Majesty,' said Gravel, disappearing speedily. Gravel was not the sharpest sword in the King's armoury, but he had learnt one or two goblin-saving tricks, such as "doan be dere if der Queen got der angries".

'Good,' declared Avalanche, 'now you need to hunt for food, dear.'

'GOT DER FOOD. FOOD IN DER STORE,' grumbled Hammer, as inaudibly as only a large goblin king could.

The Queen wondered, at times, if her beloved husband was truly as obtuse as he seemed.

'No, love of my life, there is hardly any food left in the store.'

Noting the look of abject bafflement on Hammer's face, she tried again.

'Store empty. Need to hunt for food.'

'WOT HUNT DEN?' moaned Hammer almost imperceptibly.

'Those!' replied Avalanche, pointing to the immense throngs of animals roaming amongst the rocks, shrubs, and trees near the goblin encampment.

'Can you see them? There must be thousands of them!' she continued.

'FOUL SANDS?'

'No, thousands…lots of them! Look, sheep, pigs, cows, goats, deer, chickens, ducks, and fish swimming in the river there!'

Hammer was looking puzzled again. Once more, a simpler approach was required.

'The things with the fluffy meat, the grunt meat, the horn meat, the flappy meat, and the splashy meat. Hunt them.'

'YEAH, HAMMER HUNT DEM,' he grudgingly whispered. He trudged off, returning with his four-foot sword, battle club and battle axe.

'No, Hammer, not those. They are for fighting in war. I want no more wars. Take your spear with your bow and arrows.'

'NO SHARPEN DER WEAPONS?'

'No! They can wait. Now, you need to go hunting.'

Reluctantly, the king gathered his hunting equipment.

'YEAH, DO DER HUNTING DEN,' he moaned faintly, as he marched away.

Aiming his large finger at all of the nearby goblin warriors, he announced so gently, that the ground shook, 'ALL GO DO DER HUNTING.'

CHAPTER FIFTY-TWO
Discussions at The Meadow

At The Flooded Meadow in Little Merritiddle, Helen and Ewan Earth were lunching at their usual table. As it was a quiet day, Frank and Pearly Wisdom had joined them.

The other table regulars, Onion and Flaky, were absent for different but connected reasons. Onion was not present as he was attending an urgent call at Great Merritiddle. The cottage wall, of an elf named Strawberry Sundae, had been partially demolished in a car accident. The perpetrator of the accident was Logan Berry, a young elf "joy riding" in a car owned by his parents, Holly and Rowan.

Flaky had many faults but a lack of generosity was not one of them. He walked Strawberry's dogs, Basil and Chocky, regularly. When she asked him to "mind" the dogs, while Onion worked on her cottage, he was pleased to help. Strawberry was so pleased with Onion's speedy response and Flaky's help that she cooked them lunch in the undamaged end of her kitchen.

'Flaky was in earlier,' remarked Frank. 'Shovelled his lunch down so quickly I barely saw the goings of it.'

'Yes, he was definitely in a hurry,' said Pearly. 'Mumbled something about an accident in Great Merritiddle and some dogs he has to look after.'

'Certainly, sounds like Flaky. Wherever there's a problem, stands to reason that he is involved somehow,' stated Ewan.

'Yes, couldn't agree more,' said Helen. 'He's like a magnet for trouble.'

'For once, he might not be to blame,' said Pearly. 'It was a car accident. An elf crashed his car into a wall. Obviously not Flaky. He cannot drive.'

'Just as well, really,' commented Helen, 'can you imagine the disasters if he ever learnt to drive? Flaky behind the wheel of a car does not bear thinking about!'

'Extremely worrying,' agreed Ewan. 'Although if you ask me, it would take Flaky about twenty years to learn.'

'Or more,' added Helen. 'Did you see him at the Spring Dance yesterday? Danced the wrong way, clumsily bumped into everyone. I don't believe he managed to get any of the dance steps right. How would he ever master car driving?'

'I, for one, hope he never does,' observed Frank. 'I still haven't forgiven him for making me shoot myself in the foot with a crossbow bolt.'

'Oh, come on!' laughed Pearly. 'That was your own fault for having a loaded crossbow in the bar. All Flaky did was walk in.'

'Trust you to take his side,' muttered Frank.

'You're too harsh on him. He can't help the fact that he's not too bright or the fact that he's a bit awkward and ungainly. He means well. He is big hearted. He is always willing to help.'

'I, for one, wouldn't want his help,' replied Frank. 'I have learnt from experience never to ask Flaky to help with anything. He is probably the stupidest elf in Underside. Certainly, the clumsiest. Every time he comes in here, he knocks something over or falls off his chair. No wonder he was rubbish at the dance!'

'That's enough, Frank! We know you don't like Flaky, but he is really not as bad as you make out.'

Unlike her husband, Pearly liked Flaky. She felt quite protective towards him. She believed that fate had dealt him a bad hand. She was convinced that Flaky just could not help how he was. Frank wilted under the fierceness of Pearly's angry, accusatory stare. Sensing it was a good time to change the subject, Helen interrupted.

'We were stocktaking yesterday, so we couldn't make it to the dance. What is this we hear about Flaky having a girlfriend?' she asked.

'Oh yes, she seems very nice,' stated Pearly. 'I believe she is called Lemon Puff. It was obvious to everyone that she really likes Flaky. She spent most of the evening laughing with him.'

'Laughing at him, more like!' mumbled Frank.

'Don't be nasty, Frank. Go and wash some glasses or wipe down the bar.'

'Humph' was Frank's solitary reply. 'I'll check the barrels in the cellar.'

'He can be such a miserable beggar when the mood takes him,' Pearly observed as Frank disappeared. 'Now, where was I? Oh yes, Lemon. A lovely elf. Not too clever herself but cheerful, easy going and considerate. She could be just the companion Flaky needs.'

'Well, that's an unexpected surprise,' noted Ewan.

'But a very pleasant one,' added Helen. 'Perhaps Flaky will bring her here one lunchtime.'

'Possibly not, she lives in Babbsley Reach,' Pearly revealed. 'They may decide to go to The Duck Inn instead.'

'The old Duckweed?' queried Ewan. The Duck Inn pub in Babbsley Reach did not have a good reputation. Ewan was not alone in considering it "a bit of a dump".

'The Duck Inn? Not the best place to take your girlfriend,' agreed Helen. 'Let's hope Flaky thinks better of it.'

'Let's hope he doesn't,' said a grumbling voice from below. 'Rather there than here.'

'Frank! I won't tell you again,' shouted Pearly, staring furiously down into the cellar.

CHAPTER FIFTY-THREE
The Dark starts
outlining his plans

The Dark entered the hazy, dusty cavern, which he thought of as home. The bats, which were his only fellow residents, skittered around the walls and the ceilings in a vain attempt to avoid the light from his smoky torch. Although, this light was bright it flickered as he moved or if stirred by the movement of the stale air. Repeatedly, its glow was partially obscured by the pungent, unpleasant vapours the torch emitted.

The Dark flicked a switch on the wall. Once more, the bats scurried about as the overhead fans extracted the worst of the musty fumes, introducing a supply of fresh air. Whilst he enjoyed the dark, atmospheric gloom of his lair, The Dark also appreciated the need to breathe.

He assessed his surroundings. He had been absent from his home for many weeks. Too many weeks. He lit the wall torches from the one he was carrying. Then, picking up a bundle of kindling from the stack in one corner, he swiftly started a small fire in his fireplace. He added a large log, which he selected from his pile. It hissed and crackled, creating an obnoxious retch-inducing stench, accompanied by a murky, cloudy, blue-tinted fog.

The Dark hummed tunelessly, as he searched through his collection of suitably dramatic classical music recordings. He was not sure which piece would suit his mood. With the addition of his recently acquired hypnosis skills, he was sure he had everything he needed to complete his plans. What was best for triumphant yet serious, plotting? At last, he settled for "Pictures at an exhibition" by Mussorgsky. It was ideal. Sombre, intense, and bleak, but also rousing, uplifting and hopeful with a glorious, celebratory finale.

Switching on the cave's subdued overhead lighting, The Dark started the activation sequence of his display screens. While they flared into life, his selected music commenced. For four or five minutes, he sat listening to the orchestra in contented appreciation.

The oily, black smoke from his torches intermingled with the sharp, gaseous fumes from the roaring fire, which was now burning magnificently in his hearth. A peculiar, thick, green-yellow smog hung menacingly in the air.

The Dark sighed. 'Ah, that's better already! Now it feels like home again.'

✵✵✵

Kuppa Broth stared at the board in the main police office, which was known affectionately by her officers as "The Chief's Dark Questions", wondering why nobody had heard anything from The Dark recently. She knew enough about her "Most Wanted" felon to be concerned at his unexpected continuing silence. She understood that The Dark's ego demanded attention. This quiet period must mean that not only was he totally preoccupied with his current scheme, whatever it might be, but also that the result was likely to be substantial as well as unpleasantly dangerous.

The truth was that The Dark had been far too busy to spend time composing one of his threatening yet "fun" messages. He had invested months of his time in preparation for this latest malevolent exploit. He wanted this to be the one deed for which he was remembered. His most fantastic criminal achievement. He hoped that this one act would compel the inhabitants of Underside, finally, to recognise him for the mastermind which he already knew that he was. The Dark craved respect. He believed that once he had accomplished this magnificent misdemeanour, his name would be mentioned forever in the same breath as Underside's most famous terrorist, Sedge (Mad Jack) Warbler.

For the Dark's plan to succeed, he needed to utilise misdirection; the kind typically employed by an expert illusionist. As The Dark's conjuring knowledge was best described as sparse, his first task was the simple one of visiting a library to gather information. Not just any library, however.

If an elf needed detailed information on any subject, it was recognised that Hollow Earth University library afforded the finest selection of reference material in Underside. Moreover, the University librarians were so proud of their collected works that, for a nominal fee, they allowed all Underside citizens to visit the reference sections. It was the perfect location for the intensive study The Dark required.

Naturally, the librarians did not allow any elf to remove material. They could make notes during their visit to the library and visit as often as their research required. (Amongst the visiting elves there were those who were so dedicated that the library became their second home.)

The librarians were exceptionally tolerant of their visitors, but they were extremely strict regarding two rules. Making notes within a particular volume or defacing it in any way resulted in severe penalties. These varied from a ban on using the library for a specified time, or in the worst instances an undefined but appropriately lengthy ban. Theft or vandalism always resulted in a lifetime ban. The gravest cases were reported to the police for potential prosecution.

In reality, this type of punishment was rarely required. The library had a secret weapon – the Head Librarian, Mistress Ida Downe. Ida considered the library to be her domain. Here she was queen. The works of literature were her charges, to be protected at all costs.

Ida was an atypical elf. She had never enjoyed life. In fact, she had never found any reason to enjoy life. She could not understand the happy elves that surrounded her. Their happiness merely irritated her. Had negativity required a sponsor or spokesperson, Ida was the ideal choice. Ida's glass was never half full. Equally, it was never half empty. It was always completely empty. Strangely, this did not concern Ida. Nothing mattered to her, other than the library and its contents.

Even though Underside was beneath the surface, away from the vagaries of climate which the world above experienced, there were localised underground weather conditions. In particular, the vast complex of caverns regularly acted as wind tunnels, producing anything from a light zephyr to a blustery gale. Those elves toiling regularly in such winds, tended to develop a "healthy glow". This was not the case with Ida, who never stepped outside the library for any occurrence other than a dire emergency. As a result, her complexion resembled the colour of old dust, such as might be found in the corner of an ancient, disused property. Neither her eyes nor her hair improved her appearance. Her eyes were an exceptionally pale, unattractive, liquid blue, while her hair closely matched the tone of an old, used tallow candle.

Over the years that she had commanded the position of Head Librarian, Ida had developed a facial expression which reflected her personality. Thunderously stern, and miserable. It was truly a terrifying sight. Any elf failing to adhere to the library's rules risked confronting that face and experiencing Ida's wrath. Most elves had no idea what this entailed but they were not keen to find out.

The Dark, acting as Cornflower, was entirely aware of Ida's reputation. As The Dark did not wish to draw attention to himself while researching in the library, he was especially careful. His treatment of the library's books, leaflets and other papers was almost reverential. As it happened, Ida did notice Cornflower, albeit in passing. She looked him over briefly and was impressed. "Now there is an elf who knows how to treat literary works," she thought. Beyond that, she took no further notice of him. He was so unimportant to Ida that, despite his striking blue skin, she would not recognise him, if she passed him in the street.

One visit of approximately one hour was sufficient for The Dark to obtain the information he required. In his mind (or rather that part of Cornflower's mind, which he controlled), this was a small but important task now completed.

CHAPTER FIFTY-FOUR
The Dark continues
his planning

The next part of The Dark's plan required not only misdirection but also a degree of fairy-like cunning and deception. He arranged for Cornflower to visit his cousin Denim Blue in Wind Stop. In a month's time, it would be the birthday of Denim's daughter Skye. Although he saw her rarely, Cornflower was fond of Skye. Naturally, The Dark disliked her in the same way that he disliked any elf.

Usually, Cornflower sent a parcel for Skye's birthday. This year, Cornflower, under The Dark's direction, intended to call in person. A great pleasure for Cornflower but an even greater convenience for The Dark.

Cornflower's social call would allow The Dark to post a letter from Wind Stop, which was vital to his plans. His present to Skye was also part of his scheme. A selection of face paints for celebratory occasions. The Dark had deliberately bought more than he needed for Skye's present, keeping the remainder for himself. These were another necessary item that he required for his devious plot.

When a small truck derailed, outside Hollow Earth Central station, just as it was about to be attached to a train, everyone assumed it was an accident. The truck tipped on its side, emptying the contents across the adjacent tracks. The H.E.T.T. employees were so focused on attempting to move the truck and its spilled cargo to safety, away from the rails, they did not notice that one of the helpers, a certain Cornflower Blue, had placed several items into his holdall.

The H.E.T.T. accident investigators determined that the derailment resulted from a wheel axle that had sheered away. They failed to notice that the axle had been deliberately cut. The truck's contents were police uniforms. The investigators were unable to ascertain if any had been lost, as the truck's inventory was missing, assumed lost in the crash.

That evening, The Dark arrived back at his secret hideout with a bulging holdall, containing two complete police uniforms, the truck's inventory sheet, together with a modest, yet powerful, electric saw. This had proved quite capable of cutting through the truck's metal axle.

'That was simple,' he stated, gloatingly. 'Sometimes these elves are so trustingly naïve. That's a further one of my requirements obtained.'

Sniggering, hooting, and crowing loudly, he broke into a chaotic, madcap dance around his gloomy home.

[As always, this was purely for The Dark's entertainment. It is unlikely that it would have impressed any judges on a TV dance show, but he did not care.]

The following morning, a selected few of The Dark's criminal associates were at work in The Galaxy Mall. The work in question involved them in careful pickpocketing. PC Mountain Boncebasher barely noticed the elf that bumped into him, apologising profusely.

'See dat, Cliff? Der elf wot do der bump but den do der sorry after. Sed sum elves nice.'

'No elves nice. All nasty crimnoes.'

While this intellectual discussion was occurring, The Dark's criminal confederates were engaged in copying the policeman's ID, which they had "borrowed". Just ten minutes later, an elf approached PC Boncebasher.

'You dropped this, Constable,' he stated, passing the ID back to Mountain.

'Fanks, sir,' said Mountain.

Turning to Cliff Wallbreaker, he remarked, 'Wot der nice elf! See, Cliff, not all der nasty crimnoes.'

[Unlike Cliff, who was a lost cause, Mountain was beginning to grasp the finer points of language. In his own goblin way.]

The "nice" elf had rejoined his companions.

'What a couple of clowns! We need to pass this copy ID to one of The Dark's runners. I gather he wants it urgently.'

The Dark was overjoyed. For an elf of his talents, turning this copy into a believable fake ID was child's play.

Once again, The Dark cackled manically.

'Just need to create fake beards from my wig supply and I will be all set. Time to make merry. Time for celebratory music. Now what do I have in my calypso section? I only need to hope that my plans are not spoilt by some stupid elf!'

***

At that precise moment, Flaky Pastry was approaching The Duck Inn, in Babbsley Reach. Lemon Puff had arranged to meet him there.

'It's my local but it isn't the best pub. Not as nice as your local,' Lemon had told him.

In truth, even the Duck Inn's regulars thought it had become jaded. The pub had stood empty for four months, after the last tenant, Eva Brick, died. Initially, her son, Howse, was reluctant to take over The Duck Inn. He had an excellent job in Hollow Earth. Landlord of a pub did not appeal to him. But finally, his wife, Laya, persuaded him.

'It's run down now but I think we could make a go of it,' she had said.

In the four months that it had stood vacant, the premises had been occupied by squatters, who had used the building as a convenient storage space for a range of stolen goods, which they sold on to unsuspecting locals.

With the Elite's help, Laya and Howse had cleared the pub site. However, returning the Inn to its previous high standard was proving difficult, time consuming and expensive. Presently, the pub was partially restored, decorated outside with half-painted walls and scaffolding. The interior had been repainted but the pub's chairs and tables had been vandalised by the squatters, so Howse had obtained a mixed batch of cheap, somewhat rickety, wooden benches and tables until new modern furniture could be purchased.

Ewan Earth was by no means the only elf that thought The Duck Inn had become "a bit of a dump". As admitted by Laya, at this time the Inn was run down but she could recall how good an establishment it had been when Eva was still alive. She hoped to return it to its former glory. An enjoyable, friendly venue where elves might visit with their friends and families, confident of a pleasurable visit with tasty food and drink.

Laya was not happy that the village locals considered The Duck Inn to be "a bit of a dive" or that, with its recent history of "dodgy dealings", the less charitable regulars thought it should be renamed "The Duck Inn and Dive Inn". Nevertheless, a part-renovated building, with shaky furniture was the best that she and Howse could manage for the time being.

Sadly, for Laya, the combination of Flaky Pastry with wobbly bench seats and equally wobbly tables was an accident waiting to happen. As he walked in, Flaky spotted Lemon at one of the tables. He could see that she already had a drink, so he waved happily then span around quickly, heading for the bar. Unsurprisingly, Flaky span too quickly. As he picked himself up from the floor, he waved to Lemon once more before turning to order. He did not recognise any of the beers on offer. In the end, he chose a pint of Thirsty Frog. He was presented with an insipid, unappealing lager.

(As Laya and Howse were still in the process of re-establishing connections with good suppliers, most of their beverages were similar. Somewhat "lacking" or "below standard".)

Flaky carried his pint to the table, with special care. Flushed with the unexpected success of not tripping over or dropping it, he tried to sit on the bench seat. Immediately, he almost fell over, spilling beer onto the floor. He was grabbed by Lemon and another elf, who happened to be sitting at the table.

'Careful, fella. Don't want to lose your drink. Although that stuff is pretty dreadful,' said the elf with a smile, noting the colourless pint which Flaky was holding. Flaky was not sure what to say but as he was always polite, he smiled, and said thank you.

As Flaky attempted to place his beer on the table, both the bench and the table wobbled, which meant, of course, that he spilt some more of his beer.

Lemon giggled. 'Go and ask the landlord if he will top it up for you, Flaky. I'll come with you to help carry it back to the table.'

As Flaky approached the bar, he stumbled again, throwing the rest of his beer into the landlord's face. *[An accidental (make the beer disappear) trick he had performed on more than one occasion previously at other locations.]* Lemon burst out laughing.

As Howse stood, dripping with beer, Laya came to the rescue, handing him a hastily grabbed towel.

'Go and get cleaned up, dear. I'll serve these good people. Don't want you losing your temper and banning them. We haven't enough customers as it is.'

Howse sloped off, muttering under his breath, as he left.

Three minutes later, with Lemon carrying his beer, Flaky was able to sit down at last. This time, successfully, with no further spillages. Cautiously, Flaky placed himself next to Lemon. Opposite them was the helpful elf, who introduced himself as Aaron Head, and another friendly elf, who introduced herself as Aaron's girlfriend, Fleur Matt.

Both Fleur and Aaron were typical examples of the elvish race. Aaron was approximately six feet two in height with near-black wavy, mop-like hair surrounding his mid-brown face. His earthy brown eyes were framed by "laughter lines", which supported his obvious, friendly nature. Fleur was a shade under six feet tall with a paler tone to her face than Aaron. It was best compared to creamy caramel in colour. Her hazel brown eyes peered out from under a neatly trimmed fringe. Her apparent long, straight, honey-blonde hair was misleading. In reality, Fleur described her hair as "just ordinary brown". She disliked both the colour and the slight wave of her lengthy tresses. As a result, she customarily both dyed and "straightened" her hair.

In her otherwise relaxed, carefree, cheerful personality, this was Fleur's one serious obsession.

Aaron smiled across the table. 'Lemon has already introduced herself to us. From what she said, you must be her boyfriend, Flaky. Have you got your balance back now, Flaky?'

'Oh yes, I think so. Um, thank you. Oh, and thank you for catching me.'

'No problem, although losing your beer would not have been so bad. That looks like Thirsty Frog you're drinking. Horrible, weedy stuff. If you are staying long enough for another pint, try the Old Coal Scuttle. It is the only decent pint they have at the moment.'

'Perhaps we could have that with some food, Flaky?' asked Lemon, looking at the menu.

Flaky studied the menu in front of him.

'That would be nice. I wonder what this Chicken Chaser is?'

'I think it's called Chicken Chasseur, Flaky,' said Fleur. 'It's a recipe someone picked up when they were Topside. Not that it matters, as I know their oven went wrong this morning, so they won't have any cooked food, just sandwiches. Although, their sandwich toaster is still working so you would still be able to get a toastie.'

'Maybe I can get a Chicken Chaser toastie?' wondered Flaky.

'I don't think you can put Chasseur in a sandwich,' replied a slightly confused Fleur.

CHAPTER FIFTY-FIVE
The Dark travels to Wind Stop

I t was fortunate for The Dark that Denim Blue and Skye lived in Wind Stop, rather than River End or Peak Rise. Of the three other major cities, Wind Stop was, by far, the closest to Hollow Earth.

Until the new rail links were completed, The Dark's only travel option, for longer journeys, was to drive. Once a traveller left Hollow Earth, they were faced with roads that were only designed for local use. Although it was possible to navigate these to your required destination, many were little better than narrow village lanes or cart tracks. Even the larger of these roads were often poorly maintained. On most roads, high speed was impossible. Any elf achieving a top speed of thirty to forty miles an hour on any stretch of road, considered themselves fortunate. In some places, the top speed that could be achieved was between five to fifteen miles an hour. It was estimated that trains on the new rail links would travel at speeds of up to one hundred miles an hour.

For an intrepid voyager willing to undertake the trip, a journey to Peak Rise, the most remote of the cities, might take two to three months. River End was achievable in a four-to-five-week trek, with virtually non-stop daytime driving. Due to its closer distance, The Dark expected to travel to Wind Stop in four to five days. Even for this shorter drive, he would need to stop periodically as well as staying somewhere overnight. The Dark had persuaded his other self to book six weeks' leave. This was, supposedly, to give Cornflower time for travel to and from Wind Stop, time to stay with his relatives, but also time to visit his family's original home in Wind Stop. His employers at H.E.T.T. understood fully. Most elves thought that family history was important. The Dark did not. He had no such interest. He only wished to ensure, by hypnosis, that Cornflower thought it was how his time had been spent.

Cornflower Blue did not own a car. At least, not one of which he was aware. Since his emergence as a separate personality, The Dark had established various other alternative identities, each with their own bank account. This was convenient for him. After all, every arch criminal requires somewhere to store their ill-gotten gains. The Dark, using the identity of Walter Darknight, had purchased a car. Consequently, as Cornflower Blue was, albeit unknowingly, The Dark, it could be argued that Cornflower Blue also owned a car. Just a car of which he was unaware. The Dark would travel to Wind Stop in this car.

Over time, a wide selection of hotels, inns and hostelries had appeared along the road routes. While the residents of Hollow Earth, River End, Wind Stop and Peak Rise were looking forward to the vastly improved travel between the cities, the rail development was bitterly opposed by the owners of these businesses.

When The Dark left for Wind Stop, he gave no thought whatsoever to that problem. Had another elf asked for his opinion on that matter, in his guise as Cornflower he might have commented, "It's a shame. I hope the impact is not too severe." As The Dark, he did not care in the slightest. He disliked all elves equally. Why should he worry about the misfortunes of one particular group?

For The Dark, his excursion to Wind Stop was unexceptional. For Cornflower Blue, it was fractured and strange. He could remember packing for the journey (including packing a substantial selection of face paints for Skye, which he was sure he had not purchased), but he could not recall setting off on his travels. He was certain that he must have taken breaks on each day, but he had no recollection of stopping. His memory was of an unbroken, steady five-day drive.

The Dark's memory was different. Also, it was far more detailed. The particulars of each hotel, inn, or guesthouse, at which he stayed, were indelibly stamped in his mind (or that section of Cornflower's brain that he occupied). As were all of those extremely kind managers that had offered him an upgrade to the best room at half the regular cost, with a free breakfast the following morning. It was the same story for every café or restaurant on his route. Inevitably, he was offered his drink or meal at dramatically reduced prices. The Dark left a trail of bewildered individuals in his wake, who were wholly unaware that they had been hypnotised.

When Cornflower arrived at the Blues' residence, The Dark relinquished his control. He could imagine nothing worse than several days in the company of Cornflower's relatives, particularly Skye. Unlike Cornflower, The Dark did not like children. In fact, he hated children more than he hated adult elves. He decided to "hibernate" in Cornflower's mind, for the duration of the visit.

Cornflower stayed with his cousin's family for three days and nights before leaving for home. They were exceptionally welcoming. Denim's wife, Lavender (who resembled her name, with her lavender face and lilac hair), was a friendly, but busy doctor who flitted in and out, depending on the demands of her job. By her own admission, she was a dreadful cook. However, this was not a problem as Denim loved cooking. He was an excellent cook, albeit a terribly messy one, who regularly spattered whatever he was concocting over his mid-blue face or his navy-blue hair, as well as the clean clothes he had put on that morning. Cornflower felt relaxed and "at home", even though he remained confused regarding his journey.

Skye was delighted. She did not see Cornflower very often, other than in online links. Occasionally, there were service interruptions to these links, which led to jumpy, blurred, or patchy images, which were not synchronised with the voices of the caller or recipient.

[I have been told that elves have the same problems as us, with that specific technology.]

Although Cornflower was not her uncle, Skye always referred to him as her "lovely Uncle Corny". As expected, she was thrilled with her present and, with help from her parents, had already painted her face, before attending a friend's party. Instead of its usual pale blue, her face was now a light orange with accompanying deep orange stripes mimicking a "marmalade tabby" cat. Somehow, her natural short, straight, misty blue, toned hair contrasted perfectly with her face.

Cornflower set off the following morning with mixed feelings. He had thoroughly enjoyed his time with his relations and was sad to depart, but he remained baffled over his continuing memory blackouts. He resolved to arrange a further appointment with Annie Payne as soon as he arrived home. As it was, his journey home was similar to the one he had undertaken to Wind Stop, which meant he would have yet more to relate to her.

As previously, The Dark's recollection was entirely different to that of Cornflower. He recalled the voyage in vivid detail. He had resumed control shortly after the departure from Denim Blue's cottage, including pausing at a post office to mail a letter to Kuppa Broth, which he was confident would arrive ahead of him. As before, The Dark stopped repeatedly but he ensured that he did not revisit anywhere he had stopped en route to Wind Stop. He was aware that hypnotic effects were not permanent. He was not keen to encounter an irate hotel manager, who had just recalled how they had been duped.

***

The Dark was overjoyed as he relaxed in his rank, hazy lair inhaling the noxious, sulphurous vapours that hung in the air, while listening happily to the chittering of the bats who shared the space with him. His plans were coming to fruition wonderfully. Through Cornflower, he had access to the railway tunnels, explosives, smoke flares and the full range of equipment the elves used for mining or tunnelling. Shortly, once his letter was delivered to Kuppa, he would have a means of admittance to police headquarters. During his brief stay with Denim and Skye, he had overheard some exceptionally useful information, regarding a General in the Elite. Information that fitted exceedingly well with his plans. Information which he had incorporated into his letter to Kuppa.

In his absence, The Dark had arranged for his assistants to conceal black masks and clothing in each of the new rail tunnels in boxes labelled "Explosives. Handle with care". The Dark knew there were stacks of such boxes already present. His assistants were instructed to ensure that the boxes they left were at the base of the stack. One of his helpers, an excellent thief, had been told to "help himself" to an Elite guard's uniform and "doctor" it so that it indicated the Eastern Elite rather than the Southern elite.

Kuppa had received The Dark's letter that morning, purporting to have been sent by General Earnest Lee of the Eastern Elite. In the letter, the General explained that he was retiring but had "set in motion" various initiatives before he left. One of these was to commence establishing a police force, similar to that of Hollow Earth. To that end, he was despatching one of his soldiers, a Private Owen Space, to Hollow Earth, on temporary secondment for one month, to both "learn the ropes" and help where he could.

When she received The Dark's letter, Kuppa was puzzled as well as suspicious. It was strange that the General had not contacted her earlier. She called the Eastern Elite base, speaking with a Captain Lorne Mower. The captain was mildly amused.

'I'm afraid that was the General in his last few weeks, before retiring. He had become extremely forgetful but determined to make a number of changes ahead of leaving. It would be just like him to have this idea and then forget to inform anyone. He was a fine officer, excellent in his role but, even before his memory started going, he was a notoriously poor communicator.'

Kuppa's scepticism continued, but with the delivery, that afternoon, of a package addressed to Temporary Constable Space, Kuppa felt less perturbed. PCs Barry Tone and Cole Slorre had noted it had been left outside the main door and had brought it to her attention. A brief examination of the contents revealed it to be two full police uniforms.

On checking with Bingo, she found out that although he knew nothing of the delivery, he deemed it likely that Lottie had dealt with it, while he was away in Topside. As Lottie was now in Topside herself, Kuppa decided to wait until the arrival of PC Space.

The delivery had removed most of Kuppa's concerns. She reasoned that if General Lee had taken the time to order a uniform for PC Space, together with a spare, it was likely that his request for this temporary secondment was genuine. What she could not know was that these were the uniforms that The Dark had "saved" from the rail crash. Additionally, she could not know that they had not been delivered by the usual parcel delivery service, or that The Dark had arranged for one of his retinue to make the delivery.

CHAPTER FIFTY-SIX
Constable Space arrives

General Lee had not provided Kuppa with a photograph of her new temporary starter. Consequently, she had no idea what to expect. She had to trust that the Constable would introduce himself, on arrival.

The following Monday, Sergeant Sally Forth was on duty at the Police Enquiries/Information desk when an elf, smartly dressed in an Elite guard's uniform, marched up to the counter. The sergeant had never seen this elf before but aside from his immaculate uniform, he was the least notable elf she had ever encountered. A more typical, almost nondescript, elf would have been difficult to find. His skin was a deep brown colour, which was characteristic of many elves. When he removed his cap, she could see that his hair was darker. It was almost black, as was his beard. Such black hair was similarly characteristic of numerous elves.

The Dark was fully aware of typical colouring for elves. Whilst his blue colouring was, by no means unique, nevertheless it was noteworthy. He did not wish Constable Owen Space to be noteworthy. The real reason for his purchase of face paints was now revealed. With some experimentation, he had found a paint that resulted in a satisfactory dark shade of brown. As The Dark customarily retained a wide selection of clothes and wigs, he soon found a suitable black wig with an accompanying false beard.

Sergeant Forth addressed the stranger standing in front of her desk.

'Good morning, guardsman. How can I help you?'

'Good morning, Sir. I am Private Owen Space of the Eastern Elite on temporary secondment as a Constable. Hopefully, I am expected.' The Dark smiled. When it suited The Dark, he was able to borrow a convincingly genuine smile from his Cornflower self.

'Right, I'll speak with the Chief. Please wait here, Constable. I am Sergeant Sally Forth.' She returned The Dark's smile. 'You don't need to call me Sir. Sergeant or Sarge will suffice. No doubt the same as a Sergeant in the Elite.'

'Yes indeed, Sergeant.' (Inwardly, The Dark cursed himself for such a stupid error. He could only hope that the Sergeant would not consider it important or worth remembering.)

The Sergeant returned a few minutes later. 'Follow me, Constable. The Chief will see you now. Please note, she does not like being called Ma'am so make sure you call her Chief.'

'Yes, Sergeant.'

The Dark was shown into The Chief's office. Kuppa Broth looked up at him. This would be a test for his disguise, as Kuppa had met Cornflower Blue before. If she recognised him, The Dark would need to alter his plans quickly and radically. Fortunately, Kuppa gave no indication of recognition.

This was a new situation for Kuppa. One where she believed a serious attitude was required. Before talking, she assumed the most authoritarian appearance she could manage.

'Please sit down, Constable. I am Hollow Earth's Chief of Police, Kuppa Broth. I will be frank with you, Constable, I am not entirely happy to have you foisted on us at short notice but that is the fault of your superiors not yours. Therefore, we will accommodate you as best we can, and an extra pair of hands is always welcome. I understand from your commanding officer, General Lee, that he wishes you to see we how we run our police force, to gauge what is necessary to establish a similar force in Wind Stop.'

'Yes, Chief.'

'Now, we cannot have you parading around headquarters in that uniform, Constable. I will ask Sergeant Forth to show you the locker we have allocated to you, where you will find two police uniforms. Change into one of those and report to PC Jersey Pullover and PC Avva Biscuit in the administration section. I have asked them to show you how the day-to-day administration is carried out, but I am afraid, for security reasons, they are under strict orders not to allow you to access the computers.'

✿✿✿

Within a few days PC Space became a familiar sight to most of the other police, with just three exceptions.

'Hoo dat?' asked PC Granite Rockearth.

'Hoo Hoo?' replied PC Mountain Boncebasher.

'Hoo dat dere?' asked Granite again.

'Wot Hoo?' said Mountain helpfully.

'Dere! Der new police,' insisted Granite.

'Dat Space,' explained Mountain.

Even goblins know what a space is, so Granite tried once more.

'Not der space! Hoo dat dere?' he said, pointing furiously.

'Dat Space,' stated Mountain yet again, holding his large arms out to the side of his body, while offering an explanatory shrug.

As was often the case with any conversation involving goblins, confusion now reigned supreme.

Granite was becoming irritated. 'Dat not der space,' he maintained. Waving his arms to indicate every direction, other than where the new police officer was standing, he continued.

'Dat der space! Dat der space! Dat der space! Dat der new police!'

'Yeah,' agreed Mountain. 'Dat der new police. Der PC Space.'

'Der PC Space?' growled Granite. 'Stupid name. All der elves got der stupid names!'

'Yeah, all got der stupid names.'

There was silence for a minute, as the two goblins nodded at each other.

The silence was broken by a voice from lower down.

'Hoo dat?' asked Cliff Wallbreaker. With impeccably awful timing, he had contrived to appear immediately after the conversation ceased.

Swiftly, Granite held up his arm, in front of Mountain's face, before Mountain could speak. 'Dat der new police, Cliff,' he declared. 'Der PC Space.'

'Der PC Space?' echoed Cliff. 'Dat der stupid name.'

✳✳✳

The Dark was amazed at the way fate was providing him with a helping hand. He had not anticipated the bonus of his own personal locker. When Sergeant Forth explained to PC Space that his locker was completely private, he struggled to believe his good fortune. It gave him the perfect location in which to store his explosives. The perfect location to store the bomb, with which he intended to destroy the police headquarters.

On his first day, The Dark had carried in with him an excessively unattractive kitbag. In the past, it had most probably been merely a plain, homely, beige bag. Now, it was the very definition of shabby, tattered to the point of distress. It was riddled with holes; the straps were frayed with threads hanging down around the bag. It featured a selection of unknown stains or scuff marks. The other officers took little notice as PC Space opened the holdall to remove a flask and some sandwiches before storing the kitbag very carefully in his locker. They recognised an old, favourite friend, no doubt originally a school bag retained for nostalgic or sentimental reasons.

At first, The Dark had been concerned about keeping this bag hidden somewhere, but his locker had provided him with the ideal storage space. The other members of the police were completely correct in their assumptions concerning his kitbag. As they suspected, it was Cornflower's old school bag which he had kept for emotional motives rather than for its continued practicality. In his desire to appear as mundane as possible, The Dark had decided that it added to his ordinariness. Of course, no-one but The Dark could know that the bag now contained explosives rather than schoolbooks and would eventually contain the bomb he was constructing.

During his stay at Police Headquarters, as PC Space, The Dark had gained access to an empty locker. The day before he was due to depart, he had relocated his bomb surreptitiously into this empty locker, ensuring that not only was it locked securely but also that he "accidentally" misplaced the locker key into a pocket in his guard uniform.

At the end of his "secondment" to Kuppa's police force, PC Space left as quietly as he had arrived. He changed back into his guard uniform, emptied his few personal effects into his dilapidated bag, passing back his locker key with the two PC uniforms to Sergeant Forth. PC Space thanked everyone, especially Kuppa, for their tolerance and help. They, in turn, thanked him, wishing him well for the future.

The Dark left in the car which he had used to travel to Wind Stop. The car which Cornflower Blue was unaware that he owned. After travelling a few miles, The Dark turned his vehicle off the main road into a small winding lane. This led to a recently constructed secret entrance down into a small car park. From there, The Dark had a short walk along a tunnel leading back to his lair.

CHAPTER FIFTY-SEVEN
The Dark activates his plan

The Dark added an extra log to the fire in his lair. As the blue/grey smoke curled up from the fire, towards the ceiling of the cave, the bats fluttered around, in agitation.

Usually, The Dark favoured the intense or the dramatic, in his musical preferences, but there were times when he desired music that was lighter, more celebratory. This was such an occasion. His selected album contained a variety of jigs, reels, and hoedowns. He giggled, at his own antics, as he pranced around the impromptu stage, provided by his secret hideaway. He could not believe how clever he had been. Everything, for his master plan, was organised.

Abruptly, he ceased his dance and turned off the music.

'Now is the time!' he announced, theatrically, to his non-existent audience.

Later, he made his way back to Cornflower Blue's cottage. The following morning, The Dark exited Cornflower's front door, ensuring he was seen by several villagers, before catching the tram to work.

✻✻✻

The Dark was a meticulous planner, but it did not matter how thorough his preparations had been. They could not allow for every contingency. Often, a chance decision by another person is all that is required to "throw a spanner into the works" of your perfect scheme. He did not know this yet, but this was a lesson The Dark was about to learn.

After PC Space's departure, PC Jersey Pullover and PC Avva Biscuit checked his locker to confirm that he had not left anything behind. Initially, they were impressed by the condition of the locker. It was immaculate. Of course, Avva and Jersey were typical police officers. An immaculate locker seemed strange. It did not take them long to become suspicious.

'Do you know of any officers that keep their lockers this clean?' asked Jersey.

'Well, I can't say for all of them,' admitted Avva, 'but my locker is certainly not that pristine and I've always thought I was one of the tidiest officers here!'

'He was allocated an empty locker. As he was only here for a couple of weeks, perhaps PC Space did not have time to make it untidy?' wondered Jersey.

'Maybe, but I'm not convinced. There's another empty locker at the end of the row. Let's check that.'

Jersey attempted to open the locker. 'It's locked,' he declared. 'Maybe, the handle's just a bit stiff.' He gave the handle another pull, shaking the locker as he did this.

'Avva,' he said, 'it's ticking.'

✻✻✻

Cornflower's return to work the following day was well received by his fellow workers in the new H.E.T.T. rail tunnels. They were delighted to see him, flooding him with questions about Wind Stop, his relatives, or details of his lengthy car journeys to and from Wind Stop. Journeys which the other elves deemed to be astonishingly arduous as well as unbelievably difficult. None of the elves were able to imagine travelling for five days in a car over often treacherous roads, let alone traversing those roads twice. They felt that Cornflower was incredibly brave, fearless, or courageous. Cornflower would have been happy if he could just remember undertaking any of the journeys.

The only exceptions to this adulation were the dworfs that were assisting the elvish tunnel constructors. Elves are industrious workers but compared to dworfs they might be seen as half-hearted slackers. The dworfs could not understand anyone taking a holiday when there was so much "fun" work still to complete. In fact, the dworfs could not understand why anyone ever took a holiday.

[Ask any typical dworfs about holidays. Without fail, they will inform you that interesting, challenging work is all the holiday they ever need.]

Journeying for five days and back, merely to visit a relative was an incomprehensible concept to the dworfs. Dworfs never undertake a lengthy voyage, unless they have an incredibly specific reason for travelling, such as attending an important family event, or aiding an ally beset by enemy forces.

In his first two days back at work, Cornflower familiarised himself with the progress made in his absence. Additionally, as one of the three senior engineers overseeing the work, he found much of his time taken in resolving minor complications which had arisen.

In the main, it was clear that excellent headway had been achieved. The three crews tunnelling from River End, Wind Stop and Peak Rise towards Hollow Earth had just begun to meet those tunnelling outwards from Hollow Earth. The tunnel workers had an unofficial sweepstake on which tunnel would complete first. Against all the odds, the two halves of the tunnel to Peak Rise were completed ahead of the others, despite the greater distance involved. This was closely followed by the River End tunnel. The tunnel to Wind Stop had suffered three time-consuming setbacks, so, much to the frustration of those elves, who were convinced they were backing the favourite, it was the last to complete.

The final linking of the tracks was expected to take no more than two to three days. Nevertheless, extensive testing and safety checks were required before the elves would attempt the first trial run of trains through the new tunnels. Although Cornflower was pleased to learn that all the tunnels were completed, as the senior engineer most involved with the Peak Rise tunnel, he was particularly thrilled to hear that those crews had finished first.

Sitting in the recesses of Cornflower's mind, The Dark did not share Cornflower's pleasure at the completion of this key stage of the project. However, he was elated for a completely different reason. In each instance, the three tunnels had met at almost the halfway point between Hollow Earth and their destinations. Fate decreed that those were the perfect locations for the bombs that The Dark intended to place.

Periodically, along the length of each tunnel, the elves had incorporated safety shelters. These were intended to provide somewhere for maintenance workers to take refuge when a train was passing through the tunnel. Some were no more than a recessed alcove in the wall, just deep enough to accommodate a standing individual for a short period of time. Others were larger, more deeply recessed with lighting. These offered a small table with one or two chairs, where a maintenance operative might sit to work on an intricate mechanism. Of course, they also afforded a convenient location for elves to stop for a quick game of cards, while eating a late lunch.

Where the tunnellers had met at the approximate halfway points, large shelters had been built, allowing essential equipment to be stored in addition to chairs and table. In the few days since his return, The Dark had ensured that Cornflower retrieved the three boxes labelled "Explosives. Handle with care", which his helpers had added previously to the piles of other similar boxes in the tunnels.

In the guise of Cornflower, The Dark placed one of his "fake" boxes in each tunnel, adding an additional message, "H.E.T.T. instruction. Not to be removed".

There now resided a box, of which elvish tunnel workers were unaware, beneath the table in each of the three larger tunnel shelters. As H.E.T.T.'s employees were proud to work for such a prestigious organisation, they always followed instructions. The Dark was confident that his boxes would remain untouched.

Had any of the elves looked inside one of the boxes, they would have been shocked at what they found. They would have seen a device, looking uncannily like a bomb, with wires connected to explosives. They would have observed a timing device and a detonator, apparently intended to be triggered by a remote telephone call. But, as none of the elves opened any of the boxes, they did not see this. That pleasure was still to come!

CHAPTER FIFTY-EIGHT

The Dark sends
Kuppa a message

The morning after The Dark had placed his boxes in the tunnels, Cornflower set off for work, content in the knowledge that the tunnel project was nearing completion. As he approached Hollow Earth Central station, he spotted Flaky on his way back to Little Merritiddle, with a supply of wood for Onion. He gave Flaky a smile and a cheery wave, which Flaky returned, before braking suddenly as he nearly slewed off the cycle path onto the road. By then, Cornflower had just entered the tunnel development, so he failed to see Flaky's latest, near-mishap.

Recently, The Dark had realised that he could hypnotise his other half into believing a fictional narrative, invented for him by The Dark. This was an improvement as Cornflower would now believe he had been busy working, rather than having an unexplained blank in his memory.

As Cornflower entered the tunnel complex, The Dark took control. As Cornflower undertook his imaginary day, The Dark, wearing his black mask, sought out his closest confederates – his runners. He had ensured that several of these runners were H.E.T.T. employees, although whenever they were needed by

The Dark, they ceased their H.E.T.T. duties in order to carry out his commands.

The Dark instructed six of his runners that, at two o'clock that afternoon, they were to waylay each of the three tunnel supervisors. Naturally, as Cornflower Blue was one of those elves, he was, in fact, ordering them to organise his own kidnapping. A fact of which his runners were ignorant.

The Dark's instructions were clear, if somewhat surprising to his accomplices. They were to take the supervisors to where his explosive devices were stored, in the safety alcoves, but he stressed that he did not wish them to use undue force. Each of the supervisors was to be taken to a separate tunnel. There they were to be made to sit on the seat in the alcove, with the bomb on their lap. They were to be gagged and tied to the chairs but not so tightly that they would be unable to free themselves within a few minutes. Once more, this confused his sidekicks, but they knew better than to argue with The Dark.

At all costs, they were to ensure they were not observed by any of the tunnel workers.

With this stage of his plan achieved, The Dark put his newly acquired mesmerising techniques to use. Pleasing music was customarily piped into the tunnels in order to assist in providing an enjoyable working environment. Surreptitiously, The Dark replaced this with a recording he had made, which was subtly hypnotic. It also included a hidden, subliminal message.

Next, The Dark completed a communication to Kuppa Broth, which he had drafted in outline prior to his trip to Wind Stop. He had set his computer to send this to police headquarters at fifteen minutes to two.

Unlike his previous announcements, The Dark's notification to Kuppa was not broadcast generally. This time, he had concluded that it was "more fun" if the sole recipient was the new police chief. In his warped mind, The Dark saw Kuppa as a troublesome irritation, who had an annoying habit of ruining his wiliest plots. He could no longer endure the torment of watching her thwart his plans.

At quarter to two, Kuppa's computer at the police station turned itself on, displaying the black cloaked, black masked figure of The Dark.

He commenced his message with an onslaught of unsettling, screeching laughter. The source of his merriment was unclear. Nonetheless, the effect was appropriately disturbing.

'Chief Broth, please accept my apologies,' he croaked, through his customary vocal distortion. 'It is such a long time, since I contacted you. You must have wondered if I had retired. The recent crime wave must have been a clue that I had not. I am sure you had guessed that I was behind it, keeping you and your police busy.

'You have been very clever in the past, always stopping everything I try to do. This scheme may be more of a challenge. I have arranged for three unexpected presents to be left in the new rail tunnels. But that is not all. The added complication for you is that I have arranged for the three tunnel supervisors to be taken hostage. Each of the hostages is now tied to one of my explosive devices. All my gifts are timed to go off at two-fifteen.'

The Dark snorted derisively. 'Can you get to the hostages in time? Defuse my little offerings, before it is too late?' he asked, before breaking into a further bout of manic cackling. 'How jolly! Watch out for the Bang! Boom! Blast!'

The Dark paused, before adding, 'If that is too simple for you, my dear Kuppa, do not forget the station. It's an extra puzzle for you. Have I also left something at the station?'

Kuppa smiled as her screen darkened.

For the first time in her dealings with The Dark, Kuppa had foiled part of one of his terrorist schemes, without his knowledge. When Avva and Jersey had reported an empty locker was ticking, at the police station, she guessed immediately that it might be a bomb. With Lottie and Bingo's assistance, her new bomb squad had disarmed the device, rendering it harmless. Kuppa knew it had to be The Dark's "extra puzzle". No doubt, he had expected his obscure reference to "the station" to mislead her. The discovery of his bomb at the police station meant she would not need to waste any time or resources hunting for it at the railway station.

At the exact time that he launched the message to Kuppa, The Dark sent a signal to the three devices to activate their timers, with a thirty-minute delay. When he contacted Kuppa, he was sitting in the safety shelter of the new Peak Rise tunnel. To The Dark, with his distorted world view, it made perfect sense to familiarise himself with the locality, which he would be occupying in the near future, as a hostage.

Nearby was a stack of similarly labelled boxes, all with the wording "Explosives. Handle with care". He checked that the top box was his fake box, containing black masks and clothing. Removing his own mask and black cloak, The Dark inserted them into the top of box. He collected a jacket from the back of the chair. This had been left there earlier by one of his runners. A trusted servant, who knew better than to ask any questions. The Dark put on this jacket, as he was strolling back to the entrance of the tunnel. It was bright red in colour. One of Cornflower Blue's favourites.

Carefully, The Dark sat down on two wooden sleepers placed beside the entrance. These doubled as an impromptu table and chair. He pulled a sheaf of papers from his jacket pocket, which he studied closely, feigning interest in their contents. None of the tunnel workers took any notice when they walked by. The tunnel supervisors often checked their notes, near to the tunnel entrances.

Concealed within Cornflower's brain, The Dark waited patiently for his abduction.

CHAPTER FIFTY-NINE
Fire in the tunnels

T he Dark expected a full contingent of police officers to
arrive at the railway station by ten to fifteen minutes past
two o'clock. He did not anticipate any other significant attendees.

Fate had other ideas though. Onion did not need him that
afternoon, so Flaky decided he would watch the trains near
Hollow Earth Central Station. The Dark had been concerned
that "some stupid elf" would upset his painstakingly fashioned
arrangements. With the arrival of Flaky, Fate had duly obliged.

Following instructions given to them previously, The Dark's
runners lit smoke flares behind each hostage once they had
secured them. They waited near the entrance to the tunnel
complex until Kuppa's police began to arrive. They ran out
towards the officers, yelling, 'Stay back! There are bombs in
the tunnels!'

As they circled around, waving their arms about, their
apparent fear was extremely persuasive. Kuppa and Chief
Inspector March Doubletime were amongst the first to arrive
at the scene. As The Dark's runners darted out of the tunnels,
Kuppa held up her hands to slow them down.

'We know this is a frightening situation for you, but it will
not help if you panic. Now, can someone tell me what they have
seen? Exactly what is causing your distress?' she queried.

The Dark had anticipated the likelihood of such an exchange with the police. His runners had a well-rehearsed script to follow.

'We have a fear of The Dark, Mistress,' stated one of The Dark's runners.

'Sorry, I don't understand. You have been working in the tunnels all this time, but you are scared of the dark?'

'No, fear of The Dark. We have no fear of darkness. We fear the elf who calls himself The Dark. We have seen him in the tunnels frequently recently. He is quite mad. Insane. He's threatening to blow up the tunnels.'

As this discussion was happening, the subliminal instructions in The Dark's recording began to influence the actions of the tunnel workers. They started donning the black masks and clothing stored in the tunnels. Dozens of elves, dressed as The Dark, flooded out of the tunnels, frantically attempting to escape an unseen fate.

As they rushed past her, Kuppa endeavoured to ask the names of the escaping elves.

'I'm The Dark,' claimed the first elf she approached.

'I am The Dark,' declared another.

'No, I'm The Dark,' insisted a third elf.

'You can't be. I am The Dark,' disputed the fourth.

'No, you're not. I am!' argued the next elf.

Kuppa smiled. "Well, masked or not at least I know they are elves," she thought.

Eventually, a figure appeared that was not masked. By now, after hearing twenty to thirty elves claiming to be The Dark, Kuppa was becoming frustrated.

'I suppose you are another elf called The Dark?'

'How dare you, Mistress? I am a dworf!'

Slightly embarrassed, Kuppa continued.

'I am most terribly sorry, sir, but are you also claiming to be The Dark?'

'No, of course not.'

'I see, may I ask what your name is, sir?'

'I'm Spartacus!'

'Spartacus?'

'Yes, Spartacus Draper.'

'I see, Mister Draper. May I ask why you are here?'

'This is where I am meant to be. I am an engineer assisting your elvish colleagues. I work for H.E.T.T. in the new rail tunnels that are being constructed but you need to look in the tunnels yourself. Not everyone came out. I heard voices calling for help. Follow me. I will show you the way but put on the safety helmets, goggles, face masks and high visibility coats just outside the entrance before you go in.'

As he said this, a figure sprinted past, fell over and got up again before dashing off once more.

'Flaky, wait for everyone else!' yelled Kuppa, but he had already disappeared into the tunnel complex.

✸✸✸

When Flaky had spotted the commotion outside the railway station, he had leapt onto his tricycle, fallen off, remounted, and then cycled urgently toward the tunnels. He knew that his friend Cornflower was inside, in danger. As he drew near, he had heard the words "bombs in the tunnels". In his anxiety to reach Cornflower, he tumbled off his trike once more. Discarding it, he had decided that he would get there quicker if he ran.

Although, Flaky had been instructed on the use of the safety equipment on a previous visit with his friend, in his alarm he could barely remember anything he had been shown. At the entrance, he grabbed a coat, putting it on back to front and inside out. He jammed a safety helmet on his head with the peak at the back. Unsure what to do with the face mask, he fastened it securely under his chin. He placed some goggles triumphantly around his neck.

By now, the smoke flares were accomplishing their purpose. Smoke filled the tunnels. As he tried to run into the middle tunnel, where Cornflower worked, he was spotted by an elf who was just exiting. Assuming this was an over-enthusiastic rescuer, the elf called out to him.

'Wait there! I'll adjust your safety gear, sir.'

He helped Flaky to put on his jacket, helmet, and face mask correctly. As he repositioned Flaky's goggles, he switched on his helmet light and gave him a friendly grin.

'That's better, sir. Best not to run in this smoke. You're likely to fall over. Was it tunnel two, the middle tunnel, you were heading to?'

'Yes, my friend Cornflower works there.'

'Good, you are just in time. I heard cries coming from that tunnel. Go straight forward from where you are but watch your footing.'

'Thank you,' replied Flaky, as he lurched forward.

As he disappeared from view, the other elf shook his head.

'What training do they give these rescuers nowadays?'

Flaky moved forward slowly. He could hear someone calling out.

In the tunnel, The Dark, thinking to add drama to his eventual escape, had delayed his extrication from his bonds. Additionally, he had hoped this would guarantee that he would be amongst the last elves leaving the tunnels. But he had not allowed for any unforeseen accidents. Sparks from the flare in his tunnel had ignited wood shavings behind him. The Dark staggered around, surrounded by fumes from the flames, which were mingling with the smoke that was already present. He was no longer sure which way led him out of the tunnel. His eyes watering with the stinging smoke, he coughed repeatedly. He was struggling to breathe. The extent of his miscalculation was clear to him. He recognised that he might perish in this fire. He called out in genuine, desperate terror.

'Help! Fire! Fire! Please, help me! Is there anyone there?'

A light appeared before him. As he collapsed, a figure caught him.

CHAPTER SIXTY
Flaky, the rescuer

O utside the tunnels, order was being restored. The process was necessarily careful, methodical, and cautious, but the rescuing crews were confident that they had control of the situation. The station staff had been well-drilled, in anticipation of incidents such as fires or bomb threats. Kuppa was receiving regular progress reports.

'All the smoke flares are extinguished, Mistress Broth,' reported one elf. 'The ventilation systems will soon clear the remaining smoke. The fire in tunnel two caused some concern but it has now been smothered. Fortunately, there was minimal damage.

'Happily, when we discovered the devices in the tunnels, we realised they were all fake and quite harmless. All three had pop-up messages. One had "Bang" written on it, another had "Boom" while the third said "Blast". Someone's idea of a joke I expect, but none of us found it amusing! Our biggest worry is two missing elves. One is Cornflower Blue, one of our supervisors. The other is an unknown rescuer, who went to save him.'

At that moment, a sooty, dusty Flaky stumbled out of the tunnel complex, supporting a similarly soot-covered Cornflower. They were grabbed by Kuppa and March, who helped them to a nearby bench.

Kuppa called out, 'Can we get stretchers over here urgently? We need to get these two to hospital.'

'That was a brave thing to do, Flaky,' Kuppa said quietly. 'Probably a bit foolish but very brave!'

Flaky coughed heavily before croaking out a reply. 'Sorry, Mist Chief Kuppa, but my…my friend was in trouble.'

'You could have been killed if those bombs had been real,' remarked March.

'But thankfully, you weren't,' said Kuppa. 'Looking at how that fire was raging before they managed to put it out, I think you saved Cornflower's life.'

"And mine," thought The Dark, who was wondering how his perfect plan had ended in such disarray.

Kuppa watched as the two elves were stretchered away. Grinning, she leant across to March.

'I expect I will need to give him another medal,' she remarked wryly.'

'At this rate, he will soon be able to open up his own trophy shop!'

The safety equipment Flaky had been wearing had been extremely effective. After a quick check up, the medical staff decided that he could be released, as he had no noticeable problems.

'You're fine,' the doctor told him. 'You can go home whenever you like, Mr Pastry.'

After a short pause, Flaky remembered that he was 'Mr Pastry'.

'Oh, yes. Thank you, Mister Doctor, Sir. I'll go then. Thank you. Goodbye.'

Just as he was about to leave, Flaky stopped.

'Oh, oh, I forgot. My friend, Cornflower Blue, was with me. Has he left already?'

The doctor looked at his notes. 'Mr Blue? He is too ill to leave, Mr Pastry. Suffering from smoke inhalation. He will be with us for at least three weeks. Leave your details, so we can call you when he is well enough for visitors.'

This was something Flaky knew how to do. Onion was always telling him to ensure that he left their business cards with all their customers. He had a bunch in his pocket but like Flaky's clothing they were rather singed. Finally, he produced one to pass to the doctor. It was sooty and slightly burnt but just legible.

'Thank you, Mr Pastry. We all heard what you did. It was very brave.'

Flaky was lost for words. 'Oh right. Thank you, Sir Doctor.'

Onion was waiting outside, when Flaky exited.

'Hi Flaky, I heard that you were being discharged. Let's get you home so you can get cleaned up.'

***

As expected, when approached by Kuppa, Potter had agreed immediately that Flaky should be awarded a medal to recognise his bravery. Kuppa thought that this medal should be presented by someone from H.E.T.T rather than herself. Their current chairperson was Tank Shunter, a stately, almost regal looking individual who invariably wore a double-breasted navy or black suit, complementing his hessian carpet coloured face and slicked back mocha toned hair. Tank was surprised but delighted to find himself nominated by Kuppa.

The company retained a supply of medals to use for awards such as Employee of the Month. These already contained the H.E.T.T. name and logo. Tank knew that they had several skilled engravers working for them. Within an hour, he had a medal in his possession that stated "H.E.T.T. Bravery Award" on one side with "Presented to Mr Flaky Pastry for exceptional bravery" on the other.

The following day, Tank invited Flaky to attend the station for a "surprise".

For once, Flaky managed to receive his award without any "accidents", although as he was exiting, in his now predictable way, he repeatedly held up his medal to Onion, stating, "I got another medal!"

As Onion drove them home, Flaky was unexpectedly quiet, staring at his medal with a perplexed expression. Finally, as they pulled up at Onion's yard, Flaky asked, 'Onion, what does "expect it all bravery" mean? Is it a special kind of bravery?'

'Expect it all bravery?'

'Yes, I think it might be this word here.' Flaky pointed at his medal.

Onion chuckled. 'That says "Exceptional bravery".'

'So, is that good then?'

'Yes, it is. Exceptional is a bit like saying special. "Exceptional bravery" is his way of saying you were very brave, Flaky. I am sure everyone agrees with that. I certainly do. I'm very proud of you.'

As they walked indoors, Onion considered the words special and exceptional when applied to his friend.

"Flaky certainly is exceptional," he thought to himself. "There is no other elf like him. He truly is special!'

CHAPTER SIXTY-ONE
Flaky prepares for
an evening out

Following events at the railway station, Flaky was "the hero of the hour".

Lemon wanted to celebrate with her hero by taking him for a meal. As Lemon, Flaky, Fleur and Aaron had enjoyed each other's company at The Duck Inn, Fleur suggested that it would "make a nice change" if they all went to The Flooded Meadow, for the evening.

'It will let us meet some of your other friends, Flaky,' Fleur pointed out. 'I expect they will want to welcome their brave hero!'

Apart from Onion Gravy, had the regulars at The Meadow heard this, they might have baulked at the idea that they were believed to be Flaky's friends. They thought of themselves merely as acquaintances or associates of Flaky. In some cases, they were customers of his dog walking services, but none were truly his friends. The majority of the regulars tolerated Flaky's stupidity or clumsiness with good grace or amusement, whereas others found his actions quite annoying.

The owners of the pub had markedly different feelings about Flaky. Pearly Wisdom was fond of Flaky. She had always felt sorry for him, believing that he could not help his lack of mental acuity or clumsiness. Lemon's pride in Flaky, following his recent heroics, was shared by Pearly.

'I know you have no time for Flaky,' she said to her husband, 'but he is loyal to his friends and very brave.'

Frank Wisdom was not convinced. He had no tolerance for Flaky. He was certain that Flaky was the dumbest elf in Underside. Had it not been for Pearly, Frank would have banned Flaky on the grounds that he was an idiotic menace, who was a danger to all of their customers.

'Brave? The idiot ran into a fire,' Frank observed. 'Deliberately! That's not brave, that is plain foolish! And I hear they gave him another medal for it!'

'That's enough, Frank!'

'Alright. I know. I'll clean some glasses!'

✿✿✿

Prior to Flaky's visit to The Meadow that evening, Onion had been working on two projects, with Flaky's assistance. Onion's first project was for Dora Jarre, an elf who lived approximately two miles outside Little Merritiddle. She had an old outhouse which had been repaired repeatedly but was now beyond repair. She had asked Onion to build her a new one. Onion kept a sizeable supply of wood at his premises, but he knew he would need extra supplies, which he would ask Flaky to collect later.

Onion's day had started well. He was happy that, for once, it had been free from Flaky incidents. Well, almost free.

As he liked always to be useful, Flaky had offered to help load Onion's van with the tools and equipment for the outhouse job. There were eight boxes to be loaded. Most were helpfully labelled "This way up". The box on the top contained a selection of weighty items, which Onion had added belatedly, but which he had failed to secure as effectively as he should have. Therefore, in this instance, it might be considered unfair to blame Flaky for what happened next.

Flaky picked the box up, tilting it away from him to read the instruction on the side to ensure that he was holding it the right way. As he did so, the stress on the top of the box proved too much. The full contents spilled onto the road, behind Onion's van. Looking at the inadequate taping on the box, Onion realised that this was his mistake, not Flaky's.

'Sorry, sorry, Onion,' said Flaky apologetically. 'I'll pick everything up.'

'It's alright, Flaky. I'll do it. It was my fault. I didn't tape the box properly, but while I'm tidying this up, I have an important job for you.' Onion handed Flaky a sheet of paper.

'I am short of a dozen or so items of wood for the outhouse job. Can you take your tricycle and trailer and pop up to the wood store, about a mile outside of the village, and get these for me? I'll tell them you are on your way. Be as quick as you can. You will need to go on the road for a bit but get back onto the cycle path as soon as you can, for safety.'

Onion's second project was not initially on his list for the day. He had just collected together all the items accidentally spilled on the road, placing these in a fresh, firmly fastened box. He was completing the last of his drawing plans for the outhouse when he was contacted with a request for an urgent repair. The repair was to a tram stop, near Little Merritiddle, to which he was alerted by three members of the police on their way to work. Sergeant Brass Button, PC Brekkie Rawle and PC Willie Woantee were travelling on a tram, which was halted by debris in the road ahead.

Apparently, a car had swerved to avoid an elf furiously riding a tricycle, pulling a wood-laden trailer. The elf was pedalling frantically, veering erratically across the road, as he endeavoured to dodge every pothole. Unexpectedly, he turned sharply, without signalling, onto a cycle path.

Happily, the unidentified cyclist was not damaged. Happily, the car driver was not damaged. Unhappily, the car driver's vehicle *was* damaged. As was the tram stop he crashed into when he ran his car off the road, swerving to avoid the mystery elf.

Flaky returned just after Onion received the call about the tram stop incident.

'Did you see the car that crashed into the tram stop, Flaky?' he asked.

'No, Onion, I didn't see anything.' He paused for a moment. 'I did hear something though. There was a loud bang behind me, as I cycled towards the village.'

After this, the rest of the day passed peacefully. Onion constructed a temporary repair to the tram stop. As Sergeant Button, PC Rawle and PC Woantee were witnesses, Onion booked the additional work to his schedule, knowing that H.E.T.T. would pay for it, as they would consider the incident to be "simply an unavoidable accident". Amazingly, Flaky was able to assist Onion, quite successfully, with only one or two, minor "problems" arising.

On the other hand, Flaky's evening dog walking was dreadfully problematic. Dora Jarre had heard of Flaky's dog walking from Onion. She was the proud owner of three small, extremely hyperactive dogs: Cuddles, Fluffy, and Sparky. She was keen for Flaky to include these on his evening walk. When he left, he was leading a veritable pack of dogs. The three new dogs were delighted to be walking with Flaky, but their excitement meant that they were all determined to travel in different directions.

The walk ended badly. Cuddles, Fluffy and Sparky had over-stimulated the rest of the pack. Flaky stumbled back with every dog's lead wrapped around his legs. He looked more like a maypole than a dog walker. Onion laughed loudly as he disentangled his friend.

'I'll hold onto them now, Flaky, until their owners arrive. Why don't you get ready for this evening and then I'll drive you over to Babbsley Reach to meet with your friends.'

CHAPTER SIXTY-TWO
A friendly evening
at The Meadow

Aaron did not drink. Consequently, he had offered himself as driver for the evening at The Meadow, with the stipulation that he be given directions. Naturally, this task fell to Flaky, as a resident of Little Merritiddle.

There was just one tiny drawback to this notion. Whenever Flaky was travelling between the villages or Hollow Earth, Onion had told him repeatedly to travel on the roads, only where he had to. He told him to travel on the cycle paths, wherever he could, as they were safer for an elf riding a tricycle. He would not risk being hit by a car, plus there were far fewer potholes. Flaky knew that Onion was intellectually superior to him or, as he would say, "Onion is more cleverer than me", so the routes that Flaky followed customarily, made heavy usage of these cycle paths.

It was not long before the first difficulty presented itself.

'Straight on down here, Aaron,' Flaky directed with confidence. After a mere ten yards, Aaron brought the car to an abrupt stop.

'We can't go down here, Flaky.'

'It's the way I always travel, Aaron. It's quite quick.'

'It may be quick, but it's only for pedestrians, cycles, and horses. We're in a car.'

'Oh, right! Sorry, everyone. I got it wrong again, didn't I?'

Aaron backed up onto the road.

After another half mile, a turning was visible, but it was poorly lit, as two streetlights had failed recently and had not been replaced. As a result, Aaron could not see the sign clearly. He tried Flaky again.

'Do we turn here or continue straight on, Flaky?'

Staring into the half-dark, Flaky was uncertain. It looked like a place where he would usually travel beside the main road, on a safe cycle path. He guessed a left-turn was the correct answer but was worried that he would lead them the wrong way again.

'I think it must be left here but I don't know,' he admitted.

Once more, Aaron turned the car into a cycle way.

[Really, quite a remarkable magic trick!]

This time there was the significant hint of a group of wandering pedestrians ahead of Aaron to tell him that this was not a road. When they returned to the road, Flaky spotted a turning that he knew must take them in the right direction. Unfortunately, by now he had lost all belief. He was convinced that he was always mistaken, so he decided to say nothing. As a result, they needed to execute a three mile backtrack to regain their route.

After continuing setbacks, where Flaky had instructed Aaron to turn his car onto cycle paths or where he had missed turns, Aaron decided just to follow the road signs, trusting that once they reached Little Merritiddle, they could locate the pub.

Eventually, after several detours, countless apologies from Flaky, and a massive amount of laughter, they arrived.

✳✳✳

In direct response to the increased terrorist threat posed by The Dark, General Zingor had commissioned a new initiative for The Elite. They conducted military drills around Hollow Earth on a regular basis. Now, she ordered the troops, based at the Southern border, to complete a series of comprehensive manoeuvres in the areas surrounding each of the villages, which had been designated as locations for the Elite to defend. That afternoon, significant military operations were accomplished, with enormous precision, around Great and Little Merritiddle, Upper and Lower Tinkerton, Great Riverstop, Lower Riverstop, Dingleberry, Greater Dingleberry and Babbsley Reach.

At the conclusion of the activities, the General was so impressed, not only did she declare them an enormous success, but also, she decided that no further exercises would be required for at least three months.

As luck would have it, the guards ended their operations in Little Merritiddle. The Flooded Meadow had an excellent reputation, so the majority of the soldiers headed that way. As a result, the pub was unusually busy. Both Frank and Pearly Wisdom were serving drinks as quickly as they could manage.

When Flaky's party entered, Flaky stopped in amazement. He had never seen this many elves in his local before. It took extraordinarily little to confuse or disorientate Flaky. Consequently, he was uncertain which way he needed to go in order to meet Onion and the others. Ultimately, it was Lemon who nudged him, pointing at one corner of the pub.

'Isn't that your friend Onion, over there in the corner, waving at us?'

'Is it, Lemon? Oh yes, there he is. Hello, Onion,' he called out, returning Onion's wave, before falling over a bar stool. 'I'm fine,' he stated, leaping to his feet.

Onion smiled. He saw Flaky's wave but, with the background noise from the crowd, he could not hear what Flaky called out. 'Hmm, traditional Flaky entrance,' he observed quietly. Flaky led the way to where Onion and the others were seated, at "their table" in a comfortable corner of the pub. By Flaky's standards, this was a successful exercise, as he only tripped over four customers on his way. His apologetic 'Sorry, sorry' was repeated on each occasion, to the growing amusement of the pub's customers, who were seated nearby.

As he neared the table, Ewan and Helen Earth spotted him.

'Pleased to see you, Flaky,' said Helen. 'We heard about your bravery at the railway station. Well done! You are a hero.'

'Yes, couldn't have put it any better myself,' agreed Ewan. 'You certainly are a hero. The man of the hour.'

Flaky was not used to receiving praise. He responded by turning a bright red and mumbling a thank you.

'Who are your friends, Flaky?' asked Helen.

Flaky attempted introductions in his own inimitable, unnecessarily nervous, style.

'Umm, hello heavy one, I mean everyone. These are my friends, Fleur Shop … no, sorry, sorry, that's not right, I mean Fleur Matt and her girlfriend, no, no, I mean boyfriend, Aaron Head. They live in Babbsley Reach with Lemon Puff, my, my, err…'

'Girlfriend?' suggested Lemon with a chuckle.

'Oh, yes, if that's alright, Lemon. This, this is my, my girlfriend, Lemon Puff.'

Turning his attention, such as it was, to those already seated at the table, Flaky announced 'These are the others' and sat down.

Giving him a friendly but nonetheless quite sharp dig in the ribs, Lemon whispered 'What are their names, Flaky?'

Flaky leapt to his feet, barely avoiding falling across the table.

'Sorry, every buddy, I got it wrong again, didn't I? These nice people are Helen and Ewan Earth, and this is my friend, Onion Gravy, who looks after me and lets me help him with his work.'

Flaky sat down again, almost falling off the seat due to his abrupt descent into a seated position. At this juncture, Pearly Wisdom turned up to collect empty glasses.

'Hello, Flaky, who are your friends?'

'Allow me,' said Onion, in order to avoid a further attempted set of Flaky-style introductions. 'These are Fleur Matt, Aaron Head and Lemon Puff from Babbsley Reach. Lemon is Flaky's girlfriend.' Flaky pinked noticeably as this was said. 'Fleur, Aaron, and Lemon, this is our friendly innkeeper, Pearly Wisdom. The elf behind the bar is her husband, Frank.'

'Frank doesn't like me,' noted Flaky.

'Nice to meet you all,' stated Pearly, wisely ignoring Flaky's comment. 'It's very crowded up at the bar. Can I get you all some drinks and bring them over? In honour of Flaky's heroics, this round is on the house…but don't tell Frank. What do you fancy?'

'Just a lemonade for me, with some ice, please,' said Aaron.

'I'd like a nice, strong bitter,' declared Fleur. 'What do you recommend?'

'We've just stocked a new ale today called Dark Mill. Would you like to try it?'

'Yes, I'll have a pint of that, please.'

'I'll try that as well, please, Pearly,' said Lemon.

'Do you others want the same again or will you experiment also?'

Ewan, Helen, and Onion all looked at each other and nodded.

'Dark Mills all round, please Pearly.'

'That just leaves you, Flaky. What will you have?' asked Pearly.

'Oh, I'll have some Mark Dill, as well...I mean Dark Mill, please.'

Pearly walked away, grinning to herself. "And that's before he's even had a drink," she thought.

Onion waited three or four minutes, after their drinks arrived, before asking what the others thought about the army activities around the village that afternoon.

'There's certainly a load of soldiers in here tonight, after all that military action this afternoon. Do you think there is another war coming?' he asked.

'No, I don't think so,' said Ewan. 'It looked as though they were just ensuring the Elite are ready if required.'

'Yes, stands to reason that they need to keep alert and prepared,' agreed Helen.

An Elite guard, who was standing a couple of yards away, leaned in to add a comment.

'Sorry to interrupt but you are quite right. There is no need to worry, folks. These were only manoeuvres to keep us sharp,' he said.

'Thought as much,' Ewan concluded. 'I overheard one of your senior officers, a General I believe, say how pleased she was with the manoeuvres today.'

Flaky was struggling to understand the meaning of this conversation. Stretching across, he whispered to his friend,

'Onion, why was the General pleased with their man hoorahs?'

As with many of his dealings with Flaky, Onion sighed heavily before attempting a reply.

'Not man hoorahs, Flaky, but manoeuvres,' he explained. Seeing that Flaky's face was now displaying a look of total bafflement, he tried again.

'Manoeuvres are when soldiers practise their skills, but no-one gets hurt. It's simply pretend fighting.'

Flaky nodded as if this now clarified everything. However, Onion suspected that, in reality, his friend did not understand fully the explanation he had been given.

CHAPTER SIXTY-THREE
An update for Potter

The elvish military leaders met periodically with Potter, as Commander in Chief of all elvish forces. Potter was keen to hear their report on the recent military operations.

'Everything was most satisfactory, Potter. The troops performed admirably,' stated General Zingor. 'I have an Elite to be proud of once more.'

'As well as that, now the Elite is back to its full strength, most of the volunteers that were involved previously in the fighting have been able to return to their normal occupations,' said Captain Ponsonby-Smyth.

'It also means that we no longer need the Auxiliary Special Reserves Volunteer Unit to provide elves to cover on guard duty at the border posts,' added Captain Carruthers. 'We'll have professional soldiers on duty again not…well, you know who I mean, Ponsers?'

Captain Ponsonby-Smyth allowed himself a small smirk.

'Do you mean, by any chance, those sterling volunteers, Privates Gravy and Pastry? They were, perhaps, slightly below standard…'

'Below standard? I cannot imagine they would have fooled any fairies that might have been spying on us,' commented General Zingor, with just a hint of a growl. 'No attempt to look as though they had any military bearing whatsoever!'

'But, General, in their defence, they were unpaid volunteers with no training. They were just keen to help out.'

'Yes, once I'd volunteered them!' laughed Carruthers.

'One of them looked like he had walked straight off a building site before rushing onto guard duty. Unkempt and untidy. Had not even buttoned his uniform correctly, but he was not the worst. Who was the scruffy, bony one with the uniform that looked two sizes too big?' asked the General. 'With all that straw-like hair sticking out, looked more like a scarecrow than a guard.'

'Ah, that was volunteer Private Flaky Pastry, General,' said Ponsers.

'Oh yes, I've heard about him,' she remarked. 'Did something heroic at the railway station, I've been told. Enthusiastic, means well but a bit of an idiot by all accounts. Still, good chap for volunteering. Shows backbone if nothing else. Some of our best troops have been a bit lacking in the brains department but made up for it with bravery.'

'Yes, Flaky saved a railway worker's life, General,' stated Potter. 'You are right, he is not too bright but he's as brave as a lion and always keen to help. Those of us who know him well, would not change him a bit. Now, I need to change the subject somewhat. I am concerned that we still have nearly all of the Elite guards based at the southern border. Can you start looking at repositioning our troops, to spread the numbers between the four outposts?'

'Of course, sir. We will start on that straightaway. Captain Carruthers, Captain Ponsonby-Smyth, you chaps are good at planning. Can you look into this and present me with outline plans as soon as possible?'

'Certainly, General,' answered Ponsers.

Carruthers merely nodded, smiling at his friend. In reality, he preferred action rather than planning, but he would help, as best he could.

'Excellent,' said Potter. 'Thank you all. I will look forward to hearing the troop repositioning plans.'

CHAPTER SIXTY-FOUR
At the teashop

Later that day, as Potter and Wendy both had a free afternoon, they decided to relax with a stroll around one of Hollow Earth's numerous parks. Instinctively, their walk took them towards the shopping precinct, in good time for afternoon tea.

'The Galaxy Mall?' Wendy asked.

'Good idea, we could try this new tea shop that has been advertised recently. Ye Olde Tea House, they've called it.'

'Oh yes, I know where it is. Close to Howte's the jewellers.'

Potter laughed. 'Interesting reference point!'

Wendy grinned. 'Well, a woman has to know where to buy the best jewellery, even if she cannot afford it.'

A five-minute saunter led them to the teashop, which was busy but not overcrowded. There was no difficulty finding a table but as they sat down, they realised they were being waved at from an adjacent table.

'Look, Potter!' Wendy exclaimed. 'There's Mary, Mark, and Archer. They are signalling for us to join them.'

'Excellent, we can find out how Archer is settling in,' declared Potter.

'Oh, Pottsie! I expect Archer is enjoying his afternoon tea. He may not want to talk about work.'

'Alright, I'll keep it light, Wendy. I promise.'

Wendy chuckled. 'That'll be the day, Mr Serious!' she observed teasingly.

On approaching the table, they noticed a young female elf sitting beside Archer. It was clear that she was feeling awkward. Her head was tucked down into her chest, so that her short, bobbed, black hair obscured her face.

'Good afternoon, Wendy, Potter. Will you join us?' asked Mary.

'We'll be delighted. Hello, everyone,' said Potter.

'Let me introduce you to Lacey Ribbon,' stated Archer. 'She has been my guide around Hollow Earth. Apart from Mary and Mark, she is the first friend I have made since I arrived. Lacey, these are Wendy Panboil and Potter Teasready.'

Lacey looked up from warm, brown eyes, displayed within a pleasant face, the colour of which was akin to a sandy beach on a sunny day. Wendy noted that Lacey was holding firmly onto Archer's hand for reassurance. She wondered if they were destined to become close friends, as time passed.

Having been introduced, Lacey seemed to relax. 'Pleased to meet you both. I am particularly honoured to meet you, Mr Teasready. Lately, I have been meeting so many important people. First, I met Archer, our new Santa. Then I met Mark, the former leader of the High Council of Elves. Now I am meeting with you, Mr Teasready. Every elf has heard of you. Not only our current council leader, but also the clever, resourceful Commander in Chief of our armed forces. I am just an ordinary elf. I'm a bit daunted meeting with so many celebrities!'

'Please, please, Lacey! None of us are celebrities. We are all just ordinary elves, like yourself. Please call me Potter, not Mr Teasready.' Potter noted that Wendy was giggling. He turned to her, with a grin. 'Alright, what's amusing you, then?'

'Clever and resourceful eh, Pottsie? When we leave, you'll struggle to get your head through the door!'

Potter laughed. 'Hmm, clever and resourceful is a bit much. How about fairly smart, Wendy? Will you give me that?'

Wendy chuckled again. 'OK, you can have fairly smart, Pottsie.' She glanced around the table. 'Have any of you ordered yet?'

Deciding what to order took no more than two to three minutes as everyone fancied afternoon tea. Three "Afternoon tea for two" were swiftly ordered.

'So, how are you settling in, Archer?' asked Potter, ignoring Wendy's slight frown and her silently mouthed message of 'That's work, Pottsie!'.

'Where to start, Potter? Firstly, I have to thank all of you for giving me this opportunity. In particular, I want to thank Mary and Mark for all their help in making the transition into the job so smooth. Also, for keeping me calm whenever I began to worry or became stressed at the magnitude of my position.

'I really need to thank you, Mary, for organising my move to Underside and assisting me in setting up my cottage. I doubt very much if I would have managed on my own. Mark, thank you for guiding me through the fundamentals of becoming Santa. I really appreciate your help. I am sure I will continue to need that during my first Christmas. Lastly, I must thank Lacey. She has shown me Bingo's cracker-making factory, the Teddy Bear Stuffing factory, and countless other fascinating places.'

Archer chuckled, 'Perhaps I should stop now. I'm beginning to sound like someone at an awards ceremony!'

'Fully understandable, Archer,' Potter remarked. 'How about any other elves you might have encountered? Any of them appear troubled by their new Santa?'

'Not at all. Apart from Mary, Mark and Lacey, no-one knows that I am the new Santa. Once I have the outfit on with the magic dust to disguise my true appearance, it's as if I have always been Santa. Every elf I meet, greets me warmly. Most of them will address me as Santa but it feels a bit odd when any of them call me Sir. I have never been called Sir before, not even when I was teaching.'

'You'll get used to that,' laughed Mark. 'After a while, it will seem normal.'

'I expect you are right. I will get used to it, I'm sure.'

'Excellent,' said Potter. 'Well done, Archer. Or should I say well done, Santa.'

'Are any of you still experiencing these time leak problems?' queried Mark.

'Yes, less often,' noted Potter, 'but I experienced an odd one just yesterday. I heard footsteps behind me. When I turned, I could see about a dozen versions of myself walking the path I had just trod, with the nearest merely a couple of steps behind me. As I watched they all began to merge with each other until the nearest caught up and joined with me. It was most disturbing. It left me quite disorientated. Really edgy, in fact.'

'That explains why you were so distracted when I met you yesterday,' remarked Wendy. 'That reminds me, I was chatting to Kuppa yesterday about the leaks. Although there are less nowadays, she gets to hear about most as nowadays elves choose to report time leaks to the police, instead of the elite guards or the council. Thankfully, these are minor, and she assures me that they are no more than a nuisance or minor confusion. Except, of course, when the incident is reported to one of her goblin constables or even worse when one of them is present.'

'In what way?' asked Potter.

'The other day was a perfect example. She came across an elf who had been arrested by Cliff Wallbreaker and Granite Rockearth. It took her almost twenty minutes to determine why he had been arrested. The elf had actually been on his way to the police to report a time leak. Kuppa would not divulge the elf's name as he is innocent of any felony.

'When she spoke to him, he stated that he had been followed by himself all morning.

'Regrettably, he parked outside the station just as Granite Rockearth, Mountain Boncebasher and Cliff Wallbreaker were departing. Then he drove up and parked again three more times. As he entered the car park for the fourth time, PC Wallbreaker stopped him. According to the arrested elf, Cliff said the following to him or words of an extremely similar nature.

'"You, der elf. Why do dat – der cross der road in der car, den cross der road, den cross der road, den cross der road? Dat der danger."

'Then Kuppa said that Granite agreed, saying something like, "Yeah, dat der danger to der udders. Hands up! Under der arrest."

'As you might expect, the elf had asked him why.

'According to Kuppa, Granite's response was "Under der arrest for der driving dat not safe".'

Everyone at the table, including Wendy, was attempting to avoid laughing.

Even Potter sniggered. 'I shouldn't laugh really, but do you mean the elf was arrested for dangerous driving?'

'Yes, I'm afraid so,' Wendy confirmed. 'The poor, innocent party spent an hour in the cells, when his only fault was to be the unlucky target of a time leak. Kuppa says she apologised to him and offered him compensation for his lost time. Fortunately, he saw the funny side of the incident and marked it down to experience. Kuppa asked him to continue reporting any time leaks to the police. Also, she told him that she would be speaking to the officers concerned.'

'An incident like that is very amusing,' Mark observed, while still grinning, 'but I think it is a problem that needs solving quickly, Potter.'

'Yes, I agree. I have already spoken with Merlin. If anyone can solve this perplexing conundrum, it is Merlin.'

At that moment, two waiters arrived carrying the afternoon teas.

'Now that's what I call a well-timed natural break,' said Mary. 'It all looks delicious!'

As they were tucking into their afternoon feast, Merlin appeared suddenly, out of nowhere. 'Ah, this is not the moment,' he muttered before disappearing as abruptly as he had appeared.

Potter laughed, 'Classic Merlin. As mystifying in his arrivals or departures as he is with his magic.'

'Was that Merlin?' asked Archer. 'I was hoping to meet him.'

'Don't worry, he often turns up when he doesn't mean to. No doubt he will return later.'

Mark grinned knowingly at Potter before changing the subject.

'I gather Flaky won another medal recently, Potter,' he noted.

'Yes, he did. Ran into a fire in one of the tunnels at the railway station to rescue his friend, with no thoughts for his own safety. He was presented with a bravery medal. Richly deserved, I think!'

'Well done, Flaky!' stated Mary. 'Yes, indeed,' agreed Wendy.

'Sounds like another to add to my list of people to meet,' observed Archer.

'He has had a busy few months!' admitted Potter. 'Previously, he was awarded the "Citizen of the Month" medal for identifying the elf who murdered a robber named Morty Vicker and attempted to murder a jeweller called Peter Howte.'

'I can fill you in on the details of that episode later, Archer,' stated Lacey.

'Fortunately, we have not experienced any further murders, Archer,' added Potter. 'Actually, while I think of it, everyone, we have an interesting development regarding the charges brought against our suspected murderer, Isaac Lubbe. Unbelievably, despite his extraordinarily lengthy catalogue of past episodes of aggressive, criminal behaviour, he has decided to enter a plea of temporary insanity.'

'Really? Astonishing!' said Mark.

'I suspect his lawyer may have something to do with this decision. A relatively simple case of deliberate murder, and for that matter attempted murder, has now become complicated by considerations of his sanity. Still, regardless of this new, unlikely change in the case against Mr Lubbe, it does not detract from the excellent work by Flaky.'

CHAPTER SIXTY-FIVE
Flaky and Lemon's picnic

U naware that elsewhere he was the subject of such interest, Flaky was existing in his own joyful little world. There is little doubt that had he been a character in an animated movie, his clothes would have been flashing through a vast array of cheerful, psychedelic hues, as he pedalled through a beautiful flower meadow. Surrounding him would have been a happy flock of multicoloured songbirds. As he cycled, gentle fluffy clouds would have moved out of his way to let him through.

In reality, Flaky's legs were pumping up and down furiously as he sped along the recently resurfaced cycleway. He did not notice this improved pathway. His head was filled with too many other matters, some of which he could scarcely believe. He had saved his good friend, Cornflower. He had been told that he was a hero! He had another medal! More importantly, he was on his way to meet his girlfriend, Lemon Puff, in Babbsley Reach. Then she would drive them to their favourite picnic place, near Hollow Earth Central station.

Flaky was so absorbed, that he cycled clear past the turning for Babbsley Reach. He travelled a further mile, before he realised that he was heading in the wrong direction. By the time he finally arrived at Babbsley Reach, he was not only late but also quite flustered.

'Sorry, sorry, I'm a late lemon,' he declared, with a typical, moment of Flaky-inspired confusion.

Lemon laughed, giving him a hug.

'Not to worry, Flaky. I will get the car. You can park your tricycle in the garage. We won't take long to get to the station. Did you bring anything for the picnic?'

'Oh no, I forgot again.'

'You are a silly, but it won't be a problem. I have plenty that we can share.'

As the couple were picnicking, watching with interest as the trams and trains arrived or departed from the station, Onion pulled up in his van. As he climbed down, they noticed that he was sporting a pair of binoculars. Focusing them on the train about to depart from the station, Onion muttered, 'Yes, there it is.'

Grinning, Onion looked over to where Lemon was sitting with Flaky, on a colourful blanket, which served as their table on the ground. On it was spread an extensive array of foodstuffs, supplied by Lemon. There was easily sufficient for three or four people.

Lemon was used to Flaky's chaotic, disorganised approach to life. In her eyes, his confused, messy, even muddled activities, together with his forgetfulness, merely added to his charm. They were part of the reason she could not help liking Flaky, but they were also the reason she always packed more food than might be needed. She could rely on Flaky to forget to bring anything.

Onion strolled over.

'Good afternoon, you two. You might want to stand up to watch the departures for a few minutes. In particular, watch the carriages on the next train.'

As it pulled out, cruising slowly past, Flaky and Lemon read the names painted on each carriage. As the last one passed, Lemon tugged at Flaky's arm excitedly.

'Look, look. Can you see what that one says?'

Emblazoned on the side were the words "The Flaky Pastry".

'Is that me?' asked Flaky.

'I believe so,' said Onion, beaming happily at his friend. 'That is why I am here. Potter told me that they were going to be including a new carriage on this train today, named after you. I wanted to see for myself. Anyway, I am interrupting your day off. I've work to do. It's time I left.'

'Do you want anything to eat or drink before you go?' asked Lemon.

'No, thank you, Lemon. Very kind, but I've just eaten. See you later at The Meadow, perhaps? Enjoy the rest of your picnic.'

With that Onion departed, with a cheery wave out of the window of his van.

After their excellent picnic and the wonderful surprise of the new Flaky Pastry train carriage, Flaky was ecstatic.

'Lemon, they gave me a medal for saving my Cornflower and ... and, now they have given me a train as well! It's exciting, isn't it?'

Lemon grinned. 'It certainly is, dear. Shall we visit your friends at The Meadow, tonight? You can tell them all about it.'

Lemon had never felt so happy; so relaxed in another elf's company. She decided that Flaky was everything she could ever hope for in a partner. She loved him with every part of her being.

Grinning, she turned to him.

'Flaky, have you ever thought of getting married?'

CHAPTER SIXTY-SIX
Merlin reappears

At Ye Olde Tea House, with his mouth still partly full of cake, Potter looked around to Mark, Mary, Archer, Lacey, and Wendy. He took a final swallow before saying, 'Well that was wonderful. I'll settle the bill. Next time, it will be someone else's treat.'

Just as the group were about to leave, Merlin reappeared.

'Ah, now *this* is the correct moment!' he stated with confidence.

'Potter, I must talk with you urgently,' he continued. 'I have important news to impart. 'I know that I may trust its confidentiality with you, Mark, Mary, and Wendy. Please accept my humblest apologies and excuse my directness, but may I enquire who you young elves are?'

Archer stood. 'Of course you may, Merlin. I am delighted to meet you. My name is Archer Upbowes. I have the honour to be Underside's new Santa. My friend is Lacey Ribbon, who is my excellent guide around Hollow Earth.'

Potter glanced at Merlin. 'You may trust them as you would me, Merlin.'

'Excellent. In order to place my news into its proper context, I am afraid I will need to request your forbearance, while I update you on recent events involving the fairies and goblins.'

'Has there been more fighting, Merlin?' asked Potter.

'There have been particular instances of "almost" fighting. Not between the goblins this time but the goblins attempting to raid the fairies.'

'Sounds intriguing. What happened exactly?'

'The two parties of goblins banded together into one formidable army, with the clear intention of attacking the fairies. The fairies were prepared. It was obvious that they were aware the goblins intended to attack with a massive force. They must have realised that they could not defeat such an immense legion of goblin warriors in a straightforward battle, but fairies have their own strengths they can employ in battle. Trickery, cunning and devious deception are potent weapons.'

'It is difficult to imagine what the fairies could do in order to give themselves any chance of defending their realms,' noted Wendy.

'The principal advantage the fairies possessed was trickery. A skill which was beyond the lesser intelligence of their goblin foes,' explained Merlin. 'Prior to the arrival of the goblin army, they constructed a collection of signposts which they positioned in key locations leading both into and around the fairy lands.'

'Arthur and I determined swiftly,' added Merlin, 'that the signs were intended to be confusing or misleading. As such, they were exceedingly effective. A significant contingent of the goblin warriors became lost in the fairy swamplands, while approximately a quarter of their forces inadvertently imprisoned themselves in Elderberry's castle. The remaining goblins returned to their homelands in defeat.'

'Excuse me for interrupting,' said Archer, 'but when you say Arthur, you don't mean King Arthur surely?'

'No,' laughed Potter. 'Merlin is referring to Arthur Moe. He is the head of Classified Intelligence and Secret Services. Our chief spy if you prefer. A close friend of Ena Minnit, who I believe you have met already.'

As Merlin was smiling it was evident that he had not minded the interruption. He proceeded with his narrative.

'From what we have seen, the goblins are no longer preparing for war. They are focused on practical matters, such as burying their dead, repairing their dwellings, and hunting,' Merlin summarised.

'That sounds like excellent news,' stated Potter with a little smile. As he spoke, he put a barley twist sweet in his mouth, having surreptitiously placed them on the table two minutes earlier.

'Hopefully, war against us is no longer a consideration for either the goblins or the fairies. Barley twist, anyone?'

'Oh yes please,' Wendy replied, helping herself. 'Sorry, Merlin. Please continue.'

'Thank you, Wendy. I have covered the necessary background. Now, I will address the crux of the matter. As you know, King Elderberry's forces defeated the attack on his castle by his wife, Queen Parsnip Mash together with her sister, Lady Butternut Risotto. We know that King Elderberry used The Seven to cast a spell banishing them both from all fairy realms in Underside for fifty years. Thankfully, the Seven were not used by King Elderberry in this latest dispute with the goblins. It would seem that they have departed.

'The Seven's spell is exceptionally powerful. Not only does it banish Queen Parsnip Mash and Lady Butternut Risotto from fairy realms, but additionally it bans them from any interaction with other fairies. Moreover, if they attempt to break this spell, the result will be agonising pain for them or any fairy attempting to help them.'

'A horrendous fate indeed, as we have discussed before,' remarked Potter, 'but why raise it as an issue now?'

'In essence, this is why I needed to speak with you urgently. *This* is the fundamental problem. Since their banishment, our spies have lost contact with them. We have no idea where Parsnip and Butternut are currently.'

'I see,' said Potter, although in reality he did not. 'Surely their absence is good news for us or is there something I'm missing?'

'It is my belief that these two powerful fairies may continue to pose a threat,' declared Merlin. 'If I am right, not only could they present a threat to other fairies but also to every elf.'

Seeing the puzzlement on the faces of the others at the table, Merlin allowed himself a further barely noticeable smile.

'Let me elucidate,' he said. 'The wording of this banishment spell ensures they can have no contact with other fairies. It does not stop them seeking assistance from other beings. If these two fairies are operating outside the view of our scouts, they must be residing in an area that is not controlled by elves, fairies, or goblins. Logically, the only possible place they might be is The Wastelands.'

'The Wastelands?' queried Archer. 'What are they?'

'An area controlled by no-one, where all manner of disturbing, tremendously dangerous creatures exist,' Merlin explained. 'I visited it once. I consider myself fortunate to have survived the experience. I will not return there again, by choice. Nevertheless, two potent fairies might have the guile and strength to persuade some of these treacherous fiends to join with them. Such an army might sweep all before them.'

'The notion of such a potent, monstrous army marching from The Wastelands into Underside is terrifying,' noted Potter.

'We can only hope that the two exiled fairies do not succeed in raising such a hideous army and that this remains merely a concern. However, I think we should consider another worry that has just presented itself to me. If King Elderberry considers this outcome, he might decide to join forces with his ex-wife, with the aim of declaring war on us once more. I have no idea how we might repel such a force. If they attack, it may signal the end of Underside as we know it. On that rather sombre note, perhaps we should leave and let the restaurant have their table back? Thank you, Merlin. You have given us plenty to think about.'

CHAPTER SIXTY-SEVEN
At the hospital

Cornflower Blue adjusted his breathing mask. Feeling around, he located the bed remote control he had been given to allow him to raise or lower his hospital bed. The medical staff had placed him in a virtually horizontal position. They had informed him that he needed to lie on his back while recovering. As someone who habitually slept on his side, he did not find this easy or comfortable. Tentatively, he raised the top of his bed a fraction, hoping none of the staff were watching.

Cornflower was struggling to understand why he was in the hospital. The doctor attending him had explained that he had been rescued from a fire in one of the tunnels at Hollow Earth Central railway station. He was told that he was recovering from minor damage to his lungs caused by smoke inhalation, together with minimal burns to his hands and face. "It explains all these fetching bandages I'm wearing," he thought to himself.

Cornflower's last memory was of a normal day's work at the station. The doctor had asked him what he could remember of the accident. When he had replied that he could not recall anything, he had been told not to worry as his memory would return in time. Cornflower was not so sure. He was not surprised that he was unable to recollect the fire. By this time, he was used to periodic gaps in his memory.

For his alter ego, The Dark, there was no confusion. As he had been in control of Cornflower during the recent incident in the railway tunnel, he knew exactly what had occurred. The Dark was irritated that his plan had gone so entirely amiss. He was disheartened. The damage at the tunnel was insignificant. His bomb at the police headquarters had been discovered and defused. His plan had been an abject failure. His only success was in damaging himself. Even worse, there was the humiliation of knowing that he had been rescued by that idiot, Flaky Pastry.

The Dark rarely suffered any doubts but he began to wonder if he truly was the evil genius he imagined. Was he cut out for the role of frightening terrorist? He allowed himself to continue to reside in the back of Cornflower's brain. Observing but no longer controlling. Merely sulking dejectedly.

'You have some visitors, Mr Blue,' announced a voice.

Turning his head slightly he could see one of the nurses. Behind her were Flaky Pastry, accompanied by Onion Gravy. Cornflower could only manage a contorted grimace in welcome.

'Thank you for coming to visit me,' he croaked from behind his breathing mask and bandages. 'I am pleased to see you both.' Talking was difficult but he hoped Onion or Flaky might know the full details of what had happened.

'They tell me,' he continued, 'that I was in a fire at the station, which someone rescued me from, but I cannot remember anything at all. I would like to thank my rescuer, but I have no idea who they are.'

Onion grinned widely. 'H.E.T.T. are still investigating the origin of the fire but I can tell you who your rescuer was. In fact, he is standing right beside me. Flaky rescued you. Other elves told him not to go into the fire, but he went anyway. Thankfully, he was wearing safety equipment, so he was practically unharmed.'

'I am very glad you came after me, Flaky,' said Cornflower. 'By all accounts you saved my life. Thank you.' ("Yes, thank you," thought The Dark grudgingly.)

The nurse re-entered. 'He needs rest. You will have to leave now, gentlemen.'

Flaky looked round to see the gentlemen the nurse was referring to.

'The nurse means us, Flaky,' explained Onion.

Flaky turned to the nurse. 'Can I visit him again, Mistress Nurse?'

The nurse chuckled. She had been called many names before, but Mistress Nurse was a new one. 'Of course,' she replied 'He will be with us for a couple of weeks to recover from his injuries. He inhaled a great deal of smoke, and he needs treatment for some minor burns, but he'll live.'

'Thanks to you, Flaky,' remarked Onion.

Flaky did not know quite what to say so he gave an awkward, embarrassed grin and mumbled, 'Get well soon, Cornflower. I'll come to see you tomorrow.'

Cornflower unsuccessfully attempted a smile through the bandages and rasped, 'Bye, Onion, Bye, Flaky, and thanks again for saving me.' In the back of Cornflower's brain, The Dark thought, "Alright, don't praise the fool too much!"

'Goodbye, Cornflower,' said Onion. 'I'll make sure Flaky has plenty of time off so he can come to see you.'

As they were leaving the hospital, Cyan Hope was about to enter.

'Good afternoon, you two,' said Cyan. 'Have you just been in to see Cornflower?'

'Yes,' replied Onion, 'but we could not stay long as the nurse asked us to leave. She told us Cornflower needed to rest.'

'Oh well, never mind. I'll have a word at the reception desk. Find out what time I can visit this evening.'

As Cyan walked into the hospital, Onion smiled at Flaky.

'Let's go home and tidy ourselves up. I think Lemon and you planned to head for The Meadow this evening to get something to eat and drink. I've arranged to drive over to Lower Tinkerton to pick up Karva this evening. I can take you across to Babbsley Reach afterwards. Shall we see if Lemon wants to join us in the van to go to The Meadow or drive herself?'

'Yes please, Onion.'

CHAPTER SIXTY-EIGHT
Discussions at The Meadow

That evening, Onion drove his van to The Meadow, with Karva as his very willing passenger. Lemon followed closely behind, as she was still unfamiliar with the route. Beside her she had Flaky, her equally willing passenger.

When this mini convoy arrived, they were all surprised to see an Elite vehicle parked in front of The Meadow. Immediately, on entering the pub, they spotted the reason for the army truck outside. Baton Burg and Redd Shooz had taken part in the recent manoeuvres around the villages. Both remembered the visit to The Meadow afterwards. They had been impressed by the quality of the food, together with the wide range of beers on sale. As they both had a free evening, they had successfully persuaded their girlfriends that they would enjoy an evening out in Little Merritiddle. Actually, this act of persuasion was exceedingly easy, as both Candy and Kuppa were keen to see this place that they had heard so much about.

Helen and Ewan Earth were seated at their favourite corner table talking fervently with Candy, Baton, Kuppa, and Redd when Karva, Onion, Lemon, and Flaky arrived.

As usual, the Little Merritiddle experts had an excellent grasp of the general trends in Underside.

'I heard that the goblins and fairies are no longer a threat to us,' announced Ewan.

'Absolutely. Well at least not for the foreseeable future anyway,' agreed Helen.

She glanced up as the others walked over. 'Oh, what a pleasant surprise. You must join us. Drag that spare table across. Ewan and I will find you all chairs.'

In addition to the chairs, Ewan passed around menus. 'We haven't ordered yet. We may as well order at the same time.'

Onion quickly took his group's drink orders and headed for the bar with top-up requests for the two soldiers. Once everyone was settled with a drink in front of them, the Earths continued with their mission, which, as far as they were concerned, was to update everyone on every important piece of news in Underside.

'I believe Potter and Merlin are worried that there may be an imminent threat from the exiled fairies,' stated Ewan.

'Yes,' acknowledged Helen, 'I understand that they think they might gather together an army of monsters.'

'You are quite correct. My sister Wendy has hinted the same to me,' said Candy. 'It is most concerning. All we can do is wait. See what happens. Still, changing the subject, what is this I hear about H.E.T.T. honouring you, Flaky?'

As was often the case, Flaky was present physically but not entirely present mentally. As a result, he did not hear everything Candy said. He looked at Onion with a puzzled expression.

'Your name on the train,' whispered Onion helpfully.

'Oh yes, I have a train called Flaky Pastry,' Flaky stated with an air of misplaced confidence.

'Wasn't it a train carriage, named after you?' asked Ewan.

'Yes, surely it was a train carriage,' added Helen.

'No, it's a train, not a train garage,' declared Flaky.

Seeing the utter bewilderment on everyone's faces, Onion joined in.

'Never mind, Flaky. It's a huge honour.'

"I'll explain it to him, later," Onion thought.

Lemon giggled, giving Flaky a big hug. 'Well, I'm pleased they named it after you, Flaky. You deserve it.'

Over the lengthy period of time that they had known Flaky, Helen and Ewan had noted his trouble with words.

'We haven't seen you in our shop for a long time, Flaky. You should pop in to see us sometime,' suggested Ewan.

'Yes, we could sell you a dictionary,' agreed Helen. 'It can help you with all those difficult words.'

'Why do I want to buy someone called Dick Chunnery?' asked Flaky.

'It's not a person, Flaky. A dictionary is a book that tells you what hundreds of words mean,' explained Onion. 'Might be helpful.'

'We could also sell you a Thesaurus, Flaky,' said Ewan, hoping for a further sale.

'Oh no, thank you,' replied Flaky. 'I don't think I want a dinosaur. We haven't room for one of those.'

Onion grinned. 'It's not a dinosaur. It's another type of book.'

'Perhaps you should come to see us in the shop tomorrow, Flaky,' offered Helen.

'That sounds nice,' declared Lemon. Linking arms with Flaky, she continued. 'I'm due another day off. I'll drive over and have a look round with you, dear.'

Flaky blushed. 'Yes, please. I would like that.'

CHAPTER SIXTY-NINE
The fairies

The fairy rulers were assessing their situation. Currently, neither war with the elves nor the fate of his ex-wife and her sister were on King Elderberry's mind. He was discussing the recent goblin incidents with his son, Prince Dandelion. Dandelion was fighting to stay awake, while his father droned on in his usual, astonishingly tedious way.

'I think the goblins, our erstwhile allies, and our more recent enemies, have lost heart after the absolute embarrassment of their recent encounters with us. As I am sure you know, my son, goblins need to feel they have the upper hand in any battle, in which they partake. In particular, they are only truly comfortable if they have superior numbers. When, as has happened on this occasion, they had superior numbers but were still defeated, there can be no doubt that they will have become dejected. It has always seemed to me that goblins do not believe they should ever lose a battle. When they do lose, as they most certainly have in their attempted attack on our kingdom, they are notoriously poor losers. Typically, they sink into depression. Fortuitously for us, not to mention the pride of their kings, the goblin queens have taken control. Our scouts have reported that the queens have them occupied on mundane everyday tasks, such as burying their dead, rebuilding their abodes, hunting for food and so on, rather than pursuing their favoured pastime of fighting. Are you listening, son?'

'Sorry, Father. Of course,' Dandelion replied, while endeavouring to conceal the yawn he had just stifled. 'You said they were burying their dead. I did not think we inflicted any casualties.'

'No, quite correct, Dandelion. I believe the only damage we inflicted was to their pride, but before their incursion into our lands, they were fighting among themselves. I have been informed, by my spies, that the conflict was with their cousins from the north. This led to wholesale slaughter and destruction. Of course, this is common among goblins. I often wonder how they maintain their numbers.'

'So, may we consider our realm to be safe now, Father?'

'I am not sure, Dandelion. I have to remain cautious. The goblins may have agreed to a ceasefire for the time being, but can we trust them to keep their word in the future? Also, I fear that there remains a larger problem for us to contemplate. Your mother is still out there somewhere.'

'But she has been banished, Father,' Dandelion protested.

Elderberry allowed himself a wry smile.

'If I know Parsnip, she will not let a trifling matter such as banishment hold her back for long. I have no doubt that she will be busy plotting. Planning some kind of revenge.'

✿✿✿

In that part of Underside referred to by most as "The Wastelands", two forlorn figures sat huddled in front of a pathetically tiny fire. Behind them was rickety arrangement of branches, twigs and leaves which was the only shelter they had managed to construct.

It was clear that Parsnip Mash and Butternut Risotto were not natural builders.

A small spear and a branch were suspended over the fire. Six shapes had been pushed onto them. By appearance, the shapes might once have been rats.

'Any luck, Butternut?'

'None whatsoever, Parsnip. I found a sprite. She was quite pleasant but unfortunately, we discovered that as sprites are so closely related to fairies, she was affected by The Seven's exclusion spell in the same way as any other fairy. She became ill just attempting to talk to me. She rapidly excused herself and left.'

'How did you fare with that nymph we saw?'

'In a word, badly. I did not know that the elves had so many allies. She yelled at me to go away. Her exact words were "Leave me alone, frightful fairy. Surely you know the elves are our friends and fairies are our enemies". Worse still, a gnome passed by at the same time. He threw a spear at me. Nearly hit me in the leg.'

'Threw a spear at your leg, Butternut?'

'Yes, remember gnomes hate all fairies. They will attack us on sight. They can be quite aggressive.'

'Yes, but why did he throw a spear at your *leg*?'

'Do not forget, sister. They are exceptionally small. It was as high as he could reach! I shouted at him but when I started to give chase, he ran away with the nymph following close after. Still, he did leave his spear behind.'

'Lucky for him that I did not see him,' observed Parsnip. 'I would have chased after him and run him through with his own spear! On the other hand, you are not the only one having trouble with these diminutive menaces. I had my own problem encounters with miniature folk today. To begin with, I encountered a pixie.

The horrible little monster kept playing nasty tricks on me then rushing off before I could get at her. In the end, I was forced to concoct an invisibility spell. Once she could no longer see me, she became bored and left but no sooner had she departed then that imp, we saw the other day, reappeared.'

'What that one that was so disrespectful?'

'Yes, the same one. Again. Screamed at me, "Leave, mortal! You do not belong here. This no place for your kind." The cheek of him. I was furious but the little beggar flew away so fast I was unable to catch him. If I had caught him, I would have torn his wings off.'

'I think he might be right in one way,' mused Butternut. 'This is no place for ladies such as us. We used to have status, position, dignity. Other fairies followed our orders. When we issued a command, whatever it might be, our commands were obeyed. Here we cannot even command respect.'

'Yes, here we have nothing. It is an intolerable situation. I will not accept it much longer. I will find a way to change our circumstances, if it is the last thing I do.'

'Exactly, Parsnip. Here we have no standing. Creatures that most individuals ignore elsewhere, have more importance than us. Do you remember that Yeti we saw a week ago?'

'Yes. If I wasn't so annoyed with him, I might have found him amusing. How can a Yeti pass by, size us up and declare "*You* do not exist"? If there was one creature in The Wastelands that I thought might have been sympathetic, surely it would be a Yeti?' declared Parsnip.

'Precisely my point. It was the same with that giant last month. The one who tried to eat you.'

'One of my few moments of pleasure, recently. That spell I created while he was heating his oven and preparing his seasonings certainly brought him down to size.'

'Oh yes. It was good to have something to laugh at,' Butternut confessed. 'He looked so ridiculous when you reduced him. It is not often you see a giant so pathetically tiny that he has to run a way from a mouse!'

Parsnip paused in thought momentarily. 'Of course, that troll we encountered a few weeks back was bigger than the largest giant. He was immense, but I suspect his brain was nowhere near as huge as his bulk. Do you recall that when I tried to engage him in conversation, he was merely bewildered? Just kept looking around him, obviously wondering where the voice originated.'

'That's right. When he finally looked down and spotted us, he seemed even more confused. Even had the impudence to pick us up and smell us as if we were some kind of peculiar animal.'

'Indeed. Then announced, "*You* are not goats!" as if we might ever have been mistaken for such appalling, smelly animals. The nerve of him!' complained Parsnip. 'Only his massive size saved him. There was no chance that I could generate an enchantment capable of affecting him.'

'Talking of nerve, sister, what about that family of hideous, repulsive ogres we saw yesterday?'

'Yes, had the audacity to call *us* ugly, then march off as if they owned the place. I was so taken aback; I did not have time to reply let alone cast a curse on them.'

'We cannot continue like this, sister,' stated Butternut.

'For once, I agree with you entirely,' said Parsnip. 'We need a plan.'

'Perhaps I can help,' said a voice, behind them.

THE END

[The identity of the mysterious owner of the voice will be revealed in the, as yet untitled, third Underside adventure.]

ACKNOWLEDGEMENTS

I want to thank my wife, Lesley (Les), for her ever-present love and support. My constant "rock", especially throughout the lengthy writing process. I want also to thank my son Dave. My local IT expert. How they both put up with me I will never know!

Thanks also go to my parents for giving me a wonderful childhood, and for always being there when needed.

Further, I would like to thank all the friends I grew up with and the exceptional people I encountered during my working years. Those who made employment tolerable or even, on occasion, enjoyable. In particular, I need to thank my "second family", who I worked with at Gratte Brothers Catering Equipment Ltd.

Finally, may I thank my editor, Ruth Lunn, at UK Book Publishing, for presenting me with the opportunity to publish both my previous book and this sequel.

ABOUT THE AUTHOR

Ray Lewis Halliday resides in Hertfordshire. When he retired from full time employment, he was determined that he would spend his retirement constructively, rather than vegetating watching endless hours of daytime television.

Ray's chief desire was to write. After numerous false starts, Ray decided which type of writing he enjoyed. His first book, a comedy adventure story, entitled "Potter Teasready: Reluctant Hero – An Underside Adventure" was published towards the end of 2024. This latest book "Where is The Dark (or Flaky's medals)" is the second in Ray's Underside series.

Ray is currently developing a book of short stories, which he hopes to have published Autumn/early Winter, with a third Underside Adventure book to follow next year.

www.ingramcontent.com/pod-product-compliance
Lightning Source LLC
Chambersburg PA
CBHW050902250626
47155CB00001B/68